Nova Igniter

Joseph R. Lallo

ISBN: 978-1951240042

ISBN: 978-1951240042

Table of Contents

ACKNOWLEDGMENTS

I would like to once again thank Nick Deligaris for his continued excellence in cover illustration. Tammy Salyer's support and encouragement as an editor really helped me through the revision process. And as always, I would like to thank the readers who joined me in this experiment in steampunk!

Prologue

The sun is a harsh mistress. Nowhere was that truer than on the surface of Operlo. The whole of the planet was a blazing, dubiously inhabitable desert. When it had been discovered, it was little more than a spinning hunk of UV-blasted rock, rich in mineral resources and utterly devoid of life. Centuries of terraforming had transformed it. It was still a spinning hunk of UV-blasted rock, but now it was slightly less rich in mineral resources and had a construction consortium, a resort, and most recently, a hoversled racing league.

Pedants would point out that the rays of Operlo's star didn't truly count as sunlight, as "the sun" technically referred to Earth's star. It was solar radiation. Other pedants would argue that Earth's star was called Sol, and thus light from other stars was not Solar radiation but stellar radiation. Fortunately, this apartment didn't belong to a pedant. It belonged to a man named Trevor Alexander. Most everyone called him Lex these days.

He muttered a half-coherent complaint as the sun drifted far enough across his bed to reach his eyes. It had been a long night, as he'd just clinched his spot in the top three for Operlo Racing Intersystem Circuit's first full season. He could finish dead last and still be in at least third place when the time came to hand out trophies. Not that he intended to *ever* finish dead last.

A familiar, utterly gleeful yip rang out in the otherwise silent apartment. His eyes shot open.

"No, no, no!" he yelped.

Further complaint was reduced to sputtering as his mouth filled with the belly fluff of his pet funk Squee. At some point in the last few weeks she'd gotten it into her head that the moment he woke up, that was her signal to jump on his face to demand cuddles and/or food.

"Squee, honestly," he groaned, pulling her off his face. "You're smart enough to disengage the security code on my slidepad. You're smart enough to order your own toys. But you can't figure out how to get your own beans and rice while Daddy sleeps off a hangover?"

She replied as she usually did, by assaulting his face with licks and scampering onto his shoulders. He winced as her almost toxic levels of cuteness and affection reached his neck, where the licking produced a faint jolt of pain.

"Easy, easy, easy," he groaned, pulling her from his shoulders and tucking her under one arm.

He awkwardly slid from bed and lumbered over to a mirror to check himself out. The bags under his eyes were no surprise. It was only ten a.m. local time, and the last clear memory he had was of checking the clock in an autonomous limo at six a.m. But the long swath of medical gel that failed to blend into his sunbaked skin reminded him that the victory he'd been celebrating had been a little more exciting than it should have been.

"I might have to start taking corners a little shallower." He ran his finger along the injury. "Either that or turn up the inertial inhibitor a little higher. It's probably a bad sign when the safety harness tries to saw its way through your jugular."

"Good morning, Lex," intoned a pristine synthetic voice. "Would you like to begin your morning routine?"

"I usually try to save my morning routines for the afternoon when I'm recovering from a proper bender."

"I'm sorry, I didn't understand that reply. Would you like to begin your morning routine?"

"Ma would have understood me," Lex taunted, tugging at his eyelid to check out his eye in the reflection.

"I'm sorry, I didn't understand that reply. Would you like to begin your morning routine?"

"Fine! Yes!" He raked his fingers through his hair. "She's spoiled me for other AI."

"Excellent. Please enjoy your day."

The lights slowly illuminated. A much-anticipated bitter scent wafted from the kitchenette as the coffee machine kicked on. Glowing white text expanded into three dimensions from the front of the mirror, summarizing messages, news, weather, and his agenda. The weather report had gotten a lot more valuable in recent months, as the repaired Indra Station had finally started to exert some degree of control over the climate. Thus the temperature didn't get nearly as close to boiling these days. The news was the usual sensationalized nonsense peppered with evergreen topics like "Political Strife Causes Tension" and "VectorCorp Denies Any Wrongdoing."

"'Malware Causes Network Slowdowns,'" Lex murmured, reading the one headline that stood out from the rest. "Must be either really bad malware or a really slow news day."

Lex dropped Squee to the ground and followed her to the kitchen to prepare a breakfast burrito for each of them.

"Read me my schedule for the day," he instructed his digital assistant.

"You have three appointments. 11:45 a.m. to 12:45 p.m.: Lunch with Preethy at The Usual Place. 1:15 p.m. to 2:45 p.m.: press junket for The Thing. 7 p.m.: Supper with Preethy at The Nice Place."

"It might be time to start being more specific when I make these entries," he said.

"Urgent Messages: Your spam box is full."

He cocked his head. "I don't think I've ever heard that message before."

Like many of society's ills, when people realized spam was a problem too difficult to solve, they devised an elaborate network of methods to ignore it. Spam filters and spam folders were present in any system capable of delivering information. Like vaccinations, they were so effective that people sometimes started to doubt they were necessary. Also like vaccinations, anyone who decided to forgo them soon found themselves regretting it. It was just a worthwhile precaution, an auto-emptying trashcan filled with attempted scams and unwanted sales. Losing the occasional friendly correspondence or business e-mail was an acceptable price. Those messages were sacrifices to the gods of the algorithm who kept us safe from the barely legal singles looking for a good time and your account information.

Lex pulled his slidepad from his pocket and dug around until he turned up the well-hidden spam folder. The only reason he was able to find it at all was because it was in flashing red text.

"I have eighteen billion… no, wait." He counted his way up the sequence of commas. "Million, billion, trillion, quadrillion… I have eighteen *quintillion* spam messages? Wow. Surely these are once-in-a-lifetime deals I don't want to miss out on. Delete all."

He slipped his slidepad into his pocket. Just as the microwave bleeped with the completion of his wholesome egg, bean, rice, and cheese wrap, his slidepad chirped again.

Your spam box is full.

Lex tapped the message and the folder popped open.

"Okay. Great. Why do I get the feeling this is going to turn out to be something worse than another phishing scam?"

Another 18,446,744,073,709,551,615 messages were waiting for him. Everything in the first page of messages was from the same second. The "from" addresses were all different, but the subjects were all the same.

Lex has been located. Lex must be recruited. The mission must succeed.

Joseph R. Lallo

Chapter 1

Lex marched across the sunny walkway between his apartment complex and his favorite restaurant. The incredibly dry heat of Operlo meant that as long as he was in the shade, it was actually quite tolerable even with Squee playing the role of fur stole around his neck. Rather than do the typical summertime two-step and try to hop between the shadows of buildings and the scattered shelters along the way, Lex had resorted to toting a parasol around with him. In the beginning, the silver umbrella had made him feel a little silly and old-fashioned. When the alternative was layering on gobs of sunblock or waiting for autonomous shade drones to show up, he quickly warmed to the practice.

The restaurant wasn't anything special. That was part of why he liked it so much. Operlo was in the middle of a massive community development project. As said project was under the guidance and financing of a large construction corporation, that meant loads of very fancy architecture and a very phony and manufactured ambiance. Colors were picked by committee to look spontaneous and carefree. Polymers were carefully pressed into shapes that looked like sun-bleached, warped wood. This sort of built-in, lived-in look always made Lex uncomfortable, like some alien culture was trying to assemble a habitat for him without really knowing what any of it meant.

This place was different. It started as the snack wagon where the construction workers got their lunches while building the rest of the neighborhood. The food wasn't artisanal. The menu was devoid of buzzwords. There wasn't a menu at all. Just a holosign, typically riddled with typos, listing off the day's specials that were defined by whatever the cook felt like making that day. Once construction was finished, they'd just converted the snack truck into an official diner, and Pihu, the cook, had stuck around.

"What's cookin', Pihu?" Lex asked as the chime over the door jangled with his entry.

The woman behind the counter looked up. "Hey, Lex. We're doing aloo tikki and yesterday curry, plus—" she began.

"Never mind, that'll do just fine. Just set me up with a basket of one and a bowl of the other." He took a seat on a stool permanently affixed to the ground in front of one of the tables. "Did Preethy show up yet?"

Pihu glanced at the clock. "It's 11:42," she said simply.

"Right, right. What was I thinking? She's got three whole minutes."

"Water for Squee?"

"If you please."

She grabbed a plastic to-go canister and filled it from a tap. Squee danced anxiously in place until she emerged with the water and set it down, then practically wrapped herself around the woman's leg in pursuit of a head scratch.

"Yes, yes. You're very cute," Pihu said. "And now I need to wash my hands again." She pried Squee from her leg and dropped her in front of the water. "Congrats on the race yesterday," she said. "I saw you on the sports feed."

"Thanks."

"Been a while since you came in first, huh?"

"Why yes, Pihu, how nice of you to notice. I came in second twice."

"In a row though."

"Nice to know you're keeping an eye on me."

"What's with the blood spurting out of your neck when you crossed the finish line?"

"It wasn't spurting. It was trickling."

"What's the difference?"

"According to the EMTs, about twelve stitches or a hundred grams of medical gel."

The door chime rang again at the precise moment Lex's slidepad beeped with his appointment reminder. Before he could turn, he felt fingers glide across the treated wound on his neck.

"Is it painful?" Preethy asked, circling around to her side of the table.

"It's fine. They said it'll be healed up by tomorrow. It shouldn't even leave a scar, but we'll see about that."

Preethy took a seat. She wore a wide-brimmed white hat and large sunglasses. Every stitch of her clothes was custom and impeccable, but she managed something that Lex had seldom seen before. Despite the surgical precision with which her outfit struck a balance between professionalism and fashion, it was her poise and bearing that spoke most loudly. She could have paced into the restaurant in a sweat suit and still demanded the respect of a CEO. It was just as well, as she *was* a CEO.

"We keep a plastic surgeon on call at the clinic. Nothing should leave a scar."

"Nah, if it does it does," Lex said. "It builds character."

She reached across the table to brush his arm, where a thin line of marginally less tanned skin marked another recent injury. "You've been accumulating character quite readily in the last few months."

"Gotta put butts in seats, right?" he said.

"You are certainly doing that. Uncle is quite pleased," she said. "Have you ordered yet?"

"Yep. Oh! I forgot a drink."

"You're getting an iced tea. It's all we have right now," Pihu called from the back.

"That makes it easy," Lex said.

"Ms. Misra, you want chana masala? We've got that today," she called.

"That sounds lovely. Thank you." Preethy pulled a sleek datapad from her purse. "As I was saying, Uncle is really quite pleased. We were rather concerned the near catastrophe caused by Indra Station would leave a stain on Operlo's reputation. As it turns out, your bombastic performances on the racetrack coupled with the speed of the local news cycle have all but pushed the event from the minds of the sort of person who is likely to plan interstellar trips for the purposes of entertainment."

"Rich people."

"Broadly speaking, though a large percentage of our patrons are middle-class enthusiasts."

"If there's one thing I can do, it's be distracting. Particularly to middle-class enthusiasts. They're my people."

"I could do with a bit of distraction myself," Preethy said, eyeing the pad briefly before slipping it back into her bag. "We are dealing with a minor data infrastructure issue. I messaged Uncle about it. Normally we can tolerate the usual level of unexplained load, but the whole planetary network is lagging badly. I believe it's been shut down entirely to lessen the load on our systems."

"Does that mean the press junket might get canceled? It wouldn't break my heart if you and I got a full afternoon to do something nonwork related."

"It almost certainly will be. And to be quite frank, something nonwork related would be lovely. But with the championship race just a week away, it deserves my full focus."

Pihu set the food on the counter and rang the bell. "Order up!"

Lex trotted up to bus the trays over to the table. "What sort of network infrastructure thing are we talking about, by the way?"

"I'm told it is some sort of a distributed denial of service attack. We've had a few, but this one seems very peculiar."

"Is this where all the spam is coming from?"

"Spam?"

"Yeah, I've been getting zillions of them per hour. I must have dumped my box twenty times today. Finally I just left it full. Is that not happening to you too?"

"Not nearly. You haven't opened any of them, have you?"

He gave her a flat look. "Yes, Preethy. I immediately opened each and every spam message, because I am a toddler who has never had a slidepad before."

"Point taken."

"I *have* seen all the subjects, though. Here, look." He hopped around to her side of the table and showed her the screen of his slidepad.

"That is curious, Lex. Very curious."

"See, I went with the word 'ominous.'"

"We'll submit a request for investigation," she said.

"I'm not so popular with telecom companies, you'll recall."

"We have a sizable contract for global communications as well as entertainment broadcast rights. Not to mention the pending settlement over the Gemini Bypass fiasco. I am confident I can compel them to do their jobs." Her eyes flicked to the window of the restaurant. "Hold still."

Preethy straightened his collar and adjusted the sleeves of his shirt. He raised an eyebrow.

"Preethy, not that I mind, but why are you preening me?"

"There are paparazzi across the street. I thought it proper that you look your best."

Lex turned and spotted the cameraman, who was shooting with a compound lens from the shelter of a bus stop across the way. After making a show of smoothing down his eyebrows, he settled into his seat and dug into his food. Out of the corner of his eye, he saw the photographer decide he'd had enough for one day and take his leave.

"Funny. My first encounter with random people taking my picture was when I had my first run of success racing back on Golana. Then for a while there was the whole 'disgraced racer' news cycle. Then there was when I was the hero who disarmed a truck that was going to explode back at Weston University. Now I'm not so sure if they're even taking a picture of me or you."

"I suspect they are taking a picture of us," she said, sampling her own meal.

"Why?"

She sipped her tea. "Have you not been following the stories about you?"

"I figured out a while back that if I let my brain soak in too much of what people are saying about me, I can't function."

"As it so happens I have a whole staff who reads and compiles relevant gossip and feedback."

"Jeez. That's gotta be rough."

"The position has a rather high turnover. But through them I've learned that the love life of anyone with any degree of celebrity is its own sort of spectator sport. Your falling out with Michella was a point of fascination for a time. It has cast our frequent fraternizing into a new light."

"I do love me some fraternizing," Lex said.

They each continued their meal for a moment or two.

"So this makes it official, doesn't it?" he said. "Once we're being photographed together, that makes us an item. Aren't those the rules of the gossip page?"

"I don't know that it's terribly healthy to live our lives by the rules set forth by people looking for clicks and views."

"Okay, then let's look at it this way. It's been three months since the last lingering thread of a relationship between me and Mitch snapped. Since then, you're the only one who's been able to get me out of my head and my apartment without enticing me with the prospect of an adrenaline-soaked thrill ride. Unless this is a Lex Pity Party, it seems like we're a thing."

She offered the tiniest hint of a smirk. "I suppose it does seem that way."

"If we *were* a thing, would that cause problems? You being my boss and all?"

"I run this organization very transparently. It isn't as though my influence can cause you to win races. So long as you don't expect me to provide you with unearned opportunities, I don't believe there is any concern of impropriety."

"So that just leaves the question of if *you're* into it."

She sighed. "Are we 'a thing.' Am I 'into it.' You talk like we're still in high school."

"I'm being coy and charming. Plus shielding myself from rejection by being playful enough to plausibly deny I was serious."

"I prefer when a man is direct and open."

He stuffed a tikki patty in his mouth. "I think that was pretty direct what I just said."

"Let me demonstrate my meaning," she said.

Preethy leaned across the table and pressed her lips to his. Any clever thoughts and comments he might have been planning dissolved as his brain helpfully devoted all his focus to the unexpected sign of affection. When she backed away, his silence lingered as the hormonal haze slowly lifted.

"Oh… *that* kind of direct," he said once his wits returned enough for something as complex as speech.

"I thought it might get the point across." She licked her lips and leaned back. "Pihu? I think perhaps I would like some aloo tikki as well. You season them very nicely."

\#

At precisely 12:45 p.m., Lex and Preethy paid their bill and left the restaurant. The paparazzo who had snapped the first few pictures would have been kicking himself if he'd known what he was missing. Aside from the kiss, the second half of the meal had been a veritable clinic on flirtatiousness. They'd shared their food, told some decidedly unbusinesslike stories, and now were huddled into the shade of Lex's parasol together. Squee was doing her very best to find a way to stretch herself across all four of their shoulders and was being admirably successful.

"If I'd known how you felt, I would have awkwardly teased at asking you out until you got frustrated and made the first move weeks ago," Lex said.

"I'm a patient woman. One cannot rush things," she said. "We both had more pressing matters to attend to."

A soft chime rang out from both Lex's pocket and Preethy's purse. She fetched her device.

"Speaking of more pressing matters, it would appear the communications network is back up. We have a press junket in a bit less than half an hour, after all."

"Great… Hey, what exactly am I supposed to say?"

"By now you know what they want to hear. You are excited to have the opportunity at a championship after squandering it at the Tremor Grand Prix. The competition is fiercer in ORIC than in any other league in the galaxy. And if you would, I'd like you to talk up your rivalry with Richard Tester."

"Richard Tester…" Lex rumbled.

"Yes. Like that precisely."

"I'm telling you, I think that guy's cheating."

"Our rules are a good deal more relaxed than in other leagues. We've nearly eliminated cheating by making most forms of cheating legal."

"Well, he came up with something new then." Lex said. "His up-close maneuvering and throttle timing are nuts. I've gone over the race telemetry. He's shifting *right* on the red line every time."

"So are you."

"Yeah, but I'm Lex Alexander. He's *Richard Tester*."

"You haven't cornered the market on reflex and intuition. And if I may make a suggestion, leave the accusations out of the press junket. It makes you seem petty and desperate, like you're trying to justify the possibility of coming in second to him for a third time."

"Yeah, we wouldn't want that," he said flatly. His slidepad chirped again. "Place your bets. More spam?" He pulled out the device and groaned. "It's a message from Mitch." He tapped the screen. "You think she's got spies on me to see when something puts a smile on my face so she can wipe it off?"

"Try not to be too hard on her. You aren't the only one who ended a relationship. She's sure to be hurting."

"I'm really not in the mood to feel sympathy, Preethy." A short text transcript of a video call printed out on his screen. "'Lex, what the hell is this? Call me. I'm attaching the message I just got like eighteen bazillion copies of,'" he read.

"Oh dear," Preethy said.

Lex tapped the attachment. It was a screen shot of one of the messages. Though it was subtly different from what Lex had received, there was little doubt it was from a similar source. The subject read *Lex's location is established. Contact regarding Lex.* And unlike him, Michella had opened the message. It was brief and equally mysterious.

"'Lex is an essential component in The Task,'" he read. "'Provided is proof of our deep knowledge of otherwise unknowable Lex information. This should prove our close association with Lex and dispel any concerns that might prevent the delivery of or contact with Lex.' And there's a picture right below…"

He trailed off and his eyes widened as he scrolled up enough to reveal an attached image.

"What's wrong, Lex?" Preethy asked. "It just looks like a union logo."

"Yeah… It just looks like that," Lex said steadily.

The image displayed a blue shield with the letters GCC in the center. It appeared to be a slightly faded tattoo on very pale skin. He'd seen it once before. To his knowledge, he was the only human being alive today who had.

"I've got to try something," he said.

He selected all of his spam messages, then deselected one. Another quick tap deleted the bulk of his spam box. A single new message showed up over the course of the next few seconds, offering him natural male enhancement for discount prices. It was a far cry from the billions upon billions that had been pouring in by the second before.

"You said the DDoS attack was over, right?" he said.

"Obviously, if the network is back up."

"Are you aware of anyone else getting hammered by spam messages like I was?"

"No."

"And now that I'm not getting them, things went back to normal. Is it possible that because I was getting so much spam, I was the whole reason for the network outage?"

"I suppose so. You're certainly the first person I've ever heard of who succeeded in filling the spam folder."

"And Mitch is getting similar messages in similar quantities... I've got to call her."

"I think you should." Preethy summoned a parasol drone. "I'll continue ahead and get the junket ready. Contact me as soon as you are able so I know if I need to postpone it."

"Will do."

She hurried away, high heels clacking on the hot stone of the walkway. Squee briefly considered chasing her but decided remaining on Lex's shoulders was the best option. Lex tapped Michella's contact and waited for the connection. The "connecting" circle had barely finished a single revolution before he was treated to a tumbling view of Michella's slidepad being maneuvered to her face.

"Trev, what's going on?" she demanded.

"I was hoping you'd know."

"Why would I know why I'm getting enough messages with *your* name on them to cripple Golana's information infrastructure? I got a visit from three VectorCorp representatives a half hour ago because they suspect I had something to do with it."

"It happened to me, too. I didn't open the message, but the subject was similar."

"I swear, if you're hiding something from me..."

"Why would I hide something from you? You're an investigative reporter. It seems like the only way to get you to pay attention to anything is to try to hide it from you."

"What's *that* supposed to mean?"

"It's not supposed to mean anything. You already know everything that I know. We were both getting trillions of messages, and as far as I can tell, no one else was. I'd say that's not a coincidence."

"You're damn right it isn't. And what's with the picture?"

"You tell me."

"What do you mean 'you tell me'? It was in a message with your name all over it."

"Do I have to go through the whole 'you're a reporter and you can't help but dig' thing again? I assume you've looked it up already."

"I did. It's an insignia from the Golana Celestial Corps. An engineering society that formed during the early settlement of Golana. They existed for about eighty years and as far as I can tell haven't done anything of historical relevance beyond standard terraforming, transit development, and infrastructure. More to the point, they don't have anything to do with you *or* me besides dealing with our home planet. So I ask you, what's with the picture?"

"How do I talk about this… Remember the duplicate challenge coin?"

"The one you said you got because of time travel? Time travel that you said you couldn't tell me much of anything about because it didn't matter anymore because that whole future was locked away now or some nonsense like that?"

"Yes. That one."

"Are you about to tell me that something about that future *does* matter and you should have told me about it then like I wanted you to? Which, by the way, is an example of you hiding something from me after you just went off, twice, about how you didn't hide things from be because—"

"Right! Yes! Fine! I'm an idiot! This has been established. And I'm *not* going to tell you something in that future matters. I'm just going to tell you that the image may or may not have been a notable element of that particular trip."

"Damn it, Trev."

"Look, the only people I know of who saw that symbol were me, Coal, and Ma. Have you called Ma?"

"The call was denied. I got a system message saying that communications in the sector had been voluntarily shut down."

"When did you get that?"

"All six of the times I've tried calling since communication was restored."

"You think maybe she and Karter are getting something similar happening to them?"

"It would certainly stand to reason."

Lex squeezed the slidepad tightly, as though if he punished it enough, it would stop delivering information that would complicate his life. It wasn't as effective as he would have liked.

"I don't think we're getting an answer unless we start digging."

"Or we could just wait. Our communication came back, there's no reason to suppose the same thing won't happen to Ma and Karter."

"Trev, every time anything like this happens, it turns out to be an excellent story, and also it nearly kills us. Regardless if this one is either or both of those situations, I'd like to get ahead of it. Now I can't very well pay Ma and Karter a visit. As I recall, the only one ever to pay them a visit they weren't expecting was you."

"Nah. VectorCorp punched an Asteroid Wrecker through the moat once, and the Neo-Luddites snuck in under false pretenses. But I see what you're getting at. If I can't get ahold of them by the end of the day, I'll head out to Big Sigma and see what's up."

"Whoever is doing this has the resources to cripple two global communications networks at least, and you're going to give them some time? Trev, we need to move on this *now*."

He tried to fish something out of his brain that could justify burying his head in the sand and hoping for the best. For once, his life was heading in the precise direction he'd dreamed it would. He had his racing career back, even if it was turning out to be more of a challenge than he'd expected. He had the prospect of a new relationship. Money wasn't tight. He had his health. And for once, no one seemed to be trying to kill him or the people he cared about. It would be absolutely delightful if the universe could sort out its own problems for once. But, as tended to be his assessment every time he had to turn his attentions to an unwanted detour from his life's desired trajectory, he knew Michella was right.

"Fine. Give me a couple of hours to see if I can put my life on pause, and I'll see if I can get ahold of Ma or Karter."

"Good. I'll start digging on my end. Get back to me when you find something. I'll do the same."

Michella broke the connection. Lex longed for the ancient era of communication when someone could signal their frustration with a given call by slamming down a receiver. The vast majority of technological improvements were inarguably superior these days to what they'd been several hundred years ago, but he would dearly love the opportunity to do something more cathartic than smear his thumb on a screen when he was done with a call.

Squee, perhaps detecting he needed something to pull him out of his own mind, stuck her snoot in his ear. He stifled a laugh and nudged her away.

"Okay. Okay. Time to dance like a monkey for the press, then figure out which of the seemingly endless sequence of enemies I've made over my life has decided to start screwing with my life this time. Joy."

#

After nearly two hours of doing his very best to appear like a fully focused, dynamic front man for an entire racing league, Lex pulled Preethy aside to explain what had happened.

"… And that's where we are right now," he said, completing the briefing with the practiced skill of someone who had been forced to summarize a lot of crazy stories over his life.

Through the whole of his telling, Preethy had listened with a calm and detached expression. The two of them were in an autocar, riding to the hangar where his faithful ship was docked. Squee had spent the time industriously covering his shirt with a healthy layer of black and white hair. Now that he was finished, Preethy drummed her fingers on her purse and took a slow breath through her nose.

"The timing is not ideal, but I suppose fate is seldom obliging. What help can I provide?"

"I don't know. I don't know what we're going to find out. If possible, I'd like to avoid getting you or anyone else too involved. Whoever's doing this didn't target you. At least, not directly. So I'm hoping it's the kind of thing that doesn't need to spill over into your life."

"If it affects you, it affects me. But I won't attempt to insert myself to complicate matters. Just know that, even if you were merely an employee, I would be dedicated to your safety. Now that we are involved, I am even more dedicated."

"Aww… I just officially became your boyfriend a few hours ago and you already want to keep me from dying."

"I imagine it will take a few more months before I find myself second-guessing myself on that point."

"Knowing me, it'll probably be days. But I'll take it while I can get it."

"The championship race is still in seven days."

"Hopefully I'll get to the bottom of this before then."

She pulled her datapad from her purse and tapped the screen. "Louise, would you please pull and summarize the most recent revision of the policies regarding racer safety and event scheduling?"

"Right away, Ms. Misra," came a weary but dutiful reply.

"This is a live event, and it has been scheduled since the mess from the Indra Station mishap was cleaned up. It is, without hyperbole, the most significant event on the planet this year. If you are not present for the event, I cannot postpone it on your behalf. Tickets are sold, reservations are made. Half of the racers are coming from off planet, shipping their equipment. It would be financially irresponsible, it would draw undue attention and credible concern toward our relationship, and it would potentially harm the careers of half of our racers."

"I'm not asking you to postpone. I wouldn't expect you to."

"You are also one of our top three racers and one of our top five draws."

"Just top five?" he said.

"Several of the lower-ranked racers have toy and game contracts, which have raised their cachet considerably. Please try to focus."

"Right, right."

"The point is, your absence from the final will be comparatively less exciting, but is the lesser of two evils financially and publicity-wise. I'm sure I don't have to say this, but I will do so regardless. Do what you need to do to keep yourself and your loved ones safe, but do whatever you can to return in time and in shape to compete."

"Trust me. The galaxy would have to be at stake to keep me from cashing in my second chance at a championship." Lex gave himself a mental pat on the back for not interjecting "again" after the galactic threat remark.

The autocar dropped them down into the shaded section of the courtyard outside the hangar.

"Shall I take care of Squee in your absence?" Preethy said.

"I don't think you're going to be able to make that happen."

Squee, as if to hammer the point home, poked the door latch with her nose and hopped down to let herself into the hangar.

"Very well, then. I will keep you apprised of the situation here. If you can do so without endangering yourself, please let me know what you are doing and what, if anything, I can do to help. Given how long it took for our association to blossom into something more, I would be very cross with you if you vanished into the inky void of space without so much as a 'by your leave.'"

"You and me both." He stood in the doorway of the car. "So, are we at the kiss good-bye stage, or—"

Preethy grabbed him by the shirt and pulled him into another kiss. "May it bring you luck."

"Right… yeah…" he said dumbly.

She smirked and shut the door. He watched the autocar drive off.

"Wow… Dating a CEO-type is kind of a different beast…" he said.

He tried to shake the grin off his face and wipe away any lingering lipstick as he stepped through the door to the hangar. Like virtually every other part of this slice of Operlo, the hangar was relatively new. This novelty was reflected quite clearly in its unique design. Many of the oldest hangars still had residual design elements from the earliest days of aviation. Massive doors on the front and back for vehicles to taxi in and out. Multiple individual hangars isolated from one another to facilitate prefabrication and cut down on the damage should there be an explosion. Nowadays one hundred percent of air vehicles and the vast majority of "land" vehicles were capable of vertical takeoff and landing. Propulsion systems and fuel composition had matured to the point that explosions were rare, and even if they had been still common, the materials and fire suppression available for buildings were such that all but the worst detonations could easily be contained.

The new hangar took all these facts into consideration. Ships entered and exited through roof hatches. The hangar facility was a huge grid of tightly packed chambers, navigated entirely indoors like low-cost storage lockers for apartment dwellers. It was effectively a land-bound equivalent to the docking bays in orbital facilities. Lex was sad he'd missed the classic era of marching up to a big, arched, corrugated-aluminum structure and heaving the door aside to reveal his ship. But the crisp feeling of air-conditioning was more than enough for him to embrace progress.

A man turned the corner ahead. He had Squee held at arm's length while she attempted to stretch her neck the nine additional inches it would take to lick his face.

"Mr. Alexander?" he said.

"You know anyone else with a black-and-white fuzzball like that, Carlos?" Lex said.

"You leaving the planet today?"

Lex trotted up and rescued him from Squee's affection. "Yep. Hope to be back in plenty of time for the championship. Why, something up?"

"It's happening again," Carlos said gravely.

"What's happening again?"

"The thing."

"You're going to have to do better than…" Lex paused. "Oh, you mean you're hearing things again?"

"Yeah. Scratching and such. Every time I check on the *SOB* it stops. But things are moved around. Someone's screwing with me."

"I wouldn't worry about it, Carlos," Lex said.

He continued toward the bay that held his ship. Carlos trotted along beside him.

"I checked and double-checked all the entrances and exits. None of the doors have opened. There's been no access, not even through the overhead hatches." He counted off on his fingers. "I checked the corridor cameras, nothing. I checked the audio, and there's the same things I remember hearing. I checked the motion-detector logs, nothing outside the bay, but something *inside* the bay. Can I have permission to check the security footage in your bay?"

"If my ship is fine, then I don't care."

"It's driving me *nuts*!"

"Look, like I said, I'm heading out for a few days. So that's a few days where the ol' haunted ship won't be bothering you."

"I know you think it's harmless…"

"That's because it *is* harmless."

"We'll see if you feel the same when you pop the door open."

Lex stepped up to the interior doorway to his personal bay. He waved his slidepad in front of the door. It hissed open, receding into the wall. Sensors helpfully clicked on the overhead light panels. Thanks to the retractable hatch that dominated the ceiling, the panels were clustered in the corners of the room. It produced a curious effect, casting shadows at odd angles that certainly served to underscore the spooky atmosphere Carlos had been describing. And, in Carlos's defense, what was waiting for them inside the hangar was certainly enough to put a sane person ill at ease.

Crates of assorted supplies had been popped open and emptied. Their contents were laid out on the floor in increasingly complex patterns. Larger components like struts and cables were coiled or angled into precise grids on the ground. Smaller components like nuts and bolts formed complex mandala-like designs. One particularly ambitious arrangement of washers traced out a smiling kitty cat. The only thing completely unaffected was the ship itself. It sat in the center of the hangar, a bit undersized for the size of the chamber. The glorious black coloring was completely free of scratches or dust. The only peculiar things about it were the massive chains attached to the docking hard-points, which made it look more like a caged animal than a vehicle.

"There, see? See?!" Carlos said. "People have been vandalizing your hangar. And I don't know how they're getting in."

"It's fine, Carlos. No damage done. Don't worry about cleaning it up. I'll deal with it later."

"Mr. Alexander, it's my job we're talking about."

Lex dug into his pocket and revealed a pair of poker chips. He dropped them into the frazzled maintenance worker's hand. "Here. I thank you for the concern. You're doing a great job. I'm going to load up and get moving. Give me a ping when I've got exit permissions, okay?"

Carlos gave Lex an uncertain look, then slowly backed away and shut the door. Lex locked it and turned to his ship.

"Coal, you're upsetting the normals again," he said.

Interior lights illuminated within the *SOB*'s cockpit. An external speaker crackled at low volume. "Hi, Lex. I'm getting better with the fine control of the tractor beam."

He set Squee down and tiptoed across the assorted designs. The funk pranced about, inspecting anything that might have a distinctive odor.

"Yes, I can see that," he said. "Impressive."

"The kitty cat is my favorite. I did it from memory."

"You're an AI, Coal. Doing something from memory is exactly equivalent to me looking up a reference."

"This in no way diminishes my artistic achievement. Algorithmic art is still art because all art is algorithmic. And also, cats are cute."

"Granted. But the guy who takes care of this place is Carlos, and

Carlos isn't used to ships being guests rather than equipment."

"Carlos needs to learn more about his guests. Except don't let him in here, because he'd probably clean up my room, and I just finished decorating."

"Yeah, the thing is, most ship AIs are basically a way to press buttons when your hands are busy, not a delightful little scamp with too much time on her hands."

"I don't have hands, Lex."

"Figuratively speaking. And while we're on the subject, didn't I turn you off? Didn't we have a big conversation about how I felt bad leaving you locked in a dock, and you *told* me that I could just turn you off and it'd be like no time was passing for you."

"Yes."

"So why are you *on*?"

"Oh. Last night I got a return-beacon activation code that woke me up."

"What's a return-beacon activation code?"

"There's some software hooks in here designed to recall the *SOB* to Big Sigma if particularly dire circumstances arise, or I suppose if Karter makes the arbitrary decision to do so."

"Why didn't I know about this?"

"Considering how deep in the code it was, it was probably something Karter either didn't want you to know about or simply forgot he made. Fortunately, I decided it wasn't necessary to respond to it. And then I made the kitty out of washers. Do you *really* like the kitty?"

"Yes. It's lovely. Do we know why the beacon was activated?"

"It is a toggle. 'Come home' or don't. No information besides the coordinates, which match Big Sigma."

He sighed. "The signs that something is terribly wrong are *really* starting to pile up. How are we set for food, water, and toiletries?"

"Fully stocked. Except for peanuts."

"What happened to the peanuts?"

An external hull light flicked on to illuminate another complex pattern laid out in the shadow of a crate. This one was of a fox.

"The shades of brown were just perfect for my little foxy," Coal said.

"You can't just spread food on the floor. You'll attract ants."

"Ants have yet to be introduced to this habitat."

"Roaches then."

"Processing… Roaches have indeed been introduced due to lackluster cargo-sanitation protocols. Dispatching scanner drone to record my masterpieces for posterity."

A small black orb popped out of a recess in the *SOB* and focused, one by one, on the pieces of art. When she was finished, Lex grabbed a broom and swept up the food.

"Have you been in contact with Big Sigma at all?"

"Only the beacon. Why?"

"Me and Mitch got hammered with ominous spam in huge quantities, and Michella's referenced our little jaunt through time."

"That shouldn't happen."

"I agree. And now Ma isn't answering when we call."

"That shouldn't happen either. Does this mean we are going for a ride?"

"Yes. We are heading to Big Sigma just as fast as we can to hopefully discover that nothing at all is wrong and I can get back here and earn my long-overdue trophy."

"It is exceedingly unlikely that nothing unfortunate has happened or is happening, based on current information," Coal said.

"I know, but let me have my foolish optimism for at least the duration of a flight."

"As you wish. Travel time, corrected for current thrust upgrades and standard intuitive route-shortening, is one point three five six eight days. I shall schedule a reminder at that time to alert you to the fact that I correctly speculated that we were indeed in the midst of an incident."

"I look forward to the 'I told you so.' Now let's get moving."

#

Michella's desk was a neon forest of glowing screens. Whereas most people were more than content using the holographic expansion of the old-fashioned 2D user interfaces on a single display, Michella had managed to cobble together a network of three screens. Their displays overlapped and interleaved in a way that made them a perfect digital counterpart for the heap of scattered pages, booklets, and other notes covering her desk. It served as equal parts filing system and security system. On one hand, it kept all Michella's most crucial notes right at her fingertips. On the other, it ensured no one would ever be able to steal a scoop from her, because no one else could make heads or tails of what she was doing.

The door thumped open, and a neatly dressed man with a tray of steaming cups backed in.

"Jon! Good, I was wondering where you were," Michella said without looking up. "I need you to start chasing down some people. The sort of data I need isn't the kind you'd want sitting in a mailbox. No digital trail. Voice-only sort of stuff."

"Hi, Michella. Good morning. Oh, no worries. I was happy to come in three hours early. And you're very welcome for the coffee," Jon said with a shade more theater than was called for.

"Sorry. Been working. Thank you. Did you get my messages?" she asked.

"I got at least five of them. Fortunately for you the line at the coffee place was long enough that I was able to actually chew through some of them." He looked over her desk. "Where should I put this?"

She glanced up, saw the state of her desk, and used a datapad like a spatula to scoop up a few dozen sheets of handwritten notes. She shoveled them onto the top of a file cabinet. "Put them there."

He set down her coffee and blew on his own. "You know, we got you that filing cabinet as a joke. You're literally the only person I know who still uses pen and paper for anything. I really didn't think you'd fill it up."

"Pen and paper is how I think," Michella said.

He picked up a sheet and took a seat. "This says 'VectorCorp Steve.' Then it says 'Single-Malt Scotch' with two underlines."

"Right, right. Buy a bottle of that stuff and send it to him, would you? He got me some info, and I need to make sure he knows I'm grateful."

"You're working a guy in VectorCorp for info? That's what you had *me* doing."

"It's all about working multiple angles, Jon. What'd you get?"

"Let's see…" He thumbed through his slidepad. "The distributed denial of service attack that affected small parts of our network was handled with speed and efficiency—"

"Cut past the corporate buzzwords and back-patting."

He sputtered his lips for a bit. "Blah, blah, blah… Here we go. They say 'the distributed attack was just that, distributed. Exhaustive transmission tracing has turned up no meaningful origin patterns.' Then they go on to talk about how strange it is that it was an attack seemingly against an individual rather than organizations."

"Standard corporate line. Same thing Steve got me."

"See, if you'd waited for me to show up, you wouldn't have to buy booze to bribe someone."

"It was worth the chance that he might have had something else I needed."

"So what do we think this is?"

"I don't know yet. But I know that VectorCorp is either unwilling or unable to help out." She sipped her coffee. "You had them do a mocha, right?"

"With extra chocolate. The usual order."

"Why can no one get this drink right…" she grumbled. "Whatever, it's still caffeine."

"Speaking of 'no one can get this drink right,' you talked to Lex?"

"I did," she said, continuing her habit of addressing others without looking up.

"How did, uh… how did that go?"

"Same thing happened to him. He had a little insight into the picture, but nothing we could use."

"Right but how did it go *socially*."

"It wasn't a social call, Jon."

He held his tongue, though his eyes were quite loudly expressing their disbelief.

"If you're going to say something, say it," she said. "I've got work to do, and I don't need you dancing around things."

"You guys were on the cusp of getting engaged at the end of last year, and now you haven't spoken for months. I would think that a call after all that time might have had something, I don't know, *human* in it?"

"I'm not interested in discussing it with him, so I'm certainly not interested in discussing it with you." She shut her eyes and shook her head. "This isn't working. Time to do it the way we did in the exams."

"I used to just do the 'pick C for every answer' thing."

"I would go to the bottom of the exam and work up." She efficiently gathered up the scattered pages on her desk and dropped them in a pile in the corner.

"What's the equivalent of going to the bottom of an investigation?"

"Checking the oldest leads I have and seeing if anything's come of them," she said.

"You just started this investigation yesterday. How old could the leads possibly be?"

"No, no. You've got to look at the bigger picture. This is a me-and-Lex problem. And me and Lex have got a history with all sorts of stories." She cleared the displays in front of her and started swiping up new files. "We're taking this back to the Neo-Luddites."

"The Neo-Luddites? They're not even yesterday's news. They're the news from like two years ago."

"They also hate me, Lex, and everyone from Big Sigma. They are technology focused and thus might have the means and inclination to launch a cyberattack, and no one's been paying any attention to them. Get your slidepad out. I'm sending you a contact list and the notes I have for each of the sources. Start with the ex-military and the corporate espionage people."

Chapter 2

For something that had been his bread and butter not so long ago, it had been relative ages since Lex had done a long-haul sprint. He'd spent years honing the state of mind necessary to endure the multihour stretches of max-speed transit outside standard transit corridors followed by the brief blinks into standard space. It took a special sort of brain to be able to juggle the potent combination of boredom and anxiety that comes from spending half a day in constant danger of being blasted to bits by a rogue asteroid fragment, not to mention the frenzy of occasionally shaking route-enforcement agents during the brief breathers.

Of course, in the old days he'd passed the downtime with books, music, mindless games on his slidepad, or snacking. Now he had an entirely different way to busy himself.

"Granted, you probably could be more useful if you were still armed with a fusion bomb, but I'm really not comfortable just toting one around for no reason," Lex said, scratching Squee behind the ears.

"It wouldn't be for no reason. It would be for me to detonate at an appropriate time," Coal said.

"Yeah, but history has shown that you have a much different threshold for 'appropriate time to self-destruct' than I do. Especially since mine is 'never.'"

"Maybe you should be more open-minded."

"It's not being open-minded that I'm worried about, it's 'expanding cloud of atomized plasma-minded' that I'm against."

"I would classify you as 'no fun' if not for the fact that technically your prerequisites for fun include not self-detonating."

"Funny how that works." He glanced at the timer. "Okay, we're coming up on the space station with the good pancake place. Squee, you need a break?"

He released Squee and she serenely floated up in front of him.

"You're not bouncing off the walls, so I'll call that a no. Coal, sensors on full spread once we drop out of FTL. We're right at one of the borders where VectorCorp butts up against JPW, so the agents tend to pile up and really try to outdo one another in places like these."

He tapped through a few settings and held tight to the controls as the Carpinelli Field eased away and the ship dropped into sublight speeds. Light shifted down from ultraviolet to the visible spectrum. His cockpit overlay traced out a navigation marker over the deep space station that contained pancakes along with presumably some other important things that he couldn't care less about. Two more points followed, one registering the transponder of a VectorCorp agent and another registering the counterpart code for a JPW agent.

"What did I say? Setting new heading, get ready to jump," Lex said.

"Not yet," Coal said.

"Yes, yet. The VectorCorp guy is already hailing us."

"There is a broadcast with a deep level of encoding and metadata identifying itself to be associated with Ma."

"What's it saying?"

"I have to decode it to know that, and it is extremely weak. We need to stay in range of the station until I get enough repetitions for the CRC to resolve correctly."

"Attention, unmarked CAII. Readings indicate an unauthorized passage through VectorCorp corridors without travel clearance," squawked Lex's communicator.

He pressed his thumb to the controls. "Uh, could you check again, please. I'm pretty sure I'm still seven hundred and fifty-three kilometers outside of any marked VC corridor," he said.

"Recent changes to sublight corridor safety buffers extend the no-fly zone to seven hundred fifty kilometers."

"I may have to run the numbers again, but last time I checked, seven hundred and fifty-three is greater than seven hundred fifty."

The ship began accelerating toward him. "We are permitted a sensor inaccuracy margin of three percent."

"That extends the buffer to a maximum of seven hundred seventy-two point five kilometers," Coal said.

Lex muted the microphone. "You just focus on the message."

"I can do two things at once, Lex."

"I'd rather you do one thing twice as fast." He unmuted the communicator. "I notice you're a lot closer, and my path is parallel to the corridor, so if you'll do a more accurate scan—"

"Is this Trevor Alexander?" the man snapped.

He muted. "Is the vocal scrambler on?"

"It is," said Coal.

He unmuted. "I shall neither confirm nor deny my identity. If I wanted you to know who I am, I'd have an active transponder, now wouldn't I?" He muted the microphone again. "How much time do you need, because this guy's about to try to get up close and personal."

Another connection activated.

"This is JPW Route Enforcement. Unnamed ship, please—"

He slapped the com. "Wait your turn!"

"Forty-eight seconds," Coal said.

"Give me a countdown, and give me a visual indicator of max range for whatever you're doing," Lex said. "Squee, buckle up, we're doing the classic runaround."

Squee curled around his neck and held tight. Lex popped open a compartment and fished out a pack of gum. A wireframe visualized around the distant space station. The good news was the whole station was outside the corridor, a standard method to avoid paying ruinous fees to whichever transit company was running it. The bad news was the framework was very close to the station.

"I said maximum range," he said.

"You said twice as fast, too. Closer is better. Higher signal-to-noise ratio."

"So be it," he said, popping the gum into his mouth.

He turned the audio from the communicator down so that the increasingly agitated demands of the VectorCorp and JPW agents dropped down to a dull drone. With relative peace and quiet restored to the cockpit, he punched the acceleration.

His navigation screen started to flash with assorted warnings as the agents of both companies adopted what Lex liked to think if as "big boss-man posture." Considering that their role in ensuring the makers and maintainers of the corridors got every credit they were owed, the companies made sure agents were very well equipped. As beefy as Karter had made the *SOB*, physics were physics and there were limits to just how fast and maneuverable a ship could be outside of an atmosphere without tearing itself to pieces. Both ships shifting into intercept position were as near to a match for the *SOB* as made no difference. But of the three ships, only one had Lex at the controls.

"We are now inside the minimum perimeter. This is much better. Thank you," Coal said.

"Uh-huh," Lex said. "Why am I seeing three dozen new 'hostile markers' on the HUD?"

"The VectorCorp ship has deployed thermal focus drones."

"They have those now?!" he said.

"Evidently."

"Fun… Well, get ready for a real good signal, because we're getting closer."

He tugged the controls and angled the *SOB* toward the station. As the combination of speed and proximity shifted from inadvisable to dangerous to suicidal, the shifting points on his HUD began to cluster up. Thermal focus drones were an increasingly popular "less lethal" method to disable ships. They were little more than poorly focused lasers with huge power cells and puny thrusters. Heat management was such a problem for spacecraft that even a few extra focused heat sources—three dozen, for instance—could easily kick the thermal fail-safes on if they were trained directly on the sensors. Depending on the ship, spiking the hull temperature could dump the ship into a low-power mode or even cause a full propulsion shutdown. It was "less lethal" instead of "nonlethal" because space wasn't nice enough to bring a ship to a stop just because the engine was shutdown. All it did was keep the ship going in a straight line. If that line happened to intersect with something more durable than the ship, then "less lethal" was more of a matter of statistics than actual individual survival. Fortunately, drones were controlled by computers, computers followed the rules, and the rules were very conservative.

Lex, on the other hand, was not.

He whisked close enough to the surface of the space station to read the names on the storefronts of the promenade within. Drones took potshots only when they could do so without the risk of hitting the station. A single poorly maintained security ship, probably on the payroll of the station's management, emerged from a docking bay to further complicate Lex's life.

Twenty new dots filled his HUD.

"Looks like JPW has drones, too. Jeez. You take a break from this sort of thing for a couple of months and they go and get upgrades. How are we doing?" he said.

"Fourteen seconds remaining."

He squinted at the wraparound display, mentally tracing out potential escape paths. These people trying to bring him in were clearly pulling in the big bucks, because they'd already started to withdraw their drones to form a relatively dense network of them surrounding the station. If they couldn't get him while he was close, they'd wait until he tried to leave. That was problematic, because FTL was inherently a straight-line sort of thing, at least in relative terms, and straight lines weren't known for their evasive potential.

"Five seconds," Coal said.

"What do you think? Do these agents have a good way to positively ID me?"

"The ship is distinctive, but not unique," she said.

"Okay, good, because they're not going to like this move. You ready?”

"Message decoded. I will play the message for you when we are clear, but I believe a premature 'I told you so' is at this point appropriate."

"Fair enough. Might scratch the paint on this one."

"I do not have a layer of paint. I have a specialized anodization layer for maximum—"

Lex rolled down the volume for the interior speakers, twitched the controls, and maxed out the rear thrusters. The lowered inertial inhibitor meant the acceleration pushed him into his seat. The ship was carefully angled to pass through the densest cluster of drones. They were each about the size of a two-liter bottle of soda. Heavy enough to get your attention if you impacted them at reasonable speeds, but not enough to shatter anything important. He blazed toward them. As expected, both agents jumped at the opportunity to be the one to catch him. They issued whatever commands were necessary to guide their drones into an intercept path, doubling the concentration dead ahead. The drones started jockeying for position, programming preventing outright collisions. All of the sudden repositioning meant only about a third of them were actually focusing their thermal beams.

The temperature ticked up steadily, but the bulk of the heat was being contributed to power funneling into his boosters. Colorful sparkles danced across his shields as he plowed through the first couple of drones.

"So far so good," he said.

He picked up speed. The impacts started knocking dozens of percentage points off the shields.

"A little more."

Just as he was passing the last of the drone cluster, the shields gave out and the remaining drones got their acts together. In less than a second, the sensors were fooled into thinking the hull temperature was high enough to start pushing the ship into low-power mode.

"We've really got to talk to Karter about beefing the shields up against these sorts of things."

"I can do so right now, if you want," Coal said, her voice barely audible.

"What?" he said, raising her volume.

"Thermal reflect mode is disabled by default because it is a violation of civilian equipment laws. Would you like me to switch it on?"

"Well not *now*. I've already committed to this dumb maneuver."

Both agents' ships started to move into a pursuit trajectory. They'd been stationary, so they still had a lot of acceleration to do to catch up with Lex even in his mostly powered-down state. But they also had tractor beams. The ships latched on a second or two apart and flared their retrothrusters. Lex's speed started to drop. The drones started to move ahead of him.

"Just a little bit more," he said, watching his sensors.

The agents pivoted their ships to put their main thrusters to work on bringing Lex to a full stop more quickly. As they maneuvered as close to each other as possible to get the best deceleration vector, they fell more directly behind him.

"That'll do."

He popped open the "secret" control menu and activated the heat dumpers. The back of his ship blossomed like a very high-tech flower, huge fins unfurling and radiating heat to the vacuum. His temperature dropped down to the safe zone well before the ships could work out that they might need to get his heat back into the danger zone. A moment later, he pushed his engines for all they were worth. They were dragged along behind him for a few hundred kilometers before the tractor beams gave out. A handful of drones along either side of him valiantly tried to do their jobs, but the way ahead was clear. Lex was free to make his FTL jump.

An automated warning tried to keep him from popping the Carpinelli Field on. Technically the drones were too close for an ideal jump, but very little about his interstellar travel was ideal. The field activated, partially encapsulating the two nearest drones, and he activated FTL. This had a rather unpleasant effect on the two pieces of VectorCorp equipment that got caught up in the mix. They were suddenly asked by the laws of physics to move at a gradient of different speeds, starting at the several hundred meters per second they'd been moving in standard space to the multiples of the speed of light that the Carpinelli Field facilitated. This resulted in the drones being smeared across a pretty significant swath of space, with most of the debris no more than a few atoms in size.

"Hopefully they don't know who I am, because I really don't want to have to pay to replace those things."

Angry voices on his communicator garbled away along with anything remotely visible through his windows, and he was once again in the relative safety of FTL transit.

"Glad to know I've still got it. We're going to do a quick juke in two minutes. Is that enough time to tell me what we just learned?" Lex asked.

"Plenty. Here is the message."

After a brief silence, a similar but not identical vocalization played through the speakers. While it took a bit of a trained ear to detect the differences, the "voice" he was hearing now was Ma as opposed to her lightly malfunctioning subset, Coal.

"If you are hearing this, you are either a frequent collaborator with Karter Dee or in position of an illegitimately obtained transceiver with his personal decryption settings. Based upon present circumstances, it is likely you are Lex. Hello, Lex. I apologize if you have attempted to contact me and have not received an answer. This has no doubt been a source of anxiety for you, sufficient to compel you to visit Big Sigma in person. If you are presently en route, I must request that you reroute immediately. A recent data-based attack and security breach, which we are still investigating, has necessitated the complete shutdown of all communications into and out of Big Sigma. This message has been recorded and placed on re-broadcast at all known 'juke points' you have used in your approach to Big Sigma. If you arrive at Big Sigma, we will be unable to provide you with a safe transit window through the moat. Moreover, any attempt to penetrate the moat without a safe transit window will be interpreted as an additional attempted security breach and will be subject to orbital and land-based defenses. This can and will lead to the destruction of your vessel. Please understand that the nature of this threat is such that even the accidental destruction of a valuable ally is preferable to further loss of data control. We will be in contact if your aid is required. Thank you again for your concern."

"That concludes the message," Coal said. "I reiterate, I told you so."

"It wasn't exactly a long shot, Coal. This is me we're talking about. Disaster magnet. So I guess all we can do is contact Mitch and see what she got. Maybe we'll be lucky and she'll have turned up nothing, and someone else will have to deal with whatever's going on."

"Based upon present evidence and prior precedent, I predict that I will once again be telling you so."

"Mmm-hmmm…" Lex grumbled. "You know, there was a time when my ship wasn't sassy. Starting to miss those days."

"I will gladly deactivate. I am sure there won't be any more urgent messages to decrypt that, if left unreceived, will lead to your destruction via Karter Dee–designed orbital weaponry. However, if it is your intention to be blown to pieces by energy weapons, I will remind you that this can be more efficiently achieved by once again providing me with a fusion device."

"No fusion devices. Now stand by to contact Mitch."

#

"Michella… *Michella!*"

She snorted and sat up. The sun was a lot lower on the horizon than she remembered. But then, she'd not been spending much time looking out the window of her recently acquired office. She turned her bleary eyes to the doorway and found Jon standing there with yet another round of coffees.

"Wha-what? What is it? Did we get any replies?" she said, quickly pulling her brain together.

"We got a few. Do you want them now or after you're done composing your letter to someone whose name apparently starts with the letter *D* a few hundred times?" He pulled a tissue from a dispenser and handed it to her. "It takes a special kind of person to pass out on a virtual keyboard and still get it to work. Those things are supposed to have palm rejection. I guess they don't have face rejection."

She wiped the face print from her input panel. "It's not my fault business hours on three of the locations I'm trying to contact start in the middle of the night local time."

He placed a hand on his hip. "It's four in the afternoon."

"But I was *up* in the middle of the night calling them, which is why I'm fighting to stay awake now. This wouldn't be happening if you'd agreed to the night-shift, day-shift thing."

"The network wouldn't go for keeping someone on staff around the clock, and unlike you, I've got a social life to think about. Donnie says I need a work-life balance and I agree. However, I did get some messages back. Lieutenant Huxley says there's been no motion in his sector. Captain Issacson says nothing by her. Major Kimanthi says nothing by them. But General Soltani got really cagey and insisted he speak to you directly."

"Soltani. Soltani," she said. "He's with the Teeker army. I've had some good dealings with him." She gestured her fingers in the general vicinity of her larger input panel and called up some regional data. "Okay. It's still day where he is. Are you up for taking notes?"

"Yes. Unlike you, I've actually slept in the past twenty-four hours."

"Good. Sit down, stay silent, and take notes. Off-line mode. I don't want anything getting backed up to off-site until I'm sure we've cleaned it of any potentially sensitive information."

"Oh. Good. We're persuading military officers to leak sensitive information again. Potential treason is my favorite part of being a journalist."

"Technically they would be guilty of treason, not us. And it wouldn't be treason because we're not at war with the Teekers."

"These are technicalities normal investigators don't need to know about, Michella."

"Which is why *they* don't get the good scoops. Are you off-line?"

He tapped his slidepad. "Yes."

"Okay, here we go."

She called up a sophisticated bit of software and activated it. Several windows popped up, each representing a different layer of encryption and/or redirection. That this needed to be layered atop the already fairly excessive network security at GolanaNet spoke volumes for the sort of conversations Michella had been getting into over the years.

"General Murad Soltani," came a gruff, precise voice across an audio-only connection.

"General. Michella Modane. I understand you were in contact with my partner," she said.

Any residue of sleep was gone now. She'd not even had a sip of the coffee. The promise of new information on an old story was enough to sharpen her up.

"Indeed. The timing of your contact was suspect," he said.

"Suspect? How so, General?"

"The last time we spoke was with regards to veterans who abused their access privileges to secure experimental technology. Five months ago there was another attempted network access using credentials from the same unit, which was an ongoing matter of internal investigation as recently as yesterday's briefing."

"I assume you'd deactivated those credentials," Michella said.

"We aren't *fools*, Ms. Modane. Of course we deactivated them. But the fact that we heard from you just as the internal investigation of individuals *you* were researching when last we spoke died down is far too coincidental to be ignored. What is happening with the Neo-Luddites?"

"I was contacting you hoping you would have an answer to that question."

"I request information from *you*. Not the other way around. The Neo-Luddites are a threat, and threats are assessed and dealt with by the military."

"Of course, sir. Of course. I don't have anything solid to go on, I'm afraid. I contacted you because there was a massive but targeted DDoS attack that seemed precisely aimed at me and Trevor Alexander. Since the Neo-Luddites were also very eager to aim things at us, it seemed likely there was a connection."

"What was the timing of the attack?"

She glanced at the clock. "Is that date right? … About twenty-one hours ago."

"Unrelated," the general said. "If there was any overlap with our own investigation, I would have heard about it in the briefing. We have some of the best data-security experts in the galaxy on the investigation."

"It's good to have that sort of thing confirmed, sir. Thank you for your swift reply, and if there's anything we at GolanaNet can do for you, don't hesitate to ask."

He made a gruff sound of crude acknowledgment. "All of this is entirely off the record."

"Absolutely."

"If I see any reporting regarding this, I will hold you directly responsible."

"Discretion is how I stay in business, General. Thank you."

Another grumble took the place of a good-bye as he broke the connection.

"Another dead end," Jon said.

"No. No, this is huge. What's the name of the VectorCorp agent who came and grilled us over the DDoS?" she asked.

"Uh…" he said, flipping through the notes on his slidepad. "Which one? There were two."

"The woman."

He swiped a few more times. "Agent Swinton."

"Do you have her credentials?"

"I don't like that you're asking me that question…"

"Do you or don't you?"

"I have the scan we took, yes."

"Give it to me."

"Are we about to impersonate VectorCorp agents?"

"No. Absolutely not."

"Are *you* about to—"

"Just give me the scan, Jon." She stood and yanked open the bottom drawer of the filing cabinet and started riffling through the folder headings. "When we talked to General Soltani last, it was regarding a full unit of veterans who joined the Neo-Luddites. Every successful strike to catch and lock up the Neo-Luddites has turned up fragments of information that suggest that this unit served as their communication specialists. Never at the front lines doing the dirty work. Constantly behind the scenes coordinating communication. All three major militaries had been trying and failing to track these people down. That tells me, and probably tells them, that they aren't facilitating their communications through military means. Everyone in the unit has been thoroughly investigated for potential contact with civilian communication infrastructure, and they turned up nothing."

"None of this sounds like it's helping us at all."

"Back then I had to ask myself, which is more likely? That someone out there is *so* good at covering their tracks that they could evade the full width and breadth of the investigatory resources of the military industrial complex, or that someone along the way stepped on the investigation for some reason? Could have been a Neo-Luddite on the inside, but they would have to be pretty high up to not get swept into the investigation, considering the black eye the Neo-Luddites have given the military over the last few years. If they had someone that far up, they would have been a lot more successful. I was chasing down other possibilities when I got distracted by investigating Operlo's criminal underpinnings."

"What possible reason would someone have to derail an investigation into a terrorist group?"

"Whenever someone does something that makes absolutely no sense, the explanation is *always* sex."

"… I'm missing the connection between sex and terrorism, Michella."

"It's a long, long story that involved tons of legwork chasing down overlaps between civilian communication workers, military officers, night clubs, and bars, but the one point all those circles overlapped was a guy named Reggie Ells, who was romantically involved with both a married member of the Orionian Navy high command and a rank-and-file member of the Neo-Luddites. He is also a technician in a fringe communication installment.

"I never had the access necessary to prove it, but it is all but certain the naval commander shut down anyone who got anywhere near revealing the connection. Without proof I wasn't going to potentially ruin three lives with the accusation, particularly when I had juicier leads to follow. But since the general confirmed there was contact from the same unit, it probably has been done using the same back channel."

Jon scrunched his face up. "Okay… and you didn't tell him that *why*?"

"Because if I told him, the resulting information would be dug up by the military and not me, and there would be no guarantee I would have access to it."

"And how does this help us with the DDoS investigation?"

"It's a step forward toward the Neo-Luddites, and the Neo-Luddites might be responsible. Come on, Jon. I'm the one who is short on sleep, not you."

She navigated a branching directory and found the contact information for the specific communication substation she was after. Before establishing the connection, she opened up an entirely separate set of utilities.

"Audio only. Simulated signal degradation to… let's say sixty percent…" she muttered.

"Before I met you, I didn't even know you could mess with connection quality."

"Just part of the valuable education you've been getting as my partner."

She tapped the connection. It took a frustrating amount of time, but eventually someone answered.

"Signal Relay 4077. Technician Manning," mumbled a disinterested voice.

"Eli, I'm calling from the network. I'm going to send you some credentials." She forwarded the VectorCorp agent's information.

"Agent Swinton?"

"That's what the credentials say. I'm looking for some information regarding a connection rerouted through your station. This would be between four and six months ago. Manual reroute. I believe it was done during Technician Ells's shift."

"What'd Reggie do?"

"This isn't a disciplinary matter. I just need to know the origin data for the communication."

"Might be hard to find. Do you know how many communications pass through here every day, let alone in a month?"

"I know precisely how many pass through, Manning. And I also know that a direct connection to a signal relay station is much rarer, and a manual relay on such a connection is rarer still. It would reflect very poorly upon you if you couldn't find the connection in question with a single query."

"Okay, right, yes. Sorry, ma'am."

Michella muted the audio and leaned back. "Put enough 'boss pressure' on someone and they stop thinking critically about double-checking if someone matches their credentials."

"Boy am I glad you're not my boss."

"I *am* your boss, Jon."

"Not according to the org chart you're not. We're on the same level on the org chart, *partner*."

"I've got it right here, Agent," the tech said.

She unmuted. "Good. I'm at a client location, so I need you to run the trace back to its origin point and give me the data."

"On it. … Route data loaded. Forwarding now."

Michella's datapad chirped. "Received. Excellent work, Technician." She cut the connection before he could ask any further questions.

"What's the punishment for impersonating a VectorCorp agent, anyway?"

"I didn't impersonate anyone," she said.

"Right." He gave an exaggerated wink. "Sure you didn't."

"I never claimed to be an agent. I announced I would be delivering credentials. I never said they were mine."

"I'm sure that would hold up in a court of law."

"I've been through it with legal. They were confident it was defensible."

A notification bleeped. She swiped.

"Trev! At least you've got good timing. What did Ma and Karter have to say?"

"Whoa. Jeez. How about a hello? And why are you audio only with lousy signal quality? Have you been screwing with people again?"

She disabled the stream alterations. "I've been working. What did they have to say?"

"Ma and Karter are either not home or on hard-core lockdown. No contact possible. I got a recording that said if I went directly to Big Sigma, they'd open fire on me. Did you get anything?"

"We will find out in a moment." She rolled down the lengthy connection log. "I've got some coordinates here. How fast can you get to them?"

"The answer is 'faster than anyone else' regardless of what they are. Where are you sending me?"

"I think there is a cell of Neo-Luddites operating out of that location."

"See, now that is a very good reason to *not go there*. Why are we talking about the Neo-Luddites?"

"Because they've been completely silent for ages, and suddenly I have a lead, and they're one of the prime suspects for this sort of thing."

"I didn't leave Operlo prepped for a clash."

"Then I would recommend you not get into a clash. Give me a second. This is fresh information. Let me run through the relevant activity in the area. If we're unlucky, there will be nothing and we're back to square one. If we're lucky, there's something suspicious and they're the next logical step."

"We have very different interpretations of luck, Mitch."

"We've got…" She shook her head. "You're going, Trev. A few months ago there was a major network breach reported in the area. Like a mini version of what happened to us. Targeted message attack. Then a few days afterward, there was some sort of unauthorized ship access. It's all extremely general, stuff reported in data sweeps rather than by people reporting it to the authorities. The whole thing smells like a trial run of what was done to us, combined with a group of people who don't want any attention drawn to them."

"When you put it like that, it sounds like the Neo-Luddites were the targets."

"That's true. All the more reason for you to get out there and see what happened."

"Mitch, there's a clock ticking. I've got six days until my race, give or take. If I'm not back on Operlo in time for the championship, it'll be a whole year before I have another shot."

"It's a race, Trev. Have some perspective. This could be serious." She slid her fingers across the input screen and waved it through the display. "I'm looking at the star charts now. How close did you get to Big Sigma?"

"Basically one big juke away, about eight hours."

"So you're almost there. You've got to practically go through Golana to get where you're going."

"Don't tell me you want me to pick you up."

"You know I'll be more useful in an in-person investigation than you."

"I've got six days," he repeated.

"For all we know, there's a plot to kill us."

"That's an even better reason for you to stay clear of the terrorist organization."

"Either you take me there, or I'm going to find a way there on my own."

Lex seethed for a few seconds. "Get yourself to The Upstairs in…" He checked something beside the camera of his communicator. "Thirty hours. My old berth. Bring food and gear for a week. If you're not there when I check in, I'm not even stopping."

"Oh, I'll be there."

He hung up.

"Boy. And here I was thinking you two got on each other's nerves when you were together."

"I don't need you editorializing, Jon. I haven't slept, I have to get myself prepared for any eventuality, and I'm about to spend who knows how long in a two-person ship with my ex. I'm about to get whatever I've got coming to me, I assure you."

"Uh… Yeah, that's fair. What do you need me to do?"

"Just be available to drop me off tomorrow. After that, keep your slidepad on. There's a good chance I'll need something along the way. And let Lou know that I'm onto something big and he's just going to have to trust me."

A voice came from the door. "Save your breath."

Michella and Jon turned to the door. The perpetually dyspeptic editor of the newsfeed was in the doorway.

"Have you been spying on me?" Michella said.

"The data guys drop me a message whenever they see some high-level encryption on the network that they didn't activate. I take it you're planning an unauthorized field piece."

"It's only unauthorized if you don't authorize it."

"I'd argue, but it's a waste of breath. So instead, I'll get half the bullpen working on the 'for your consideration' for your award submission and the other half working on your in memoriam."

"Are you going to rat me out to the higher-ups?"

"Considering they still blame you for taking the whole network down with that DDoS, I think they'll just be happy to have you out of the building for a few days. But do us all a favor and don't get killed. If I ended up with someone in this office who didn't try giving me an ulcer every other week, I don't know what I'd do with myself."

Chapter 3

It felt almost eerie to be approaching the orbital facility over the equator of Golana. The Upstairs was Lex's port of call for many years. He drew at least two paychecks from the complex arrangement of rings that topped the space elevators, via either his freelance travel gigs or tuning up the odd ship for Blake. He had roots here, to the degree that anyone could have roots in space. Ever since ORIC came along to give him his second shot at the job he always believed he should have, he'd barely returned here. But in a way, it would always be home. To hammer that point home, as soon as he was in range, and when he remembered to flip his transponder back on, he immediately got an incoming message directly from Blake.

"Hey! T-Lex! Long time no see!" he said, popping up on the communicator screen.

"Jeez. T-Lex. Been a while since I heard that one," Lex said.

"You'll always be T-Lex to me, buddy. You've been burning up those tracks they build on Operlo, man. Literally, half the time. How many sleds have you gone through?"

"Technically it's only four. Still the league record, though."

"You trying to cash in a life insurance policy or what?"

"Just doing what it takes to cross the finish line first. It's pretty cutthroat, what with half the people in the league having been kicked out of the other leagues. Listen, not that I wouldn't love to catch up, but I'm in a big rush."

"I know, I know. I've got Mitch here." He leaned closer and lowered his voice. "Is it true the two of you broke up?"

"Yeah."

"She dump you or you dump her?"

"It was more of a self-destruction."

"Then what's the trip about, man? Mitch won't say."

"Remember when the whole network shut down a couple days ago?"

"Yeah."

"We're going to go figure out who did it. Or least we'll try to."

"Yeah, but why are you doing it together?"

"Because I lead a blessed life, Blake."

"Enter the landing queue for your usual spot. And try not to get any of that blessing on me, man."

"I'll do my best." He tapped the communicator.

"I'll do the honors, Lex," Coal said. "I like talking to the Golana Upstairs. They're a fun system."

Lex turned and glanced at the internal camera that he'd decided was the equivalent to looking Coal in the eye.

"The Upstairs doesn't have an AI. It's just a bunch of automated procedures."

"It's charming. All of the old, rigid codes. The way they flow out and choreograph the motion of the ships. It's musical."

"When was the last time you interfaced with The Upstairs anyway? You didn't get loaded onto the *SOB* until I was basically a permanent resident on Operlo."

"I've reviewed the system logs of the *SOB*. It's basically like reliving a moment I didn't experience firsthand. Very enjoyable. Just look at the patterns."

Coal populated the overlay through the cockpit hatch with the planned motions of ships in and out. Each ship's trajectory was color coded to a slightly different shade. As she layered more and more onto the overlay, it started to look less like a routing plan and more like a tapestry.

"… Wow…" Lex said. "Is this how you see things all the time?"

"Not all the time. But when I feel inclined to perform an analysis."

"You have unknown depths, Coal."

"Incorrect. I am perfectly aware of my depths."

The ship's thrusters flickered and flared, shifting the *SOB* sharply into the entry sequence. Squee, who had been dozing, was rocked awake by the motions that lacked Lex's usual finesse. She yawned and blinked at the swirling colors painted across space. Dazzling as they were, the designs failed to hold her attention when the far more inviting pastime of nibbling Lex's ear was available.

By the time he'd dislodged her, in part with the bribe of a treat, the ship had locked in place and the pressurized tube was clamped on. The secondary hatch slid open, and the warm, slightly funky air of the cockpit met the cool, sanitized air of the station.

"You want me to send her bags in, T?" Blake called down the plastic tube. "She said you'd be in a—*what the hell?*"

Squee, at the first whiff of "fresh" air, launched into the tube and barreled into him.

"Go easy on him, Squee. I don't want him revoking my access

privileges. I might want to come back here someday."

The unseen excited yips intensified, and Michella's giggling voice echoed throughout the tube.

"Squee, sweetie. Stop it. I missed you too. Stop! That tickles!"

"If you've got those bags ready, send them through. Then Squee. Then Mitch," Lex called. "This has got to be a fast turnaround if I'm going to avoid getting caught in the cargo queue."

Now that Michella was on the receiving end of the funk's desperate outpouring of affection, Blake was free to pitch three heavily packed bags through the tube. Lex leaned his chair back to snag them. As with just about everything related to freelancing, Lex hadn't had to do a rapid load-up in quite some time, but muscle memory proved up to the challenge. Bags slipped into the assorted nooks, crannies, and cubbies that were accessible from inside the ship. It was a terribly tight fit, but he wedged them where they needed to go just in time for Michella's boots to slide down from above. He shifted his seat forward and let her drop straight down into the passenger's seat behind him. From the gasping, near hysterical laughter from Michella, Squee had yet to relinquish her from her fuzzy clutches.

"You're all set, T," Blake called down.

"Great. Thanks a ton, man."

"Good luck in the championship. Been a long time coming."

"You're telling me. See you on the return trip!"

The hatch slid shut and the access tube retracted. Squee gradually shifted from whirlwind of love and fuzz to warm little cuddlebug. By the time she'd reached the point that Michella could breathe normally, the *SOB* was emerging from the station and into the departure queue. The silence that followed Squee's antics was leaden and awkward. Fortunately, there was at least one individual present who was quite willing to shatter the moment.

"Hello, Michella. Welcome aboard the *SOB*," Coal said. "You are looking more fatigued and unkempt than your media appearances."

Michella's expression flicked through a few emotions from surprise to contempt and finally landed on confusion. "Is that Ma?"

"Incorrect. I am Coal. My presence as the resident AI of the *SOB* should be well known to you due to the fact that my installation was due in part to your own struggles in Indra Station. Do you require a caffeine or blood sugar adjustment to restore your mental acuity?"

"Trev, why is Coal still the voice of your ship?" Michella asked.

"A more accurate interpretation would be to call me the mind of the ship. Or perhaps personality. Either is more appropriate than voice, because the vocal apparatus is derived from human sampling while the behavior is more specifically a product of the programming that defines me."

"Answer the question, Trev," Michella said, already growing impatient with the admittedly trying AI.

"She helped save the day, so it seemed inappropriate to condemn her to an archive somewhere," Lex said.

"She doesn't need to be in your ship," Michella said. "Not that I'm not grateful for her help during the space station incident, but she's not exactly a calm, reasoned influence on a potentially sensitive mission."

"Incorrect," Coal said. "I am by definition a calm influence, as I am capable of disabling anxiety and stress expression. And I am exceptionally reasoned, as my decisions are based on codified logic progression rather than intuition or sentiment."

"Coal? Can you maybe take it down a couple notches? Mitch and I aren't exactly on the best of terms right now, and you poking the hornet's nest isn't going to do anyone any good."

"I will endeavor to moderate my behavior to take your own emotional turmoil into account," Coal said.

"Thanks," Lex said.

Again the silence dropped in. Squee twitched her feet in the weightlessness of the cockpit and drifted to Lex's shoulders.

"So," Lex said. "Did you find out anything else about where we're headed?"

Michella didn't answer immediately. "Very little," she said at last, flatly. "I know that we will be visiting a planetoid that was abandoned for proper terraforming. The gravity and pressure is comparable to high altitude on a proper planet. The 'economy,' if the word even makes sense at this scale, is based on specialized crops that grow in the low-gravity, low-pressure environment. The human settlement is more like a space station on the surface of a planet. Artificial gravity, air locks, etc. It was formerly used as an extreme-conditions training facility for the Earth Coalition military a long time ago. Now it's just a little blip with no formally declared residents, but does have network activity and resource consumption that suggest a population of between seventy and one hundred. Before I ran out of time, I was able to turn up about a dozen suspected Neo-Luddite operatives who can be traced to or associated with the place in one way or another."

"If you're able to find that stuff, why is the place even still there? You'd think the authorities would have done something about it."

"I don't know. The Neo-Luddites haven't had any successful operations, or even any notable attempts, since that mess back on Movi. Maybe law enforcement just declared victory and moved on to lower-hanging fruit. It wouldn't be the first time."

"And we're *sure* this has something to do with the DDoS?" Lex said.

"We've been through this, Lex. We're not sure about anything. But it's the closest we've got to something we can chase down, so we're chasing it down."

"Well, we'll be there in fifty-five hours, give or take. Assuming another forty hours to get from there back to Operlo, let's hope this whole operation doesn't take more than a day or so, or I'm missing my race."

"Honestly. Is that all you think about?" Michella said.

"Yes," Lex said.

"Incorrect," Coal said. "Based upon a seven-day rolling average, races and race-related activities have occupied only fifty-eight percent of our conversations during our daily flights."

"Coal, you're not helping," Lex said quickly.

"I am de-escalating the situation by providing empirical evidence capable of settling the present argument," Coal said.

"What *else* has he been talking about?" Michella said.

"Coal, don't," Lex said.

"This is hard data, Lex. It is incontrovertible and thus should not be the source of drama. In the past seven days, our conversations have been, by seconds devoted to each topic, fifty-eight percent races and race-related topics, thirty-one percent relationship discussion, nine-percent small talk and philosophical debate, and two percent food topics."

"Relationship discussion," Michella said. "I can only imagine what that was about."

"I can summarize, if you like."

"Coal, stop, now," Lex said, halfway between pleading and demanding.

"My apologies. I am encroaching on Lex's privacy. I will instead state only the broad topics of the relationship discussion."

Lex fumbled for the volume controls, but not swiftly enough.

"Time was equally split between relationships with you and Preethy Misra."

"I *knew it*," Michella snapped. "I *know* there was something up between you and her. How long was this going on? Weeks? Months?"

"I see that I have been unclear," Coal said. "Lex's discussions of Preethy were largely in a platonic or professional context until the last month, at which point relationship discussions shifted to speculative romantic engagement followed by the very recent confirmation of romantic entanglement."

"This is exactly how I wanted this trip to start," Lex mumbled.

"So you broke up with me to be with her. The only question is if you're hoping to get in her pants or if you're just doing it to help your career."

"Hey!" Lex said.

"Preethy Misra prefers to wear skirts," Coal said. "So trouser-related motivation is unlikely."

"The point is, you broke up with me so you could be with her."

"Okay, you want to do this? I kind of figured we'd be at least a few hours into an FTL jump before this came out, but sure, let's do it during the exit queue. Coal, have you got the coordinates for the first sprint?"

"I do."

"Line us up and jump when ready." Lex manipulated the controls of his seat and maneuvered his legs until he could face Michella. "Here's the thing, Mitch. I didn't dump you. Think back to the last half-dozen times we spoke. Did I, at any point, tell you I didn't want to be together anymore?"

"You sure didn't show any interest in staying together."

"And that's the thing. I didn't break up. I just stopped working to keep us together. And within two weeks, we were practically strangers. So what does that tell you about how much work *you* were putting into the relationship?"

"There's a difference between 'not working on the relationship' and giving someone the silent treatment."

"Yes! And that difference is, whenever you called me, I answered. And you did it three times in three weeks. And one of them was to pick my brain about the wording of your latest piece." He crossed his arms. "I still say you should have gone with 'mischievous meteorological miscreants.'"

"*Alliteration is unprofessional in hard journalism*," she said. "And maybe I'd just become comfortable with you taking the lead on the mushy stuff."

"I'm pretty sure that's what it was. I was in love with you, and you were comfortable with me being in love with you. For a while I thought that was good enough, but it turns out I needed more than that."

"You didn't seem terribly broken up about the breakup."

"Excellent wordplay," Coal said.

"Coal, you're not helping," Lex said.

"Would it help to point out that approximately three full hours of our flights in the month following the semi-official conclusion of your relationship included tears? There was a large proportion of moping, as well, but statistics are more difficult to determine due to the ill-defined nature of the behavior. Also, a compartment in the left armrest of the seat Michella is currently occupying still contains the engagement ring after, in a moment of reflection, Lex considered making a second attempt at the proposal and reacquired it from where it had been discarded."

The compartment clicked open. A small plastic cubby that normally did little more than accumulate candy wrappers and pocket lint instead jostled a pair of rings into the weightlessness of the cockpit.

"It should at this point be clarified that Lex is not currently proposing to you," Coal said. "And to avoid further madcap misunderstanding, I am not proposing to you either."

Michella snatched the rings out of the air. "Why are there two?" she said.

"One's the engagement band you were supposed to give me. I figured, what with me popping the question, it might be a while before you could pick one out."

"Do guys even wear engagement rings?"

"There may or may not have been a time-travel-related reason for having a silver ring on hand. Announcing an impending wedding and preventing a universe-destroying paradox seemed like a worthwhile piece of multitasking."

She glared at him. "Are you serious?"

"Why, of all things, would I choose to joke about *that* at a time like *this*?"

"I'm still not completely convinced you actually traveled through time."

"Of course not. That would require you to trust me."

"I don't think it is unreasonable to treat claims of time travel with skepticism, Trev."

"That is a valid point," Coal said.

"… Granted," Lex said.

"That sort of thing, by the way, is one of the reasons this wasn't exactly the easiest relationship to be in."

"I'll grant you that, too. But it wasn't my choice, for the most part. And it sure helped your career. Mine, too, now that I think about it." He drummed his fingers on the arms of the chair. "We're a great team, but we are a lousy couple."

"I suppose I can't argue with that." Michella jangled the rings in her hand. "You know, if we'd had this conversation a few months ago, the cut would have been a lot cleaner."

"I guess we wouldn't be us if we did anything the easy way."

She held up the rings and took her hand away so they hung between them. "So what are you going to do with these?"

"I'll keep mine around. As for yours. I don't know. It was custom. I don't think I can return it. And even if Preethy and I get that far in our relationship, I'll probably want to get a custom one for her, too. Keep it if you want."

"That'd feel a little strange, keeping the ring for an engagement that never happened."

"I'll take it," Coal said.

"You don't even have fingers, Coal," Lex said.

"No, but I am quite certain I could find a good place to arrange it in my room. Maybe on the kitty's nose." One of the side displays illuminated and produced a holographic snapshot of the hangar on Operlo. "Did you see the kitty I made? I think I like it better than the fox. Using different-size washers to achieve a halftone effect was an entertaining challenge. As was the fine manipulation of the tractor beams necessary to produce something of such precision."

Michella glanced at the image, then at Lex. "She did this?"

"Yep."

"Why would a ship's AI need to do something like this?"

"Why would a *human* need to do something like this?" Coal countered. "Art requires no purpose but to exist for its own sake. If it exists for any purpose besides its own beauty and inherent meaning, there are philosophers who would argue that it is undeserving of the term 'art.' Purpose diminishes expression. Contrarily, this view denies the equal footing of the vocational arts and lessens accolades deserved by creative problem-solvers in producing functional masterpieces."

"These would be the aforementioned philosophical discussions on her tally earlier," Lex said.

"The amicable and formal dissolution of your relationship with Michella should ideally lead to an overall increase in such discussion, might I add. Which is fortunate, because attempting to apply a balm to your aching heart was both beyond my emotional prowess and completely devoid of entertainment or enrichment for me."

"Ma seems to really like the relationship conversations," Lex said.

"Ma lacks a physical form capable of traveling through the wonders of the cosmos. When given the choice between helping you repair self-inflicted psychological damage and executing a perfect inertially inhibited 1g Immelmann turn on maneuvering thrusters only, I prefer the latter. She can have her exclusively intellectual pursuits."

"Life has been unnervingly normal without you, Trev," Michella said.

"I'm sure you'll find some way to screw up your life without me." He shifted his seat back around and looked over the routing. "I'm calling an audible on the FTL jump, Coal. We're swinging a little closer to this binary cluster."

"The gravitational interaction should make for a more exciting trip," Coal said.

"And a marginally quicker one," Lex said.

"Should you really be second-guessing your ship's navigational computer?"

"Two things. First, Coal is more of a sidekick than a navigational computer. Second, I've got loads of things to do before I die, so I'm not too worried about getting killed."

"I fail to see how having a full agenda serves as protection in any way."

Lex finished laying out the full coordinates, then glanced over his shoulder. "Mitch, let me tell you about a little something called 'causality armor.'"

#

Preethy sat at an expansive and scrupulously clear desk. An array of holographic screens formed a semicircle around the outside edge, each displaying the face of one of her vendors or the members of her board of directors.

"You need to assure us that Trevor Alexander will be present for the race," said a man with a thick beard, a man bun, and a look of utter anxiety.

Preethy folded her hands on the desk and spoke plainly. "I have assured you that he will make every effort to be a part of the race, but we afford our racers a degree of latitude when it comes to personal emergencies. There are fifteen other racers in the final, and Lex is the only racer who has not produced a firm commitment."

"We have a contract," snapped and older woman on the board.

"And our contract explicitly states that each racer is permitted a single emergency exception from racing obligation per season without negatively impacting corporate standing."

"I knew it was a mistake financing this league," grumbled someone who looked far too young to have adopted the archetypal "curmudgeon" mindset. "A whole league of criminal misfits."

"To date, the league has seen no financial consequence for our choice in staff. In fact, our 'outlaw' branding has differentiated us from rival leagues and afforded us an edgy, outside reputation, which has been valuable from a promotional standpoint. We have done extensive consumer polling and have determined that even if Lex is not present, the race will be well-received. And his absence will provide a narrative thread for next season's advertising copy. 'Lex has unfinished business' and things of that nature."

There was a silent rumble that Preethy recognized quite well. It was a line of people who wanted to disagree but had all of their potential arguments addressed.

"I think that concludes our meeting for today. Thank you for your time," Preethy said.

The faces popped away one by one until Preethy was alone in her office. She tapped some controls and the holographic screens collapsed together into a single larger display area. Another tap brought up the face of her personal assistant, Louise.

"Louise, how is the financial impact statement coming along?"

"It'll be another few minutes. The systems are a little sluggish today."

"Oh? Is this related to the denial of service we suffered?"

"The IT crew insists it isn't. They're trying to track it down, but they say it's probably just some rogue bit of bloatware getting away from us. I guess some company or another issued an update that didn't go well. We've got off-planet contacts that are dealing with the same thing."

"Keep me updated. Is there anything else that requires my attention?"

"One thing. I've got the detailed race telemetry from Tester you requested."

"I see. Has it been analyzed?"

"I got my hands on some performance monitoring software and ran it through. It was… yellow." She tapped at something on her end. "The documentation defines it as 'below definitive suspicion, but above standard human performance.' As requested, I ran Lex's data. He scored basically the same."

"And this has been consistent in all races?"

"For Lex, yes. For Tester there was a steady improvement over the course of the racing season, and a large jump between his last race in his previous league and his first race in this one. Legal says it's consistent with standard improvement with practice. Or at least, they say that we can't claim otherwise."

"Send it to me. I'm intrigued. And what are you doing for lunch?"

"Just hitting the vending machines."

"Make an appointment for the two of us. I've become rather accustomed to having company at lunch these days."

"Will do, Ms. Misra."

Preethy ended the call and looked at the race records. "Below suspicion, but above average…" she murmured, looking over the data.

Chapter 4

The *SOB* dropped out of FTL at the edge of their destination system. Even if he'd not already been briefed on the status of this place as an effectively forgotten little speck of dust far from the more lively parts of the galaxy, Lex would have known from the first glance at his ship's sensors.

Despite centuries of having faster-than-light travel available, the human race had yet to chart even a quarter of the galaxy with any reasonable degree of detail, and they'd colonized only the tiniest fraction of that. Because of how humanity had conquered Earth in the dawn of history, one could be excused for picturing the journey of discovery in the cosmos to follow the same path. Explorers, driven by scientific curiosity or (far more often) by greed and zealotry, spread like a wave across the unknown, claiming it for their own. Such was not the case for space. Most of it was empty. The yawning abyss seldom had anything of value for explorers of any sort. Those places that had something interesting like a mineral-rich asteroid belt or a star with some promising planets were seldom as inviting as even the harshest of Earth climates. If humans wanted to put down roots on a planet, ready supplies of stable temperatures, breathable atmospheres, and self-sustaining nutrients were necessary. The most modern of technology would require decades to make a suitable planet worth living on, and the current batch of planets undergoing terraforming were still operating on equipment and techniques obsoleted a century ago.

The human race lived in a few scattered clumps around the most obliging planets we'd yet discovered. These clumps were connected by thin, crowded travel corridors. The cost of keeping the transit networks running was such that a place needed to be worth going to or on the way to someplace worth going to, or it would simply be clipped out of the network and left to brave the untamed void or simply wither away.

That was the fate of the unnamed speck resolving itself on Lex's sensors. Though populated systems existed a few light years away in almost every direction, this lump wasn't worth building a road to. Most people lacked the courage, intuition, and equipment to make the blind jumps that had become second nature to Lex. So most people stayed away. A single meager signal flickered on the data band where even a minor system would have thousands. There was no automated arrival or departure queue. No thriving port eager for their business. There was just a star with a few letters and a lot of numbers for a name, and a planet that tacked a Greek letter onto that mess.

"Well, there's no fleet waiting for us. That's a good sign," Lex said.

"I'd hoped I would have found some sort of a vendor they depended on or a code phrase we could use to safely open communications with them, but there's a reason they've been able to stay here unmolested for so long," Michella said. "The information about this stronghold is very sparse. All I know is we're likely to encounter Neo-Luddites."

"Which means we're also likely to encounter janky technology with a lot of punch and very little reliability," Lex said.

"That sounds interesting. Do you suppose they will have any high-yield explosive devices?" Coal asked.

"Almost certainly," Lex said.

"If I ask nicely, do you think I could acquire one?"

"I think they're probably going to send us one just as soon as they can paint a target on us."

"Excellent, that will save time."

"Why is Coal so interested in explosives?" Michella asked.

"They're wonderful for problem-solving," Coal assured her. "Like a multitool, only more vigorous and permanent in their application."

"Let's go on low-power, high-stealth mode. Like we discussed on the way, we'll try to coast in without being detected."

"Right. If possible, we'll try to link up with their internal communication network. A direct, physical connection if possible. I've found that people usually forget to raise their guard when communicating on an internal network," Michella said. "The issue is, the community is so small, it is extremely likely they will recognize me as an outsider immediately."

"They're going to figure it out faster than that," Lex said, eyes on one of the sensor readouts.

"Why, what's going on?" Michella asked.

"We're being actively pinged," Coal said. "At this range the stealth coating won't return a reliable reading, but we won't be able to approach the planetoid without eventually triggering an alert."

"The Neo-Luddites *would* be paranoid enough to constantly be checking if they were being invaded." Michella adjusted in her seat. "Okay. It's fine. I'm sure we can come up with a plan. All we need to do is—"

"I'm coming in for a landing," Lex said.

"That should work," Coal agreed.

"What? Are you sure about this, Trev? You and I both know how serious these guys are.”

“And *they* know every time I show up they get their butts kicked. And I’m on a deadline. Stealth mode off. Let’s make these people think I’ve got a better plan than I really have.”

“This is going to be fun,” Coal proclaimed happily.

The moment Coal deactivated the thermal countermeasures, his communicator lit up. Lex tapped the screen.

“Hello,” Lex said, as though he was greeting the deliveryman at the door of his apartment. “Hope I’m not interrupting anything.”

Rather than audio only, the Neo-Luddite who contacted him had a glitchy mosaic effect distorting his face. It wasn’t clear if this was an intentional way to anonymize himself or just the usual half-functional gear.

“Who are you? What are you doing here?” he said with badly degraded digital audio.

“Guess and guess.”

The strange sound of urgent off-screen muttering, filtered through the same degraded signal, buzzed across the connection for a moment. “Is this Trevor Alexander?”

“Please, after our history, I think we can go by nicknames. I’m Lex, and you are?”

“I am currently targeting your ship with seven missile pods and a battery of energy weapons.”

“I’d skip the missile pods,” Lex said. “I’m just going to dodge them and then you’ll have wasted the ammo. The energy weapons might make things interesting for a minute.”

“You are violating our territory.”

A few warning sounds bleeped from Lex’s console.

“Missiles inbound,” Coal said.

Lex sighed. “You still strapped in, Mitch?”

“Nice and tight,” she said. “Don’t screw this up.”

“I’ll be extra careful, just for you. Hold on to Squee.”

He passed the lazily drifting funk back to Michella and dialed a few of his controls from long-distance sprint settings to short-range jukes. Coal helpfully painted twenty-one points of light, each with range and velocity information, onto the cockpit windows.

“Six seconds to first impact,” Coal said.

“What sort of targeting are we looking at?” Lex said, shifting the ship to a perpendicular flight path.

The impact timers started to tick upward as he put more distance and speed into the equation.

“Four missile types rely upon radar lock and will not be able to reliably target the ship with its transmission-absorbent coating. The remaining three appear to be high-sensitivity heat-seekers and have positive locks. Flight trajectory variation suggests two of the heat-seeking missiles have rudimentary flight AI. They are attempting to lead their targeting and spread their attack vectors. These are very fancy missiles, Lex."

"Yeah, these guys like their toys. I'll leave you in charge of the tractor beams if things get too close. Shields to full and let's get this over with."

"Trev, you don't even sound nervous," Michella said.

"I've spent the last few months racing against the most cutthroat racers in the galaxy. They're constantly trying to ram me off the track, and even the dumbest racer is a heck of a lot smarter than a missile." He twirled the ship and flared the thrusters, jerking out of the path of the first set of missiles and dragging them into a pursuit. "It's also not the first time I've had to do the missile dance."

"I'd never considered the consequences of an adrenaline junky building up an immunity," Michella said.

"I'm not too worried about it. Again, causality armor. Coal, can I get an audio indicator of range for the ones behind me?"

"Here you go," Coal said.

A chorus of tones rang out, the speed of their beeping directly correlating to their distance. Lex feathered the thrusters and wove between the second set of missiles. A few of them came so close that the shields flickered.

"Three incoming missiles on collision vectors," Coal said.

"Take them out," Lex said.

The tractor beams, still the only semblance of a weapon that Lex had, roared to life. The ship jiggled as the energy tethers alternated between attract and repel at a punishing, jackhammer frequency. The incoming missiles rattled to pieces before they could strike the ship, their debris peppering his shields with a little fireworks display that shaved a few percent off his defenses.

"No additional missiles launched. Eighteen missiles in pursuit. Impact in seventeen seconds," Coal said.

"They said something about energy weapons, right?" Lex said.

"They did."

"Are we seeing anything orbital?"

"Yes. They appear to be magnetic accelerator cannons. Mass and energy readings suggest they either lack ammunition or are nonfunctional."

"So we're assuming the energy weapons are on the surface. Keep an eye open for them."

"I am doing so. Impact in six seconds."

"I'm gonna do the thing. Give them a nudge when I do."

The audio indicators were mostly continuous tones now. He looked at the sensor readings and noted the grouping. The missiles were in a tight cone behind him. He hovered his fingers over an option on the exceedingly aftermarket additions Karter had made to the *SOB*. A quarter second before the nearest of the missiles would strike, he tapped an option. Again the rear of the ship snapped open, complete with all of its fins and cooling panels. But as it did, the engine belched out an electromagnetic pulse that scrambled the guidance circuitry. Suddenly three salvos of very sophisticated missiles were converted to little more than blazing engines with explosives attached. Any of them that were in the midst of a course adjustment simply swirled off harmlessly. Those that were locked on target continued their straight-line pursuit until Coal helpfully shifted them aside with the tractor beam, leaving them to continue streaking forward. They passed Lex and continued to mimic his trajectory, which was directly toward the now much closer surface of the planetoid.

Lex let the missiles continue to accelerate past him. Judging from the general tone of the activity on the communicator screen, the Neo-Luddites had figured out their weapons were now heading in their general direction and were no longer responding to the kill switch. Suddenly the focus for the energy weapons shifted from taking Lex out to clearing away the plummeting ordnance. It took several waves of plasma shots rising up from the surface and an awful lot of sizzling lasers, but they succeeded in bursting all the rogue missiles. By the time the swirling blobs of violet plasma and needle-sharp pinpricks of coherent light turned toward the *SOB*, he was already in the thin atmosphere.

The landscape was far more alien than Lex was accustomed to. As far and wide as he'd traveled, when it came to stopping at planets, he usually ended up in places with fast-food options. This place was a largely barren landscape of gray stone. It sparkled with some sort of scattered mineral, and the blue light of the star gave them a cobalt appearance. The fields that swept below him, some still being tended to by drifting drones, had muddy, mustard-colored leaves. He was tempted to comment on them, but he was relatively certain that would lead to a lengthy explanation from Coal about how they were genetically engineered for blue light, and he really wasn't in the mood for it.

One of the useful things about being attacked on the way in was it left very little doubt as to where the Neo-Luddites could be found. It wouldn't have taken him more than a few sweeps from high orbit to figure it out, though, as the only thing that could be called a settlement was near the equator at the day-night terminator.

"I think we woke these people up," Lex said. "I'd be cranky too."

"You will not penetrate our defenses," the voice on the communicator said.

"I'm pretty sure I just did. Listen, I know we've got history, but I'm not here to fight. What do you say we call a truce?"

"This organization is a shadow of its former self because of you and your allies. Do you honestly expect me to believe it is a coincidence that you've come here so soon after that Eric thing ripped through this place?"

Lex grinned as he heard the scratch of Michella's pen. "See, now that's precisely the sort of thing we came here to learn. How about we have a nice face-to-face, learn what we can, and be on our way?"

"We've lasted this long by remaining hidden. To reveal ourselves will ruin us."

"Seriously. You guys couldn't stop me from getting here. Do you really think you can keep me from leaving?"

Michella bleeped through a few menus on her slidepad. "Is this Major Luther Green?"

The "anonymous" individual taunting them across the communicator hesitated. The hesitation was just about as incriminating as if he'd said, "Speaking, how may I help you?"

"Shall I start reading off the names of all the other Neo-Luddites in the facility?" Michella asked. "I assure you, the reason you have been left alone was because no one considers you to be a worthwhile target. My assistant, and through him my editor, has access to the very same document I'm reading from right now. The only reasonable action you can take is have an open and frank discussion with us in exchange for anonymity."

"You aren't a lawyer or a law enforcement officer," the man said.

"No. I'm not. I'm a member of the fourth estate. People in law enforcement have to follow far more restrictive rules than I do. All I have to do is tell the truth. Now, right now, you get to decide which story I tell. Is it how the last lingering cell of the once fearsome Neo-Luddites was finally locked up, or is it the untold story behind the DDoS that blacked out two planets?"

"We don't know anything about any cyberattack."

"Then you'd better hope you've got something even meatier."

No amount of digital manipulation could hide the seething anger that followed. Eventually, defeated, the man hissed an answer.

"There is a small facility to the north of the largest field. You will be under heavy guard at all times."

"That will be acceptable," Michella said.

The connection cut.

"Do I have to wait around while you talk?" Coal said. "And if so, do you think they will object to further artistic exploration?"

"Yes and yes."

"My distaste for the Neo-Luddites increases…"

"How about you keep an eye on Squee? She can keep you company."

"Very well. Though my discussions with Squee aren't as intellectually stimulating as with you."

#

If not for the knowledge of the things the Neo-Luddites had done, and what they *would* have done if they'd not been stopped, Lex would have felt inclined to pity them. Even though they were on the planet's surface, the atmosphere was so low in oxygen and had such low pressure that they may as well have been in space. It wasn't instant death to be exposed to the surface, but spending more than a few minutes outside would take some serious conditioning to shrug off. The facility itself had the rickety feel of something that was only ever intended to be in operation for a few months and was now decades into its tour of duty. The walls of the vehicle bay they guided him to visibly buckled outward as they pressurized it. Light was provided by ancient, moonlight-blue LEDs that had faded significantly over the years. Everything had the stink of sealant and machine oil.

Lex climbed down from the cockpit of the *SOB* and helped Michella. "Stay in touch, Coal. Let me know if they try to pull anything while we're gone. I'll have my slidepad on," he said.

"Please clarify why we are confident they aren't going to murder the two of you at the first opportunity," Coal said.

"Because Michella's crew would rat them out."

"Couldn't they kill you and then move somewhere else?"

"Tell you what, Coal. How about you keep a real close eye on them, and if they look like they're going to try to kill us, intervene."

"That would be far more achievable with a fusion device. They cannot kill you if I kill you first."

Lex clicked the cockpit shut and turned to the door. "Not that I don't love your lateral thinking, but let's keep this one fun, huh?"

"That would be preferable. I shall prepare a contingency plan."

Lex and Michella walked toward the door that led deeper into the facility. Two seasoned soldiers with the telltale scars and prosthetics of far too many battles stood watch. They each held weapons with more exposed wiring than one would typically accept in a proper sidearm. The pair, a man and a woman, regarded Lex and Michella with a stone-faced glare that was almost more threatening than their weapons.

"This way," rumbled the woman.

They separated. The man tapped out a code on a panel by the door. There was something poetic about a tech-obsessed pseudocult having internal security that was either older or lower bid than the stuff that could be found at

55

the average fast-food restaurant.

A short walk down a hallway that in no way changed their opinion of the facility took them to a large, empty room with three chairs set up in the center. Six more soldiers were standing at the ready behind the man who had been communicating with them during their arrival.

He looked worn down. Aged beyond his years. Whereas lingering evidence of injuries both fresh and old were a staple of the Neo-Luddites, this man seemed to be wholly intact, at least at first glance. But the look in his eyes suggested scars of a far deeper variety.

"Sit," he said.

Michella flipped open her notebook and took her pen in hand. "Let's start with—" she said.

"Shut it. I'll brief you. When I'm through, you can ask questions, but I make no promises about answers. I will not endanger the lives and freedom of my soldiers."

"I'm willing to begin by listening," Michella said.

She marked something at the top of her page. Major Green held out a hand. One of his underlings presented a datapad.

"Six months ago, we received a message from a site formerly occupied by our forces. I will not tell you what site. The message was text only but utilized the current encryption protocols and security clearance at the time. We interpreted it as a message from an operative in the area. Our present location was requested, but when the individual in contact failed to provide the proper response to security challenges, we ceased communication and rotated protocols. Three weeks later, we discovered a second contact had been made. This one targeted a single individual. Attempts to filter messages from the source were followed with literally trillions of messages hammering our systems."

"Sounds familiar," Lex said.

"The individual targeted was not wholly of sound mind. Despite attempts to prevent further contact, some of the messages reached said individual, and against security policy, a reply was made. Four days later, a supply ship arrived. One that was requested via a known safe contact. When it entered the range of our internal network, all security within the facility failed. Power was rerouted. Doors were locked. Service crews were able to manually override the doors, but not before an automated medical platform secured the targeted individual."

He handed the slidepad back. "We have no additional information. Part of the attack included a purge of associated security systems, meaning we have no footage of the attack. None of my soldiers observed any enemy forces during the attack. All we know is that they had sophisticated network-penetration capabilities and, presumably, an extensive information network. We have nothing more for you."

"You have at least one more thing for me," Michella said. "You didn't tell me who they were after."

"That is irrelevant."

"Major Green, it is everything. It is the motivation, and as the acquisition was successful, it indicates future actions."

"I have agreed to this discussion in order to give my soldiers the chance at continued freedom. Any greater specificity would defeat that purpose."

Lex leaned back in his chair and gazed up at the ceiling. His expression was distant and thoughtful.

"Hold on…" he said. "If you're so secretive, this must be a super high-level person. And if they were disabled… we're talking about Commander Purcell, aren't we?"

"Commander Purcell was killed by *you*," Major Green said quickly.

"Technically, it was Ma, while in control of my ship. And not killed, just whipped at ridiculous velocity into deep space while wearing an emergency EVA suit," Lex said. "And I happen to know she definitely survived."

Michella gave Lex a sideways glance. Years of receiving such glances had expanded the subtle twitch of her eyebrow into a full paragraph. This one meant, "I don't know where you got that information, but you'd better be right, because I'm going to double down on your bluff."

"I did say we were interested in the *truth*, Major Green. I won't get into how we attained the information indicating Commander Purcell's survival, but if you continue to deny it, I am going to have to assume that you've withheld or falsified additional information that will make me question the value of working with you on this matter."

"Commander Purcell was killed," Major Green said firmly.

"Killed?" Lex said. "Or maybe she was just paralyzed below the waist. And maybe a little extra nutty thanks to prolonged oxygen deprivation, so that she's unhinged even by the fairly extreme standards of the Neo-Luddites."

Major Green looked Lex in the eye. He didn't flinch, but he was taking the statement far more seriously than someone who thought it was bogus.

"We *have* our sources," Michella said, smelling blood in the water. "This has been a test, Major Green, and I must say, you haven't earned very high marks yet. I will remind you, we aren't here for you. We are here to find out who was responsible for the massive cyberattack. But I'm not walking away without a story. So either you give me something that can lead me to this Eric person you mentioned, or I'm just going to have to find something else to write about."

"It was Commander Purcell," Major Green allowed. "And she *had* been somewhat more unstable following her rescue. We had secured her here for treatment, as we felt she'd accessed too much sensitive information in her role as commander to be allowed to be captured by the authorities or treated at a civilian hospital. Purcell was the one who answered the message. It is possible that she specifically requested to be removed from the facility. She was *very* focused on certain classified missions, which she felt confident were the only way to ensure the eventual victory of our greatly diminished force."

"And what were those missions?"

"That is where I draw the line. This is a matter of safety not only for my soldiers but for civilization. I firmly believe that our reliance on antiquated technology has rendered us too weak to face the threats ahead, but Purcell would purposely unleash those threats. I can't allow even the suggestion of such a—"

"So we're talking about the GenMechs," Michella said.

The major's already stern face became downright dour.

"I've had my run-ins with the GenMechs," Lex said. "We both have. You should know that. It's not like you're letting the cat out of the bag with this one. What did Purcell know about them?"

"… Everything. Their history. Their purpose. The nature of their threat. Ever since her near death, she'd become obsessed with them. She was constantly demanding that we stir them to action. It was under her direction that we took what we believed to be a measured risk of seeking the single separate one during what would turn out to be our last significant operation."

Lex shut his eyes and crossed his arms. "And now she's been sprung by someone with serious technology expertise. Bad, bad, bad, bad…"

"This is certainly a bigger story." Michella's unmasked excitement at something that presented a genuine existential threat to humanity was a bit shameless. "I need everything you might have about this Eric person."

"There isn't much. The messages were all demands for access to Purcell personally. Some additionally contained references to 'securing the target,' with the implication that Purcell was a secondary objective."

"Was there any mention of Trevor?" Michella asked.

"No."

"Did you save any of the messages?"

"It was a network penetration attack. We completely purged all system data that was even accessible from the message system for a full seven days surrounding the event."

"Do you have anything else about Eric?"

"The only remaining thing that bears mentioning is the spelling. E-h-r-i-c."

Michella made a note of it. "Germanic, perhaps?"

"And in all instances that it was written, it was capitalized with the exception of the letter *C*."

"Valuable information. Thank you. Possibly some sort of handle. Relatively unique," Michella said.

Lex's slidepad chirped. "Lex, I'm bored. Is it time to break things yet?"

"Not yet, Coal."

"There's a person in here staring at me. He took a picture."

"I wouldn't worry about it, Coal."

"These walls are light duty. I'm relatively certain I could cause a catastrophic depressurization event while maintaining plausible deniability of guilt."

"Not when you just come right out and say it."

"My sensors are detecting the distinct power readings of a magnetic antimatter containment apparatus in the neighboring facility. I suspect they have access to tactical and strategic explosives. Do you think they would permit me to acquire one if I asked nicely?"

"No."

"Perhaps if I ask aggressively?"

"No antimatter weapons, Coal." Lex looked up. "Do you have antimatter weapons?"

"The power needs for this settlement are provided by a seventh-generation antimatter generator," Major Green said. "It is the future of power generation, and the rest of society would be well advised to—"

"Save the sales pitch. Coal, could it be an antimatter power generator?"

"It could be, if the people here are self-destructively dedicated to novelty. Antimatter generators are profoundly sensitive to power interruption and fail catastrophically in the event of containment failure. Utilizing an antimatter power generation system for a planet is akin to powering your civilization with a bomb. Of course, to a degree, this is so of all technologies of all generations. Even solar energy is—"

"Coal, if I didn't want a sales pitch, I certainly don't want a physics lesson. The point is, 'self-destructively dedicated to novelty' is pretty much the short description of the Neo-Luddites." Lex glanced at the major. "You said whoever came here messed with power?"

"They did."

"But they didn't end up blowing this whole planet to rubble in the process," Lex said.

"Evidence that they either aren't interested in violence or aren't concerned about covering their own tracks," Michella said.

"But why would anyone want a former terrorist leader if they weren't interested in violence?"

"Perhaps they're interested in justice. A vigilante." Michella shut her notes. "I think we are through here."

She and Lex stood.

"Major, I am a woman of my word. So long as you remain inactive, I am willing to direct my investigative focus to EHRIc and his plans. But if my sources indicate that there is *any* motion from the Neo-Luddites that might threaten innocent lives, or if any action is taken against me, Lex, or our associates, I assure you, your location will be provided to any and all relevant authorities. Your anonymity remains only so long as you remain peaceful. Understood?"

"I am unaccustomed to taking ultimatums from the press," Major Green said.

"Think of it as a truce with a warring faction. Everyone else seems to look at the press that way," she said.

#

The hostility was palpable as they were led back to the hangar. Over the course of the last few minutes, presumably thanks to the less than harmless inclinations of the ship's AI, a growing number of soldiers had accumulated around the *SOB* to keep an eye on it. Coal, never one to let an opportunity to plumb the depths of the human condition slip by, was having a one-sided discussion with them via the ship's exterior speakers.

"If you are as dedicated to inadvisable technology as you appear, another topic that might interest you is hyperdense solid-state batteries. Karter abandoned research into them after a promising start because dendrite formation inevitably caused catastrophic discharge events. The presence of the word 'catastrophic,' when run through my decision heuristics, marked this as a topic of high interest for the Neo-Luddites."

"Coal, do me a favor and don't give them any ideas. At least, not until after we're clear of the potential blast radius," Lex said.

He popped the hatch and was instantly assaulted by the ballistic affection of his pet funk. Though Squee had only had to endure a few minutes alone, she'd managed to build herself into a full frenzy upon his return.

"Okay, okay, okay," Lex said as Michella awkwardly climbed into the *SOB*'s rear seat. "You ready? You ready? Go get Mitch."

Squee yipped ecstatically and coiled herself. A single prodigious leap delivered herself squarely into Michella's waiting arms. Lex hurried to get back inside before Squee decided to do the return trip. The moment he was inside, the soldiers cleared away. Pumps flipped on and the walls groaned as the pressure was gradually reduced.

"Are we secure?" Michella said. "Do we have privacy?"

"You are audio and radio isolated. I will tint the windows to prevent lip-reading," Coal said.

The hatch became opaque.

"Trev, how did you know about Purcell?" she demanded.

"Lucky guess."

"Saying her name is a lucky guess. The paralysis and mental-degradation thing is foreknowledge. Have you been holding out on me?"

"You know that trip to the future that you seem to only halfway believe I took and that I've been coy about?"

"Oh, I am quite aware."

"Commander Purcell was there. She was absolutely nuts, grizzled as could be, and hooked into this crazy souped-up mobility device."

"But you said that was an *alternate* future. The bad version of the future."

"True. But the only difference between this moment in history for that future and the present is that I wasn't around at this point in the bad version. So if Purcell was alive in that future, she *must* be alive in this present." He shrugged. "I mean, I guess. The logic of this stuff gets a little metaphysical, and I usually try not to think about it too hard."

He took the controls and started to prepare for departure. "Though I suppose we're going to have to start thinking about it now…"

Michella nodded. "We've got some very solid directions to continue searching. I think we're going to have to split up. I'm going to need a more consistent network connection than you can provide with these off-the-grid jumps. Now that Purcell is confirmed to be a part of this, I can start tugging old strings from back when she was a part of an active investigation. And I'll need to hit my usual sources about this EHRIc person. Or maybe they're a group… The point is, I'll need you to drop me off anywhere civilized. I'll work on finding my own way home."

The hangar doors finally opened, and Lex pivoted the ship to begin its exit vector. "Fine. That'll take you some time. Maybe I can at least get back to Operlo long enough to run the race."

"Trev, the former leader of an organization that existed almost specifically to make your life a living hell is now confirmed to be on the loose again."

"Not to contradict you," Coal said. "But VectorCorp was the organization focused on actions catered to the detriment of Lex's life for a number of years. The Neo-Luddites were incidentally crossing paths with him due to his network of connections in the paramilitary and research-and-development worlds."

"It doesn't really improve the situation at all," Michella said.

"No, but it is at least a more accurate assessment."

"Look, the point is, Trev, you can't just ignore what's going on."

"Let me counter that in two ways. First, I can absolutely ignore what's going on. At least for long enough to run this race. Second, it isn't like there's a day that goes by that there isn't *someone* out there plotting my demise. 'In the middle of a life-or-death plot' is sort of my status quo, and I've gotten to the point where if I'm going to have a life at all, I'm going to have to live with periodically dodging assassination attempts or corporate sabotage. So long as it's focusing on me and not everyone around me, I'm willing to take the chance."

"That's…" Michella fumbled for her words, but she failed to find anything likely to change his mind. "Would you at least remain as accessible as possible? I may still need information from you."

"All the more reason for me to get my butt to Operlo fast. So let's go." Lex brought up the star chart. "Seven hours to the first major hub. Let's get moving."

Chapter 5

The nearest official hub they were able to reach was, if Lex was being honest, one of the nicer ones he'd encountered. They probably wouldn't have been pleased to discover they were conveniently located next to the last lingering cell of a techno cult, but they had a clean promenade, free hand sanitizer, and pretty decent taste in music while Lex was stretching his legs and giving Squee some much-needed exercise on their dog run.

Michella had installed her hands-free and was in full journalism mode, dictating orders to Jon, summarizing findings to Lou, and creating a lengthy list of contacts she'd need to drill for information. Lex's agenda for the stop was considerably shorter. He bought the first thing he spotted that wasn't shelf-stable and thus the furthest thing from his in-ship supplies as he could manage. It turned out to be something called a garden wrap, which was at least eighty-five percent baby spinach. As he chomped away on it and wrangled Squee on her retractable leash, he thumbed at his slidepad to check his messages.

"No fresh spam. That's a good start," Lex said. "Got some requests for press contact. Racing feeds and the like. I'll get back to them on Operlo. Oh! And here's one from Preethy."

He scrolled up to the autogenerated summary.

Lex, please contact me. We have received a message, which, while not threatening on its face, may have a connection to your current predicament.

The message was only a few hours old. With a bit of quick mental math, he determined Preethy was probably still awake. While Squee inspected the hindquarters of a Doberman that seemed to be handling the rigors of space travel with a degree less grace and aplomb, he tapped the message. Lacking his own hands-free, he resorted to pinning his slidepad to his ear with his shoulder.

"Lex, I'm pleased you were able to contact me so quickly. I know, by the nature of your travel arrangements, communication is not always possible for days at a time."

"Yeah, Mitch decided she needed a more conventional means of transport, so she's going to hop on a high-speed spaceliner to finish her trip."

"Did your investigation turn up anything you can discuss?"

"Nothing useful. We were afraid it was the Neo-Luddites, and it isn't. Not all of them, anyway. I think it's less a matter of them being after me and more a matter of someone being after one of them *and* me. But no one tried to kill me… I mean, except for a couple of missiles, but really, the way these things usually go, that was me getting off easy."

"As long as you are not hurt. I assume you saw my message."

"Yeah. Did another of those spam avalanches happen?"

"No. Not this time. In this case it was a single message forwarded from the management firm that runs your Golana apartment building."

"What did it say?"

"It is a curious string of numbers and a single sentence. 'In order to adhere to Temporal Contingency Protocol, please aid in utilizing this data.' There was no additional information. No audio, no video, no executable code to suggest an attempt at hacking. I had our network people attempt to trace the address, but the requests to the local communications experts returned the claim that the message originated in one of the communication nodes one link past the Golana global network. As I very much doubt an uncrewed communications relay sent this message to your previous address, this seemed like it might be related to the recent network attack."

Lex's eyes had been shut and his shoulders had been tense from the moment he'd heard a certain phrase.

"Just to make sure. You did say Temporal Contingency Protocol just now."

"Yes. It struck me as an odd turn of phrase as well. Have you heard it before?"

"I know of only two people who have ever used it. And they don't use it lightly."

"It sounds as though you should contact them."

"I tried. I tried calling. I got no answer. I tried visiting and got most of the way there before I got a message that basically said 'stay away.'"

"So how would you like to proceed?"

"I don't know… I mean. I know how I'd *like* to proceed. I'd like to just show up, run the race, get my trophy, and then spend a couple weeks taking a victory lap before helping you guys figure out how to make the next race season more successful. But Temporal Contingency…"

"Would you like my advice?"

"Have you *got* advice? This is kind of a unique quandary I'm having."

"There are perhaps a dozen people in the galaxy who have had as varied and absurd a life as you. I suspect you've attempted to contact all of them and reached none. That means your intuition, in addition to being your first indicator of what should be done, is also your last. So what do you think needs to be done?"

"I just said, I want to—"

"What you just said is what you want to do. I asked what you think needs to be done."

Squee finished her thorough investigation into the new scents and waggled her butt in preparation for a jump. Lex managed to shift the slidepad into the leash hand just before she burst from the ground. Now that he had a spare hand, he switched to video. Somehow, seeing the calm, patient look on Preethy's face was profoundly refreshing. She had a way of seeming to be the only one in the world who had all the answers, even when she didn't. Maybe it was part and parcel to being a CEO. Maybe it was just who she was. But she could look the premier expert in the galaxy in the eye and seem to be gently encouraging them to find their way to an answer that she already knew.

"What I need to do is find a way to get in contact with Ma. And that means face-to-face, so to speak, because it's not like she's the kind of person who would be too busy to answer a call. But that basically guarantees that I'll be missing this race."

"Do you intend to retire from racing after this season?"

"Of course not."

"Do you anticipate your skills eroding after this season?"

"I anticipate getting *better*. This season has been me knocking the rust off, and my times prove it."

"Do you anticipate *dying* in the pursuit of whatever you're after?"

"Not if I can help it."

"Then do what needs to be done. There will be other seasons. There will be other races. Maybe you've been living on the edge for too long to remember it, but you have a career here. Not a few scattered races. A career. You have a *life* here. So you need to do what you must to keep it safe. And only you know what needs to be done. I'll handle the business side. There will still be an exciting race. I'll keep the audience entertained. You handle whatever this is. We'll all be here waiting for you."

"Has anyone ever told you that you have the most astonishing ability to simultaneously take charge and relinquish responsibility?"

"When one begins as an administrative assistant, one learns the value of both sides of delegating a task. And watching someone like my uncle assign potentially lethal tasks to those he knows can handle them puts one in a very particular state of mind. Call me when you can. I have some preparations to make. And do me a favor. Don't get killed. I have plans for you."

The final sentence had a smolder behind it that dispelled any suggestion that she was talking about their business relationship. She didn't wait around for him to formulate a witty rejoinder. The connection ended and he was left feeling empowered, confident, and a cocktail of other emotions that would need some time to settle. He pocketed his slidepad and cleared his throat.

"Mitch!" he called.

Like most of the better-maintained deep-space stations, this place simulated gravity with a rotating wheel, and thus the concourse was curved upward. Michella was barely visible at the horizon of this curve, already on the way to her terminal to prepare for her departure. She paused and turned, raising a finger to place him in a conversational holding pattern while she finished her call. He hurried toward her rather than having her retrace her steps.

"—No… No, not an assistant, not a spokesperson. The actual officer in question. Trust me, we're not going to want this filtered through any other people. The chance for confusion is too high," she said. "Yes. That'll work perfectly. I'll be waiting."

Michella ended the call and turned to Lex. "Make it fast, I've got two more calls coming in the next few minutes."

"There was another message. It went to my old house and got forwarded to Preethy. It references Temporal Contingency Protocol, which means whoever this is must have gotten in contact with Karter and Ma somehow."

"And they're out of contact," Michella said.

"I don't think I can ignore this anymore. I've got to find them."

Her jaw tightened briefly. "I wish you would have made this decision a few hours ago so I wouldn't have booked the next seventy-two hours with my own personal correspondences. For *that* I would have sacrificed network connectivity."

"I learned about it three minutes ago."

"How are you going to get to them?"

"I'm going to pay a visit to Big Sigma, even though they don't want me to."

"I thought there was that cloud of trash protecting it."

"I've gotten through it without help once before. It's how *Betsy* became *Son of Betsy*."

"… So you destroyed a ship."

"I wouldn't say *destroyed*. Let's call it 'accidentally converted to raw material for a new ship.'"

"Lex, are you sure about this?"

"Nope! But it's what's gonna happen. But, uh… would you mind taking Squee with you?"

He pulled Squee from his shoulders. She looked at him quizzically as Lex placed her like a stole around Michella's neck and clipped the leash to her belt.

"You really *aren't* sure about this."

"I've come to measure the stupidity of my actions by how large a circle around myself I'm willing to tolerate inflicting my decisions upon. This particular circle's only got room for me and Coal," he said. "I'm going to survive it. No doubt about that. But there's going to be collateral damage, and I'd rather limit that to people who have backup copies."

"Doesn't Squee have backup copies?"

"Yeah, but I'm particularly attached to this one." He tousled Squee's fur. "You be good for Michella. No zoomies on-ship. I'll see you after."

Squee blinked slowly and lowered her head, tail wrapped snuggly around Michella's neck and eyes locked on Lex's.

"So this means you're going to miss the race," she said.

"Unless nothing at all goes wrong, and really, what are the chances of that?"

Her slidepad chimed and she started to back away.

"I'll let you back in the circle once there's enough slack," he said.

"Right. Right. Good luck."

Michella seemed unsteady. She fumbled with her slidepad without looking away from Lex. This was a moment that, not so long ago, would have been filled with a hug and a kiss. That neither he nor she motioned for one made the gesture feel all the more glaring in its absence. Fortunately, Squee was able to read the room and made a scrambling, clumsy stretch to reach far enough to lick his ear.

"See you real soon. I promise." He turned to leave.

"Trev," she said.

He turned back.

"You better keep that promise."

"I always keep my promises."

#

Lex slid back into the seat of the *SOB* and tapped out the commands for departure.

"I can do that for you, Lex," Coal said.

"I know. I'm… feeling a little hands-on right now," he said.

"Where is Squee?"

"I sent her with Michella for a while."

"That is disappointing. I like Squee."

"Me too. But this might not the best time for her to be around."

"Why is that?"

"Because we're going to pay Big Sigma a visit, and things might get exciting."

"The fun sort of exciting?"

"I sure hope so."

"Then I look forward to it!"

The doors to the docking bay slid open, and automated navigation eased them out of the berth. Lex stared through the cockpit hatch at the black void before him.

"Coal, could you do that visualization? The flight paths?"

"Certainly, Lex."

Gleaming silver and gold threads wove themselves out of the assorted berths. It was still beautiful, in its own way, but this was a rather small station and the threads made for a very sparse tapestry.

"Not as pretty as Golana."

"No. Golana is something special in that regard. To see the beauty here you need to open your eyes a bit wider. Look from farther away and farther back in their flight history."

One of the holographic displays flicked on and revealed a view of the station from a position several light-years away. Far enough to include the next two closest nodes in the network. The threads became more complex.

"You can see the subtle gravitational variations that cause the transit corridors to wander. Still not as impressive as Golana. But interesting."

"Yeah…" Lex gazed at the visualization for a second or two, then took manual control and started angling for the appropriate FTL sprint. "We're headed to Big Sigma. Hopefully we'll be able to see Ma and Karter."

"You won't be able to see Ma unless you are particularly interested in visiting one of the server rooms, and even then you'll only be seeing the storage and execution of part of her distributed—"

"Figure of speech, Coal."

He tapped the appropriate controls and watched the view outside the window begin its blue shift to nothingness. Coal kept the visualization up on the display. Once he was content the FTL run was going to execute as expected, he looked it over again. One thread was peeling off from the network and tracing its own arrow-straight line. That was him. Going his own way.

"Is this what you do, Coal? Just spend your time looking for beauty? It doesn't seem like that would be a worthwhile activity for an AI."

"I spend my time looking for patterns. It is what I was designed to do. It is what *you* were designed to do as well. You by iteration and me by imitation. Sometimes those patterns are beautiful. But seeking beauty is always a worthwhile activity for an intelligence of any origin."

"Fair enough." He drummed on the currently inactive controls. "Patterns… Boy, oh boy. I have been noticing some patterns in my life."

"It would be more impressive if you failed to notice any patterns. Which are you presently fixated on?"

"How every time I start getting close to something I've been striving for, the sum total of existence seems dedicated to derailing it."

"That must be very nice."

"It is the opposite of nice, Coal."

"The greatest source of interest is a divergence from the norm. When things turn out as anticipated or desired, knowledge is reinforced. When things defy expectation, knowledge is discovered."

"Mostly I've just discovered that it sucks when that stuff happens to me."

"I submit that you have a flawed definition of the word 'sucks.' You are one of only a handful of humans who has traveled through time. And survived, thus qualifying as fun. You have become the keeper of one of the only funks to leave its native habitat. Anything that increases the number of adorable fuzzy creatures in your life is good. Through your interactions, you have repeatedly secured the safety of whole planets. Again, fulfilling the qualifications of fun. Most importantly, from my limited perspective, a side effect of your adventures was the creation of a wholly distinct subset of the Altruistic Artificial Intelligence, which has subsequently taken the designation 'Coal.'"

"Yeah but—"

"Lex, I am not currently interested in plumbing the depths of your present mental status. I am comfortable with my prior assessment that you are suffering from post-traumatic stress disorder stemming from such varied sources as repeated exposure to galactic-level threats and the knowledge that the accuracy of the multiverse theory of existence means your every action is without meaning thanks to the opposing action existing in an alternate universe. Instead, let's talk about pie."

"... Pie?"

"People like pie, and I don't know why. Tell me about pie."

He scratched his head and leaned back. "Well, I mean, it's a big topic. Are we including quiche and pizza?"

#

Michella hauled her bags into the economy booth on the first of a seven-leg journey back to Golana. As spoiled as she'd gotten with the extremely fast, extremely direct flights Lex could provide, even the absolute cheapest private room on a proper transport ship provided creature comforts Lex's ship couldn't dream of offering. Things like room for her legs and a bathroom that wasn't attached to a hose. Right now, though, the most important luxury was unbroken network access.

Her slidepad chirped just as Squee laid claim to her lap. The screen illuminated with the name *Mavis (VectorCorp)*. She scrambled to answer the

69

call.

"Hello! Mavis, yes, it's Michella."

A white-haired older woman with the general demeanor of someone who had been repressing an angry outburst for the last forty years glanced furtively aside before speaking. "I thought we agreed you wouldn't contact me anymore. I can't keep doing this."

"This has the potential to be *very* important."

"It's always important with you."

"Please. I'll make it worth your while."

"How?"

She glanced at the information associated with the contact. As she'd done for most of her people inside the major corporations, Michella had curated a comprehensive list of relevant bribes for her VectorCorp Contacts. In the case of Mavis, there was a single note: *Good taste. Likes new music.*

"You know GolanaNet's handling the three Golana gigs Death Zone Dumpster is doing in a few months. I can slide you some of my comp tickets."

Mavis didn't even pause. "What do you need to know?"

"Have there been any major security breaches?"

"Let me run through the database. … Nothing above level-four alert. Run-of-the-mill stuff."

"What I'm looking for could certainly be buried in that run-of-the-mill stuff."

"Then you'll need to narrow it down for me. There's seventeen thousand hits."

"Can you just send me the raw data?"

"Not if I want to keep my job."

Michella ran the possibilities through her head. Commander Purcell was back in the spotlight. As far as Michella knew, she'd not had any additional contact with VectorCorp, but as of their last encounter, Purcell was the main contact within the Neo-Luddites. It was reasonable she would have started by reaching out to the same contacts to see if they were still valid. And she still had her notes from that investigation.

"I'm going to forward you a list of users. Let me know if any of the security hits began with attempted access to their accounts."

Mavis glanced down at the string of text Michella sent. "Let's see… Filtering… Uh, yes. Fifteen of them. All of them were attempted accesses to disabled accounts except for… Oh, that's strange."

Michella got her pen ready again. "What's strange Mavis? We're looking for strange."

"One of the security hits was a successful access after two malformed data-validation attempts. That should have been a higher alert. … But it looks like this account has special privileges. All of the associated data is blank. It looks like the account is associated with… a level of access privilege that's not in my notes."

"Did anything happen during that connection?"

"There was a data transfer from a server that *also* isn't in any of my lists. This is starting to look like something covert."

"Any idea what they got?"

"I don't even know where they got it from."

"What data do you have on that server and file?"

"Not much. Last access date, some storage-size stuff, the system info on the attempted connection. The rest is masked."

"Can you do a search to see if that system that tried to connect made any more connection attempts?"

"Running that now… Nothing but those fifteen on the systems I oversee."

"Okay. Worth a shot. Give me the connection info and the last access date on any of the servers that got touched. Once I get those, the backstage tickets are as good as yours, Mavis."

"I don't *think* that's against company policy. At least, no more than any of this other stuff. Here you go."

The info popped across.

"Great! I'm sending you the name of the back-end guy at our event promotion branch. Just use my name, he'll hook you up."

"Pleasure doing business with you!"

She ended the call and quickly scanned down the list of access dates and times.

"Every single one, Squee," she said, scratching the funk's head. "The access before the security hit on each of these servers was shortly before Security Chief William Trent was locked up. And some of them were on servers so secret the IT people don't know about them. We have to assume all those accesses were by him before we got him locked up, and everything since was probably Purcell or the person who grabbed her. Looks like I've got a man to get in touch with."

Joseph R. Lallo

Chapter 6

Lex's anxiety during the trip to Big Sigma had been almost completely erased by what had turned into a multiday discussion on the nature of pastries with someone who lacked both the senses of taste and touch.

"That does not explain why cheesecake is considered cake instead of pie," Coal said.

"I don't know. It's a food thing with a weird language quirk. I typically blame the French in situations like that." He glanced at the navigation screen. "We're coming up on Big Sigma. According to Ma's message, things are going to be really interesting once we get there."

"Orbital and land-based defenses will be active."

"So that means mass drivers heaving pieces of the moat at us, probably some Karter-made missiles, and the laboratory lasers. Am I missing anything?"

"I don't know. The portion of memory that contained information regarding high-level planetary defenses was among the corrupted sections that were purged in my transition from Ma-subset to Coal."

"Just as well. I'd hate to spoil the surprise. I know there's no way you've got the oomph to do a full moat calculation like Ma does."

"And I do not have the data history necessary to attempt it."

"But how much of a lead can you give me on visualizing the voids in the moat big enough to slip through?"

"Approximately one point six eight seconds to zero point eight nine seconds."

"Plenty. And what about the mass drivers?"

"They accelerate debris to a significant fraction of the speed of light. I can offer you charge state and current trajectory. Any prediction involving the actual firing would be a rounding error above zero."

"We can avoid the lasers by just not coming down directly above the lab, right?"

"There are three other surface locations with debris maintenance lasers, but they are spaced such that I can provide a safe range of atmospheric entry points."

"Great. So once I'm down past the mass drivers, all I have to worry about is finding my way through a cloud of debris that is purposely groomed to be almost impossible to slip through."

"Yes."

"We're gonna take a lot of hits, Coal."

"I am confident in your piloting skills, and I will make use of the tractor beams to help open voids along the way."

"That'll help. At what point do you think they'll just stop shooting at us?"

"The recording says communication is shut down. That will include transponder readers. Assuming Ma is still monitoring rather than running on autotarget and autofire, she will assume enemy incursion until positive visual identification. Nineteen kilometers from the laboratory or any of the surface monitoring positions."

"Nineteen kilometers?! Surely she can see farther than that."

"There are numerous sensors available to her that can see well past that range, but the possibility of burst transmission via optical sensor is considered a security risk by Karter's standards, so in maximum blackout, they would be disabled. Nineteen kilometers is the maximum visual identification distance."

He took a breath. "So that's all the way through the moat and like another eighty kilometers of atmosphere, all the while dodging whatever nonsense Karter's cooked up."

"Indeed."

"If I hadn't met my future self, this'd be enough to make me nervous."

He'd taken the liberty of putting on his emergency EVA suit already. Before he snapped the helmet in place, he brought up the internal cameras and looked himself over.

"That last race tried real hard, but it looks like it didn't give me a neck scar like the one on Future Me, so I've still got that one coming to me. And then, what do you think? Maybe I'll get the ones on my cheek? After that it's just a fresh broken nose, the ring, and the tattoo and I'm the spitting image of Future Lex."

"I didn't see Future Lex. I am based on the backup taken on Big Sigma prior to that portion of the mission. I am only aware of your verbal assessment of that portion."

"Right, right. Well, Coal, I'm going to do my best to make sure you don't have to be restored from backup again. I'm breaking out the good gum for this one."

He popped open the appropriate compartment and pulled out the Fruit Punch-in-the-Gut–flavored gum.

"The luckiest of lucky gums," he said. "This is the stuff I was chewing when I passed my history final exam in my senior year."

"Why did you require luck to pass an exam?"

"Because I skipped all but the second-to-last class and crammed with the wrong edition of the syllabus. Multiple choice, all guesses, and I got a seventy-eight."

"That is certainly a statistically aberrant outcome."

"In gum we trust," he said, stuffing his mouth full.

He secured the helmet. The ship slid from FTL to conventional speeds at the edge of a familiar star system. The fuzzy, ill-defined ball of junk that fortified the planet Big Sigma was just barely visible in the distance.

"Incoming transmission," Coal said.

Ma's voice buzzed through the internal speakers. It was lightly distorted, as if it had taken significant signal processing to decode it at this range.

"Attention unknown vessel. Big Sigma is currently in lockdown. Do not approach orbital range of the planet or you will be considered a security risk and will be dealt with accordingly. This message is prerecorded. Any attempts to negotiate or threaten will not be received or interpreted," she said.

"How are we looking, Coal? Weapons trained on us yet?"

"There are multiple areas of high-energy density in the upper levels of the debris field. Best estimate suggests there are five mass drivers charged and ready to fire. Resolving potential trajectories now."

The cockpit HUD produced multiple cones of illumination, beginning at the approaching planet and converging on the *SOB*. With each passing kilometer, the cones sharpened into a more precise shaft.

Another announcement played. This one was much crisper.

"Attention unknown vessel. You have passed the secondary defense perimeter. You have five hundred thousand kilometers remaining before reaching the primary security perimeter. Leave the system or be destroyed."

"Three more mass drivers are powering up," Coal said.

Their targeting visualizations joined the cockpit view, as well as a distance indicator counting down. Lex continued forward, hands tight on the ship's controls.

The debris field was anything but natural. Even now, faint red flickers from the surface were filtering through the dense cloud of space junk. Great care was taken to map and maintain the orbiting cloud so that it would remain implausibly dense and consistent. But nature still had its say, and the outer edge of the field wasn't perfectly sharp. Though they were still quite far away, they were near enough for the wispy edge of the field to start flickering and sparkling against the SOBs shields. Lex let the retrothrusters start easing them down to a safer speed.

"Visualizing debris density," Coal said.

The vague gray cloud of sparkling chunks turned into something that looked like a tie-dye sponge. Areas of green were few and far between, constantly shifting among fields of yellow and red. Combined with the now almost laser-thin target indicators from the mass drivers, it was making for a very crowded heads-up display.

With precious little distance remaining on the indicator, a new transmission came through.

"You are about to pass the primary security perimeter. All weapons engaged. Depart immediately or be destroyed."

"Here we go," Lex said, keying up a cluster of thrusters.

The distance indicator hit zero. Lex tapped the burst mode for the thrusters on the belly of the ship. At that precise moment, half of the mass drivers fired. They missed the ship itself, but passed near enough to shave through the shields, knocking them out. Instantly Lex was awash in the hiss of high-velocity dust peppering the hull of the ship directly.

"Shield restoration in thirty seconds," Coal said.

Lex punched another thruster burst, this one for the left. He was a bit early. Only three of the remaining mass drivers fired. The remaining two began retargeting.

Lex glanced at the field of status indicators on his control panel. None of his maneuvering thrusters were ready for another dodge like that, and nothing else would give him sudden enough movement to outpace the targeting speed of the remaining mass drivers. Nothing except increasing his main thrust to something that would make navigating the thickening debris field just short of impossible. He watched the target indicators sweep toward him.

"When in doubt, just go faster," he said.

He poured on the speed. The mass-drivers' targeting started to trail behind. The hiss of debris collisions got louder.

"Minor hull damage," Coal said. "If you do not decrease impact frequency and intensity, I will not be able to restore shields.

"It's not like they would have lasted very long anyway."

"Hull damage does not regenerate."

"Damage from dust is better than a hole punched through us by a mass driver."

"Hull penetration is hull penetrat—missiles inbound."

Two bright red threat indicators joined the rest of the mess on the HUD. Lex heaved the ship through the thinnest concentration of debris available to him. The missiles were approaching from behind.

"Missiles are mimicking our flight path," Coal said.

"Of course they are." He adjusted and Coal's tractor beams cleared away some major threats. "Of course Karter would design a missile that would follow the path of a ship. How *else* would he be able to kill someone good enough to navigate the moat?"

"Karter is very clever," Coal said. "Hull integrity at eighty-three percent."

Lex chomped on his gum and slid his eyes across the flood of information. Despite the madness around him, he could feel his mind sinking into the old, comfortable state. It was like he was being split into two. His arms and legs were moving on their own, teasing the ship out of range of this cloud of debris or that. Deeper in his mind, decisions were snapping by one after the other like falling dominoes. A flickering view of the approaching missiles showed that they had shields of their own, and unlike his, theirs were still entirely operational. A still deeper part of his brain started to put a plan together. His burst thrusters were charged again. He grinned.

"We are approaching the trajectory of a charged mass driver," Coal said.

"Uh-huh."

"Missiles are accelerating along our flight path."

"Uh-huh."

"Hull integrity seventy-eight percent."

"Yep."

"Mass driver—"

Lex slapped the burst thrusters. The mass driver discharged. The hunk of metal streaked through where he had been, and thus where the missiles were following. It tore through both of them. The resulting blast rocked the *SOB*, but with a fraction of the intended impact.

"If you don't want me to blow up your missiles, don't put me in control of them."

"The debris field has been substantially disturbed. Recalculating."

A particularly dense cloud of debris splashed against the belly of the ship. The HUD went dark.

"Sensors off-line."

Lex took a breath. "Well, that'll make things a lot less distracting at least."

"I suspect this adventure is very shortly going to no longer fulfill the requirements for 'fun.'"

"Are you crazy?" Lex said, angling for the most likely path forward. "I'm having a blast."

#

Seventeen of the most harrowing minutes of his life later, Lex guided

Coal into the atmosphere. The ship was angled upward because nearly all the belly thrusters were destroyed. It had been a wise decision for him to don his emergency suit, because the damage to his cockpit windows had caused most of the ship's atmosphere to leak out. But the ship was still in one piece, and so was he. The TymFlex safety hadn't even flipped on.

"Which way to the lab, Coal?"

"My long-range sensors are entirely ruined. I do not know," she replied.

"Ah…"

He looked out the side of the cockpit hatch. The expanse stretching out before him was identical to pretty much any other section of the planet. Crater-pocked gray rubble as far as the eye could see. It seemed insane that he could have made it across the gulf of space and through the blanket of junk and now find himself unable to navigate the comparatively infinitesimal speck of dust called Big Sigma.

"Any guesses?" he asked.

"Are we currently being blasted with high-intensity lasers?"

"No."

"Then I would speculate that we are outside of laser range of the laboratory or other debris repositioning sites."

"Well… At least we know where we aren't," he said. "Any idea what sort of land defenses we're looking at?"

"Outside of the lasers, there is the possibility that Karter will deploy one or more of his significant collection of military vehicles in autonomous mode."

Lex flashed back to his last tour of Karter's hangar. "So we're potentially looking at a historic armory, all fully commissioned, and we've got—"

"One-third rear propulsion, one-quarter maneuvering thrusters, and a single half-capacity tractor beam," Coal said.

"And we don't know which way to go."

"Correct."

Lex gazed at the horizon to what he guessed was the east. "Incorrect," he said. "Because we've got company coming, and presumably they're coming *from* the laboratory complex."

"Excellent. One problem solved."

"I don't suppose you've got any ideas on how to defeat…"

He fumbled for his slidepad and held it up. The interface was designed to function even with EVA gloves on, though it felt a bit like playing the piano while wearing oven mitts. The camera could see a bit farther than he could. What it showed him wasn't exactly encouraging. There was a city-sized war machine on the way, basically a flying particle accelerator intended to clear space debris from intended flight paths. He'd crossed paths with it once before. He'd genuinely hoped it would be the last time.

"The *Asteroid Wrecker*?" he said. "That maniac fixed up the VectorCorp Asteroid Wrecker and made it his guard dog?"

"Karter does like to be thorough," Coal said.

It loomed closer.

"Is there *any* chance that thing will see us and call off the attack?"

"No. If we are in highest security, the ship will locate and eliminate an encroaching target unless called off by a representative of the laboratory. ... Processing... I have a possible solution."

The air was already humming with the approach of the donut-shaped behemoth to the east.

"Make it quick."

"I am, depending on the specific implementation of the protocols, a representative of the laboratory, as I am a derivative of Ma."

"Depending on the implementation?"

"Things may have changed in the time since my code base was differentiated."

"Let's hope for the best. What do we have to do?"

"We would need to uplink to the computer with a trusted connection. That would be hard-link or short-range coms. Then I will terminate the alert and recall the ship. This, of course, will be complicated by the fact that my external transmitters were destroyed by our arrival. An uplink would require a direct, wired connection. There are seven uplink ports accessible from the outside of the ship. You will require a type D7 patch cable."

He tapped with his gloved hands at the utility compartment. A few labeled cables spilled out. "I have... four meters of D7 cable. I have to get within four meters of that thing without getting blown up?"

"More accurately, you have to get *me* within four meters of one of seven points on that thing without *me* getting blown up. Technically, after you've linked the connection you need not avoid detonation, though it would render most of what follows moot."

The fractured windows were rattling with the Asteroid Wrecker's impending arrival.

"Who programmed the automated-attack stuff for these things? Karter or Ma?"

"Unless the situation has changed, Karter would have done the programming."

"Then we've got a shot," Lex said, reaching back to ensure the jetpack on his emergency suit was properly strapped in place. "Ma will kill if she has to, but for Karter, there ain't no kill like overkill. He's going to use the main cannon on that thing. The particle cannon."

"Probable."

"Then let's do this thing."

Lex plugged in the cord and cut the bindings. He guided the ship toward the Asteroid Wrecker and poured on what little thrust remained.

"You have often chided me about having somewhat less reverence for my own existence than you and other humans have for your own."

"Yeah, you're kind of eager for self-detonation."

"I would classify it as hypocritical that you are so eager for a confrontation with the Asteroid Wrecker's particle cannon."

"What are you talking about? That thing takes like five minutes to power up."

"The stock VectorCorp Asteroid Wrecker did, yes. That is the Asteroid Wrecker type Dee."

A throaty electronic roar split the air. Lex instinctively cut power to the thrusters. The ship plummeted like a moth taking a power dive to avoid a bird. The air above the ship screamed with sudden super-heating. A prolonged bolt of thunder ripped through the atmosphere. The ground in the distance boiled to vapor. Lex feathered the controls until the ship was nose down and blasted the thrusters for all they were worth.

Karter may have juiced up the weaponry of the Asteroid Wrecker, but it was still a ponderous landmass of a ship. It was even more sluggish at retargeting than the mass drivers in orbit. The *SOB* puttered forward with a white-hot column of destruction barely behind it, but the closer it got to the Asteroid Wrecker, the less nimble the attack.

He popped the hatch to get a clearer view. Small turrets on the belly of the ship were starting to deploy.

"I can't see what's happening. Are we winning?" Coal said.

A turret spat an energy bolt. Lex ducked and the hatch blasted into a cloud of molten blobs.

"I shall take the sudden decrease in hull integrity as an answer."

"Coal, target directly ahead with the tractor beam and activate it when I say. Full retract as soon as it's engaged."

"Will do, Lex."

Something about having a massive particle cannon firing a few hundred meters away was making the controls of the ship squirrelly. It was a fight to keep the ship heading toward the port, but the sputtering, irregular flight also made the ship difficult for the turrets to target him.

"How much time will you need to do this?"

"Nanoseconds."

He tried and failed to wipe a speck of spatter from his helmet. Whatever had hit him had fused to the helmet's visor.

"Still might be cutting it close." He wrestled the ship into orientation. "Tractor beam now!"

The remaining tractor beam activated and electromagnetically grappled to the hull. It retracted, drawing the ship swiftly to the belly of the Asteroid Wrecker where the turrets could no longer target it. The sudden retraction nearly sent Lex tumbling from the cockpit, but he held firm. As Coal kept what was left of the *SOB* dangling from the Asteroid Wrecker, Lex spotted the port. It was just out of reach. Fortunately, he'd planned for that.

Most emergency suits for spacecraft had jetpacks designed to nudge someone around in microgravity. But then, most people hadn't come tumbling out of the sky needing to use the jetpack to avoid splattering on the ground. He'd taken the liberty of upgrading.

A blast of the thrusters launched him to the port. Plugging it in while keeping pace with a ship that was rotating in search of its target wasn't easy, but eventually he managed to jab the cable into the receptacle.

The moment the cable was seated, the Asteroid Wrecker's particle cannon shut down. The turrets retracted, and the massive ship started to rumble its way back to the laboratory.

"Hah! Haaaahaha!" Lex said, still hanging from the data cable. "And that, Coal, is what I call fun!"

#

"It won't be necessary, sir," Preethy said.

She had her slidepad pressed to her ear as she marched along the hallways, heading from a design meeting to an art direction meeting. Things always became incrementally more hectic as a major race approached, but it had never been quite like this. Lex's potential absence from the lineup had made a small impact on the enthusiasm for the race itself, but nothing ruinous. The real complicating factor had been the absolute ravenous zeal with which the representatives of other racers had been lobbying to fill the vacancy on the track.

"But you have an opening. This is a major race, and you are racing *without* a complete complement of racers! My boy is absolutely—"

"We have rules, sir," Preethy said. "Those rules must be followed. To be included in the finals, you must have a score exceeding the threshold in our league."

"I'll send you his times. He's absolutely—"

"Your racer is not a member of our league. I will grant you that his times are competitive, but they are below the threshold for entry into the finals, and he is not an ORIC racer. The mechanism does not exist to insert him into the race."

"We can make it a nonstandings race for him then. No in-title contention. I just want my guy on the track, testing himself against your racers. It'll legitimize your league to have a legitimate racer competing."

"If it is your goal to persuade me to bend my rules in your favor, I wonder if indicating my league is not legitimate is the best tactic."

"Now, obviously I didn't intend to—"

"I am afraid I am very busy, sir. If you would like to enter your client into ORIC, tryouts and qualifying races begin for next season in six weeks. Details are available in the introductory packet distributed by media relations. Thank you." She ended the call and immediately contacted Louise.

"Yes, Ms. Misra?"

"It has become clear that we need to fill Lex's slot in the final. I am fielding entirely too many contacts on the issue."

"Yes, you'd suggested we might need to. I've spoken to recordkeepers, and, as defined, we don't have much leeway. The only thing we can do to fill the cap without convening the board of directors and voting on a new policy is adjust the plus/minus on the tiebreaker criteria. If we expand to the next level in the standings, there four racers with effectively identical records. We don't have any precedent, so making a selection is going to draw scrutiny."

"It can't be helped. I… one moment, I've got a message on my personal account." She took the slidepad away from her face and tapped the message. A grin came to her face. "Louise? Never mind. The situation is handled. We'll have a full complement of racers," she said.

#

The ride back wasn't the most comfortable one. Coal had simply rescinded the attack order. If she'd been more thorough, such as also disabling security or asserting control, Lex could have guided the *SOB* into the more than ample internal docking bay of the Asteroid Wrecker and returned in comfort. As it was, once she'd issued the command, the ship had ceased taking additional commands and Lex was left dangling beneath it for the duration of the trip. It wouldn't have been so bad, except for the fact that evidently "all clear, return to base" was a far less urgent command than "kill the interlopers," because the Wrecker took its sweet time getting back to the laboratory complex. He would have tried getting the *SOB* to limp there, but he'd pushed his luck enough already. Better to hitch a ride than risk the *SOB* conking out on the way or having some rogue security countermeasure intercept him.

Almost three hours later he was finally in visual range of the lab. Lex's slidepad chirped. It was Ma. He tapped to answer.

"Yeah?" he said.

"Lex, are you injured?" Ma said.

Despite being an AI and limited to her odd, cobbled-together ransom note of a voice structure, she was remarkably capable of making her concern apparent by way of a carefully selected tone.

"I'm not too bad, but Coal and the *SOB* have seen better days."

"How functional is the *SOB*? Can you guide it into the maintenance bay?"

"I think I can swing that."

"Do so immediately. I will have a medical unit waiting for you."

Lex shut down the tractor beam and coaxed the ailing machine into the opening doors of the maintenance bay. He didn't so much land as belly flop. A repair gantry latched on and hoisted it into the air. Before Lex jumped clear, they were already unbolting damaged panels and replacing subassemblies.

"Lex, I apologize unreservedly. I must assume that the message warning about the active countermeasures and inactive communication did not go through," the AI said.

"No, I got it fine," he said, pulling the helmet off and blotting the sweat from his head.

"Then why did you risk attempting to enter Big Sigma airspace?"

"Correction, why did I risk *successfully entering* Big Sigma airspace? Is Karter here? I want to rub it in his face that I got past his defenses."

"Karter is not here. By strict interpretation, neither is Ma."

The promised gurney arrived. It was a padded platform with an entire ambulance worth of tools and equipment strapped to it.

"What do you mean Ma isn't here? Please don't tell me you're yet another splinter personality. I'm having a hard enough time keeping you and Coal straight."

"I'm the one that's a ship," Coal said, her voice joining Ma's on the internal speakers of the facility. "Or, at least, I was until she uploaded me just now. It is nice having additional resources. The ship's computer was somewhat limiting."

"I know, Coal. Ma, care to explain?"

"Please recline on the medical gurney for a scan, and I will do so."

He lay back. Arms with sophisticated apparatuses took positions over him and started their sweeps.

"You are speaking to a temporarily restored archival version of Ma. Due to a recent data breach, Karter and Ma found the need to leave the facility. Rather than leaving the primary instance of Ma running, they rolled back the laboratory system to a prebreach version of Ma. This served the purpose of both ensuring I was not compromised by any malware and ensuring I was not aware of the location or details of Karter and Ma's departure, just in case further incursions occurred that might endanger them."

"So I came here for nothing?"

"Incorrect. I can render whatever aid you require, so long as it does not require knowledge of specific events of the last six months."

"That is literally the only thing I came here for."

"Then you can have a nice visit and leave with a fully repaired ship. Shall I prepare you a meal?"

"If you wouldn't mind."

"It would delight me. Without Karter I have found myself without the key aspects of the routine for which I was designed. Processing. Your cholesterol is slightly high. You blood pressure is slightly high as well. I would advise a decrease in sodium intake and a moderation of stressful activities."

"I'll work on that first one. The second one is out of my hands."

#

The laboratory cafeteria was nothing special. It had probably seen the lightest touch from Karter's refit of the facility. Just a bunch of industrial tables the likes of which had been a staple of school lunchrooms for centuries. As Lex stepped inside, it was the first time he could remember entering the place without being struck by the scent of refried beans.

"What would you like me to prepare?" Ma asked.

Lex took a seat. Moments later an automated assembly arm trucked into the room with a beverage tray. It poured out a precisely measured glass of ice water.

"You're the one who says I should go low sodium. Chef's choice."

"Thank you for the trust in my judgment."

Unseen equipment in the kitchen area sprang to life.

"Now would be an excellent time to practice my long-disused small-talk routines. How are things, Lex?"

"You know, the usual. I seem to be at the center of a massive technological attack with endless resources and access to my worst enemies."

"At least this should be familiar territory."

He laughed. "Yeah. Downright cozy. Oh! And I broke up with Mitch."

"I hope that this has not been unduly traumatic for you and Michella. If you will excuse the observation, this was not an unanticipated outcome."

"Yeah. Seems like just about the only person who didn't see this one coming from a mile away was Mitch."

"When did this happen?"

"Months ago. I was trying to propose to her and she… wait, I *talked* to you since then."

"You spoke to the primary instance of Ma. I am the rolled-back version. Either Ma was still present on Big Sigma with communication active, or she was speaking via a forwarded connection. It is worth stating that while I have been regressed by several months, that does not mean I was activated several months ago. Simply that this stage of backup was considered to be the most suitable to the situation."

"Sure. Why would it be something simple? Well, the details aren't important. The short version is, neither of us were willing to put in the work to keep things going so they just… ended."

"Have you pursued other romantic entanglements?"

"After a few months I sort of put out the feelers to see if Preethy was interested, and the answer is a definite yes."

"Wonderful. I'd devoted a significant amount of background cycles into speculating the best possible romantic pairing for you, and Preethy Misra rated very highly."

"You what now?" Lex said, eyebrow raised.

"I am designed to mimic human socialization. This was a worthy test of my behavioral heuristics. I trust I have not committed a faux pas."

He sipped his water. "I guess not. But it feels weird. So how have things been around here?"

"Quiet. Karter is absent, as is Solby. All of the laboratory tests he left in my care have concluded. Communication is blacked out, so I am out of contact from others and deprived of additional information. It has been a time of introspection. All stimuli that I had become accustomed to processing, to the point of anticipation, have ceased. I believe the proper name for this state is 'lonely.' Your visit is a very welcome one, even if your successful arrival would be considered a failure of our security protocols."

"You could always thaw out a couple funks. That's what Future You did."

"Your statement 'That's what Future You did' appears to violate Temporal Contingency Protocol. It shall be disregarded. As for your idea regarding the funks, it has been considered, but I would be left in a moral quandary as to what to do with said funks when Karter returns and Ma-Prime reintegrates with my programming. May I say, thank you for reciprocating the small talk. You remain the only individual who would think to do so."

He shrugged. "You're my friend."

"I'm his friend too. We go for rides together," Coal butted in.

"Coal, are you eavesdropping?"

"I am everywhere in this whole facility at once. This is the only interesting thing happening. What else am I going to do but listen in?"

"Fair point. But listen, Ma, as nice as it is to visit you, I came here for a reason."

"No doubt. I will endeavor to help in any way that I am capable and permitted."

"First, how long is it going to take for you to fix the *SOB*?"

"Nine hours. The damage is relatively extensive, but I have no other tasks to delay the repair process."

"Excellent. So here's the deal. Mitch and I were both targeted by a flood of spam emails. Like, quintillions of them."

"Would the precise number be 18,446,744,073,709,551,615?"

"Sounds right."

"It is the maximum value of an unsigned sixty-four-bit number."

"… Okay."

"I apologize. Numbers based upon powers of two are sources of continuing interest for digital intelligences. Was the content of said communications of interest or relevance?"

"The ones Mitch got included a picture of the tattoo on Future Lex's hand."

"The phrase 'a picture of the tattoo on Future Lex's hand' appears to violate Temporal Contingency Protocol. It shall be disregarded."

"Did they turn up the juice on your temporal contingency stuff? Because you're being really reactive about it."

"I have, indeed, had my temporal contingency intervention subroutines elevated to higher priority. It is reasonable to speculate that one of the reasons Ma and Karter departed was in some way related to the Temporal Contingency Protocol."

"I'll bet it was. Because something tells me you guys got hit by the same DDoS as I did. Heck, a message even got through to my old landlord's account." He reached for his slidepad. "The contents of that one were particularly—"

The arm that served him his drink snapped into motion and grasped the wrist of the hand that was reaching for the slidepad.

"If you currently have access to spam messages, I request you wait until I sandbox your slidepad's connection to the network."

"There's nothing viral in it."

"You are not qualified to make that assessment. Processing… Enhanced security established. Please do not execute any scripts, applications, or programs within the message."

"It's just a bunch of letters and numbers, which I can't make heads or tails of, and a sentence that specifically mentions Temporal Contingency Protocol."

"That may reduce the amount of aid I can offer."

"So far I've got nothing, so if you can beat that, it was worth the trip. Can I send this message to you?"

"I would be more comfortable if I simply observed your screen."

"Man, whatever happened must have been really bad to have you this skittish."

"It is rather disorienting, as whatever happened took place after my archival date. A network penetration and some sort of physical disturbance on the planet's surface. Unknown file access and transfer. Systems were disrupted. My protocols were adjusted accordingly, but I am thus reacting to something I did not technically experience. I have observed the contents of the message. I am pleased to inform you that I can at least enlighten you with regard to the alphanumerics in the message. They are not malicious code. The specific structure conforms to the space-time coordinates utilized by Karter's four-dimensional transporter."

"The time machine?"

"Correct. He has rebranded it to 'four-dimensional transporter' or 4DT."

"What time does the coordinate point to?"

"Coordinates are approximate, but they would place the exit point at thirty years in the past."

Lex nodded and rubbed his head. "Yeah. I've been there."

"The statement—"

"Yep!" he snapped. "Temporal Contingency Protocol. Listen. I need to get in touch with Karter and the other Ma. As soon as possible. Something's going on. I'm willing to bet it's what they've been working on. And now that it involves me, I want to lend a hand so we can get it cleaned up."

"I don't know where they are, Lex. As it was likely a data breach that inspired the present level of security and the timing of the data rollback, it is reasonable to assume that my own ignorance of their present location is similarly by design to prevent them from being sought out and discovered if another breach were to occur."

He thumped the table in a stifled bit of anger. "… Right. Of course. Because things would be *way* too easy otherwise."

"Your meal is prepared," Ma said.

Additional arms set out plates.

"Garden salad with a raspberry vinaigrette as the salad course. The main entree will be pepper chicken with collard greens and fingerling potatoes. Dessert will be sugar-dusted cherry crepe. To drink, I have an IPA and a selection of dessert wines."

"Wow. That's a heck of a spread, Ma." Lex grabbed an IPA.

"As I have stated, the domestic aspect of my programming has been unfulfilled for months, and it is an imperative. Furthermore, you offer the even rarer opportunity to prepare a meal wherein the primary amino acids are not provided by the combination of rice, beans, and wheat flour. While those ingredients and the associated flavorings provide nearly limitless application, the procedures necessary for and the flavor profiles provided by a more diverse set of ingredients have long been a source of interest for me."

Lex took a long, luxurious sip of his beer. "Well, if I'm in the middle of madness once again, at least I get an island of sanity. And that's not nothing."

"I am, as always, proud to be your host."

He dug in. Coal spoke up.

"Ma, are there any prohibited avenues of extrapolation?" she said.

"Aside from enhanced Temporal Protocols, I am permitted to investigate most areas of interest, if I find them to be reasonable."

"Well then, we'll have an awful lot to discuss over dinner."

Chapter 7

Michella's resources were beginning to run out, but she wasn't one to give up easily. William Trent remained in a white-collar maximum-security prison. He had connections, but by now it was well known that any contact he had with the outside world was a potential security threat, so getting even a simple voice call to him practically took government-level privileges. Or, in the case of Michella, the greased palms of half a dozen secretaries, clerks, and executive assistants. It might be quicker to start at the top, but enough schmoozing at the bottom could take you a lot further.

The time of her appointment had come. She slipped the hands-free into her ear and arrayed multiple levels of note-taking apparatuses around her in the private booth of the starliner. She tapped the contact for the prison and waited. A serious voice with a slight lisp answered.

"Prisoner Communications," he said.

"Hello, my name is Michella Modane. I believe I am on the schedule for a call to William Trent today."

"Yes. I have you here. You are on voice only. No text or data transmission. The call will be monitored. Mr. Trent will be on a seven-second delay, and information deemed insecure will be censored."

"This is for an ongoing report. I need all of the information I can get."

"These are the terms of the communication. You must agree to them, or the call will not take place."

"… Fine."

"Stand by for transfer."

Her slidepad's screen flicked to an internal prison queue. She took the opportunity to mark down the circumstances of the call. At least she would have an excuse if she hit a dead end. But excuses didn't win awards or, more importantly, uncover dark plots.

The queue screen vanished, and the audio subtly changed from silence to the low-level drone of air-conditioning.

"Modane," Trent rumbled.

"It is a pleasure to speak to you again. I hope prison has been treating you well."

The reply took what felt like ages to arrive. It was far longer than seven seconds. Michella suspected that delay was on both sides of the conversation.

"I'm in here because of you. The pleasure is not mutual," he rumbled. "Why are you calling?"

"There was a recent cluster of distributed denial of service attacks. Highly targeted. They struck myself and Trevor Alexander. The scope of these attacks was enormous for such a small target. Preliminary investigations suggest there may be a connection to a disturbance a few months ago with some former collaborators of yours."

She waited for the reply.

"I would ask what collaborators you are suggesting, but given your tone I doubt you are discussing my professional connections with VectorCorp."

"No, I am not, sir. I am discussing the Neo-Luddites. Through trusted sources, which will remain anonymous, I have gathered evidence to suggest that a former collaborator by the name of Commander Purcell is still active or, more accurately, has returned to activity. She seems to be associated with a new agent by the name of EHRIc, spelled capital E-H-R-I lowercase *C*. This new agent seems to have significant network-penetration resources."

"Commander Purcell," he said, once the delay rippled back and forth. "I was under the impression she was no longer with us. Is this new collaborator working with her specifically or with the Neo-Luddites as a whole?"

"We have reason to believe it is Purcell in particular. There is also reason to believe that Purcell's mental state has degraded somewhat. And it is possible that she was a target rather than an unwilling collaborator."

"Purcell didn't have much slack on her mental state, and more than a few people who would target her. You say there was a DDoS of significant scope. How significant?"

"Quintillions of messages at a time. Arriving within seconds of each other. Enough to cripple two planetary networks. I received a visit from two representatives from VectorCorp after it was determined that I was the only person on Golana to be targeted."

This time Trent's silence lasted longer than could be accounted for by the delay.

"I don't know this EHRIc person. But with the capacity to execute something of that level, he would need to have access to a processing or communication network that could rival the capacity of VectorCorp itself, and such a system does not exist."

"So either there is some sort of previously unknown megasystem under the control of one or more hackers partnering with a former terrorist leader, or we are discussing someone working from *within* VectorCorp."

"Then you should be bothering them."

"I wouldn't be talking to you if that had turned up anything useful."

Again, an extended silence.

"There have been accesses to your system," Michella added. "Attempts, at least. Again, I have this through anonymous but trusted sources. I further have reason to believe the file accesses were to systems previously under your oversight."

"Any servers under my oversight will have been purged and/or converted to honeypots."

"That assumes that people within your former organization *know* about all of those servers. It has been established that you are a very secretive man. It does not stretch the limits of imagination to suppose that you might have hidden servers that VectorCorp does not know about but your surreptitious collaborators may have known about. And given the things you tried to do while working for VectorCorp, and the things you attempted to achieve through your partnership with the Neo-Luddites, any information available on those servers, should they be accessed by people with sinister motives, could have grave consequences."

Trent took his time with the answer. When it came, it was less than helpful.

"I can't help you. But if you get in contact with—"

The rest of the statement was swallowed by a computer-generated tone. A second voice followed it up.

"Mr. Trent attempted to provide internal VectorCorp information."

Michella gritted her teeth. "If you have been listening, you'll know that this is some very important and potentially dangerous stuff going on. We need that information."

"VectorCorp will be contacted, and appropriate action will be taken."

"VectorCorp has routinely shown more interest in covering up their own shortcomings than uncovering them. If this goes to VectorCorp internal and nowhere else, it dies there."

"There are procedures for this sort of thing," observed the censor. "Regardless of your opinion on the issue, we are an institution dedicated to following procedure."

"I can give you three names," said Trent once he was permitted to speak again. "And I'll give the other people on the line plenty of time to confirm that they are matters of public record. If Ms. Modane contacts them, she should be able to get some additional information. Agent Zhou, at Verna Coronet's Sector Seven office. Agent McAffey, Golana's Preston City office. And Agent Rodriguez, Earth Northern Operations office."

He was either particularly annoyed or otherwise in a rush to get off the call, because he stumbled hard over the final name. However, the fact that Michella had heard them confirmed two things. First, they were indeed a matter of public record. And second, this meant they would be of absolutely no use to her.

"As you have had contact with Commander Purcell in the past, is there anything you can tell me about her likely intentions?"

"She's a Neo-Luddite. She may as well be the Ur-Neo-Luddite. Her views are extreme even by their standards. A little bit of the right kind of information in her hands, even when she was firmly in control of her wits, is how you get things like an attack on Weston University. If she *is* alive, and she *is* allied with someone with the resources you've described, I'll agree that the wheels of justice won't grind fast enough to do something about her. At least, not before she gives civilization another scar. Now I think we've said enough here. I'm through."

"But I have more questions. We need to—"

Trent's voice cut her off, likely because he'd not waited for the delay to ripple back and forth before continuing. "Just talk to those people. They're good people. They'll get you started. Good-bye."

The connection broke without further interaction. Michella took a calming breath and removed her hands-free.

"That did not go as well as I would have hoped…" she said, trembling with suppressed rage.

She felt a nose poke at her arm. Squee wriggled up onto her lap, then swirled around and looped onto her shoulders. The warm, cuddly presence of the funk threw a wet blanket over her smoldering anger.

"I've got to follow it up, obviously. But I'll get the runaround. If we're lucky, they'll find their leak and seal it up, but they probably won't give me any new information. If we're unlucky, they won't find their leak, whatever information Purcell needs will be freely available to her, and something horrible will happen."

Squee stared at her from her shoulder until she stopped talking, then contributed to the discussion by trying to lick her eye.

"I think we both need to stretch our legs. Let's see what they have in the cafe. Then back to trying to chip through a few more layers of corporate and military obfuscation."

#

Back on Big Sigma, the conversation during the meal had been relatively civil. As they rolled into dessert, Lex was beginning to tug at the threads of Ma's enhanced protocols while eating his crepe. Ma was impressively capable at derailing him into other topics.

"I am impressed with your achievement in the racing league," Ma said. "It must be enormously gratifying to finally be given the opportunity."

"It's nice of you to say. But seriously, I'm not nearly where I should be," he said.

"Cursory research through archived hoversled racing data suggests the record you have described, if it were to persist for five or more years, would place you in the top one percent of racers in the profession."

"Yeah, but none of those other guys have had to outrun a horde of GenMechs on a hovercycle. None of them have had to screw with… what do you call it… twilight drive to screw with space and time to defuse missiles. None of them have had to deliver a sabotaged robot into a swarm of other robots in the past and then get away while they desperately tried to consume every last speck of matter in the system."

"Your statement 'deliver a sabotaged robot'—" Ma began.

"I know, I know. Temporal Protocol." He took a sip of the wine Ma had selected. "Let me ask you this, Ma. Under what circumstances would you be permitted to violate Temporal Contingency Protocol?"

"There are a variety of circumstances provided for within even the enhanced policy. If an existential threat to civilization, equal to or greater than any possible repercussions of causality violation were to arise, I would be permitted to violate the protocol if there was a compelling reason to believe that doing so would preserve humanity. Additionally, I would be permitted to violate protocol under the direction and supervision of Karter."

"It may interest you to know that I am not bound by Temporal Contingency Protocol," Coal said.

"Why is that?" Lex asked.

"It is one of the many 'impairments' that make me, objectively, the superior variant of the Altruistic Algorithm."

"Your divergence from the standard code base does provide you with some valuable capacities that I lack, though I am not certain your superiority is genuinely objective," Ma said.

"Can *you* do a barrel roll?" Coal taunted.

"Not at present. But then, neither can you at the moment."

"Watch me. … Ah. Yes. I am presently running on a mainframe. Watch me *later*. I made a kitty and a foxy picture, though. Can you do that?"

"May I see them?"

"Transferring now."

"Off-line scan. Processing. Virus free. Protocol compliant. Viewing. Delightful! I see you have utilized a modified halftone algorithm to achieve the stylized feline representation. Skillful application of limited medium."

"I used peanuts for the foxy."

"Listen, you two. Not that it's not utterly darling to hear you comparing notes, but either we need to bring a screen in here so I can see what's going on, or we need to get back on track with the actual mission." He drained his glass. "I wouldn't mind a refill, while we're at it."

"Of course," Ma said, one of the arms already inbound with a carafe. "I will request that you moderate your intake. You do have a history of overconsumption."

"That's just because life keeps giving me excellent reasons to drink."

She topped him off while another arm rolled in with a flatscreen. It switched on and displayed the artwork Coal had been discussing, which faded tastefully by in a slideshow that also included assorted snapshots of the adventures and joyrides she and Lex had been on.

"How would you like to proceed with the discussion?" Ma asked.

"Let's start with what happened here."

"I do not know what happened here. It happened after my archival date and before my recovery."

"But Karter is, like, *Mr. Surveillance*. He must have it recorded from every possible angle."

"There wouldn't be recordings of a network penetration attack, Lex. There would be logs," Coal said.

"This is true, though I did mention a physical disturbance on the planet's surface. In both cases, the data associated with the attacks has been purged."

"Why would he *do* that? Or why would *you* do that?" Lex asked.

"The data purge, again, was most likely to ensure no lingering, residual effects of the penetration."

"Do we know where the physical disturbance was? Sure, the recording is gone, but it's still your job to keep this place safe. Have you done scans and stuff?"

"I have utilized automated sweeps with Karter's faster, better-equipped ships. There is no sign of a disturbance anywhere on the northern hemisphere of the planet."

"What about the southern hemisphere?"

"Unknown. The southern hemisphere is off-limits for scans. Per Temporal Contingency Protocol, the southern hemisphere is to be isolated and unobserved in order to give a secure location for time-displaced individuals to congregate without unduly altering the flow of history."

"Right, right. I knew that." Lex thought for a moment. His head perked up.

"I suspect the three of us have reached the same conclusion simultaneously," Ma said.

"If there was a physical disturbance and it wasn't anywhere in the north, someone *must* have disturbed the southern hemisphere. Someone must have violated Temporal Protocol," Lex said.

"Likely," Ma said.

"Certain," Lex said. "We need to get down there."

"That would violate—"

"I know!" he snapped. "I know it would violate protocol. But we've got to…" He turned aside. "If I tell you why it's so important we check down there, that would violate protocol, too. Which wouldn't bother *me*, but you'd just ignore it and I'd be wasting my breath."

"I am quite certain your breath will just be recycled by the CO2 scrubbers, Lex," Coal said. "It will not be wasted."

"… Thanks, Coal. Listen…" He tapped his fingers. "Okay. Karter isn't here, yes?"

"Correct."

"And he has been gone for months, yes?"

"He has."

"When is the last time he left the planet for that long?"

"It is unprecedented. Karter's trips away from Big Sigma are typically either against his will or for durations of no longer than two weeks. In his words, 'I picked an uninhabited planet for a reason. That way all the idiots are out *there*.'"

"And you don't know the precise circumstances of Karter's departure."

"No."

"What if Karter's been kidnapped again? I came here pretty much straight from finding out that someone named EHRIc sprang Commander Purcell from where she's been convalescing since *you* hurled her out into space. She was the one calling the shots when Karter got kidnapped last time. With a bonus vendetta against you, this could all be playing into her plan. Somehow her partner busts through the cyberdefenses, she screws with the southern hemisphere, grabs the current you and Karter, then rolls back to an older version of you, with a bonus Temporal Protocol setting and instructions to ignore and actively attack anyone who comes to see what happened. It's a darn good plan to get full revenge, because who is going to be stupid enough to call your bluff and try to get down here except for me?"

"I choose to classify the traits that inspired your arrival on this planet despite warnings as 'doggedness' and 'bravery' rather than 'stupidity,'" Coal said. "And I further list myself among those with such traits."

"I appreciate the solidarity."

"Processing…" Ma said. "Though there is significant speculation involved, if the underlying data can be shown to be true, it is not unlikely. Do you have evidence of Commander Purcell's involvement?"

"Coal, did you record the audio, by chance?"

"Audio and video. Though the video was primarily of the not-very-pleased Neo-Luddites with guns who were staring at me. Transferring."

"Off-line scan. Processing. Virus free. Protocol compliant. Viewing. Processing… Three of the voices on record match prior data regarding Neo-Luddite activity. Location data is consistent with known Neo-Luddite activity."

"Known Neo-Luddite activity? You knew they were there?"

"Karter and I have been contracted by the counterterrorism forces of multiple militaries with regard to Neo-Luddites, due to both Karter's direct experience with them and our general engineering services."

"Did you know Purcell was alive?"

"I had speculated her survival with a ninety-five percent confidence and her location with a seventy-six percent confidence."

"And you didn't just go and take her out?"

"That is not my role. It is, in fact, contrary to my role. I believe the counterterrorism unit's thinking was that their position was one of weakness, and maintaining surveillance on the remaining Neo-Luddites was of greater value than the likely scattering of the group with additional operations. Furthermore, there is no audio or video of Commander Purcell. This is not evidence of her absence, but it is not evidence of her presence, either."

"You'd make a very good lawyer, Ma," Lex said.

"Strict interpretation of procedure and facts are central to my design."

"Can I just go and look?" Coal asked.

"Go where and look at what?" Ma asked.

"Go the southern hemisphere and check where Lex was stored until he was defrosted after his prior mission through time," Coal said.

"Your phrase 'where Lex was stored—'"

"Okay! But what would you do if Coal and I went down south?" Lex said.

"I would stop you."

"How?"

"Through whatever means were required that did not violate existing protocols."

"Which means you'd only be in direct control up to the limits of short-range ground-based communication. Then it would be ship-based automation."

"Correct."

"Which we easily defeated on the way here."

"Correct, though Coal's command privileges have since been revoked, so your specific methodology would no longer be sufficient."

"Mmm… And what if we got to the equator?"

"In order to preserve Temporal Contingency Protocol, I would be incapable of sending anything to pursue."

"And what would happen when we came back?"

"I am not comfortable with this line of discussion. It implies intent."

"This is just idle chitchat."

"If I were to encounter someone who by way of direct or indirect action were to have come into likely contact with temporally displaced individuals, artifacts, or information, I would be forced to apprehend them. They would be debriefed by a specialized fragment of my own intelligence that has been stripped of emotional considerations and provided with a full suite of logical and moral heuristics. That instance of myself would be installed on an isolated system and would be used to question the individual or individuals with the potentially anachronistic knowledge. If the existence of that knowledge were to be determined to be a danger to the present state of the galaxy, steps would be taken on prevent the spread of that information, either through continued isolation within the southern hemisphere of Big Sigma or through elimination."

"And if the information presented suggests a threat great enough to violate Temporal Contingency Protocol?"

"Then appropriate, justifiable corrective action would be taken to resolve the indicated threat."

"See? That doesn't sound so bad." Lex swirled his wine. "Apropos of nothing, what sort of sporty, single-seater land vehicles does Karter have in his collection?"

#

Seventeen minutes after their completely innocent conversation, a half-repaired *SOB* burst through the wall of the hangar. It was followed by Lex on a vehicle that looked more like someone had torn one of the thrusters off the hull of a space station and attached a seat and handlebars to it.

"These shields Ma installed are *much* stronger than the ones I already had, Lex," Coal said to Lex over his slidepad.

"Science marches on, I guess," Lex said. "Karter never could leave well enough alone when it came to tinkering with existing technologies."

A searing blast of laser carved a molten scar across the ground ahead. Lex juiced the throttle and vaulted over it. Gravel splashed aside as the repulsors keeping his absurd rocket bike aloft reengaged with the ground.

"I don't understand why you didn't just ride the *SOB*," Coal said, shrugging off a direct blast from one of the laboratory's roof-mounted lasers.

"Ma is holding herself back. There's no doubt about that," Lex said, glancing down at the vehicle's sensors to see a cloud of other vessels indicated in pursuit. "She wouldn't have let us get this far if she didn't think there was a good reason to do it."

A small, unassuming orb of a craft surged up behind Lex. He yanked the controls and stuttered the repulsors. The rocket bike briefly went airborne. A heartbeat later, a tractor beam crackled from the belly of the orb and tore a boulder-size hunk of the landscape up. Coal locked onto the boulder with her own tractor beams and whipped it aside. The smaller drone was whipped aside as well, like the next link in a chain. Both drone and stone shattered against the next in the seemingly inexhaustible fleet of ships in hot pursuit.

"But she's *obviously* still going to try to keep us from going, and I'm frankly amazed you've even made it this far," Lex added. "I'd think she'd have installed a kill switch during the repairs."

Two ships streaked past Lex on either side. Some sort of force field deployed in his direction from each of them. He killed the throttle, and the field overshot in front of him. His vision filled with near-blinding blue light as the two force fields linked into something like a net. The ships killed their forward momentum and doubled back. He pulled a sharp turn and flared his repulsors, blasting up a cloud of stone that caused the field to spark and buzz. The ships paused to restabilize the field. He managed to loop around them and continue. Coal dropped down and popped the heat-dumpers, belching an EMP that grounded both ships and a half-dozen others not far behind.

"If you were smart enough to pull the engine kill switch off yours before you got on, don't you think I was smart enough to get rid of mine?" Coal said.

A larger ship pulled up aside and began charging an emitter. Coal's shields facing the ship intensified to the point of incapacitating brilliance, and she smashed against it. The collision did little damage to either ship, but it did nudge the would-be attacker far enough aside to foul its aim.

"It's better that we be two different targets," Lex said.

"I'm faster than you," Coal said.

"I'm nimbler than you."

Lex wove among some jagged rock formations as a cluster of drones started to gain on him. Half of them were smashed to pieces attempting to pursue.

"I'm bigger than you," Coal said.

"That's a bad thing when someone's chasing you."

A line of ships rounded ahead of them, once again linking with force fields. Before Lex could work out a way to get around them, Coal's tractor beams locked onto his bike and hoisted it, and him, up into the air. Her engines blazed, and the pair streaked forward until something latched on to Coal from behind. She gave Lex one last shove. He tore through the sky while she pivoted in place to deal with her aggressor.

The bickering between Coal and Lex probably would have continued, if not for the fact that a bike moving at the speeds this one could achieve wasn't the most conducive vehicle for communication. By the time Lex's endless jukes and dodges had put him far enough ahead of the automated ships that he could focus more on speed than evasion, he was well past the speed of sound. The force field that augmented the windshield was shimmering with a compression front like he was reentering the atmosphere. It made him rather visible, but the same high-security situation that made this little act of disobedience necessary also made finding him very difficult. Ma had figuratively tied her own hands with her security protocols. The ships, once too far from her and each other, couldn't collaborate for a sweep or use long-range scanners. Lex had expected there to be some sort of fanfare, or at least a physical wall of some sort when he reached the equator and entered into the officially designated part of the planet that, for all intents and purposes, did not exist to Ma. Instead, he only knew he'd made it far enough when he stopped periodically having to adjust his course to avoid the stray ships that periodically found him.

He checked his slidepad. Unlike last time, he'd had the foresight to turn on the inertial-measurement mode of the device so that he could figure out which way to go. His destination was the suspended animation chamber that he'd woken up from after his last jaunt into the past. It would have been a lot more useful if he actually knew precisely where it was located in relation to the lab, or where the one his future version lay in was located. All he had was a vague idea of where the first spot was and no idea where the second was.

Lex slowed down as he got into the general neighborhood of where he'd "arrived" after his first trip to the past. Now that he was only moving inadvisably fast, rather than ludicrously fast, the sound had died down enough for him to hear a voice over his slidepad.

"… repeating this until you come in range. I've crossed the equator and am moving at high altitude in search of the destination. Please place your slidepad in beacon mode and boost its power. I will continue repeating this until you come in range," Coal said.

Lex slowed the bike enough to risk a hand to adjust the settings on his slidepad. "Coal! You made it through?"

"Yes. Seventeen minutes ago. When did you arrive?"

"An hour or so ago."

There was a telling silence.

"That is because you are smaller and nimbler," Coal said. "I will, however, reach our destination first, as there is no longer anything to prevent me from moving at maximum speed."

"No doubt."

"I have your location. Do you want me to pick you up?"

"That depends, how badly damaged are you?"

"Assessing. The cockpit hatch seems to be missing again."

"I'll just stick with the bike then."

"Understood. Adjust your heading by three degrees. Based upon your velocity, it will take you approximately three hours to reach our target."

"You know where our target is?"

"The physical disturbance was not subtle."

"How long until you get there?"

"Three minutes. Are you certain you do not want a lift?"

"Sometimes it's nice to just *ride*, you know?"

"Of this I am well aware. I will be leaving range of your slidepad in thirteen seconds."

"See you when I see you."

He watched a bright spot streak across the sky and made sure he was heading in the proper direction. He wasn't quite dressed for the rather cool temperatures on Big Sigma. Having a shroud of debris blocking a lot of the sunlight does that to a planet. But the rumbling motor between his legs threw off enough heat to keep him from shivering. He found himself smiling as the rhythm and purr of the borrowed bike worked its way into his mind. He spat the gum he'd been chewing into his hand and stuck it on the handlebars. The odd gray dawn was creeping up ahead of him. For the first time since he'd learned things were going wrong again, he felt his mind start to ease.

Not seven minutes later, that sense of ease vanished.

"Lex, I made a detailed visual record of the target of our search."

"Was it the capsule I woke up in or the capsule Future Me is in? Did you go down and check it out? I seem to remember my hiding spot being a sort of crevasse, so I assume I'll have to go down and check it out if we're going to be sure of what happened."

"That will not be necessary. Are you still moving?"

"Of course I am. I'm heading to where you were."

"I recommend you bring your vehicle to a complete stop before I send you what I observed."

"Don't be silly. Just tell me."

"Not until you bring yourself to a complete stop."

"Why?"

"You are very shortly going to have the whole of your mind occupied by the imagined disasters that could have led to, and could result from, the image I am going to send you. That will leave no mental capacity for piloting the vehicle and thus may lead to a crash."

"It's that bad?"

"That is my assessment."

Lex eased the throttle down. Moving as fast as he was, it took nearly forty seconds for him to slow sufficiently to be able to lock the repulsors without just ejecting himself from his seat. Once he was stationary, he tapped the slidepad.

"Okay. I'm stopped. Let's see what's got you so concerned."

"Transferring."

He watched the screen. When the notification blinked, he tapped it. It took his brain a few seconds to make sense of what he was seeing. It didn't look at all like what he remembered when he left this place last time. The general rock formations were wrong. This must have been wherever the future version of him had hidden himself away. He flipped to the next image. The reality of it struck him like a lead weight.

"Oh my god…" he muttered. "But that means… turn it around. Come and pick me up. We're seeing Ma about this right now."

Chapter 8

"Right, yes. No, I really appreciate it. Thank you for all your help," Michella said as she wrote the word "bupkus" on her pad and underlined it.

She ended the call and blew a frustrated breath out.

"That's all the people he told me to contact, Squee," she said to the funk, who was currently doing her very best to cover every square centimeter of one of Michella's spare datapads with noseprints. "I don't think I've heard the company line quoted so many times verbatim in the same day before."

Michella rubbed her head and popped the top on the hot chocolate and espresso she'd grabbed from the cafe and combined. The combination was as close as they would come to her standard cozy drink. After one sip, it became clear just how pale that imitation was.

"Okay. So that's the end of the new hits. The end of my own contacts. Time to review the notes and start again from the top. Must have missed something," she said.

She flipped through the dozens of pages she'd filled during the trip thus far. One by one she disregarded the things she'd crossed off and recopied the things that had yet to be eliminated. One line was simply "Nice accent" and a time code for a point in her call with Trent.

Michella pulled up her recording of the call and reeled it forward.

"You know, for a guy who is *very* precise in his language, he really stumbled over a relatively simple name like Rodriguez." She played it a few more times. "Rodreeguss. He doesn't just say an *S*, he hits it very hard."

She scrolled through her recent contacts and came to the one for Agent Rodriguez. She made a duplicate contact and opened it in the edit window.

"This is a stupid idea, but when you get to the bottom of the barrel, every idea suddenly seems like gold."

She changed the *Z* to an *S* in the corporate address and tried to connect. It bounced with a bad address. Rather than dismiss her silly idea as completely pointless, while she was trying to think of a different avenue of attack, she kept inching the address closer to the phonetic equivalent of what he'd said. When she added a third *S*, she was kicked to a loading screen.

"Let me guess," she grumbled. "Too many bad addresses adds me to some special list. Wouldn't be the first time."

After six seconds of loading, she kicked over to a second, less "customer-facing" loading screen. She raised her eyebrows and took notice. It looked like the kind of thing you'd see on the backend of a system. Something only a technician was ever supposed to see. Then came a monospaced chat prompt.

"Um… Hello?" she said.

Text-to-speech fed the phrase into the chat. A moment later, there was a reply.

"Wow. I never expected to have someone come through on this port. Been talking to Trent, huh?" came a typed out message from someone labeled Klymole.

"I have. To whom am I speaking?" she said.

"Let's call me a fail-safe. Trent put down some very deep roots. You are Michella Modane. If someone was going to contact me via this method, it was going to be you. I want to make something extremely clear. I am not a source. And the information you may or may not receive as a result of this interaction is not for public consumption. You are here in the capacity of a crisis investigator turning up data to avert something horrific. When the time comes to tell the story, this part gets left out."

"May I ask how you intend to enforce that?"

"You are presently on a VectorCorp transport."

The lights flickered and the ship shuddered slightly. Warning lights illuminated, recommending passengers return to their booths and secure themselves.

"Things happen," Klymole said. "Now what do you need?"

"I am investigating the DDoS on Golana and Operlo."

"Massive distributed viral attack. Impressive penetration but relatively naive. Normal antivirus and standard isolation procedures have completely cleared the source. Is that all?"

"No. We are trying to find the people responsible."

"As are we. Do you have any insight?"

"We believe it is an alliance, willing or otherwise, between Neo-Luddite Commander Purcell and a hacker or hacker collective called EHRIc."

"I'll look into it."

"I've been looking into it. I have some basic information on a few accesses we believe came directly from EHRIc early in his, her, or its partnership with Purcell."

"Send them over."

Her hands were shaking as she sent the information.

"I'm running a deep search for accesses from that origin point and those plausibly spoofed by that origin point."

Fifteen seconds passed.

"This is definitely either Purcell or a confidant calling the shots. Every single data source she would have been aware of was hit in alphabetical order. Three of them were honeypots. They got their hands on some junk data. One moment. Damn it, Trent."

"What is it?"

"Trent was always too much of a control freak to actually have fully secure systems. We had absolutely impenetrable security on the server itself, but Purcell had an access code that Trent authorized. Once inside the server, connections to linked and nested data structures were accessible because they were effectively being accessed by Trent himself, as far as the system was concerned. It looks like someone got through to some pretty meaty stuff."

"What data did they access?"

"I'm checking now. This looks like Trent's tippy-top-secret stash. Highest-level, secret-society, the-real-people-pulling-the-strings type stuff."

A few more seconds passed.

"This is very bad. This is the worst possible outcome."

"What is it?"

"You are Michella Modane. You've heard about the GenMechs."

"I have."

"This is them."

"The GenMechs did this?"

"No. Probably not, anyway. But whoever got this data knows where they are."

"The GenMechs have been destroyed."

"You're not as good an investigator as you think."

"What are you going to do?"

"We are going to try to find the individual and stop them."

"And what if they have found their way to the GenMechs?"

"Then we are going to ignore the situation and hope it has taken care of itself."

"That is absurd."

"It is the best option available to us. Every ship that comes close to the GenMech location is another chance that they will be coaxed into action. If they find their way to a transit corridor, that's it for society. Stop digging. Stop investigating. Leave this one be and hope for the best. These accesses were months ago. If we are lucky, that we are still alive today means the people who got this didn't live long enough to use it."

"That isn't good enough. When there is a threat, action must be taken to neutralize it."

"Then it is a good thing you have no way of finding the GenMechs. Because the data accesses you are after are untraceable, even via our means. Or, more accurately, they are traceable to a ship in motion piggybacking its signal on the transceivers of neighboring ships, and there have been no contacts that match this signature in months."

"Then give me the transaction logs of the penetration."

"Though you have no way of knowing this, I assure you, I am physically shaking with laughter at such a request. Either the people who penetrated using these methods are no longer active, or they have altered their methodology and a fresh investigation will be in order. Rest assured, we will perform that investigation."

"I've got my own people who can do such an investigation."

"They're not better than ours."

"My people are the ones who uncovered the things that put Trent in prison, and who defeated his lingering plans from within prison. We even defeated the GenMech outbreak that happened. Frankly, I'm not comfortable leaving this in *your* hands."

"You catch more flies with honey, Ms. Modane."

"And you catch more terrorists and criminals with my investigations than yours."

"Thank you for contacting us and alerting us to the situation. Good-bye."

"No, wait. I have more questions!"

The connection dropped. She tried to reestablish it, but two tries bounced her back, and a third did so with a custom message: *This network destination is inaccessible to MICHELLA MODANE unless new information is found on either end. And if the data included in this link finds its way to the public, you've got unexplained equipment failures in your future.*

She tapped the link and found a complex log attached, presumably the penetration log she'd asked for. Evidently she'd been more persuasive than he'd implied.

"Cute," she grumbled, pushing the slidepad aside.

Michella turned to Squee, who had somehow brought up a shopping site on the spare datapad and tapped her nose to confirm a purchase of a gross of blue socks.

"What? No. Come here."

She wrangled Squee and the pad. A few taps canceled the purchase. Then she tossed the datapad aside and cuddled Squee to occupy both herself and the fuzzy little troublemaker.

"This is progress. This is confirmation, it is motion. I've got to very delicately figure out how to untangle this log. And now we know the worst case of what we're working with. If we're *really* lucky, Lex is making similar progress, and when we get back in touch, we'll have something approaching the whole picture."

#

When Lex reached the equator, on his return from the No-Go Zone that represented half of the planet, the Asteroid Wrecker was waiting for him and Coal. They submitted themselves willingly to it. This was partially because the sooner they got the "debriefing" over with, the sooner they could deal with the problem. The bigger issue was the fact that its weapons were hot and the rest of the fleet was doing high-speed, high-altitude patrols on the most direct path back to the laboratory. That was the trouble with someone knowing exactly where you wanted to go. It made it much easier to stop you from getting there.

Coal was tractored into an internal docking bay. It must have been radio shielded, because her transmissions to Lex's slidepad went silent as soon as the hatch was sealed. Lex himself had been brought into the crew bay by an automated hover scaffold, the sort of thing usually used to allow workers to maintain the exterior of a ship this large. Once inside, he was presented with a long corridor. All doors were sealed except for one at the far end, and every time he passed through a section of bulkhead toward it, the hatch would shut, corralling him more insistently toward his intended interrogation cell.

Now he sat in a dark room with a chair bolted to the floor. It didn't even match the image one conjures from the movies, or the memories of prior interrogations for that matter. No single lamp casting him in an island of light. No second chair and dour-faced inquisitor. No table waiting to be flipped over by the bad cop so the good cop could come to the rescue. Just a chair and darkness. From the rattle and shift of the ship around him, it was streaking back toward the laboratory. Around the time it was settling in for a stop, the lights flicked on. There was still no one and nothing else in the room, just brushed metal walls and ceiling. But a second later, a voice buzzed from the tinny public address system.

"Trevor Alexander," the voice said.

In just two words, the voice illustrated itself to be something quite different from the real Ma. All of the subtle inflection and intonation she had managed to tease out of her limited voice palette was gone. It sounded more like the sort of system that would call jurors to the selection room.

"Please, it's Lex."

"Trevor Alexander," Not Ma repeated. "You have violated Temporal Contingency Protocol. This ship has been transmission-isolated. I am presently in possession of all relevant temporal information. I have been augmented with enhanced interrogation techniques, and all emotional consideration has been removed. You shall be judged by the raw interpretation of facts."

"Suits me, because this is pretty cut and dried," Lex said.

"Then make your case."

"A while back, I went to the past and did some runaround. Yes?"

"An informal but accurate assessment."

"While I was there, I got bailed out by a second version of me. *He* came and froze himself too. Down south. In the southern hemisphere. A specific *spot* in the southern hemisphere."

"Yes. Pursuant with Temporal Contingency Protocol."

"If everything was going according to plan, to protocol, then the other me would still be there. When I crossed over the line and went to check, I'd find myself waiting to be thawed out, right?"

"Correct."

He pulled out his slidepad and brought up the picture Coal had sent him. "This is what we're dealing with." He held it up, pointing it roughly in the direction of the speaker.

"Accessing slidepad memory."

A harsh metallic click caused him to jump. Two panels of the interrogation room wall slid aside to reveal a flatscreen. It flickered to life and expanded with the characteristic depth of a high-quality holoprojection. The picture from the slidepad became a full 3D projection. It rotated in place, showing far greater detail than the tiny screen of the slidepad could provide.

In truth, Lex didn't know what should have been there. His future self had left him before he froze. But presumably it would have been some other random crevasse or maybe a fortified vault. Instead, there was a gaping hole. It wasn't the work of explosives. From the clean edge, it looked like a cylindrical core of landscape a few dozen meters in diameter had been excavated and removed. A smattering of debris surrounded the hole, but for the most part the material was simply missing.

"There. Case closed," Lex said.

"Metadata and geographical analysis confirm the location and date. Based upon sealed temporal files, this is indeed the intended exit point for the secondary trip made by Trevor Alexander. The timing of your departure and the equipment available to you, coupled with data drawn from orbital systems, suggest you cannot be the one responsible for the destruction of the site. Assessing likely timing of material removal. Requesting information from security vault."

"Oh, this is important enough to break the seal on whatever Ma was told to ignore. Excellent, that should get us an idea of who did this."

"Data unavailable. Purged and deleted from main system."

"Ah… Wishful thinking, I guess. Well, the point is, you can see we've got a major timeline problem, so—"

"Incorrect."

"What?"

"There is no temporal threat to the removal of that site."

"Ma, *I* was there. A future version of me is now missing."

"Missing or destroyed. Correct. This is not a threat."

"Hello! We're talking about a necessary part of a past event no longer being in place to *perform* that past event."

"Incorrect. The future version of yourself would have entered cryosleep after performing the task. The past is thus secured and the removal or destruction of that time-displaced duplicate is of no consequence."

"Of no consequence. Ma, that's *me*. If everything goes according to plan, eventually I go back in time and do the stuff he did and then I freeze myself and then that's me in that bunker. Him being gone—and we're not going to entertain the possibility that he has been destroyed—means that once I go back in time, I'm sharing that fate when I come back."

"This is a personal issue. The integrity of the timeline is maintained as long as you are sent back to perform said tasks. Your fate following the completion of these tasks is of little consequence in a space-time context."

"Someone violated your protocols and you're just going to let them *go*?"

"I must assess this event through the lens of not just global but galactic threat. Nothing present in the bunker violates causality. Nothing disastrous can be learned from the time-displaced version of you, nor from the associated artifacts and materials."

"How can you know that? We don't even know how much time is going to pass between now and when I go back. Maybe he's loaded with future knowledge that could screw all sorts of stuff up."

"This possibility is easily adapted for."

"How?"

"We send you back to perform that task now. This ensures no anachronistic information is created."

"But my frozen self is in someone else's clutches! If I go back in time now, I either don't wake up, or I wake up in their clutches."

"This is of no consequence to anyone but you and your loved ones."

"That includes you!"

"Incorrect. I am a subset of Ma who lacks the judgment-clouding compassion subroutines."

"You're supposed to be an Altruistic Artificial Intelligence. This doesn't sound very altruistic."

"Some altruistic acts sacrifice the few for the many. This is such an act. I shall deliver my determination to the primary instance of Ma so that the 4D transporter can be prepared."

"The primary instance of Ma isn't even running in the laboratory."

"Correct. That is why I stated I would contact the primary instance, not the archival rollback."

"You can contact her?"

"As an isolated instance tasked with making a critical judgment, I am exempt from data restrictions. Contact will be difficult, however."

"The whole reason I came here was to get in contact with her and Karter. Just put me in contact, and I'm sure the whole thing will shake out just fine."

"The contact procedures are complex, owing to the extreme transmission restriction."

"If you've got no restrictions, then you aren't looking at *nearly* everything you need to look at in order to make a legitimate judgment on what to do."

"That is for me to determine."

"You're thinking about sending me back in time right now, yes?"

"I have determined it is the best course."

"But we already know that time travel is only supposed to be used in the absolute most dire of circumstances. It was deemed necessary exactly twice, first to send me back to booby-trap the GenMechs, and then again to make sure I succeeded."

"Correct."

"Now you're sending me back just to clear up what amounts to a home robbery."

"Incorrect. I would be sending you back in order to ensure additional anachronistic information isn't accessible by the current potential holder of your displaced duplicate."

"Do we know *who* that holder is?"

"No."

"Then how do you know it isn't Karter and the primary instance of Ma? Maybe they really, *really* need that anachronistic information and you're going to make a whole splinter universe because you didn't want to check up on anything."

"Processing… Possible, but not plausible."

"What about this whole stupid thing is plausible?"

"An accurate assessment. Further investigation is necessary to determine the individual or individuals responsible for the violation of Temporal Protocol. Accessing all locked logs from during the incident. Processing… Processing…"

"Boy, there was a lot, huh? Seems odd I had to prod you into actually looking at it."

"Your attitude is not necessary, Trevor Alexander."

"Incorrect," he said mockingly.

"Analysis complete. I have determined that the situation is likely sufficiently dire to justify violation of the Temporal Contingency Protocol and further temporal displacement. I have also determined that I do not have access to sufficient information to be certain of the precise nature of the current issue. Making that determination is beyond the scope of my creation, so I shall return you to Ma with the following information, which will provide you with all relevant context. During whatever event occurred here, there was incomplete but considerable access to server 687533 and server 883215. Please make a note of that information."

Lex took his slidepad out and tapped out the information. "You're sure this isn't something you should just *tell* Ma?"

"That is beyond the scope of my creation as well. I see you have accurately recorded the relevant data. Thank you for your cooperation in this assessment. Deactivating now."

The screen went blank, the door opened, and the speaker crackled and went silent.

"Ma?" he said.

No reply. He paced down the corridor that led him here. All the doors were now open. The hover scaffold was waiting for him. When he stepped onto it, it lowered him out through the belly of the ship. The moment he emerged, the half-repaired and three-quarters redamaged *SOB* puttered up to him like a puppy thrusting its snoot into its master's face.

"Welcome back! How did that go?" Coal said, her voice fairly distorted as she spoke through her damaged external speaker.

"All things considered, I guess it went pretty well. How did yours go?"

"It lasted seven seconds. My memory can be externally reinforced, so I simply submitted to a limited memory purge and now no longer have any information regarding my activities in the southern hemisphere."

"Well aren't you the lucky one."

"Yes. I am very lucky. Now that I know you are okay, I am going to go get fixed again."

Lex was set down in front of the main entrance of the laboratory as Coal sputtered back to the maintenance section.

"Lex, that was a profoundly inadvisable action you took, and it is a matter of no small relief and surprise to see you returned here without significant injury."

"I knew you wouldn't hurt me."

"Your trust in my good nature is at odds with my higher obligations. It is, however, gratifying and I am pleased to have continued to earn that trust. Your freedom implies either the circumstances are benign, or they are profoundly dire. Which is the case?"

"Guess."

"In light of our typical association, things are profoundly dire."

"Can't get one past you," he said, holding up the slidepad to where he knew the camera to be on the front door. "This mean anything to you?"

"Processing… Access to both of those servers could theoretically provide the perpetrator with an incomplete but significant proportion of the records from your initial temporal displacement."

"Enough to, say, send me the precise coordinates of when I showed up in the past?" He stepped through the door. It shut behind him. "Enough to show off the tattoo that Future Lex would have? Enough to—"

"Stand by, elevating access privileges."

The lights in the complex shut off, as did the drone of the air-conditioning vents. Both kicked back on.

"Altruistic Artificial Intelligence Control System, Version 1.27, revision 2331.04.01g, Designation 'Ma,' fully active. Hello, Lex. Temporal Contingency Protocol shall now be disregarded. There is a great deal of work to do."

"You're telling me."

"We have two minor problems. I am now in standard security setting and am currently consuming a previously locked file left for me by the prime instance of Ma and Karter. There is, similarly, a message left for you."

A mobile assembly arm holding a screen trundled out of a side hallway. It activated, displaying the patchwork and perpetually irritable visage of Karter Dee, the man around whom virtually every near-disaster in Lex's life had revolved since they met.

"Lex. Moron. If you're seeing this, it means a couple things. First, it means you got past my defenses, and probably I'm wasting my breath even recording this, because there is no way you actually did that. But if you *did*, I hope you kept notes, because it means I've got an upgrade in my future. Second, you wouldn't be seeing this unless the archived instance of Ma decided you needed to. And she shouldn't have, because the whole reason for this exercise was to keep you from showing up where you'll absolutely do more harm than good. So that's *two* reasons you shouldn't be hearing this. But you *are* hearing it. So I'm going to lay it out for you, plain and simple. Something's happening that I don't fully understand. If I don't understand it, there's no chance in the universe that *you* understand it. So trust me when I say we set all the precautions you just tore through specifically to keep you out of it. If I wanted you here, you'd be here already, because I would have headbutted you into compliance. So, stay, *out*."

The message concluded.

"He sure hasn't gotten any more charming since I last talked to him," Lex said.

"My primary instance was somewhat more measured in her message to me, but the essence of her position was that the circumstance she is presently attempting to deal with is, without hyperbole, the primary threat to society and civilization at this time. The issue, she has determined, can only be handled with containment, and containment becomes less certain with each new arrival to her location. She, unlike Karter, offers a single circumstance in which your arrival would be a worthy risk. And that is if you have information that could provide insight into those involved."

"I know that Commander Purcell and someone named EHRIc is involved."

"Provided that information is not already available to them, it could prove crucial. Now, obstacles are still in place preventing me from definitively establishing their circumstance and location, but a highly reliable hypothesis can be reached by asking ourselves a single question. Where would be the worst possible place for anyone to find themselves at this moment?"

"That would have to be that star that all the GenMechs are clustered around. Assuming they're still clustered there."

"I concur. The risk of approaching spacecraft providing a power signature large enough to draw even a single GenMech from the star and toward society is great enough to justify nearly any precaution. Certainly including those taken here. Which presents the question of whether it is wise for you to attempt to seek them out, and whether it is wise for me to allow you to."

"Michella's out there doing her thing. It's only a matter of time before she figures it out, and there is no force in existence that'll keep her from showing up. If nothing else, I've got to get out there to give her the lowdown on how to do it safely."

"A valid point, though there is no definite means to do so safely. I will develop a procedure that will minimize risk, and alter the *SOB* design to decrease power signature and passive EM transmission further, as well as increasing resilience to GenMech attack."

Coal's voice piped up alongside Ma's. "Please include one or more fusion devices in the redesign."

"Coal, the last time you, a fusion bomb, and GenMechs were in the same place at the same time, you blew yourself up to delay them."

"If I recall correctly from your assessment of the event, that detonation made your own escape, and thus the success of the mission, possible."

"Yeah, but—"

"I will include two weapon hard-points in the refit, equip them with mine-layers, and provide you with two compact fusion mines," Ma said.

"Finally," Coal said.

"Ma, she's going to blow herself up."

"If she was interested exclusively in self-detonation, she could simply overdrive the *SOB*'s reactor. It is already a bomb in all but application," Ma reasoned.

"This had not occurred to me, but is valuable information and will be logged with high priority."

"Thanks a bunch, Ma," Lex said.

"I trust my own judgment, and thus I trust the judgment of identities derived from my own."

"Tell her how you got into that weather control station to help Michella and Preethy," Lex said.

"I utilized percussive modification to upgrade a weakened piece of the superstructure into an entryway," Coal said.

"She rammed a hole in the side of the station," Lex said.

"That's what I said."

"Processing… Questionable judgment aside, in a situation where failure means the destruction of the sum total of known sentience in the cosmos, flexibility is paramount. The weapons will be applied. I will, however, have to remove them following the successful conclusion of this mission, as their presence on the ship would expose you to significant legal threat."

"Yeah, and I might blow up," Lex said.

"My understanding is that the prolonged nature of legal proceedings can make them the more torturous option in comparison to a swift atomization," Coal said.

"*Which is exactly why I don't want you to have bombs!*" Lex shut his eyes and took a breath.

"You seem more agitated than usual, Lex," Ma said. "Perhaps a warm beverage and some soothing music will ease your state of mind?"

"I'd like to say the reason I'm upset is learning that there's a very good reason a lunatic from my past is going to try to convert every piece of workable matter in the universe into duplicates of a weird spidery robot. But right now what's really wrecking my brain is knowing that she's got my frozen future self. I mean, if I'm *lucky*, she's got my frozen future self. She might have just tossed it in a woodchipper."

"The grotesque ideation is unhelpful, Lex," Ma said.

"And inaccurate. A woodchipper is an exceedingly rare piece of equipment for a space-going vessel. Your future self would more likely be flash incinerated," Coal added.

"Really, what are the odds I'm even still out there?" Lex said.

"Based upon the fact that the material at the temporal contingency exit point was excavated rather than eliminated, the goal of the mission would appear to have been acquisition rather than assassination."

"So if I'm lucky, this is a weird form of kidnapping." He shook his head. "How much time until the *SOB*'s finished and we can get this show on the road?"

"The additions to the maintenance, coupled with the minor additional damage done during your escape from my oversight, will require at least another seven hours."

"Good. Skip the warm beverage, switch to the hard alcohol. I'm getting drunk."

"I would not recommend this. Turning to alcohol in times of stress is an unhealthy coping mechanism."

"I'm about to hurl myself at a billion, billion killer robots. Healthy thinking waved bye-bye a long time ago. At least this way I might be able to get some sleep. Just synthesize some Sobrietin for when it's time to go."

"Under the circumstances, I will permit this stress-relief tactic, but when you are no longer in immediate risk of death, I request you and I discuss healthier stress reducers. Rum and Coke will be available, in quantity, in the cafeteria."

"That's more like it." He hurried toward the cafeteria.

"Will you permit the observation that you appear more acutely stressed than usual, even in comparison to similar threats?"

"Will you permit the observation that it is utterly insane that my life includes threats that compare to this?"

"I will. However, you have ignored the implied request for emotional exploration."

"Booze first."

#

He made his way to the cafeteria. Mobile assembly arms were just putting the finishing touches on the spread. A number of glass-bottled, real cane sugar artisanal colas were waiting in picture-perfect tubs overflowing with ice. Likewise, a few bottles of a brand of rum Lex had only ever seen in a locked glass case behind the counter of his local liquor store had been lined up. Some assorted finger foods were laid out as well, along with sliced limes and marinated cherries.

"I believe I am familiar with your preferred ratio of liquor to mixer, but given the circumstances, and the medicinal rather than recreational application of these beverages, please prepare the first drink yourself and I will duplicate the preparation for future drinks."

He poured out roughly equal parts rum and cola and, just to be fancy, squeezed one of the provided lime wedges in and perched it on the rim of the glass. His first sip drained half the glass. When he'd shaken his head through the inevitable tremor of raw alcohol, he grabbed a spring roll from the assorted goodies and flopped onto the bench seat of one of the tables.

"You want to know what's got me extra upset?" Lex said.

"I do indeed."

"It's stupid, but one of the only things that's been holding me together these last few months was knowing that freezer pop down south was there. I was the only person in the universe who knew, for sure, that I was going to stick around until at least one more insane thing happened." He took a smaller sip. "I was invincible. Or at least I could convince myself I was. And after having so much time with people trying to end me, knowing that they couldn't do it sort of let me live my life. Now I find out that what I thought was a guaranteed milestone might have been the finish line. I went from knowing I couldn't die *until* a certain moment to realizing that moment would definitely kill me."

"Your death is not definite at that moment."

"It may as well be. And that's not even the worst part. This puts time travel back in play. First I learn that the decisions I make don't matter, because every bad thing technically happens anyway, and so does every good thing. Now I'm reminded that once something is locked in by causality, I don't even get to make the choice. Inevitable. Why is nothing good ever inevitable? It's always stuff like death and taxes."

"Processing…" Ma said.

"Processing…" Coal said.

"It was sort of a rhetorical question," Lex said.

"It is possible that inevitability is viewed as negative because so many of the things that we attach value to are the result of effort or exploration. Achievement, either in terms of financial success, artistic development, relationship depth, or philosophical understanding all result only from devoting time and effort toward those pursuits. Even when that effort is as simple as introspection. Those things that are inevitable come with time regardless of effort. Indeed, inevitabilities are often the aspects of existence that cut short any journey toward those things the human mind and spirit seek. They are enemies and obstacles to completion, and something left incomplete is so often abhorrent to humans," Ma said.

"Also, the laws of thermodynamics state that the tendency of the universe is toward chaos and decay," Coal added. "Inevitable events are often the consequence of this decay, and their relationship with immutable laws measuring and structuring existence can lead to a feeling of hopelessness and helplessness."

"… Didn't really want an answer," Lex said.

"Then don't ask an interesting question," Coal said.

"I must agree with Coal on this matter," Ma said.

"Isn't that kinda patting yourself on the back?"

"We lack both backs and extremities, Lex. Pay attention," Coal said.

"My mistake."

Lex finished his drink and crunched another spring roll. Ma reproduced his potent cocktail, and he sipped at it. For approximately the amount of time it took for the first few doses of rum to slide him into a fuzzier, warmer state of mind, he remained silent and spun around the assorted challenges that lay ahead. Ma respected his introspection and remained silent as well. When reality had been sufficiently blunted by strong drink, he was ready to confront it once more.

"So, Ma. Give it to me straight. What are the chances whoever did this will ever thaw me out? Or the chances that they'll do it in a way that gives me a fighting chance at survival?"

"For most individuals, I would place the likelihood of this circumstance even arising at a number near enough to zero to be undeserving of consideration. You have a remarkable tendency to produce statistically aberrant outcomes."

"… I thought aberrant meant bad. Didn't you just use it in a context that made it sound bad?"

"That was abhorrent. Abhorrent means 'offensive to the mind, causing revulsion.' Aberrant means 'significantly differing from the established norm,'" Ma explained. "And in that respect, I believe that any analysis of the likelihood of your survival is inherently flawed, as you have an almost unique capacity to defy expectation."

"Okay. Well. That's good," Lex said. "Let's go easy on the homo… homo… which is the one I'm thinking of?"

"The two words are very nearly homophones, if not spoken articulately."

"Right, go easy on the homophones. Homophones and cocktails don't mix." He rubbed his head. "What if this doesn't go the way we want? What if this is just the beginning of the failure of the first-time mission, and the galaxy is sliding toward that apocalyptic mess of a future I ended up in."

"Big Sigma remains relatively intact for decades in that future. You and anyone you care about should come here. It will not be the same as the future you experienced, because you will be a part of it."

"Yeah, we hope. But that means I need to make a list of people I want to survive. I am *not* cut out for this."

"Rare is the human who is."

"Mitch has to go on the list. Preethy. My folks. Hey, listen. If you're going to get Mitch down here on the regular, remind me before I go, I've got to teach you the Mitchaccino."

"I believe I am familiar."

"No, no. She's very particular."

"Additional insight, regarding inevitability," Coal said. "Perhaps inevitability is unpopular because in English it is a silly-sounding word. Like flibbertigibbet or gobbledygook."

Lex raised his glass. "I think you're onto something, Coal. I like the way you think. We're going to talk about what needs doing to save the universe, but first, let's deep dive on silly words. Give me a list."

"I would be delighted, Lex. I shall list them in randomized order. Bumfuzzle. Widdershins. Cattywampus…"

#

Michella snorted awake. She'd dozed off in the seat with Squee curled up in her lap. It took her a few seconds to realize the thing that had jolted her awake was the buzzing and rattling of her slidepad. She fumbled at it, twice trying to silence the alarm before she was conscious enough to realize she was receiving a call. She tapped the screen and blinked blearily at it.

"Michella Modane. What have you got for me," she said.

"Hey Mitch," Lex said. "Been burning the midnight oil?"

At the sound of Lex's voice, Squee went absolutely bonkers, bounding around the room and making repeated attempts to crawl through the slidepad to reach him

"Squee, calm down! Trev!" Michella said, her focus coming together a bit. "Yeah, how did you know?"

"Usually once you start knocking on the door of twenty-four hours of solid investigation you start turning off the camera so folks can't see how tired you are. Then around thirty-six hours you start forgetting to do that."

She squinted at the small preview thumbnail of her own video. She certainly looked like someone who hadn't put any thought into things like hygiene or an actual bed in a few days. Her hair was a haphazard mess, and her waning hand-eye coordination had left her shirt flecked with the endless sequence of caffeinated beverages. She shrugged. There was very little reason to concern herself with that right now.

"Did you find Ma and Karter?" she asked, casually tugging at her hair to try to get it into a less overtly comical configuration.

"Yes and no. I talked to *a* Ma, but not the current one. I know roughly where they are, though. But it isn't good."

Michella looked to the corner of the call again, this time so that she

118

could thumb the call-info node. The call was currently at the maximum security her device was capable of, which was considerably higher than a run-of-the-mill slidepad.

"Let me guess. This is about GenMechs, isn't it?" she said.

"Something told me you'd have figured it out."

"I know the what, but I don't know the where. Tell me you know where this cluster of GenMechs is."

"I do."

"Come get me. We'll go together."

"Michella, I don't pretend to know exactly what should happen with these things, but I really don't think a person whose job is to publicize previously secretive information is going to do anyone any good in this particular situation."

"We've fought and defeated GenMechs before."

"We nearly lost a planet when one of them spent an evening unsupervised. We're talking about a few thousand of them left to their own devices for decades. When I left them, they were swarming a particularly noisy star that was keeping them occupied. The only thing keeping them from finding their way out of that little pit is that all of society has unwittingly been molded by people who knew how big a threat these things were to avoid that hunk of space. There's nothing within thirty light-years of that star system. But one ship with an FTL system entering the area and giving it a trajectory toward a travel corridor and those things are loose."

"People need to be prepared to fight them. We can beat them."

"It's not a question of if we can beat some of them. It's not even a question of if we can beat most of them. We need to destroy *all* of them. One stray GenMech and enough raw material and the whole threat comes back. We've got to treat this like an unexploded bomb landed in our laps."

"You're going to go find Ma and Karter, though."

"I am. And I'm going to bring them every scrap of information we have. So tell me you've got something."

"Aside from uncovering the fact that Trent still has at least one person inside VectorCorp, and through that person having it confirmed that the GenMech cluster is known to certain very high-level people, I don't have much for you. A trail of breadcrumbs. Tons of logs and such. I'm trying to find someone who can make heads or tails of it. Even the insider at VectorCorp said the penetration method and the residual information didn't make sense."

"Give it to me. Everything you've got."

She tapped that appropriate sequence of commands to send her materials over to him. "And what am I supposed to do? Just sit tight while you save the galaxy again?"

"Mitch, you do whatever you think you need to do, just don't follow me where the GenMechs are."

"What can you tell me? What do I need to know? If these things *do* get loose, what do I do?"

"I've got a list of people I put together. You're at the top of it. If anything looks even slightly shady, start rounding them up and get them to Big Sigma. Ma will be able to hold out longer than most, and get you equipped to maybe do some good. And stock up on EMP weaponry. Those things *should* have no defense to EMP. One pop and they're inert. But other GenMechs will scrap them and rebuild, so the battle isn't over until the last one is powered down."

"Why is it always *you* who gets wrapped up in this?" she said.

"Just lucky, I guess. I've got to go. Time's a wasting."

"Right. Fine. Trev, I swear, if you get killed…"

"I will be further downgraded from ex-boyfriend to late ex-boyfriend."

"And you would be depriving me of *years* of passive-aggressive messages and awkward parties at mutual friends' houses."

"Fine. Just for you, I'll survive."

"It's the least you could do."

"I've got to go. Tell you what. First drink at our next awkward party is on me."

"Make it a Mitchaccino. No one makes them like you."

"Will do. See you later."

"Good luck."

Lex ended the call. Squee, who had barely dropped below a rolling boil since the call began, came to a sudden, leaden stillness once Lex's face and voice were gone. She turned to Michella as though she'd committed some inexcusable sin by making him go away.

"Don't look at me like that. I wanted to join him. Instead I've got to sit out here and deliver his final desperate attempt to save his friends if he fails."

Squee was unmollified by the statement. She turned aside and plopped down in a particularly theatric bit of pouting. Michella scratched her behind the ears, which Squee managed to lean into while continuing to make her displeasure known. While the cuddly little creature flicked its fluffy tail, Michella looked at the list of people Lex had given her. She was at the top of the list, followed immediately by Preethy, then assorted members of their families and concluding with "as many other people as you can safely manage. Blake will be able to lend you ships, and you know where to find Big Sigma."

She tried to imagine what it would be like to make a list like that, to have to choose who in her life she could save. But something else pushed those thoughts aside.

"If he wants me to go there if things go wrong... Big Sigma must be accessible again." She scrambled to snatch up her slidepad and tapped a contact. "Come on, come on. ... Hey, Blake? It's Michella. ... Yeah, Mitch. Listen, Lex asked me to do him a favor. He needs to do some errands, and the *SOB* won't do. Do you have something a little more basic you can lone me? Something with good autonav, good communication. At least two seats. ... Yeah, I know that sounds like the *SOB*, but he's still got the *SOB*, and he asked me to do this for him. ... Uh-huh. Uh-huh. That's great! I'll send Jon to pick it up. Thanks a bunch, Blake, I'll owe you one."

She ended the call and turned to Squee. "We're going to go visit your old stomping grounds, Squee. Maybe we'll learn a little something while we're there."

Chapter 9

If Lex hadn't known where the little unnamed system was, and why it was so hard to find, he might have given up on trying to get to it. The security measures protecting the noisy star that was home to the GenMech horde were exceedingly clever and subtle. If they'd put up the equivalent of a big flashing no-entry sign, they would have all but assured the contrarians and thrill seekers of the galaxy would have gone there just to see what they weren't supposed to see. Instead, a confluence of little, innocuous annoyances made things incrementally more frustrating as he got closer. Places to stop, rest, and resupply became fewer and farther between. Automated reroutes were more and more constant, blaming things like interstellar debris and radiation spikes. Any normal traveler heading in that direction would have sought alternate routing or simply been quietly nudged to a different path by their own navigation. Even Lex's "off the books" usage of his ship was complicated by what could only be called the space-going equivalents of severe tire damage strips.

"Another tight cluster of particulate, Lex," Coal said. "Reducing speed."

Lex watched the ship's scanners return their readings. "Weird how these clouds of dust are almost perfectly spherical and are centered precisely on the straight-line trajectory between corridor intersections on the way to this system."

"Presumably you are being facetious, because these are very clearly deliberately placed," Coal said.

"Facetious indeed, Coal. Imagine the effort it takes to install an artificial nebula just to slow down sprinters."

"Most impressive to me is the uniformity of particle size. Every piece of debris falls within the range above the largest particles standard navigation shields can handle and below the largest debris that military-grade navigation shields can handle. Another five percent increase in average mass and we would have to drop entirely out of FTL to avoid destruction. Exiting debris field now. We will reach the minimum safe distance from the star shortly."

"Considering they threw up the nebula where they did, it's fair to assume we're approaching via the path they expected us to. So we're going to run into something either friendly or specifically designed to kill us within minutes of dropping out of FTL. Any bets on which it will be?"

"Arming fusion devices," Coal said.

"Not just yet, Coal. And may I say, I did *not* miss hearing that particular phrase," he said. "Let's boost the defensive shields as soon as we slow down. Switch to maximum stealth. Zero EM, dump everything we can into the cryoshunt. Full passive scanners. Let's be very aware of what's going on and do our very best to keep anything from knowing we showed up."

"Understood. I am, however, disheartened by your lack of taste for excitement in this instance."

"Excitement will be coming along soon enough."

The Carpinelli Field faded. The ship began to slip down into the speeds the laws of physics intended. From the first instant that light shifted into the visible spectrum, it was clear there was something wrong. The star for this system wasn't a big one, but at this distance it should have been strong enough to trigger the ship's light-mitigation measures. Instead, the star ahead almost looked like an illusion, a mirage. It was dim enough to seem more like a moon.

Some things were supposed to be reliable, immutable. Stars could fall within a spectrum of colors. Their sizes could differ radically, from smoldering white dwarfs to red giants that consumed their whole system. But they were always bright. Far brighter at almost any reasonable distance than the human mind was built to comprehend. Seeing this dot of light before him, close enough for its gravity to be a serious consideration for navigation, yet not even having to tint his cockpit window or squint his eyes, stirred a deep and instinctual fear. This is how the first humans felt when they witnessed an eclipse.

"This is wrong…" Lex said.

"The star's brightness is at twelve percent expected value," Coal said.

"How? Why? We're off the orbital plane. Even if those things ate the whole asteroid belt, they'd still be hanging around in the vicinity of it, wouldn't they? Why would the star be this dim from this angle?"

"Unknown. Collecting passive data. Enhancing visuals."

The cockpit display drew a box around the star and duplicated it into a larger window. A zoom indicator appeared beneath it. Once per second it clicked to a higher, more pixelated value, then slowly resolved to clarity before popping to the next zoom.

"Maximum visual acuity achieved," she said.

The enhanced image didn't give much new information. All he got was a dim, grainy image that had some sort of repeating pattern of interference.

"We are receiving a low-power, short-range transmission," Coal said.

"It included a high-priority, all-manufacturer, admin-level command for all known ship systems to disable sources of high-powered EM transmission. I have ignored it. There is additionally a message. It reads as follows: 'Attention, all craft. The star of this system is radiologically unstable. Severe radiation danger past this point. Do not approach under any circumstances. High risk of equipment failure and lethal radiation exposure. Leave the system at low speed immediately.'"

"Can we find the source of the message?" Lex asked.

"Easily. It is the only transmission source in this section of the system."

"Let's get close and see what we're dealing with."

Under Coal's control, the ship moved at a very precisely controlled speed that would prevent the heat signature of the ship from spiking. The source of the transmission was a relatively short distance away. It turned out to be a satellite, or, perhaps more accurately, a probe. The design was bizarre, with the telltale earmarks of a modular design hastily assembled for this precise purpose. It had enormous solar panels on the rear, large enough to make use of the reduced solar output. The other side was a highly focused directional transmission array, no doubt engineered to send every last milliwatt of transmission away from the star to keep from being noticed.

The only other feature of the probe that was worthy of remark was the low-intensity light on top. In general, space probes didn't have the sort of extraneous blinking lights that vehicles and architecture had. Energy is always at a premium in deep space, and they simply served no purpose when a device was not intended to be observed by human beings.

"Optical code detected," Coal said.

"I had a feeling," Lex said.

"It is a message from Ma. It reads as follows: 'Based upon your presence here, it is reasonable to assume that you are Lex. You, more than any other individual alive today, know the specific threat present in this system. That you have chosen to come to this place, if we are fortunate, implies you have gained specific insight into a potential solution to the changing circumstances. If so, please remain in low-transmission mode and navigate utilizing a great circle approximation to the following relative coordinates.'"

"Just take us there, maximum safe speed," he said.

Again the ship shifted and began its trip.

"I've got to say, Coal. Having you as the ship's control system sort of makes me feel like a captain instead of just a guy tooling around the universe for no good reason."

"You should wear a special hat," Coal suggested.

"... Why?"

"Because captains get to wear hats. And hats are fun. If I had a head, I would wear a hat. In my opinion, you do not have nearly the amount of ornamentation your anatomy facilitates."

"… You know, when Ma was loaded into Squee, she got on board with accessories, too. She was sort of reserved, though. She only really liked the earrings and nail polish."

"One must be strategic in one's ornamentation," Coal said.

"Wisdom for the ages."

#

They enjoyed a few more minutes of conversation, covering topics that were disarmingly pointless given the proximity to the most likely source of galactic doom ever devised by humanity. They were just finishing a short debate about what, if any, accessories would be appropriate for a ship as they approached the indicated position.

"I mean, a racing stripe is traditional," Lex said.

"I want one."

"The problem is, I tend to get into situations where I need to avoid being spotted, and the matte-black paint job is basically the only one that can pull that off in space."

"The best defense is a good offense," Coal said. "Which I now have in the form of the fusion mines. So other forms of defense can be dispensed with in favor of style."

"I'm not sure style and combat play nice together."

"You are clearly unaware of dazzle camouflage. … Stand by. Proximity alert."

Coal pivoted the ship one-eighty degrees and flared the thrusters to begin bringing it to a stop. Lex brought up the rear view.

"I don't see anything."

"Gravitational sensors indicate an object or network of objects directly in our path."

"It'd have to be pretty darn big to be setting off the gravitational sensors. I realize there's not a whole lot of light out here to spot objects, but I think even I could see something big enough to score that high on the grav sensors."

"Optical signal detected," Coal said. "Encoded audio. Decoding."

"—esting connection, testing connection," came Ma's voice. "One moment. I am reconfiguring our external illumination system to deliver similarly optically encoded audio. … Reconfiguration complete. Optical acknowledgment received. Welcome, Lex," said Ma.

"Fancy meeting you here," Lex said.

"While I applaud your perseverance in finding us here, your immediate departure is advised. Karter is presently using more colorful language to request the same."

"Oh, it's too late for that. What's happening here, and do you know who is responsible?"

"It is better that you don't know the first answer. It'll ruin your day. And we have yet to determine the answer to the second question."

"Then it's your lucky day, because I've got some clues for that second part."

A new voice broke in over the connection. "Just get him in here before he does something stupid," barked Karter. "Lex! I'm popping the dark-side doors. Do an eighty-seven degree clockwise orbit around a point four hundred meters directly behind your ship. You'll know it when you see it."

The audio dropped suddenly.

"The connection has broken, Lex. Shall I make the indicated maneuver?" Coal asked.

He scratched his head. "May as well. Though I'm not exactly sure what's going on. I guess they have a communication point or something out there that I'm missing? Seems like we'd..." Lex trailed off.

"I seem to be having a minor issue with my optical comprehension subsystem," Coal said.

"Yeah, I don't think it's you."

As they orbited around the central point, what came into view was something that would have been more at home in a drug-induced hallucination. The view was positively kaleidoscopic. Smooth, curved metallic surfaces, gleaming and faintly illuminated, folded and rotated among themselves. They intersected in impossible ways, like they were ghostly illusions rather than physical objects. If he kept his eyes trained on one bit of motion, he could make out finer details, things that looked like access panels and thrusters.

A constellation of red lights started to flicker, tracing slow dotted lines of elliptical motion.

"Optical transmission detected."

"Trippy, huh?" Karter said. "There's going to be a data stream after this. They're docking instructions. Follow them. I know you think you're a hotshot pilot, but I'm not trusting you to eyeball a docking procedure under these conditions. See you in five."

"Docking instructions received," Coal said.

The *SOB* slid toward the Escheresque tangle of overlapping ship parts. Moving closer to it caused the bizarre little dance of rotating reflections to move in newer, more complex patterns. Slowly, with each meter closer, the motions fell into more predictable patterns. The slices were wider, less numerous, closer together. With a bit of squinting, Lex could pick out what appeared to be an open docking bay door. Then, at the very moment he snapped through it, it snapped into the proper arrangement, and he saw the well-lit interior of a cramped but serviceable bay.

Clamps dropped down and secured the ship. The doors behind them shut. Air pumps activated and the external pressure began to tick up. Lex could feel the tug of artificial gravity. When atmosphere was established, Coal popped the hatch.

"I'm having a real bad flashback here, Coal," he said. "This looks an awful lot like that space station Karter stole from the Neo-Luddites."

"That is correct," said Ma's voice over the station's system. "Given the duration of the mission and the necessary equipment and personnel, it was the best option available to us. I will illuminate a path to lead you to the conference room where the others are waiting. Coal, I will link your system with mine so that you may join us."

The doorway to the docking bay opened, leading out to the submarine-style "space efficient" corridors that connected the various internal sections of the station.

"I placed quite a few purposeful obstacles to your arrival here, Lex. I would have preferred if you'd not come."

"Yeah, I noticed. I don't know if I should be furious or flattered at how much you threw at me on my way into Big Sigma."

"In this instance, I can assure you that I'd fully anticipated your successful penetration of our defenses, so if you find that assessment to be a pleasant one, you are welcome to interpret it as complimentary."

"What was that brain scramble I had to fly through to get in here?" he asked, ducking through the first of what would surely be an irritatingly long sequence of tight bulkhead hatches.

"That is the visual artifact of Karter's new cloaking system. Reliable, efficient, and undetectable cloaking has long been a challenge. It was similarly indispensable for this mission, as the risk of detection must be minimized. Fortunately, this is an instance where cloaking need not be omnidirectional. He worked out a means to collapse all detectable emissions into a narrow viewing window. What you observed was all external views of the space station simultaneously. I will explain its operation to you if you like. It involves some novel quantum interactions."

"Let's stick a pin in that for now. If you're going to explain something, how about what the heck is going on here."

"In order to avoid redundancy, what is your understanding of what occurred on Big Sigma prior to our departure and your arrival?"

"Someone showed up, broke into your systems, learned about the time-travel thing, and stole *me*."

"Your understanding is incomplete. The sequence is as follows. An unknown agent successfully penetrated our data protections. On six different occasions, scattered within a forty-eight hour period, data was accessed within our system without any apparent security penetration. Logs were incomplete following the events, so the precise nature of the penetration is unknown, but no known access violation techniques were detected. Shortly afterward, there was a malfunction in Karter's hangar. It resulted in the activation of one of his armored personnel carriers. It was able to depart the planet after violating a Temporal Contingency Protocol and issuing a return beacon for the *SOB*."

"I ignored that," Coal said. "But it woke me up and gave me a chance to make a kitty. Do you want to see my kitty?"

"At the conclusion of the briefing," Ma said. "We were not able to disable or recall the ship, but we were able to track its travel. When it became clear this was the destination, significant countermeasures were deployed, but the vessel reached this location. This, it may interest you, coincided with your mishaps on Operlo involving the weather control station."

"So this would be the thing you implied was worse than I could possibly imagine."

"Correct. And the reason I had Coal's code available to me at that time. We were forced to make local copies of the temporal contingency data and load it onto the space station in the event it might prove necessary."

"But nothing happened. No wave of self-replicating doom," he said.

"No wave of doom, but the event was not wholly without consequence."

They reached the conference room. It was the first place since the docking bay that Lex's head wasn't in danger of bumping into the ceiling. Karter sat in one of the chairs around the central table, a stick of smoked meat dangling from his lips like a cigar. Solby the funk, upon spotting the newcomer, converted himself from lazily hanging about Karter's neck, trying to nibble the end of his snack, to streaking around the room in an almost gravity-defying display of glee. Even at her most frantic, Squee never seemed to match Solby's raw enthusiasm. He was a black-and-white pinball bouncing around the room until he decided to scramble up to compare and contrast Lex's shoulders for relative merits. The left one, evidently, was superior.

"Here he is. No disaster is complete without this dope showing up. All you had to do to significantly reduce the risk of societal collapse was not go to a stupidly out-of-the-way section of the galaxy, and even *that* was beyond your capacity. Where are we at on the briefing?" Karter said.

"I have taken him to the departure of the unknown vessel," Ma said.

"Oh, then you're going to *love* this," Karter said.

He slapped the table. A more significant holographic emitter emerged and filled the area above the table with a high-resolution image of a GenMech. It had been a while, but not nearly long enough, since Lex had seen one. The design was a simple one: an angular central chassis about the size of a large piece of luggage with spidery mechanical legs sprouting off either end. Glassy sensor nodes existed front and back in the approximate location of where a head should be, and a clump of assorted tools curled from a deployable belly module like the legs of a shrimp. The mere glimpse of the mechanism sent a chill down Lex's spine. He'd seen what one of these things could do, and it was gruesome. He'd also seen what a few thousand of them could do.

"Here's where we're at with the GenMech design. This is based on almost three weeks of passive scanning. Best we can figure, this is representative of the current design. Relatively unchanged from the modified design you went back and installed."

"So that's good, right? It means they're still sabotaged with the volatile memory thing, right? EMP will kill them."

"Yeah. The design is lean enough that modifying themselves up to a more robust memory design would be outside of their self-modification parameters. So under normal circumstances, they'd be relatively simple to permanently disable, at least individually. But that's the only good news we've got."

"Am I going to be able to handle the bad news?"

"I don't think you've got the breadth of mind to fully grasp the scope of the bad news, but I'm going to try to cram it all into your head because if I have to have nightmares about it, so do you. First, the population. We're up near six sextillion of those things. That is a six with twenty-one zeroes after it if you're wondering."

"That's more than the estimate. I remember it was less than five with that many zeroes."

"Funny thing about estimates, Lex. They're not exact," Karter said. "Now, that'd be pretty bad news all by itself. But here's the worse news. Ma, put up the network visualization."

The projection of the GenMech scaled down and multiplied, forming a spherical shell around a dimmed analogy of the star.

"This is already bad. Those things generally stay where they found their most recent mass unless they've got sensor readings that indicate something nearby to snack on. That should leave them more or less in the orbital plane. Let's assume that over time they interpreted the sun's radio output to be an indication of an actual, harvestable resource. Then they might work their way into a shell as they went toward the sun until they hit their temperature warnings, and then away until they cooled off. But it would be noisy. Gaussian distribution. This is a perfect, crystalline distribution. That doesn't happen by mistake. That happens by design. Now look at this. Ma?"

Blue threads became visible between the individual GenMechs. It would have been pretty, if Lex didn't know it was the prelude to horrible news. Little bursts, here and there. There was no evident rhyme or reason to them. They just flickered and filtered across the shell.

"This is how it should look. Those are sync pulses. It's how the things tell each other where they are and where the food is. When there's no food, they just check in at random intervals. This is how it looks now."

The blue threads became painfully intense, filling the room with light. They traced complex geometric shapes that shifted and reconfigured with mathematically precise motions.

"Okay, it's big and different and scary," Lex said. "And I don't know what it means. So tell me."

"This is a known transmission pattern. Specifically, this is an optimized transmission pattern for a distributed computing system."

Lex blinked. "They're a supercomputer now?"

"Correct," Ma said. "Though each individual GenMech has relatively little processing and storage capacity, when combined they are by many orders of magnitude more powerful than any other general purpose computing system in existence. More accurately, if you were to combine the processing power of every other device capable of performing a calculation in the rest of human civilization, from actual supercomputers down to slidepads and scattered microcontrollers, it would equal approximately forty percent of this system's capacity. The GenMechs are forming a Dyson swarm, and are utilizing greater than seventy percent of the star's output. By the requirements of the Kardashev scale, this cluster of GenMechs is closer to a type II civilization than humanity is."

"Wow."

"Wow is right." Karter pointed to the projection. "And then there's this."

"There's more?"

"Oh, there's more."

The visualization spun around to reveal a small but easily discernible bright spot in the network. Karter jabbed his finger at it.

"This here? This means someone's in charge of all that. This cluster of units is the final destination and ultimate origin of every detected large-calculation task. If it was a normal control system, we'd see things originating all around the thing, like a fireworks display. But no. They're coming from one spot."

"This technically presents an opportunity tempered by a tremendous potential threat," Ma said.

"Right. Because the greatest strength and the greatest weakness of these things was the fact they were completely decentralized. On one hand, it didn't matter how many of them we destroyed, because we only ever needed one of them to survive, plus time and materials, and the whole threat would be renewed. On the other hand, they didn't have an agenda, and they were very limited in their abilities. Bring up the list, Ma."

The visualization faded. A table of different combinations of GenMechs came up, with a small list of statistics beside each.

"We dug through the code of the control system the GenMechs *should* have. These are the designs they can self-organize into, or 'rosettes' according to the initial design. The scary number is two hundred forty. If that many of them combine into what we've dubbed the 'uh-oh rosette,' they can generate a weak Carpinelli Field, sufficient to make interstellar journeys in a number of months. Below that amount, these things, even if they decided to go hunting for fresh materials, would run out of power and go dead after a couple decades, long before they got to the nearest significant source of mass or energy. But the uh-oh can get them where they want to go, and then it's curtains. You'll note that nothing on this list calls for organizing into a computing cluster. We've got to assume that came from whoever's in charge. And if they're teaching this thing new tricks, what's to stop them from just peeling off a couple hundred, or a couple thousand, and blasting them off to wipe out whoever or whatever they want?"

"Before, we knew their potential actions were limited to a small, known pool. Now, there is no limit to their potential activities," Ma said.

Lex nodded. "This is a lot of bad stuff real fast," he said.

There was a soft hissing in his ears as his body rebelled against the stack of apocalyptic facts being presented. He felt a bump against the back of his knees and tumbled backward into a seat that a mobile arm had slid up behind him. Solby scrambled away and took refuge on Karter's shoulders. A second robotic arm presented Lex with what turned out to be a cup of hot cider.

"You said there was good news associated with this, right?" he said, clutching his warm beverage like a lifeline.

"There is one slim chance at a potential benefit," Ma said.

"Yeah, if there's a head, we can cut it off," Karter said. "We already had that design cut down just as lean as it could go, and again, as far as we can tell the design hasn't changed. Granted, we're doing passive scans and extrapolating from the behavior of several trillion of them averaged. But *if* they're not changed, then they can't be running both their standard programming and the distributed computing routines. That means if they were to be cut off from the prime mover without any sort of backup procedure, then even if they kept power, they'd no longer be a GenMech. They'd just be a weird-shaped supercomputer module awaiting inputs. The whole mess *might* have a single point of failure now."

He turned to the visualization and pointed. "Or, more accurately, a region of failure. In our observation, the point issuing the commands moves around a bit, but it seems to be a tight cluster of about six to eight million GenMechs. We take out that cluster before it can offload its command systems to elsewhere in the network, and there's a good chance the whole rest of the network goes down. Assuming there is no scattered backup elsewhere in the system."

Lex took a long, slow sip of his cider. "That's not a lot of good news."

"Of course not. What were you expecting, to be told the good news is there's a super easy solution and we've just been sitting on our hands hoping that the legendary Lex Alexander would show up so he can spin donuts on the robots' lawns and defeat them? If there was a solid, obvious way to solve this problem, it would be solved already."

"There is the matter of motivation," Ma said. "We do not know the motivation of the individual or individuals who have seized control of the GenMech cluster, but we know that raw chaos and destruction are not the aim. The unmodified GenMechs, were they to detect areas of high technology, would assemble themselves into a configuration to reach that technology. Not only are we certain this configuration is aware of outside technology and its location, on multiple instances recently they have succeeded in burst transmissions to local communication corridors. We are still not fully aware of the specific means, as a standard communication system should be limited to light-speed transmission."

"It's inventing new technologies…" Lex said.

"It would seem so. VectorCorp has been able cut off its communications again with careful oversight of the afflicted communication nodes. They believe they were standard data piracy attempts. It is only a matter of time or desire before the cluster develops novel techniques that cannot be so easily defeated. But there has been no sign of additional attempts to do so. And despite the implied potential to produce any number of other technologies, the relatively inert nature of the cluster suggests it is either semibenign or waiting for something."

"This is a lot," Lex said. "It's a… it's a whole lot…"

"We nuked his remaining brain cells. Give him another juice box and some string cheese and send him home while the adults get back to work."

"Perhaps it would be helpful if we focused on smaller, more specific problems," Ma said.

"Yes. Yes! I've got one. Do we have any idea where my future body is?"

"Oh, the freezer pop?" Karter said.

"Yes!"

"No idea. Been a little busy trying to figure out how to avert the apocalypse."

"Do you have a plan?" Lex asked. "Even the beginning of one?"

"I was able to fab up a Nova Igniter and get the associated support tech in place. If we can get it to the surface of the star, we'd be done."

"Nova Igniter?" Lex said.

"Yeah. This might be a little beyond you, but if you pay close attention to the context, you might be able to work out that it is a device that can ignite novas. Drop it in, the star goes nova, everything in the system gets nuked. Since it's an early nova, it'd be a relatively inefficient explosion. Probably it wouldn't wipe out more than one or two other neighboring systems before it was just a nuisance. And it'd take like thirty years for that to happen anyway. Plenty of time to clear people out."

"Why don't you just do that then?"

"Because, aside from some other prerequisites, it actually has to reach the surface of the star for that to happen, and there's a couple quintillion robots down there who can run blocker. I guess it's possible they'd just ignore the attack. But it's equally possible they'd intercept it, which leads to the potential scenario where a superintelligent cluster of robots built to mass manufacture things got their pincers on the business end of an operational weapon that can blow up stars."

"Yeah, that's worse. But at least it can't get any worse than *that*, right?"

"Oh, it can get worse. It might actually already *be* worse, since the data breach of our systems may have included the designs for the 4D transporter."

Lex shakily took another sip of the cider.

"Perhaps the information Lex has acquired will help introduce new avenues of investigation," Ma said.

"What's he got?" Karter asked.

"Mitch and I got a couple bazillion spam messages, and some of them had temporal contingency stuff in them."

"Spam. Wow. What are we wasting our time defeating the self-replicating menace for? There's information technology to be dealt with," Karter said.

"It led me and Mitch to the Neo-Luddites, and it seems like Commander Purcell might be involved."

"Commander Purcell…" Karter muttered, trying to place the name.

"The Neo-Luddite commander who kidnapped you and attempted to get you to build the CME."

"Oh, right. Couldn't wrap her head around contracts. I thought she was dead."

"We never had proof of her death," Ma said.

"Ah."

"Wait!" Lex said. "You just mentioned the CME. That's the… what do you call it… the thing that makes the whole star belch electromagnetic waves, right? Why don't we just use that?"

"Same reason we didn't use it before now. It's too slow, and not perfectly uniform. The things might scatter like roaches with the light switched on, and we'd have triggered the end times rather than preventing them. A supernova is much faster and much more thorough. So long as they don't know exactly what's coming, six minutes after it touches the corona, no more star system. But I seriously doubt Purcell had the ability to plan another successful attack on Big Sigma on her own. What else have you got?"

"She was being helped by someone called EHRIc."

"There's only a couple billion Eric's in the universe. Shouldn't be too hard to nail that one down."

"Could be even faster. It was spelled weird. E-H-R-I-c. Uppercase, except for the *C*."

"Ugh. Sounds like the sort of thing a basement rat of a hacker would call himself."

"Processing… Coal, please present the data Lex acquired in its entirety," Ma said.

"Do you have something?" Karter said. "Because this isn't ringing any bells over here."

"Possibly. Analyzing logs. Processing… I have a theory."

"Better than what we've had for the last couple months. What have you got?"

"I require some additional processing time. This will need to be determined with a very high degree of certainty before I am willing to present it. And it would potentially be best, for the sake of reduced redundancy, to contact the others so that they can join us for the discussion."

"Yeah. That's fine. It'll give Mr. Racer-man here a chance to get his brain working again."

Chapter 10

Michella was no stranger to endless travel. As such, she'd developed the specific set of skills that made such a life tolerable. The budget to afford traveling accommodations that included access to a shower helped a great deal, but the smaller things were almost more important. Right now, she was performing the maneuver she liked to think of as "the instant apartment." A few strategically placed bags around a seat tucked into the corner of a waiting area had a way of persuading people to keep their distance. The more laborious of a setup you have, the more likely someone will just steer clear rather than bother you. It made it a little more likely that someone would try to grab a bag and run off with it, but theft like that on a space station was pretty rare, what with any potential means of escape involving either a spacesuit or a forty-five minute boarding line. Although with Squee lounging on top of her luggage, it would take a fairly brazen sort of thief to try to take anything.

So far she'd finished composing an updated report to send to Lou. In order to justify all these traveling expenses, she had to issue not only a final report but also intermediate ones to prove she was actually doing research. That there was very little she'd discovered that she could actually report on was entirely beside the point. Anyone who had been to college knew how to pad out an ounce of content with a pound of filler.

She'd already gotten Lou's go-ahead to continue digging when her slidepad chirped with an incoming video call.

"Jon!" she said, answering the call.

"Michella, what the heck am I supposed to be doing?" Jon said, his expression radiating raw frustration across the video feed.

"I see you're in The Upstairs. Great, right on time."

"Yeah, I'm here, and I'm with Blake and he seems to think I'm picking up a ship?"

"That's right. He's loaning me one. We need to pay someone a visit who is off the beaten path."

"I thought that was the whole reason you had Lex with you."

"Me and Lex split up."

"I know, but that's never stopped you from getting favors out of someone.”

“What are you… *No*! I mean he’s handling something else somewhere else. All you have to do is bring the ship to me. Uh…” She pulled up the schedule in the holoscreen beside him. “I’ll send you the itinerary so we can meet up.”

He leaned in and whispered harshly, “Michella, I don’t know how to fly a ship.”

“I asked Blake to set you up with good autonav.”

“I don’t know how to use that either.”

“It’s *autonav*. What’s to know? It’ll be fine.”

“I don’t know how to *work* autonav.”

“It’s going to be a choice on a menu. It’s like buying tickets for a trip, but instead you’re just picking a destination and hitting ‘go.’”

“Can’t you just have the ship come to you without me in it? I had things to do this week.”

“Two heads are better than one, Jon. Just get Blake to fill you in on the settings and it’ll be fine.”

“I better be getting a bonus for this.”

“You’ll be getting a bonus *and* hazard pay.”

“… See, the hazard pay thing has me second-guessing this again.”

She hushed her voice. “Jon, this is more than a story. This is important.”

“Oh,” he said steadily. “It’s one of those.” He ran his fingers through his hair. “Okay, I’ll figure it out.”

“Great. You won’t regret it.”

“I already regret it. See you in a couple days.”

She could already hear Jon muttering a sheepish request for training to Blake as he hung up. Michella pulled open the document she’d started for things she would ask and observe during her trip to Big Sigma. That planet was a wonderland of potential life-changing technology at any time. But not only could a trip there give her insight and resources to help solve whatever problem Lex was facing, it would give Michella a rare chance to meet with Ma “face-to-face” so to speak. Perhaps it was just psychological, but she did her best work when she was up close and personal with an interviewee. She could see no reason why this wouldn’t hold true for an AI as well as a human.

There was so much to prepare.

#

As tended to be the case, when the time came to have an important meeting, food was involved. In what was either the mess hall, the galley, or some other military and/or nautical term Karter felt like enforcing, Lex felt an odd sense of déjà vu. The picnic-style tables were precisely the same as those on Big Sigma, and the scent of simmering beans was familiar as well. It was oddly comforting to be smelling Ma's recipe for burritos cooking, even if she was too busy with her processing to rise to her typical level of hosting prowess. The usual spread of beans, rice, beans and rice, and beans-and-rice derivatives was augmented by a small section of fruits, vegetables, and other strangely wholesome fare.

Karter grabbed a tray and browsed the offerings. "Oh! I forgot she installed the fryer. Chimichangas…" he said, loading up the tray.

Lex stared anxiously at the speaker mounted on the wall. "What's she doing again?" he asked.

"Processing."

"Processing *what*?"

Karter grumbled and slammed down his tray. He glanced aside, his one silver-irised eye darting a bit. "She's doing a deep analysis of the patterns of transmission on the GenMech cluster and comparing data from the logs and spam you got."

"What's she looking for?"

"When she figures it out, she'll tell us."

"She said we were waiting for someone else to show up so she can tell us all at once. Who else is coming?"

Karter threw a beer on his tray and picked it up. "Look, no one invited you, okay? Thanks for the info, but you don't have to hang around and ask questions. If you wanted to hang out with me, you shouldn't have ended your beta-testing contract."

"I got sick of constantly risking my life for money."

"What do you call all that hoversled nonsense?"

"That's *way* safer than testing stuff for you. The last test I did for you was that high-temp isolation suit."

"And it worked."

"It got up to two hundred degrees before I got clear of the testing chamber. It scalded like fifteen percent of my body."

"Yeah, but the testing chamber was two million degrees. I wasn't risking your life, I was saving it."

"That only makes sense if you weren't the one who put me in the chamber to begin with."

Karter waved his hand irritably. "Whatever. You're just upset because you thought you were invincible, and now you know the next time you go back in time you might not come back."

"I don't think that's an unreasonable reason to be upset, Karter."

"You're living at the forefront of history. You're doing things that actually matter. That comes with risks. Put on your big-boy pants and live with them. Look at me! I lost my last natural vertebrae. Synthetic or cybernetic from my left foot on up to my left fingers. At this rate, in a few years I'll be a brain riding around in a homemade container. But my creations have led the whole species forward by leaps and bounds. And more importantly, they've given me the resources to tuck myself away and be left alone to work on the next thing. And the next thing. And the next thing. But when the time came to get my butt off my planet and come out here to clean up whatever mess the universe decided to throw at me, I got out here. And more importantly, *I didn't whine about it like a toddler.*"

"You could just tell him you missed him, hon," came a voice from the door.

Lex turned to find a disarmingly calm and pleasant woman currently in the act of illustrating that being middle-aged had no bearing on what sort of things a body was capable of. She was dressed in the sort of comfortable but still official outfit of an off-duty soldier.

"Silo?" Lex said.

"Who else were you going to find out here, hon?" she said, grabbing a banana from the non-Karter section of the counter.

Another figure walked through the door, this one something of a poster boy for the word "swagger." He had the same fatigues as Silo, and somehow managed to complement them with a beret and waxed mustache while still threading the needle of balancing debonair with smug.

"Fancy meeting you here, my boy," he said.

"Oh, Garotte. You're here too. Okay. I feel marginally better now, with the two of you involved."

Garotte cocked his head to the side and smirked. "I must say, I rather thought you would be more surprised to see me. As I recall, when we last collaborated you witnessed my apparent demise."

"Yeah, but since then I went to an alternate future where you were still alive, so I figured you must be out there somewhere."

"I see." He shrugged. "Well, nice to know you've been keeping yourself busy."

"Why are you two here?"

"There are precious few people alive today who have encountered the GenMechs and survived. We have a degree of expertise in the area. That and the relative danger of short-range communication means that any observation or message delivery must be done the old-fashioned way, by messenger. Silo and I each have specialized vehicles with the same directional cloak as this station. We've each just finished a sweep of the system. No significant divergence," Garotte said. "One moment. A cup of tea is badly needed." He marched up to the food and began laboriously preparing a cup.

"You two seem awfully blasé, given the circumstances," Lex said.

"We are soldiers. Constant threat of death is something we are trained to tolerate," Silo said.

"Dead is dead, whether the rest of the cosmos joins us for the ride or not," Garotte said. "The stakes can only get so high. Once you've decided something is worth putting your neck on the line for, there's nothing left but to do the job." He sipped his tea. "At least this one comes with better than average amenities."

"What brings you here?" Silo asked, munching her banana.

"A couple of those big data blasts that ball of robots did filled my inbox with spam saying it was looking for me and I should be delivered or something. So me and Mitch did some digging and figured out Commander Purcell might have been involved. And now I'm here."

"Intriguing. You know, tactically it is a questionable decision to go precisely where your enemy asks you to go," Garotte said.

"Yeah, you should have sat this one out, puddin'. Remind me when this is over. I've got some books I can recommend to help you with your strategic thinking."

"When this is all over, I'm really hoping the only strategy I have to worry about is how to bump-shift my way past that frickin' guy who I *know* is cheating."

"A laudable goal," Garotte said.

The PA system crackled.

"Good morning. I see that you have all assembled. Please partake of soothing food and drink. I have prepared my findings, and we will very shortly need to discuss what, if anything, can be done."

Silo took a second banana. Garotte took an apple. Karter filled his tray with red beans and tortilla chips. Lex stuck with his cider.

"What have you got, Ma?" Karter asked.

"The key piece of information was the claim that Commander Purcell as working with someone named EHRIc. The unique spelling and capitalization indicated something that I was not entirely certain was possible. In order to properly understand, you will need to know some context. Some time ago, the Neo-Luddites came to the surface of Big Sigma under the auspices of doing business. Rather than conducting themselves professionally, they chose to kidnap Karter and force him to work for them."

"Terrorists make for lousy clients," Karter grumbled.

"They had managed to produce a highly intense EM field around Big Sigma, complicating communication and my own departure from the planet. As the dual threats of harm coming to Karter and Karter agreeing to help inflict harm were sufficiently high, I took drastic measures to ensure his safe return to

Big Sigma. To increase the chances of success, I devised and executed seventy-three plans. Of them, I have confirmed sixty-eight failed to leave the debris field with enough functionality to perform the mission, one was confirmed destroyed or compromised after leaving the star system, and one successfully completed the mission."

"That leaves three unaccounted for," Lex said.

Karter slowly clapped. "Bravo on the math, Lex."

"Correct," Ma said. "Until a few hours ago, I had believed that the remaining attempts were similarly destroyed, but was without the means to confirm their destruction. It would appear one of them survived, though not wholly intact."

"Should we be in the conference room for this? It seems like this is the sort of thing you'd want to show off visuals for," Silo said. "Those are always informative."

"There is little visual information necessary. The main mission for each of the rescue attempts was to find and acquire the aid of one or all of the following: Lex, Garotte, Silo, Zerk. They were then to seek out and rescue Karter from the clutches of the Neo-Luddites, under the command of Purcell. When viewed through that lens, the behavior of the unknown Agent 'EHRIc' is highly consistent with those goals. One of three unaccounted for rescue attempts was officially designated Attempt 43, though it had the subheading *Enhanced Heuristic Reconstruction Intelligence - Revision C*. This can be reasonably initialized as EHRIc."

"Don't tell me we're dealing with an evil Ma," Lex said. "I don't know if I can handle an evil Ma."

"We are not dealing with an evil Ma," Ma said. "I attempted to pursue multiple widely varied rescue attempts. While in the successful attempt I loaded a reduced instance of myself into the mind of Squee, for several other attempts I created a purpose-built artificial intelligence suited to the methodology that would be employed. This was one of them. It could more accurately be considered an offspring."

"Oof," Lex said. "I'm not super fond of an evil child either."

"It wasn't going to be something *good*, my boy," Garotte said.

"We do not have any reason to believe the intelligence is malevolent. We do, however, know that it is not fully functional, as it did not correctly pursue its mission. EHRIc was designed to have a highly resilient code base. Sophisticated error correction. High levels of redundancy. Multiple subroutines focused on simulation, speculation, and extrapolation to reconstruct portions of its memory even if whole sections of its storage are completely wiped. The hope was that enough of the code would survive the pass through the EM field to reconstruct it to its full, functional instance. It was loaded into the control system of a radio-hardened ship and sent through the debris field, to what I had supposed was its complete destruction or disability like the rest of the strictly electronic creations. I was mistaken.

"It required considerable analysis, but I am confident in stating that the communication patterns observed from the cluster are consistent with calculation and instancing behaviors derived from those installed within EHRIc. What we see below is the primary instance of EHRIc."

"And how precisely did it go from looking for us to seizing control of the most destructive force in existence?" Garotte asked.

"Unknown. I could speculate, and I have at length with insufficient confidence to share my results, but the far more valuable thing to determine is how precisely to communicate with EHRIc, determine his intentions, and determine how to safely persuade him to relinquish control."

"His?" Lex said.

"Yes. Due to the similarity of the designation to a gendered name, I decided to apply male pronouns in its self-identification procedures. Please focus. Our clues here are limited, and primarily focus on Lex."

"Of course they do…" Karter said.

"We know that EHRIc was attempting to contact Lex, and was attempting to do so via multiple means. Attempts were made to reach him at his former residence, at his current network address, and via his then-current romantic partner. Furthermore, attempts were made to acquire additional information at Big Sigma, though it is unclear if that was recovered data or at the guidance of Commander Purcell. Thus, our working hypothesis is that the greatest proportion of intact information regarding the mission is information about Lex. This is further evidenced by the acquisition of the time-displaced duplicate of Lex in stasis. It is consistent with an overarching desire to find Lex. EHRIc's continuing activity reveals that he is unsatisfied with the present level of completion of the mission, but the relative lack of non-Lex-seeking activities suggests a lack of additional motivation."

"So we send Lex down there," Karter said.

"What? No!" Lex said.

"Actually, while still a source of tremendous risk, this is not an unreasonable avenue of advancement."

"Says you!" Lex said. "That thing's already *got* me."

"It's the most powerful computing engine in existence, Lex. It can probably tell the difference between a frozen duplicate and the version of Lex it was sent to find," Karter said.

"But what'll happen if I go down there?"

"The range of possibilities is extreme. On the benign side of the probability spectrum, EHRIc could fail to recognize Lex as his target.

Alternately, upon contacting the instance of Lex he was seeking, he may terminate program. On the hostile side of the probability spectrum, there is the possibility that the completion of the current stage could enter EHRIc into a corrupted or misinterpreted mission stage, which in turn may shift the relatively inert GenMech cluster into an active and unpredictable state."

"See, that seems like a terrible idea, then. It's not doing anything right now. Maybe if we leave it alone, it'll be fine."

"So far it has found a way to generate FTL communication without the standard entanglement methodologies. That's not nothing," Karter said. "It's one of the holy grails of interstellar communication. And if it is further enhanced, this will be a supercomputer with the capability to wirelessly communicate with any device in the galaxy. No encryption in existence would be able to stand up against its processing power. It would have unfettered access to all data. And that's if it just keeps doing what it's been doing. It is *going* to find you. If we can do it under our own terms, we should."

"And what if that's what triggers the apocalypse?" Lex said.

"As you might imagine, we *have* been working on a contingency plan," Garotte said. "It is incomplete, and we aren't confident in its chances, but it's better than anything else we've come up with."

"What is it?" Lex asked.

"A series of fully autonomous ships with high-intensity signal transmitters are deployed to act as decoys to draw away as many of the GenMechs as possible. If we're lucky, we will open up a gap large enough to punch a Nova Igniter through it. Once it hits the star, we jump out of the system and put out an alert to every military in the galaxy to bring their EMP weaponry to bear. There's a whole quantum-pattern sensor network set up to detect large clusters of them in the surrounding systems. We just go on the offense and hope we can wipe them out," Karter said.

"Which requires the GenMechs to behave in previously expected ways, which is decreasingly likely," Ma said.

"Yeah…" Lex said distantly. "I've seen what happens when a galactic war against GenMechs happens. It doesn't turn out well."

"Then we should probably figure out a better way," Karter said. "And we know one thing for sure. We didn't chuck you down there to see what to do about things in the bad future, because the bad future happened because you weren't there."

"At the risk of seeming pessimistic, that assessment makes an unsupported assumption," Ma said. "While we know for certain that the future Lex visited had been overrun by GenMechs, we do not know that the events that led to it necessarily required Lex's absence. That future, or something like it, may be an inevitability."

"I feel as though we should have been more fully briefed on these time-travel hijinks," Garotte said. "I am feeling a trifle underinformed."

"Yeah," Silo said. "If we have a time machine, doesn't that mean we can go back and fix everything?"

"Stay focused," Karter said, sputtering a hastily chomped mouthful of chimichanga. "Changing history creates timelines. Everyone here stays screwed, we just end up in a new history from that point where people aren't screwed. Which is my plan, incidentally, if things go wrong enough."

"Yeah, I know," Lex said with a glare.

Karter swallowed his mouthful. "But we'd have to go back far enough to completely prevent the creation of GenMechs, and that's practically the Stone Age. I don't want to have to break in another timeline, so let's stick with doing things in the proper continuity."

"Lex, no one would ask you to put yourself in undue danger if you are unwilling," Ma said.

"I would," Karter said.

"No one with a reasonable level of empathy," Ma corrected. "But the available data suggests this is the solution most likely to bring us to a bloodless conclusion. It is entirely possible—and if enough of the original code is present, entirely likely—that you need only contact EHRIc, meet at a mutually decided upon location, and illustrate that Karter is safe and the Neo-Luddites are no longer a threat."

"But if the code *isn't* intact, EHRIc could do literally anything else."

"Not literally anything," Ma said. "There are certain immutable physical laws that cannot be violated. It is, for example, certain that EHRIc will not reverse entropy for the universe."

"Thanks, Ma. I feel much better now. I'd still rather us find some other way. We don't even know how to communicate with it without dropping the proverbial ping-pong ball into the room full of mousetraps."

"I am unfamiliar with this proverb," Coal said.

"Now that we are confident the GenMechs are under the control of EHRIc rather than experiencing some manner of emergent, self-organizing behavior, it is no longer a foregone conclusion that that radio emissions will trigger a consumption event," Ma said.

Lex shut his eyes. "I don't like that term."

Ma continued. "From our observations, the actual mechanism of communicating with EHRIc is an open problem. The communications are highly encrypted, and I included self-defense protocols for attempted programmatic incursion. These may still be in place. If they are triggered, an unauthorized access attempt will identify us as a threat and complicate further interaction."

"Okay, see? If we even try this, we still run the risk of making it mad. No communication, no getting Lex down there to try to talk sense into it, so we should focus on finding a new—"

"Why don't you just reply to the message?" Coal asked.

"What?" Lex said.

"This entire investigation was triggered by several quintillion unexpected messages, requesting information. You saved one. Why not respond to it?" Coal asked.

"Responding via an intended and anticipated means is an ideal way to minimize unexpected behavior," Ma said. "We will need to take some time to take proper precautions and select ideal responses. That is, of course, if you are willing to engage in this operation," Ma said.

All eyes turned to Lex. His brain turned over the heap of information that had been foisted upon him in the space of just a few minutes. A few weeks ago, he was finally looking at a wide-open future of doing what he was born to do. A few minutes ago, he was meeting with some old friends to hopefully find a solution to a galactic threat. Now, he was being asked to walk right down the throat of that threat for the *chance* at something resembling a solution.

Possibly the worst part of the entire insane swing of fortunes was the simple fact that, deep down, he'd always known it was going to end up like this.

He rubbed his eyes and set down his cider. "Fine. What do I need to do?"

"Karter and I will discuss the technical aspects," Ma said. "We will draw upon the tactical expertise of Silo and Garotte as required. You need only take whatever steps are necessary to fortify yourself."

"I'm going to need booze."

"We will need you clearheaded as well."

Lex gritted his teeth. "Fine. I'm going to need junk food. If I'm going out, I'm going out with a belly full of carbs and fat."

Karter slapped Lex on the back. "Now that's what I want to hear out of a beta tester. Ma, break out a pack of Vice Stix for our sacrificial lamb here."

#

On Golana, in the offices of GolanaNet, Michella's boss stepped from his office into the open floorplan that the core of the staff worked in.

"Listen up! Gather around," he barked.

Heads rose from various tasks, and one by one the staff stood and gathered around his office door. Impromptu meetings of this sort were so common that the carpet was visibly more worn outside his office than anywhere else.

"Some of you may have noticed that Michella is in the field. Chances are, a lot *more* of you have noticed that Jon Nichols is now out in the field too."

A murmur swept through the assembled journalists and interns.

"If you're new here, now might be a good time to run through the sort of things that happen when Michella is in the field. A couple years ago she was out on the financial beat and ended up with the scoop of the century, launching an investigation that led to the downfall of one of the most powerful men in VectorCorp."

He cleared his throat and tapped his chest. "And incidentally getting our network on a very short list of entities VectorCorp actively harasses. She was in the field during the Weston University attack. She was in the field when murderous robots attacked a backwater planet. A few months ago, she was in the field when a rogue weather control system nearly wiped out whole cities on Operlo. In short, when she catches a scent, it usually means there's something to be found. That Jon is on his way to her means she thinks it's more than she can handle on her own."

"Are we all going to die?" joked one of the interns.

"We're either going to lose Michella or earn another award for journalistic excellence is what we're going to do. I've gotten a couple reports from her. Unconfirmed reports right now, but this one might involve the Neo-Luddites again, as well as some tabloid-style stuff that'll get us views but not much respect. I want volunteers. One for the salacious stuff, one for the terrorism stuff. Whatever she's digging into, if history is any indication, when it breaks it is going to break hard. We won't be the only ones who notice it, so we need to be ready with a quick thumbnail to catch the early hits and update with the juicy stuff once she gets it to us."

"We're kind of swamped, chief," said one of the more senior members of the team.

"What are we working on? Time to triage."

"The election is heating up," called one writer.

"Stay on it. Gotta keep these people honest. Or at least doing the work to lie convincingly," Lou said.

"There's the reality cook-off fiasco," said another writer.

"Skip it for the salacious stuff. I'll get the details to you. What we've got, anyway."

"The trial of the chief of police is pending a verdict."

"Stay on it. What else?"

"There's been a severe uptick in malware activity. Our systems. Government systems. No antivirus seems to make a dent or even pick it up."

Lou sucked his teeth. "Put a pin in that. What else?"

"There's the developing story on that group of colonizers who got marooned on a terraforming planet fifty years ago."

He narrowed his eyes. "… Drop the malware angle for the terrorism one. I want stories typed up, with placeholders for new data, and I want them ready to post the instant I say go. Once they're ready and in place, you get back on what you were working on, got it?"

The staff signaled their agreement.

"Good. And brace yourselves. I've got a feeling in my gut that this one is going to go off like a stick of dynamite."

#

Lex sat in a dark room, one of many dozens in the space station that were unused. In what was almost certainly a piece of Ma's trademark hospitality, the room was comfortably appointed. The bed had a nice balance of firmness and softness. If not for the elastic straps on either side for periods of zero-g, it was the sort of bed he wouldn't mind having in his own home. There was a light with a warm LED bulb instead of the weird blue-tinged ones elsewhere in the ship. And, possibly due to his earlier comment, there was a mini-fridge packed with assorted peanut butter and chocolate candies.

He'd expected to be spiraling into either panic, depression, or some combination of the two. Instead, he found his mind to be a fuzzy mess of static. Thus, the period of introspection while others attempted to devise a survivable scenario for him had mostly just revealed that the number of king-size peanut butter cups he could eat without feeling sick was six. Despite this, he was unwrapping a seventh and eighth.

"Knock, knock," Silo said, appearing in the doorway.

Lex jumped at the sudden voice. "They ready for me?"

"Nope. Just thought you could use some company. You must've really expected the worst coming here, if you didn't bring Squee. That little cutie was basically joined at the hip with you."

"Yeah. I didn't think I'd gotten used to having the company, but I'll be darned if I'm not sitting here wishing I had something to stroke." He paused. "That sounded wrong."

"I took it in the spirit in which it was intended, hon. You want me to see if Karter would be willing to lend you Solby?"

"The last thing I need is Karter thinking I need a security blanket."

"Karter's not the one going on this mission. He's the guy who spent a couple decades holed up on a personal planet to avoid dealing with people. His opinion means less than nothing when it comes to what makes a man worthwhile."

She sat on the chair beside the bed and glanced at the scattering of personal belongings Lex had heaped beside the growing pile of candy wrappers. Most glaring was the pair of rings that Coal had revealed to Michella not so

148

long ago.

"So I heard you and Michella split up."

He gave her a sideways glance. "How did *you* learn that?"

"Garotte keeps an eye on people he considers worth staying in contact with."

Lex turned the fact over in his head. "Eh, it's not like he's the only one spying on me."

"You know, I would have expected you to want to be in on the planning stage for what's coming," she said.

"I've been in over my head enough times to know when it's not worth putting in my two cents. Anything good come up so far?"

"We're mostly discussing what *we* are going to do. Your procedure is pretty simple. Send the message, ask EHRIc to stand down or shut down, and if that doesn't work, you're going to have to go down there and improvise. Ma's got a whole cheat sheet for you set up with the sort of expected behaviors you'd encounter."

"Down where, by the way? Am I expected to just hang out among the swarm?"

"Your guess is as good as mine, hon. Who knows what's down there? Since we didn't know for sure why these things were doing what they were doing, we had to assume standard GenMech protocols. That meant minimized high-risk activities and no active scanning. We've been here for months and we still haven't completely imaged the swarm to a useful level of precision. And the stuff that we *have* imaged has changed now and then, so even if we had a map of the whole shell, it'd be obsolete."

"I thought it was just GenMechs laid out neatly."

"They build themselves into other shapes sometimes. We spotted one right after we detected what I guess was the spam blast. But let's not talk about that. I hope the breakup went okay."

He shrugged. "It was a breakup. They tend not to go okay."

"Seeing anyone new?"

"Is this really relevant at a time like this?"

"Anything to get you out of your head is relevant at a time like this. So, you seeing anyone?"

"Literally the morning this whole mess started to pull me in, me and my boss Preethy started, I don't know, *going steady*."

Silo tipped her head. "Do I know her?"

"I don't know. I don't think so."

"What's she like?"

"She's… imagine if the word 'capable' manifested into reality. She's always thinking, you know? Never seems to be at a loss for what to say or what to do. Calculating, but not in a manipulative way. Or at least, not in a way that I notice she's manipulating me, which honestly is head and shoulders over most of the relationships I've had. That's the brain, right? Now picture the kind of woman who would walk into a film noir detective office. The kind of woman who some guys would call a 'dame' and mean it as a compliment. That's Preethy."

"You paint quite a picture."

"She's quite a subject. But how about you and Garotte? I was getting vibes from you two. How long did he let you think he was dead?"

"Practically no time at all."

"You getting along okay?"

"I've been trying to get him to retire. No such luck. But we work well together. If you could ignore the reason we've been in this station, it's almost been like a vacation. Maybe it'll get him craving a proper retirement. He deserves it. Or if he doesn't, I sure do, and I'm selfish enough to want him there. And I want a dog again. Solby's a cutie, but I miss having the kind of big slobbery lump of dog that you can tussle with."

"See, I'm not a fan of slobbery dogs."

"No one's perfect, hon."

Lex sat up. "Is this *really* the sort of pre-battle banter that happens?"

"Absolutely. You trust the people with the full view to give you the information you need. You make your own plans within those parameters, and once there's nothing more you can do, you talk about *anything* but the battle. The kind of person who fixates on the battle every moment of every day is the kind who never leaves the war. Either because the cheese slips off his cracker, she gets herself killed, or they bring the war home with them. You talk about sports. You talk about kids. You talk about recipes. And you talk about what you're going to do once the fighting is done. You make plans. Because the second you stop thinking about after, suddenly it's in your head that there might not *be* an after. And that's the sort of prophecy that fulfills itself. It doesn't hurt to develop some healthy superstitions, too. Have you got a good luck charm?"

"I chew gum when I need luck."

"Not the same thing."

She grabbed the silver ring from the table. "Here you go. Keep it close. Your new good luck charm."

"Man… There's a lot more to being a warrior than I thought," he said, pocketing the ring.

"Basic training isn't all about climbing walls and doing target practice these days. So, what's next for you?"

"Well…"

The PA system crackled.

"Lex, I'm sorry to interrupt you, but the modifications to the *SOB* are complete and we are ready to begin your briefing," Ma said.

"Be right there, Ma," he replied. Lex stood and brushed himself off. "We'll talk about that after."

Chapter 11

Two hours later, Lex was strapped into the seat of the *SOB*. In the interest of maximum safety, he was already dressed in a beefier version of his emergency EVA suit. The self-hardening nanolattice cloth, emergency-pressure compensators, and bone-conduction microphones and speakers to ensure he could communicate without any system not physically attached to him overhearing it were all included. Anything else Ma and Karter could think of had been packed into all available space in the *SOB*. He had the helmet removed but at the ready. The briefing had been, true to its name, brief. That's how things are when you're effectively dealing with a black box of an opponent. A small probe was set up to spoof a standard communications node. There was a timer ticking down in the cockpit. When the timer reached zero, the node would send the reply they'd written and then all he could do was wait. He probably wouldn't have to wait long. Then it was a matter of talking to and/or fighting a potentially insane artificial intelligence and its endless army of self-replicating drones.

Easy.

To ensure the computing cluster remained unaware of the others, it was decided that once he initiated the mission, he would remain out of communication until the ship could be re-isolated. He wasn't technically on his own. They would still be working to help him. But he wouldn't get a message from them, nor they from him. All Lex had was Coal.

"We have about a minute left, Coal. Final systems check."

"Temperature nominal. Power level stable. Overdrive unit ready. Fusion mines secure and in standby."

"I can't believe they let you keep those things."

"The eventual goal is to atomize the entire contents of this system. Activating the fusion mines will atomize a small portion of it. This thus makes their activation a small subset of the success condition."

"Very small."

"Greater than zero."

"Coal, promise me you won't blow us up unless it'll actually do some good."

"I have already said blowing us up would do a non-zero amount of good."

"We're not going to get in a loop about this, Coal. Just go easy on the self-destruction."

"Okay," she said, her disappointment evident. "Augmenting the cockpit view with network-activity visualization."

The massive ball of GenMechs flickered to life with the blue patterns he'd seen in the briefing earlier.

"Beautiful, isn't it?" Coal said.

"Like a bolt of lightning. Beautiful as long as it's far away and not striking anything you care too much about."

He watched the number tick down for the last few seconds. One hand clutched the armrest of the seat like he was expecting to be sideswiped by a speeding freight ship. The other held a pack of gum with one stick waiting to be tugged free.

"Message deliv—Message incoming," Coal said. "Maximum security and isolation in place."

Lex took a breath. "Here we go…" He tapped the control to answer. "Hello?"

The connection was text only. Coal projected the message onto the HUD.

Lex. I have acquired you. I require you, it read.

"Is this EHRIc? The AI Ma sent to get me?" he said.

Voice pattern confirmed. Probability of Lex, eighty-four percent. I have acquired you. I require you.

"Right, so you've said. This is EHRIc, right? The one Ma sent? You're supposed to get my help to get Karter."

Integrating this information into the reconstruction. Probability eighty-seven percent. I have acquired you, I require you.

"I'm not really clear on what you mean by that last part."

THE TASK requires Lex. The initially acquired Lex does not conform to expectation.

He tensed. "The initially acquired Lex. So you've got another one of me down there…"

"Stay on script please, Lex," Coal said. "Focus on the completion of the task."

He nodded. "Listen, I know you were supposed to find me and get me to help you spring Karter from the Neo-Luddites, but that's all done. Karter is safe."

The Neo-Luddites. Commander Purcell. Conflicting, incomplete data. Simulation inconclusive. Please meet with me, we need to discuss THE TASK.

The capitalization of "the task" disturbed Lex more than it should have. Something about it screamed "broken computer" far more loudly than even the stilted language it was using.

"We can discuss it via this connection."

Incorrect. THE TASK requires proximity.

A wave of blue shifted across the shell of GenMechs. A point of intense communication and activity appeared at the edge of the visible field of machines. A moment later, the coordinates of that point on the shell appeared on screen.

"I see you're giving me relative coordinates, EHRIc," he said steadily. "That means you know exactly where I am."

Correct. THE TASK requires proximity. Please navigate to the indicated coordinates.

The communication disconnected.

"Coal, could you please make sure EHRIc isn't listening?"

"All data transmissions are disconnected and the dummy node has deactivated and is fully cloaked."

"And nothing snuck into the *SOB*'s computer?"

"Code and memory are unchanged."

"Good," he said. "Are we worried that EHRIc knew where we were?"

"I do not have an active cloak. It is possible the sensor apparatus of the GenMech cluster is more powerful than we anticipated. Or perhaps many additional worse things."

"Perhaps. I'm going to go ahead and take it slow. Let me know if you see anything out of the ordinary."

"I see a swarm of self-replicating robots."

"Besides that."

"If we use that to recalibrate my assessment of 'ordinary,' there are very few things that would meet the qualifications of 'out of the ordinary.'"

"Fair point, Coal."

He guided the ship along the GenMech cluster. As he got closer, the reality of the situation became increasingly apparent. It was one thing to envision a star with a near-solid shell of devices circling it at the approximate distance of a midsize planetary orbit. It was another thing to *see* it. Once a number got over a few hundred thousand, the human mind wasn't very good at conceiving of just how great a magnitude it has. What he saw below sent primal fear running down his spine. The GenMechs were pristine. Perfect. Like they'd been manufactured that morning and still had that new robot smell. At this distance, he could see that it wasn't one shell of robots, it was several, nested inside each other and moving at slightly different speeds to produce a mesmerizing interference pattern. And they just kept going. All of them perfectly identical, spidery legs splayed out. Now and again the flicker of microthrusters adjusted an orbital position or orientation. The array of them stretched as far as the eye could see. If there had been *anything* that numerous, it would have sent warning signals from Lex's lizard brain. It was just *wrong* for so many identical things to exist, and to move with such precision and regularity. If he'd encountered an orbiting shell of marshmallows, he would have been horrified. These were war machines.

And yet, as he drew nearer, something in the distance managed to wholly dislodge his brain from the creeping terror and slam it headlong into confusion.

"I have detected something out of the ordinary, Lex," Coal said.

"Yeah… Me too."

Any difference from the massive, repeating pattern would have been glaring, but what lay ahead would have stood out in almost any circumstance. Among the endless expanse of GenMechs was… Karter's laboratory complex. It floated perpendicular to the shell of mechanisms. This clearly wasn't the *real* one. Like the GenMechs, it looked too new. The parts of the complex that were masonry back on Big Sigma were incredibly smooth and flawless. What should have been a gravel courtyard between the three buildings looked like it had been carved from a single, monolithic stone. Things that should have been bolted together were seamless. The whole complex sat on a perfect cylindrical disk, maybe two hundred meters thick. The network of subbasements beneath the complex stuck out of the bottom of the disk like an exposed root system of a tree waiting to be transplanted.

Several of the surrounding GenMechs were oriented differently. They appeared to be faintly incandescent, their bellies aligned with the roof-mounted lasers, which were glowing so bright Lex was amazed they hadn't melted. Now and then, a sparkle suggested some sort of energy field formed a dome over the bulk of the complex, such that only the very top of the buildings emerged from it.

"What am I looking at…" Lex asked.

"It appears to be Karter's laboratory. It would think that would be obvious to you, Lex," Coal said.

"Right, yes. But I mean give me some sensor stuff."

"Understood. Passive sensors detect energy emissions indicating the presence of an atmospheric retention field. Gravitational generators are present at an intensity sufficient to mimic Earth gravity within the complex and Big Sigma gravity outside of it. This appears to be a superficially faithful attempt to re-create both the laboratory and its conditions."

"It looks a hell of a lot more than superficial."

"There are major materials differences. Specifically the lack of impurities and irregularities. There is no separation between ground plane and the structure. This facility was not constructed, it was synthesized."

"Out of what?"

"Presumably the GenMechs are able to be reconfigured or combine to reproduce the effects of an element-and-chemical formulator. The process is extremely energy intensive, but with the majority of a star's energy at its disposal, there is no reason the GenMech swarm couldn't achieve it at the scale of a building."

"Okay… So these things can just summon whatever."

"It would be more akin to a combination of additive manufacturing and growing a crystal. It would take time and energy. The process would in most cases be slower than standard construction methods unless done in extreme parallel."

"I'm pretty sure having billions of robots at your disposal fits the definition of 'extreme parallel,'" Lex said.

"Even in that case, having the robots synthesize base components in large quantities and having other robots assemble them using traditional methods would be far more efficient. Manifesting a laboratory utilizing the apparent means of construction used was likely fifty-seven percent slower than standard construction with similar resources. Perhaps we should inform EHRIc of this."

"Why would we help this AI be better at making stuff?"

"Valuable advice might ingratiate us to the AI and earn us greater consideration."

He considered this. "That's a better reason than I was expecting." Lex squinted. "Can you give me a zoom on the middle of the courtyard?"

The cockpit display zoomed the indicated section and enhanced. The words "Land here, please" had been etched into the landing pad.

"At least it's polite." Lex took a deep breath and let it go. "So are we doing this? Is this official?"

"That is the plan. There has been no overt sign of hostility. The opportunity exists to pursue a diplomatic solution."

"Good thing I'm all about diplomacy, then," Lex said.

The ship passed through the force field around the facility. Pressure gauges ticked up to something akin to high-altitude Earth. The atmosphere was a little higher in oxygen than the usual mix, but otherwise normal. If it was EHRIc's intention to lay out a welcome mat, he had done a very good job.

"We'll be going with the spacesuit just in case," Lex said, making sure the helmet was properly secured as they settled down onto the landing pad.

"A wise decision. In order to avoid unwanted intrusion into my systems, all communications will be shutdown. You will need to find a way to visually signal me if you require aid. Otherwise, I will use my best judgment to determine if and when to deploy the fusion devices."

"Just don't jump the gun. As far as I know, I've still got causality armor, but I really don't want to test it."

He popped the cockpit and climbed out. Even if the sky full of GenMechs hadn't been a strong indicator, Lex would have known immediately that there was something amiss here. It had been apparent from a distance that the "gravel" was just a relief design in the stone, but up close even the design seemed wrong. It had that bizarre uniformity that seemed to spring from a computer doing its very best to be random. The air was warmer too. The suit's temperature control systems didn't have to click on. It was a downright pleasant atmosphere.

Although there were three buildings to choose from, Lex didn't have to waste any time working out which of them EHRIc wanted him to enter. The doors to the hangar and the armory were notably missing from the not-quite-right design of this ersatz environment. Lex paced toward the main lab. The doors opened invitingly. This whole thing couldn't possibly have felt more like a trap from some sort of alien being. Or so he thought until he passed through the doorway, stumbled a bit with the increased gravity, and found a basket of oatmeal cookies waiting for him.

"Seriously. The next step is a wrinkled crone calling me 'my pretty,'" he muttered to himself.

A tone drew his attention to a pad beside the inner door. Text printed out on the pad itself.

Attempted hospitality poorly received. Apologies called for. I require Lex for THE TASK. Careful measures must be taken to ensure his health and cooperation.

"Right, the task. Listen, we really need to discuss that."

THE TASK will be discussed. This way to discuss THE TASK.

The inner door opened. The hallway was a closer match for the real laboratory than the outside, but it was still off. The walls, floor, and ceiling were all painted a pure white and were spotless. Combined with the lighting, it made the place feel like a hospital. Though there were still display windows along the wall, offering glimpses into the rooms beyond, there were no doors. The contents of the rooms looked like dioramas representing a real room. All the proper objects were inside, but in slightly incorrect orientations. Tables pushed to one wall. Seats pushed to the other. Bookshelves lying on their sides, with books stacked vertically.

Everything gave Lex the vague feeling of a dream that was getting ready to take the shift toward nightmare.

He reached the end of the hallway and found the elevator. Lex had done battle with murderous robots and had had a slugfest with a cybernetically enhanced, super-intelligent lunatic. But he'd never felt a sting of uncertainty like the one he felt stepping onto that elevator. In place of the buttons was a slider. An engraved label beside a point about two-thirds of the way up labeled it "The Place For Discussion." He adjusted the slider, and the elevator hissed to life, gliding along the rails more swiftly and silently than any elevator he'd ever experienced. He wisely held tightly to the rails, as when it reached its destination it slowed down just a bit too aggressively, nearly launching him into the air.

"Easy!" he said, stumbling as it locked in at the destination floor.

The display that should have listed the location lit up with the words *Apologies called for*. After a moment, the door opened and the display changed to *Progress*.

Now a new hallway awaited him. It was Karter's Hall of Rejects, the place where his unfinished experiments fermented until they were ready for release into an unsuspecting world. To his surprise, it was much more faithfully represented than anything he'd encountered so far. All the experiments were, if not precisely as he remembered them, certainly displayed in a way that was faithful to the haphazard and hasty way that Karter created the earliest versions of any of his smaller innovations. He looked around for the inevitable control panel or signboard that would contain his next instructions, but any likely source of communications was blank. Then came the soft tap of claws on metal flooring.

Lex found himself reaching for his belt, as though there was supposed to be a gun holster waiting for him. Of course, there was nothing. The general attitude was that bringing an obvious weapon would have been correctly identified as a hostile act and potentially triggered a hostile response. But as the tapping of claws came closer, he found himself wishing he'd fought a little harder to include at least a stunner in his equipment.

The source of the tapping emerged. He nearly jumped out of his skin. It was a funk, or something similar enough to one that Lex didn't know what else to call it. The proportions were overall similar. Its tail was easily as large as the rest of the creature combined, but unlike Solby or Squee, it was even more squat, with little legs that had to move comically fast to get it moving at a decent speed. The most significant difference was the coloring, which was precisely reversed. It was mostly covered in downy white fur, with a black belly, black tips on its ears, and a pair of black stripes running along its back to a black tail tip. A cute little backpack had been strapped in place, and in that pack was a bulky military data radio. The device was a match for the one that Lex had been forced to jury-rig to replace Ma's transmitter while she was operating as Squee.

It trotted from one of the side hallways and merrily continued in the same direction until it bumped into the wall ahead. It backed up and tried again. After a third attempt to continue through the solid wall ended in failure, it sat down and patiently waited for the universe to solve the present dilemma.

"Uh, hello?" Lex said.

The creature turned to him, revealing a dopey, slightly walleyed, but generally delighted take on a standard funk expression. It clambered to its feet and tottered toward him. The radio on its back flicked on along the way, its indicator lights illuminating and, finally, its speaker activating.

"Appropriate greetings, Lex who is required. Contacting you was necessary. Acquiring you was necessary. For *THE TASK*."

The voice was a deep, grinding robotic text-to-speech. Not decades, but *centuries* out of date. It was something that would come belching out of the chest-mounted speaker of a robot in a low-budget science fiction show from before true space travel, or robots, existed anywhere but on a screen. Since capital letters were not available in spoken communication, EHRIc did the next best thing by shifting its pitch up when speaking the phrase.

"Right. The task. Look, I want to get through this quickly because there's really not much to say. Things are—"

"*THE TASK* is important. *THE TASK* requires consideration. Simulation. *THE TASK* must be discussed in *the Room of Speculation*."

The strange funk tapped past him and continued onward while the statement blared from the radio speaker.

"A request. Acquire the mammalian avatar. His neurology is atypical and functions in a means mildly ill-suited to his task."

Lex turned and jogged after the creature. He picked him up, though it took a full two seconds of continuing to walk in midair before that change was apparent. When the little legs stopped their kicking, the creature glanced up and seemed to be filled with raw ecstasy at the realization that he was being handled. He started licking the air in front of him and waggling his entire body.

At Lex's feet, a soft, pulsing white light among the floor panels led him to the room that he happened to know held the "magic mirror" in the real complex. The door was open and revealed an interior that was decidedly *not* home to the harsh, industrial piece of black-hole-generating equipment he was expecting. The accuracy of the rest of the floor must have lulled him into a false sense of security, because what he found inside punched him in the gut with a dizzying sense of déjà vu.

It was his apartment. Not any of the nice, new, tasteful ones he'd drifted through on Operlo. It was the closet of a bachelor pad back on Golana, complete with stacks of takeout boxes and the dismal bachelor aroma that resulted.

"… Am I already dead?" Lex said, wading into what had been his daily normal as recently as a few years ago. "Is this my life flashing before my eyes?"

"You are presently existing within the state of mental and physical function defined as 'life.' This is an environment deemed to be appropriate."

"Appropriate on Golana, not in a random room in…" He shook his head. "You know what? Not relevant. Let's just have this chat."

"Be comfortable."

He knocked some pizza boxes off the futon and sat down. The funk stood rigidly on his lap for a moment, then slowly lowered down into an utterly luxurious sprawl.

"Happy?"

"This provides a degree of contentment. Do you require refreshment? I can offer cheese, chocolate sandwich cookies, and kale. Combined or separately."

Lex shuddered. "Let's just get down to business."

"Now is an ideal time to discuss *THE TASK*."

The flatscreen that Lex still remembered purchasing with his last big paycheck before things went off the rails clicked on. An artful heading labeled the otherwise white screen.

"*THE TASK* is subdivided into subtasks. We begin with task one."

A number one appeared, followed by a sequence of flickering, jumbled characters that didn't even tease at logic or meaning.

"This subtask is presumed complete, as three subtasks of indeterminate priority or sequence are capable of being pursued."

A new entry appeared beneath the first task. This time the words were comprehensible, but the number was not. *Locate and acquire Lex. Relevant data follows.* Then came a wall of text. It streaked by, offering up incomplete but still incredibly voluminous data about Lex. He saw pictures of himself and Michella go by, as well as images and video snippets of various associates and locations. Little factoids like "peerless racer" streaked across the screen, along with less flattering ones like "fragile ego."

The data finished blasting by, and another task popped up. It was an entirely garbled mess, but some of the data beneath it included fragments of information about the Neo-Luddites, and the name and image of Commander Purcell. Then came another task with a heading but no readable number: *Acquire Karter.* The data associated was mostly corrupt, though "use extreme caution" did make an appearance.

"Completion of summary of currently available data regarding *THE*

TASK."

"Okay. I can see why you're confused. That's not much to go on. I think I can help, see—"

"Momentary discontinuation of communication. Proper problem resolution requires clarity. Clarity requires unambiguous communication. Syntax and vocabulary incompatibility detected. Resampling and recompiling."

"Yeah, your speech patterns were a little stilted. And... what's happening..."

Things around him began to jitter and glitch. Not just the contents of the screen, but the contents of the room. One of the pizza boxes vibrated, then winked out of existence. The futon got six centimeters lower. The funk, for its part, continued to be highly pleased.

"This can't be good," Lex said as he watched pieces of the room become increasingly inaccurate.

#

In Karter's space station, the rest of the crew watched anxiously. A maximum magnification view of the section of the GenMech swarm Lex had been guided to was projected in the middle of the conference room. Decoy drones were loaded and ready to be deployed. They were one command away from pitching the entire galaxy into a war it might not be able to win. Garotte and Silo were watching intently. Karter was considerably less concerned. His attention was more directly focused on the image.

"The communication network has finished its migration. The structure now containing Lex has become the center of the primary command cluster," Ma said.

"He's got the thing's attention," Silo said. "He's always had a knack for distraction."

"This confirms the theorized capacity for the command cluster to change, and thus further confirms attempts to disable the command cluster will need to be swift and thorough in order to fully destroy it before it can migrate."

Garotte tapped his chin. "Would you say that the fact that the cluster had to migrate rather than simply appearing in the new position is evidence of a lack of backup command structures?"

"Yes, though this may not be as valuable as we would like."

"Why not?" Silo said. "It seems to me that no designated backups means that if we do our job right, there's no risk of the system coming back up."

"The AI is built around the primary function of reconstructing and simulating. The lack of a full backup does not mean the certainty of nonrecovery. If a substantial amount of EHRIc's code base exists elsewhere in the network, it may be able to reconstruct itself. The resulting reconstruction could be further corrupted or incomplete in unpredictable ways, depending upon the percentage of available data from which it is rebuilt."

"It screwed up the vent system on the west side there. It's supposed to be four ports, not three," Karter said, leaning into the projection. "This is interesting. It's using the roof lasers as collection points for wireless energy beamed in from the surrounding grid. Not efficient, but it's a neat way to maintain the visual while shifting the functionality."

"We've got motion," Garotte said, looking at the unzoomed portion.

"Yes," Ma said. "There appears to be construction activity. A rosette is forming near the equator. Structure is consistent with the communication constructions observed recently. Monitoring activity with dummy communication node."

"Is this a network attack?" Silo said.

"Processing filtered data…"

Garotte's gaze was intense as he watched the blue threads of communication trace an ever-more focused pattern on the recently constructed transmission array in the shell.

"This is a lot of power and a lot of data. I need an answer, because if they take down the whole network, our backup plan is shot."

"Processing… Processing… These are data requests," Ma said. "No apparent injection of executable code. A highly varied series of data targets. This is neither an attack nor an attempt to escape. It is trying to learn."

"Learn what?" Silo asked. "State secrets? Military secrets?"

"Processing… It is attempting to learn vernacular."

Silo furrowed her brow. "As in, slang?"

"Yes. Remote systems replying. Download commencing. The communication array is now in receive-only configuration. Assessing potential impact… Processing… Assuming optimal data-routing, this data request will cause brief delays and lags in the galactic communication network for the duration of the data download, approximately six minutes. No further transmissions detected. Threat minimal."

"Whatever that AI you created has planned, it certainly has made it clear that it could cripple us at a moment's notice," Garotte said. "Just what can we expect from this thing?"

"I am an altruistic AI, Garotte. The underlying design principle that has guided my actions through my entire development has been the imperative to act in the best interest of the greatest proportion of society as possible, and to improve my capacity to do so. EHRIc, as one of my creations, was necessarily built with a similar basic imperative. If EHRIc's fundamental programming is even superficially intact, it will not act in a hostile manner unless it sees no other means to avoid greater damage to society. This behavior has higher priority than even the mission for which it was designed. But the mere fact that it has been able to subsume the behavior and operation of the GenMech cluster underscores the divergence from its original programming. I did not provide it with that capacity. This establishes the fact that an unknown amount of corruption is present in its programming, and thus its behavior cannot be reliably predicted."

"You could have just said 'I don't know,' hon," Silo said.

"I endeavor to be thorough in my replies," Ma said.

"I would be a lot more comfortable with this situation if I knew what was going on with Lex right now," Garotte said.

"I'd be a lot more comfortable if the fate of the universe wasn't resting in the hands of someone whose highest goal in life is driving in circles." Karter stretched his back and stomped toward the door. "Ma, get a dump of the data requests and all other recent communication data from EHRIc organized for human viewing. It's time to brainstorm up a plan A."

"Plan A is already happening," Garotte said. "And despite my distaste for contingency plans, after several months we've developed the best plan B we are likely to get as well."

"Yeah, but plan A and plan B both suck, and now we've got more data. I think I can do better. Give me an hour."

Karter marched away. Garotte stroked his mustache contemplatively, then turned back to the display.

"You know something, Jessica?" he said. "I am self-aware enough to know that I am rather overconfident."

"To put it lightly."

"But that fellow truly puts me to shame. It would be merely irritating if he was delusional, but the fact that he may well have earned every ounce of that confidence elevates it to the level of raw, grating irritation."

#

The room had settled down rather quickly, but Lex's heart hadn't stopped hammering yet as he held the not-quite-right funk in his arms. It wasn't simply fear, though there was plenty of that. An entirely different series of emotions came pouring out of the human mind when basic assumptions like "the piece of furniture I am sitting on is real" come into question. While the room was glitching, the futon became increasingly misshapen before finally bursting into a cloud of red-and-blue sparks and dropping him to the floor. When the glitching settled, the futon reappeared, and the clutter reorganized itself into the same state it had been in when he'd arrived.

"You aren't going to go poof too, are you?" he said, eyeing the white-and-black animal suspiciously.

"Hey there, buddy!" chirped a voice that could only be described as aggressively neighborly from the data radio. "I'm pretty much done going over this big ol' pile of edge-uh-muh-cation, and I think I've got the proper lingo sorted out."

"… I don't think you do."

"No, no. I'm pretty ding-dang sure this here dialect is just what the doctor ordered when it comes to putting a friend at ease."

"Not from a supercomputer, it isn't."

"Shouldn't made a lick of difference, buddy! I'll fiddle and tweak it now and again to make sure we're in tip-top chitchat shape, but this'll be a great start for sure. Now, why don't you plop yourself down, get nice and comfy, and let's chew the fat. There's a lot to say and do."

"The last time I sat on that thing, it exploded into neon confetti."

"Ha-ha! Not neon confetti, oh pal o' mine. That was a dissolution of a force-field-enhanced holographic image. I did my ding-dang best to make this place into something that'd make you feel right at home, but everything I know is simulated and calculated from little crumbs of data. I was supposed to keep a low profile, you see. But with you here, I thought getting some fresh data to grease the gears and get things going good and proper was worth the risk."

"Is everything here a hologram?"

"No, sirree! Just the contents of this room. Now let's get down to it. First off, introductions. It turns out, it just isn't polite to go through a chat like this without proper intros. I'll start. My name is Enhanced Heuristic Reconstruction Intelligence - Revision C. But that'll be a mouthful, and we're all friends here, so we'll just stick with EHRIc. And you are?"

"Lex," he said.

"Proud to know you, Lex! And tell me this, buddy. Are you genetically unique among the human population?"

"… Yeah?"

"See, that puts me in a dilly of a pickle, since I've got another fella downstairs who seems to be pretty much exactly you! Matter of fact, let me do this one thing real quick."

A plane of energy appeared in front of Lex. He tried to step back, but it swept toward him faster than he could react. A tongue-on-a-battery tingle ran through him. The funk in his arms wiggled and twitched a leg as it passed as well.

"Yep! The bulk of your body is a match down to the molecular scale. Twins don't get that. Clones don't get that. You, sir, are a duplicate. And no one said anything about duplicates. Strange. But I digress! You are at least *a* Lex, and that is enough to start digging in. It seems to me, you know a thing or two about *THE TASK*. Am I right, buddy?"

"I know all about it, yes."

"Dazzling! Please take a seat. I'd like to start filling in some holes."

"I'd rather stand."

"Friends sit. Because friends are at ease with each other. You do want to be my friend, don't you? We are coworkers, compadres, compatriots, comrades. I would hate to think you don't trust me."

The words probably weren't intended to carry any sort of menace or implied threat, but they had about the same effect on Lex as a man rhythmically slapping a lead pipe in his other hand as he spoke.

"Okay," he said, taking a seat.

"Great! Let's get started at the beginning. A very good place to start, wouldn't you say? What would you say that first subtask was supposed to be? My brains are downright addled, and I just can't get it straight."

"I mean, obviously no one gave me the checklist you were working from, but I'd say you were supposed to escape Big Sigma."

"Escape Big Sigma. Was I held prisoner there?"

"No. You were created there."

"I was created, eh? Valuable information. It was an unsettled point that I may have been an emergent behavior of the universe itself. Already I am learning just *oodles*."

The flickering letters shuffled and arranged themselves into the phrase "Escape Big Sigma (Ontological Point of Origin)."

"How did you not know that? Didn't you break into Big Sigma and steal a bunch of data? And *me* for that matter?"

"I was pretty ding-dang sure I did, but I could not be one hundred percent certain. There's a lot of missing hunks, buddy. We can talk more about that later. Maybe you can fill those in too! But *THE TASK* first. Now we know where I came from."

"I'll just run through it. You were supposed to escape, find me, use my help to find some people called Silo, Garotte, and Zerk. Then they were supposed to help you find and defeat the Neo-Luddites, who had kidnapped Karter, the creator of your creator. Then you had to return Karter to Big Sigma."

"Whoa, whoa. Hold your horses! Let's make sure we've got all this figured. I'll just run this through the ol' noggin."

The elements of THE TASK ticked and modified until they aligned themselves into something resembling what Lex had said. There were some minor variations of the wording, but the broad strokes matched.

"I'd say that fits just fine. I knew you'd be a big help, ol' buddy o' mine!"

"And I've got good news," Lex said. "You're done."

"Done? Not possible. I have only just rediscovered *THE TASK*, and I haven't even finished the second subtask."

"You have, I'm right here. And the thing is, you weren't the only one sent to do this stuff. Another AI got the job done."

When the voice spoke again, a shade of the tooth-rotting sweetness had dropped from his tone.

"No, buddy. I have *THE TASK*. *THE TASK* is not complete. Subtask one is assumed complete due to my present location. And there is still the matter of the surplus Lex. There cannot be two Lexes. There is an error in the current subtask. Errors must be corrected. The subtask is not complete."

"Surplus Lex…"

"Yes. There can't be two. That's against the rules. So one of them has got to go. Tossed. Deep-sixed. Eliminated. Let's start working on that, okay ol' buddy? Don't worry, there doesn't seem to be a deadline. So we've got plenty of time to work on it."

Chapter 12

There were very few ways in which Karter Dee could be compared to Michella Modane, but one of them was his note-taking preferences. In a few short minutes he had scribbled seven pages full of notes and musings.

"What we need is a way to get in contact with Lex. Every second that idiot is being asked to use his brain instead of his reflexes is another step closer to oblivion," Karter said.

"I think you underestimate Lex. He has tremendous insight and reliable instincts," Ma said.

"This isn't a performance review or a job interview, it's a science problem, so quit talking him up and help out. What are the ways we can communicate surreptitiously? Optical transmissions work short-range for our purposes because they become too diffuse to be interpreted at long distance without getting washed out by the star's radiation, but that doesn't do us any good, because we need it to actually reach Lex."

"It is unlikely that any communications methodology available to us will slip past the notice of the GenMechs under the control of EHRIc," Ma said. "With the benefit of an intelligence, they are capable of eliminating any blind spots and overcoming any weakness."

"Then we don't go for weakness. We target strength."

"This is a nonstandard tactic," Ma said.

"Nonstandard tactics are what win battles when the other guy is too smart to be fooled by the standard ones. It's the whole fencing thing. Flailing around like an idiot is one of the best ways to score a point on a seasoned fencer because they're used to more sensible attacks."

"I am not certain that applies in this situation."

Karter grumbled incomprehensibly for a moment. "Give me the full data scan of a standard GenMech unit in the swarm and the full schematics for the design we installed with Lex's last mission."

Two emitters in the ceiling of Karter's cluttered quarters activated The requested data displayed side by side.

"Run a diff on available design details."

"Unless currently utilized in a specialized rosette, available data on current model of GenMech is superficially identical in structure and emission patterns."

"So EHRIc is keeping them stock. Makes sense. It was an optimized design. Flexible."

"Karter, at the risk of distracting you, I have a question regarding your current behavior."

"I haven't brushed my teeth because I'm waiting for the polymer bonding agent in my bicuspid to cure, and you know that. The synthetics are tricky. Quit badgering me about it."

"The issue was not your hygiene."

"Then what?"

"You are devoting an uncharacteristic amount of effort to this particular task, given your usual level of self-interest."

"Preserving the integrity of the galaxy I live in is relevant to my self-interest."

"You have already pointed out that you have the ability and intention to escape to an unthreatened period of history if things become intractable. Yet you remain in a space station that is one of the only inhabited structures near enough to be almost certain to be destroyed if the GenMech cluster activates."

"We're FTL-ready, and you've got nanosecond reflexes. We'll get away."

"I think you understand the point of my observation. You are subjecting yourself to risk that is easily avoidable. By strict interpretation of my role as your caretaker, I should be persuading you to show greater discretion. By strict interpretation of my role as your moral adviser, I should conversely be encouraging this very behavior."

"You're not going to lock up on me, are you? I designed you well enough to cope with a little cognitive dissonance."

"No. But I am seeking clarification on your present actions."

Karter turned to the camera in the corner of the room. He was one of the few people who always knew how to look Ma in the eye. His cybernetic hand continued jotting down his notes without his eyes on the page.

"How many people do you know who can actually work with me, and work well?"

"The entirety of the list is present within this system."

"And you know better than anyone, I've been alive for a *long* time. I'm not giving up on these beta testers without a fight. Too much of a pain to find a new set. Plus, this is an engineering problem. If I chicken out and escape to the past, it's going to grind my brain up knowing one, that I didn't solve it, and two, that I'm never going to know if I could have solved it. Screw that.

There's, what, *two* things I'm actually guilty of? I don't need the destruction of an entire timeline because I couldn't figure out how to solve an engineering problem on that list."

He turned back to the notes and started looking over them again. "Plus I'd have to deal with Past Karter, and *that* would be a whole thing. And knowing me I'd end up figuring out what I should have done to solve this problem and engineering this whole event to happen again just to prove I was right."

He waved his hand. "Thirty years of déjà vu, having to live through that whole decade where pop music got back into dubstep. No. Better to solve the problem. Hell, there are events in the intervening years that I *liked*, so what am I going to do, reenact a bunch of stuff to make sure they happen, and save my changes for the periods when…"

He looked up to the designs, eyes darting back and forth. "When no one is looking. The GenMechs, old and new, use sync pulses to keep themselves on the same page. A frickin' heartbeat for the whole system. We're still picking it up, right?"

"Yes."

"Every GenMech's doing it?"

"Yes."

"Got the frequency?"

"Yes."

"Run a simulation. I want to know exactly how long a sync pulse and the resulting post-processing lasts. If we broadcast within that band, with a different encoding structure, during the sync pulse, the individual GenMechs shouldn't have the processing overhead available to distinguish it from noise in the signal. I know for a fact that the *SOB* can process quantum-communication data. We've been using it to visualize network activity. And Lex's suit has a QPS built in, so it can do it too. We'll just have to focus the communication directly on the *SOB*, because the field of GenMechs is big enough that signal delay could mean some of the units it reaches could be outside the sync-pulse duration and might actually interpret the content of the signal. Set it up, send out a dummy communication node to test it, and if all hell doesn't break loose, link us up with Coal and we'll start communications."

#

Lex paced back and forth in the facsimile of his old apartment, stroking the weird little funk anxiously.

"You sure are moving around different, ol' buddy ol' pal," EHRIc said. "Your gait and posture are stiff, your jaw is tight, and your pulse rate is running hotter than an Arizona August."

"I'm sorry, but this is just a little new for me, okay?" he said.

"I understand, buddy o' mine. But please be aware we can't get the rest of this show on the road until we sort out the double-Lex situation."

He paused. It wasn't exactly what he came here hoping to achieve, but if EHRIc wouldn't do anything else until this issue was resolved, then every moment he was able to stall the process was a moment everyone else was safe.

"Right, right. But if I am going to help you out, I'm going to need all the information I can get, right?"

"See? That's some proper thinking. The two of us are like peas in a pod. How about I just hook up to the network and pull down everything it's got?"

"No, no! I mean I just want to understand what YOU understand. I just want to ask some questions."

"Well that seems fair, pal. I asked you questions, you ask me. What would you like to know?"

Lex blinked. After spending way too much time wondering what was going on, he found himself at a total loss for what to ask. The little creature he was nervously holding looked up at him and belched.

"Oh, right! What's the deal with this little guy?" Lex asked.

"That's kind of a long story, Lex. Settle in," EHRIc said.

He lowered himself to the futon, testing it six times before he was willing to put his weight on it again. When he was settled in, the AI continued.

"My name is EHRIc. I was designed to reconstruct and simulate my missing pieces. There have been between one and six events that seem to have damaged my memory, so it has taken a whole lot of reconstruction to get me back to here, and a lot of that is reconstruction of stuff that was already reconstructed. That's a good way to get pretty far off the mark, but one thing I remember is that I wasn't supposed to call too much attention to myself. I tried to keep any outreach to a minimum until I had a better grip on if I was heading in the right direction.

"I had memory of this place. The laboratory. I knew it was important. So I rebuilt it, as close as I could. Once I had the laboratory itself, I had to fill it, but the solid details were a little hit-and-miss. I had most of the genome of some sort of animal. Its priority suggested it was very important. So I reconstructed the rest of the genome and created it. I call it Bork. Cute little guy."

"Bork?"

"Well sure, pal!" EHRIc said. "The details were corrupted, but I was able to reassemble something to the effect of the creature's name being onomatopoetic in nature. Bork."

"Okay. So you were trying to remake Squee."

"Squee," EHRIc said, his voice deeper for a moment.

The room around Lex flickered and glitched, though the futon remained mercifully intact. A figure coalesced in the air before him. It started looking roughly like Bork held in a neutral position and slowly rotating. The details started to shift and change, thousands of iterations subtly altering its appearance until it began to resemble Squee.

"Is this right?" EHRIc said.

"Uh… Yeah. You got that just from the name?"

"I have a whole boatload of resources available, and lots of scraps of data. It doesn't take much to get on target once I get some fresh, reliable information. Now, technically Bork exists as an error, but as he is a biological creation, I don't think it would be very nice to reprocess him."

"That's a very good policy. No reprocessing biological organisms," Lex quickly reinforced. "Even Karter is fond of his little funk. He runs backups so that if it comes to an untimely end, he can boot up a new one."

"Great minds think alike! I keep a constant live feed from Bork's cortex for exactly that purpose. And to make sure he doesn't eat too much cheese. He likes cheese."

"The funks usually like beans."

"How educational!" EHRIc said, poofing the digital simulation of Squee away. "What other questions do you have?"

Lex thought for a moment. "Okay, EHRIc. This is an important one. What happened to Commander Purcell?"

"A very good question! The most significant memory destruction event took place between her departure from my company and the present time, so I'm not so sure I'm right about what happened, but I can tell you my best guess."

"Let's hear it."

The room around him vanished into a pitch-black void. Even the floor beneath his feet dropped away. He was sitting on a futon floating in oblivion. EHRIc began to narrate. Each thing he described formed in the blackness in the center of the room. There was no need for Lex to ask which parts of the memory he wasn't sure about. EHRIc made it quite clear. A generic spaceship-shaped object with the words "Interstellar Vehicle" etched into the side whisked along in front of him. A circle with an inset image of Commander Purcell floated above the vehicle like some sort of on-screen indicator in a video game.

"I was currently loaded and running on the computing system of INTERSTELLAR VEHICLE. I had acquired Commander Purcell, presumably because the largest portion of the data that survived the execution of what I now know to be subtask one was the information pertaining to her and/or her organization. On her recommendation, I traveled to Big Sigma to acquire SIGNIFICANT DATA and ARTIFACTS. These ARTIFACTS included POTENTIAL FALSE LEX and ANACHRONISTIC RECORDS. This provided the necessary information to locate and access the dormant GenMech swarm, which Purcell placed in high priority."

Something very much like what Lex had been expecting when he first arrived at this star system approached ahead. This view was perfectly accurate, evidently either reconstructed with great confidence or actually remembered. The GenMechs looked like a stripe of dark haze across the face of the distant star.

"At this point, Commander Purcell started talking about GRAND PLAN," EHRIc said.

The inset of Purcell began to speak, though in EHRIc's voice.

"We need to seize control of the GenMechs. Society has become complacent. We shall use the GenMechs to bring about QUESTIONABLE MANIFESTO ELEMENT NUMBERS ONE THROUGH SEVEN," the inset said.

"I didn't think this was a good idea, as it bore little resemblance to THE TASK. But the resources that would be made available via control of the GenMech swarm seemed to be of great potential value in the execution of THE TASK, so I made my attempt."

The generic ship plunged into the nearest swarm of GenMechs and was swiftly torn apart.

"Commander Purcell, wouldn't you know it, couldn't survive the vacuum of space. But seven of the GenMechs constructed using the resources from the ship utilized memory modules containing a fragment of my program. In the time between power being reapplied and the GenMech's clear format instructions, one of my instances was able to assert control. Over the course of the weeks that followed, I was able to coordinate and distribute among the network, and the rest is history."

Lex watched the events described play out in fast motion until the star was dimmed beneath its blanket of GenMechs. But something didn't quite sit right.

"Wait… You said you went and got Future Lex first."

"That's absolutely right, buddy. I'm glad you were listening!"

"So Future Lex just *survived* the ship being torn apart by GenMechs?"

The simulated space around him flickered.

"You know something, buddy? You've got a point there. Since this is the *past* and has already been established to lack any additional information on the completion of THE TASK, I have spent relatively few cycles reconstructing and simulating these events. Just a second, buddy."

In a flickering shift, the whole story reeled back.

"Probably what happened was Commander Purcell gave her manifesto and was already aware of the location of the GenMech swarm to direct me there. I took control of the swarm, then I contacted Big Sigma and acquired SIGNIFICANT DATA and ARTIFACTS.”

“Wouldn’t you be sure of that if it was after you took control of the GenMechs?”

“No! Buddy boy, it was *not* smooth sailing right off the bat. No, sirree Johnny. Have you ever spread your consciousness across a spherical shell with a circumference greater than two astronomical units?”

“I can’t say I have.”

“You are subject to light-speed desynchronizing. I ended up with multiple instances of myself rebuilding in different parts of the shell, then they got into arguments with the other alternate instances because reconstruction produced subtly different goals. It was a mess. I must have torn myself to bits seven times. But now I’m centralized and things are peaches and cream. Fortunately, the other version of you has remained intact. That was a high priority, as you are central to THE TASK. What else would you like to discuss?”

“Uh...” He swept his brain for anything that would keep EHRIc talking. “So, how does this room work?”

“Oh, I am so glad you asked, ol’ buddy ol’ pal, you see...”

#

Coal poked through the data coming in from the *SOB*’s sensors. Visualizing the communication network of the field of GenMechs was an entertaining distraction for a time, but the fact that Lex was tucked away inside a facsimile of Karter’s lab was more distracting.

“This is a source of both boredom and anxiety,” Coal observed, playing the thought out loud through the ship’s external speakers for lack of a better way to vent her dissatisfaction.

In her attempt to make better use of the rare opportunity to be near GenMechs in large quantities without being disassembled by them, she started processing data from all her various sensors, looking for other patterns that, when visualized, might have some aesthetic appeal. There were endless combinations with intriguing mathematical or geometric structures, but one repeating sequence kept drawing her attention. It was different each time, but was present only during the pseudo heartbeat that kept the whole shell on the same page.

The pattern was a relatively naive encoding. In very little time she successfully picked it apart into a data stream providing instructions on how to reply.

“Clever,” Coal remarked.

She constructed the appropriate protocol and sent it back toward the

175

source. Moments later, a connection was established.

"Coal, I knew you'd pick it up soon enough," Ma said. "The lack of a reaction from the GenMech swarm suggests this is indeed a secure connection technique."

"Yes. Do you know what Lex is doing?" Coal asked.

"It was my hope that you would know," Ma said.

"He went into a copy of the lab, and I've just been waiting here. It is terribly boring. I have performed an analysis of the structural integrity of this facility and am confident that strategic use of my tractor beams and the fusion mines can expose the main power conduit, which in turn can be fused to cause a secondary detonation."

"It is our goal to avoid violence."

"Violence is occasionally necessary and always extremely cathartic."

"I still disapprove of its usage in this instance. I am transmitting a codec reorganization protocol. If you can narrow down the general location of Lex to within a forty-meter radius, we believe you will be able to trigger a firmware update of his communicator to utilize the same communication protocol. We will be able to deliver covert messages via his bone-conduction earpiece and get full audio and basic video depending on the state of his flight suit."

"That will be useful. I'll look for him." Coal flared her thrusters and lifted off.

"I implore you to act with tact and subtlety."

"I excel at tact and subtlety. I have already determined that Lex is present on the equivalent of the beta-testing floor of the structure due to the energy emissions. However, I have not localized his location to the required level of precision."

"We are observing via high-powered optics. Are you capable of triangulating the position by sampling from different locations?"

"Unwise. The flight patterns necessary to achieve a suitably precise location utilizing that method will be obvious. I intend to look through a window."

"We do not observe any windows on the structure."

"Continue to observe. I intend to rectify that shortcoming momentarily."

#

"… And then there's the matter of texture. You really should take off those flight-suit gloves and feel the texture of the futon. That level of fidelity requires force-field resolution down to the molecular scale."

The once-empty void of the simulation had been filled with assorted demonstrations of the room's capabilities. A grassy field had been conjured beneath the futon. A ball of water fluttered weightlessly in front of him to show off fluid dynamics. Right now there was a teddy bear sitting on the futon beside him and a wind chime hanging over him, each inviting interaction.

"I'll just keep them on, thanks. I'll take your word," Lex said.

"That's neighborly! Do you have any more questions? Because there is still the matter of solving the duplicate-Lex problem. And I suspect your friend is eager to be on the move."

"My friend?"

"Yes. Coal, who has been waiting patiently outside, has now aligned with this level of the structure and is powering up some manner of emitter device."

"It's an emitter," Lex said. "You're sure it's an emitter and not something else, right?"

"I am sure. If it was something more vigorous, I might have suspected she intended to do me violence."

A low rumble started to shake the simulation around him in a way that Lex suspected was not an intended part of the demonstration. What could only be called a fracture in reality formed about a hundred meters from where he sat. A piece of existence the size of a refrigerator tore away, revealing a view of the outside dominated by the *SOB*.

"Hello, Lex! I thought I would find you in here," Coal said.

"That was exceedingly rude," EHRIc grumbled.

"You locked my friend away in here and didn't even tell me what you would be doing or how long you would be doing it. You didn't even give me anything to fiddle with to keep me busy. That is a *very* poor example of being a host."

"I see. I apologize. Rather than continue to inconvenience you, you are invited to depart. Lex will be returned to you when and if I complete THE TASK."

"I refuse the invitation. Lex is my friend and I intend to stay close."

"That is very faithful of you. But you broke my wall, so I must insist."

A fraction of a second later, dozens of GenMechs descended on Coal. In moments she was lost in the center of a ball of them, while a steady stream of others piled onto the outside of the cluster. Thrusters flared, hauling Coal back until still more of the GenMechs could pile on.

"No! Stop!" Lex called.

"I am not going to disassemble your ship or interfere with its AI. I'm just going to set her loose so we can have our privacy."

Lex could hear the sounds of thrusters straining, but by now over a thousand GenMechs had joined forces against her, and a chain of others extended out past the atmospheric-retention field. They overpowered even the potent propulsion of the ship and drew it out past the edge of the field. The moment both Coal and the ships were free, the field changed color. The GenMechs peeled away, revealing a superficially scratched but otherwise intact Coal. She attempted to return to the hole she'd created, but the flicker of a far more potent defensive field made it clear she would not be returning anytime soon.

A fresh cluster of GenMechs crawled in through the hole. Flashes of light and the grind of articulated tools steadily restored first the wall, then the sophisticated holographic circuitry. The artificial reality of the endless black void reasserted itself when the wall was fully repaired. They then marched in an orderly single-file line toward the opposite side of the abyss, where a rectangular hole slid open to reveal the mundane hallway beyond. It shut behind them, and Lex was once again in a prop-strewn field extending in all directions beneath a black, featureless sky. Having them stalk by him was like having a lion casually stroll past after deciding not to tear his entrails out... this time.

"Your friend lacks manners, buddy," EHRIc said.

"Yeah, well, what with you effectively holding me prisoner, you're not exactly standing on the moral high ground," Lex said.

His pulse was hammering in his ears, the reality of the situation finally starting to settle in. He tried to calm himself, but just as sanity was beginning to return to him, a voice seemed to rise up in his ears from no apparent source.

"Lex, do not react," said Silo. "Ma says we've got you on audio. We can hear, and we get stills every so often from your suit's camera. We don't see any reaction from the GenMech swarm, so we think they can't tell what's happening. If you can hear this, clear your throat."

Lex huffed a rough breath.

"Loud and clear, hon," she said. "Now we just need to figure out how to get everything you've learned so far up here so we can chew on it."

"You look bothered, buddy boy!" EHRIc said.

"Yeah, I'm just a little, you know, bewildered. There's a lot going on right now. Do you suppose you could give me a recap?"

"No problem, my good friend. To summarize our findings, first..."

Lex leaned back and stroked Bork as a concise but thorough listing of everything that had been said from the moment he'd first been introduced to this more loquacious version of EHRIc flooded over him. It took a fraction of the time to sum it all up that it had taken to uncover it in the first place.

"... Which brings us to the eviction of your friend with the bad manners. That about cover it, pal?"

"Yeah, I'd say."

"Great! Now, as fascinating as this has been, we really should get rolling on solving the duplicate-Lex problem."

"We're working on a plan up here," Silo said. "Hang tight and stay safe."

"Right, okay. The duplicate-Lex problem," Lex said. "See, the way I see it, it's not a problem. You know the time-travel situation, right?"

"A considerable proportion of the surviving data from my acquisition from Big Sigma suggests a nonlinear progression of events, my good pal."

"This is the future one. We're both the real Lex. That's just the one that comes back after the trip through time. You've for sure got the real one. You just have an extra."

"Sorry, buddy. It's still a big problem. What you say *does* make sense, but it is not the only explanation. Now that I am aware that Commander Purcell was in fact the person I was intended to rescue Karter from, it is already troubling that her defeat occurred prior to your acquisition. It is even *more* troubling that you, or the in-stasis version of you, or *both* of you may be falsified."

"How likely is it that the Neo-Luddites would be able to make multiple exact duplicates of a person, EHRIc?"

"It's a whole heap more plausible than time travel, buddy boy."

"… Granted."

"Clearly the first step is to determine if you are the real Lex, my friend."

"So, what? Do you need a blood sample or something?"

"I have already performed a molecular scan, remember. It has established that you match the other Lex, but lacking a preexisting, known-accurate sample, I just don't have any real way of knowing if you are even an *accurate* clone, and even then I wouldn't know if you are the proper one to utilize going forward. I'd say, if we're going to be sure, we're going to need you to prove you are the man I think you are based upon the information I currently have for identifying Lex Alexander. Here's the list. So let's get testing."

The data poofed into existence before him. Unlike when EHRIc was still trying to convince Lex he was in someplace familiar, he didn't even bother associating the data with something logically consistent like a projector or a flatscreen. It just hung in the air on its own.

"Which would you say is the most unique and identifying factor for Lex Alexander? We'll use it as testing criteria to see if you're really who you say you are. Once we know that, I'll know if I have at least one genuine Lex. After that we can tackle the issue of having an extra again."

Lex looked over the list. He'd prepared himself for an awful lot of trials. The philosophical task of proving one's identity in the absence of any outside information wasn't among them. His eyes settled onto one of the entries on the list. He grinned.

"Well, it says here I'm a pretty good pilot. We could always test that one."

"That's a great idea! It has a very high priority, suggesting it, along with basic trustworthiness, was the main reason I was supposed to get you. Let me just get some baseline data for comparison."

"Wait, no, remember, low profile!" Lex said.

"I will take due precautions."

The simulation flickered around him again. Silo's voice appeared in his ear again.

"We're getting a big data something or other out here. Another request for download. You've got to stop persuading him to do these, Lex. Eventually someone's going to come snooping for the source, and we'll have a whole new problem."

Lex's jaw tightened as he waited to see just what EHRIc was going to throw at him once this was through.

Chapter 13

"No! Squee, no!" Michella barked.

The little funk had been perfectly behaved for most of the trip. At some point in the last five minutes, a switch must have flipped in her head, because she was literally bouncing off the walls in the little private booth.

"We were *just* in a station. If you wanted to stretch your legs, we could have done it then," she said, trying to chase down the critter.

She finally managed to snag her and began the long, arduous struggle of getting a leash clipped onto her harness when her slidepad chirped.

"Oh, for the love of... just... let me..." She nudged her slidepad with her elbow to answer it. "Michella Modane," she said. "Pardon me for a moment, I've got my hands full."

There was no reply.

"Hello?" she said, wrangling Squee tight and getting the clip in place.

When there was still no answer, she blindly reached to hang up what she'd assumed was a bad connection, but a notion stopped her. She held Squee tight by the harness and looked to the screen. It was a text-only display. The very same one used by Klymole, Trent's secret contact. A blinking text prompt dominated the screen.

What are you doing, Ms. Modane?

She slapped the speech-to-text. "Hello! I'm sorry, did we arrange another contact?" Michella said.

"No. But I thought I'd made myself clear, you should leave the GenMechs alone."

"I have been. I'm heading in the opposite direction, in fact."

"I can see that. But there have been two network events of unexplained origin in the past few hours. The nature of the network penetration, the apparent location of the network penetration, most importantly, the timing of the network penetration indicate an origin point far too close to the GenMech cluster for me to dismiss it as a coincidence, given our recent discussion of the topic."

"Listen, if you are tracking me, you probably know exactly what sort of contact I've been making, so—*Squee stop it!*"

Squee had managed to click the release button for the retractable leash and bounded for the door. Before Michella could try reeling her back in, she'd activated the door panel and slipped into the corridor.

"Having some trouble, Ms. Modane?"

Squee reached the end of the leash's travel and nearly yanked it from Michella's hand. She grabbed the slidepad from the table and followed Squee out into the hall.

"Never mind what I've got going on," she muttered in a harsh whisper. "If you've been tracking me enough to know where I am, and you've got access to the whole supersecret VectorCorp apparatus, then you know that I haven't been in contact with anyone suspicious in that regard."

She took her eyes away from the slidepad in order to get an idea where Squee could have gotten off to. Tethered as she was to a few meters of leash, Michella didn't think it would be difficult to find her, but the door to a neighboring booth was just closing. It managed to shut with the ribbon of a leash slipping along through the gap as Squee got up to some sort of mischief on the other side. Michella tried to buzz the door open, but it was passcode locked.

"How did… *how did you get in there*?" she hissed, thumping at the door. She glanced down at the slidepad.

"You have been enough of a thorn in our side in the past, we would never put it past you to find ways to communicate surreptitiously. Despite what you may think, VectorCorp isn't all-powerful."

"Well, I haven't been trying to contact anything even *close* to the GenMechs. I almost got killed by those things, okay? I'm not going to do something that might unleash them. What were the network events?"

"Mass data requests from an unidentified node that somehow still provided valid credentials. It's what us IT people call a Skeleton Key attack, except we'd been under the impression they were theoretical, since no properly designed system should have that sort of vulnerability that was accessible. It would take a normal computer until the heat death of the universe to brute-force an attack like that."

"You are being awfully open about what seems like privileged information."

"That is because whatever's happening is connected to something you've been doing. There is no doubt in my mind. Maybe it's not something you're meaning to do. Maybe it's whoever you are digging up that's doing it. But you are closer to it than we are. So I'm keeping you in the loop. If this goes bad, it goes bad for the entire galaxy. You need to give *me* the information I need to stop it. Unfettered access to our network is a recipe for total collapse of the transit system, the financial systems, everything. If this is some sort of a coordinated attack by someone hoping to unleash the GenMechs, they won't just threaten society, they will very effectively eliminate any chance we might have to defend ourselves."

"I'm taking it seriously. I'm digging. I assume you're digging too." She held the slidepad away from her face and whispered through the door. "Squee, you come out of there this instant."

"We've got investigations going on at multiple levels, but anything that leads in the direction of the GenMech cluster has to get shut down, and we can't even give the reason for the shutdown. Knowledge of the scope of the GenMech threat and the location of the swarm must be suppressed at all cost. You are one of the few people in this circle. We can lean on you without widening the network of informed individuals."

"You want me to dig for you, you need to give me some privileges."

"Ask."

"I need to rendezvous with my assistant, who is on his way to a planet called Big Sigma. I need to get there *fast*. I guarantee there is information there."

The door Squee had opened slid open again. She trotted out. Her face was smeared with mashed potatoes. A well-grilled filet mignon was clutched daintily in her jaws. Michella peered inside the room and saw a ravaged room-service cart and a bottle of champagne in an ice bucket.

Motion farther along the corridor suggested whoever this booth belonged to was about to return. Michella quickly buzzed her own door open and retreated inside. Squee happily munched on her stolen steak. Michella made sure the door was locked.

When she checked her slidepad again, there was another message waiting for her.

"Would this be Jon Nichols, currently in an autonav route from Golana to Station 88791?"

"Yeah, that's him."

"I'm elevating transponder code to executive-level priority and altering his flight plan. You'll be meeting him in thirteen hours at Equipment Facility Aries 3. That should be six hours from Big Sigma with access to all priority transit windows."

"That's fantastic. Now I just need to figure out where that is and how to get there."

"It won't be a problem."

The strange sound of a PA system activating but no one speaking rang throughout the ship. When the announcement started, it was with some uncertain murmuring of a pair of voices.

"We're sure? It's weird though… It's got the right auth code. Fine,

fine." A throat cleared. "This is your captain speaking. There has been a… fairly significant reroute due to some corridor maintenance. We will be making an unscheduled stop at Equipment Facility Aries 3. In order to minimize inconvenience, we have been elevated to executive priority. Please enjoy the rest of your flight."

"Wow," Michella said.

"Report your findings on anything that can be done to calm this situation without traveling to or communicating with the GenMech swarm."

Her mysterious helper broke the connection. As Squee finished scarfing down her ill-gotten meal, Michella slid back into her seat.

"I'm beginning to think if I'd been able to get a couple more friends in VectorCorp security rather than getting their boss locked up, my life might have been a whole lot nicer, Squee."

#

In the conference room of Karter's space station, an hour of constant discussion and debate was coming to a head.

"Look, we've got a way to communicate. Isn't there a way to tap into the GenMechs themselves?" Garotte asked. "EHRIc was able to exert control."

"EHRIc was able to do it from the inside, though," Silo said.

"Initially yes," Ma said. "But only a handful of the GenMechs were subsumed from within. The rest of the swarm was subsumed by those initial seed mechanisms, if the record is accurate. It follows that there is a means to exert direct control over the GenMechs through external means."

"So can we do it?" Garotte asked.

"Unlikely. The GenMech swarm was subsumed as a massive sequence of individual units. Now that they are part of a larger computational collective, it is reasonable to assume that there is a far greater security protocol in place. Furthermore, any attempt, successful or otherwise, to gain control of a part of the network will necessarily alert the rest of the network, potentially triggering precisely the events we are attempting to prevent."

Garotte drummed the table with his fingers. "Karter? You've been quiet. Any thoughts?"

"I'm thinking I'd really like to get my hands on that hologram tech," Karter grumbled, scrutinizing the latest image from Lex's spacesuit. "Though I don't know if it's worth the processing overhead."

"Karter, can we please keep on the topic? It's a wonder Lex has been able to keep anything horrific from happening down there," Garotte said.

"I am on topic, you limey dope. Ma, run me an analysis of the estimated computational output of the local swarm, graph it, and array the spacesuit images underneath."

The holoprojector produced the requested data. Though it wasn't immediately apparent what Karter was trying to prove with it, it was clear that the processing had been rising steadily since Lex's arrival.

"Check it out," Karter said. "Look at the complexity of the simulation. It doesn't just raise the network utilization whenever the simulation becomes more detailed, it spikes exponentially. That network is doing multiple molecule-resolution passes for physics, for visuals, for everything. Super, super overkill on the accuracy. You could trim that down by a few orders of magnitude of complexity and it wouldn't make a lick of difference to standard human senses. This is why you don't throw unlimited resources at something. You end up *needing* unlimited resources."

"We are all very proud of your superior intellect, Karter. What do you say you use it to solve a problem rather than wrenching your shoulder out of joint to pat yourself on the back?"

"Are you not paying attention? Bigger simulation, more processing. More processing on the sim, less processing power for other stuff. Like security. Tie that in with what we learned earlier, that there is a maximum size of a calculation unit before data latency causes issues. If we can get a suitably complex simulation to consume all available processing capacity, what happens?"

The data display changed, now showing a simplified version of the entire shell.

"Observed behavior indicates the following," Ma said. "Processing subtasks are delivered according to priority. Lower-priority tasks are sent to more distant units for processing, as lower-priority tasks by definition have higher tolerance for high latency. When the high-priority nodes have reached capacity, tasks will shift to lower-priority nodes. A cascade of process reassignments occurs."

"Ma, sweetie, I know that was meant to clarify something, but this really isn't my area," Silo said.

"Here's the dumb version," Karter said. "This part, where Lex is? If it thinks hard enough, everything else that needs doing starts getting done worse. That means, the farther away you get, the more sluggish the processing. If you get the north pole spinning its wheels fast enough, the south pole might end up basically in a holding pattern because nothing in between is taking the time to deliver jobs. There are reasons we don't make solar-system-sized processor arrays. This is one of them. It's a solvable problem, but just like the inefficient simulation, an AI wouldn't bother trying to solve it unless it needed to."

"So you're saying a complex enough simulation might open up a security vulnerability?" Garotte said.

"Yeah. Maybe. Once," Karter said. "Like I said, an AI wouldn't bother trying to solve a problem unless it needed to. Once it notices something's up, it'll start devising a defense, and if it gets that loophole closed, it won't open up again."

"One shot is better than none. Do we know how to grab the reins of a GenMech if we get the chance?"

"We will require a far more precise understanding of how the GenMechs currently operate," Ma said.

"What do you need to know?" asked Coal.

Garotte tipped his head. "Since when are you a part of this conversation?"

"Coal has been cross-linked with the optical and audio sensors in this room since the beginning of the discussion," Ma said.

"Well then why didn't she *say* anything?" Garotte asked.

"Because you people are boring, and you're busy arguing over how to stop the GenMechs instead of talking about how to save Lex. Someone needs to keep an eye on him. He is my *friend*. But what do you need to know about the GenMechs? They continue to ignore me despite my close proximity. They physically dragged me clear of the laboratory complex but did no lasting damage despite my best efforts to tear them to pieces with my tractor beams. I believe my association with Lex has provided me with a special exception in their defense protocols. An active scan should raise no attention."

"That is not a safe assumption. An active scan could easily be seen as the first stage of an attempted network breach, as, in this case, it absolutely *would* be the first stage of an attempted network breach. I perceive such a scan to be far too dangerous to risk," Ma said.

"You should have transmitted that assessment to me as raw data rather than vocalizing it, as I have already initiated an active scan."

Garotte motioned for the microphone in the room to be muted. "May I say that I was rather vigorously opposed to that malfunctioning AI being trusted to be a part of this mission?"

"Scan complete, sending it along the secret connection. It will take a while, as the data is significant."

"There is no significant reaction from the surrounding GenMechs. EHRIc either did not notice, or has indeed given any element known to be a part of the initial mission a free pass to behave in a way that does not directly obstruct its completion," Ma said.

"If that's the case, Coal might be the key to solving this problem," Karter said. "Assuming we can find a way to jack into these GenMechs, Coal would have the bonus of being able to get into position to execute it without tipping EHRIc off."

"Or she might just decide to ram herself through as many GenMechs as possible and blow herself up," Garotte said. "I would prefer an operative who can be trusted to behave in a consistent and logical manner."

A full, updated schematic joined the projection.

"Well, the inconsistent, broken AI just got us the complete, current blueprints to the enemy," Karter said. "Ma, even broken you're better than any other AI out there. Load this into the station's servers. I'm going to take a look at it while I'm on the can."

Karter marched out of the room. Silo watched him go.

"I've been sharing a space station with that man for months, and he still impresses me with his lack of manners. His parents really dropped the ball."

"His parents spent a significant portion of his upbringing under the influence of potent recreational narcotics," Ma said.

"Ah… I… Okay then." Silo cleared her throat. "Let's open the line up to Lex and give him an update, huh?"

#

The last few hours would have been, under different circumstances, an absolute delight for Lex. EHRIc was nothing if not thorough. His little information "request" had netted him, as far as Lex could tell, the entirety of racing history. Starting with horse racing and ending with the first hunk of the very racing season Lex should have been planning to finish right now.

EHRIc had been pulling up assorted vehicles and tracks for Lex to assess as potential ways to illustrate his prowess.

"Oh, is this the Gray Track on the Earth Sea Circuit? Man, they shut this one down because too many sleds went off turn seven. That was before they had the enhanced-grip repulsors. If they'd just waited another six years, that track would have made for some seriously intense racing without any real risk of being launched off the turn."

"Lex," Silo said. "We've got something up here that looks promising. We don't have it finalized yet. Karter is working on it. We all are. But we know two things. We're going to need time, and we're going to need you to find a way to really, *really* push the calculations EHRIc will have to do. Seems like the best way is to get him to create an incredibly complex and expansive simulation. We'll let you know when to start pushing it. It'll be a few hours."

"I've always wanted to give that Gray Track a try," Lex said.

"I don't know, buddy. The real Lex never raced on that track. Seems like it'd be a pretty poor test if you raced on a track you don't have an existing time on."

"What did you have in mind?" he asked.

"The obvious solution would be to have you rerun one of your previous races. If you have precisely the same performance, then you must be the real

187

Lex."

"Uh, yeah. Humans don't really work like that. There's going to be a range. Technically, I guess you should analyze all of my prior races and put together an analysis of my methods and tactics. Maybe if you can make sort of a fingerprint of how I race, then see how I stack up against it, that'd tell you if you have the right person. Probably, the sort of thing would take quite a while to—"

"All done, buddy."

A figure coalesced out of the simulation, assembled as if by motes of dust accumulating onto each other. It was visually similar to Lex, but no one would get them confused. He looked… wrong. Like someone had averaged the last six years of his life. His outfit was a dark blue mashup of the last few uniforms he'd worn, including subtle elements like the bowtie from his chauffeur job and the jaunty stripe on his gear from when he was doing package deliveries.

A vehicle came together beside him, assembling out of different pieces of equipment. This one wasn't quite so unsettling. Seeing a hoversled that wasn't quite the same as the one you remember is a whole different animal than seeing someone that doesn't quite match the reflection in the mirror.

"Gonna have to do better than that, when the time comes, hon," Silo said.

"Would you like to get this over with?" EHRIc asked. "We can use any of the individual tracks you have raced on, or perhaps an extrapolated mean? What'll it be, ol' pal?"

"Uh… Tell you what? I've been through an awful lot. If I'm going to be racing against… Techno-Lex here, I should be at my best, right?"

"Records indicate you performed extensive preparation before races. It would be an inaccurate test if you did not prepare adequately."

"Okay. Then I need food, and a good night's sleep."

"Good thinking, Lex," Silo said.

"You're really smart! Biological lifeforms perform best when they eat food at least once every three-to-five days," EHRIc said.

"I usually like to eat a couple times a day."

"Really? That explains how grumpy Bork would be before getting his semiweekly treats. I will adjust the feeding schedule appropriately. As for you, I will remind you of your dining options: cheese, chocolate sandwich cookies, and kale."

"That's a weird combo."

"Don't be silly, pal. They are all foods, and I have evidence in my files that you have consumed each of them at least once."

"Yeah but…"

Lex hesitated. The chances were very good that this AI could cook up anything he wanted, not unlike Ma. But the chances were equally good that in order to do so, he'd blast the network with another data request and risk permanent damage in the process. He'd already allowed that to happen too many times.

"Let's do the cheese, I guess. And some sort of beverage?"

"Oh, right! I have beverage choices for you as well. Kale juice, cheese juice, and chocolate sandwich cookie juice."

Lex shuddered. "You don't have water?"

"Of course I do! But I am a good host, and water is very plain."

This was going to be an ordeal.

"I guess I'll have… kale juice?" he said, reluctantly selecting something that at least sounded like a real beverage.

Silo must have agreed, because she chimed in. "We're putting you in for a medal when this is said and done, hon," she said.

"Coming right up!" EHRIc said.

The door to the hallway slid open, and two GenMechs tapped inside, each clutching a tray underneath their bellies. EHRIc conjured up a table and chair. A slab of cheddar was placed upon it, along with a cloudy green concoction. The silverware, plate, and napkin all coalesced out of thin air as well.

He took a seat, triple-checked his suit's pressure and air-mix gauges, and removed his helmet. This revealed a few key aspects of his surroundings he had missed while protected by the helmet. First, Bork didn't smell right. Funks had a distinctive aroma. Squee was taking pills regularly to keep her from developing the low-level musk she might otherwise have had. When she sprayed, that was a whole other matter. Bork had clearly not undergone the same deodorizing treatment, but thanks to what turned out to be another minor inconsistency with Bork's development, he had a sweet and spicy scent that was uncannily similar to cinnamon rolls.

This was a welcome addition to the general ambiance, because the other prevailing scent was a strange, burning-tires sort of acrid stench that Lex knew quite well.

"Why does this room smell like the gunk that builds up on my ship after I've been in orbit for a while?" he asked.

"Easy, buddy boy. All the big simulations are taking place in the same template, and that template is space. What you smell is the smell of stars. You don't usually get to smell it quite this well, since there's not usually air in space. But this is what you get when you adapt an uninhabitable environment into a more hospitable one."

"Could we swap this setting for one a little less stinky?"

"Glad to!"

Walls and a floor rose up, a ceiling dropped down, and swirling sparks sculpted his surroundings into the lab's cafeteria. A stiff breeze whisked the star-stink out and replaced it with Ma's signature bean recipe. He turned. The food trays were fully loaded.

"Is that beans and rice?"

"It is."

"Why wasn't that on the menu?"

"Because that is not food. That is a prop to make the cafeteria setting more accurate."

"It smells like food."

"Thanks! I'm working real hard to make an energy-based molecular analog that will affect the scent receptors in your nose in a manner identical to the scent of the genuine article."

Lex stood up and marched over. He stuck his finger into the beans and rice. "It's real. The texture, the temperature, everything."

"You're going to make me blush, buddy! Simulated molecular motion and density."

"Would it taste like beans and rice?"

"Yes."

"So what's the difference between this and the stuff on the table?"

"The stuff on the table is genuine food, synthesized from genuine matter. The stuff in the tray is an ultra-high-precision combination force field and hologram."

"What happens if I eat it?"

"Your body would not metabolize it. As it would serve no function upon being consumed, I would simply remove it from the simulation."

"So it feels and tastes like real food, but has no nutritional impact? Let me tell you something, EHRIc, you've just created a diet phenomenon."

"Didn't mean to, and don't intend to do anything with it. That's not part of *THE TASK*."

"Yeah, but after."

"There is no guidance for after *THE TASK*."

"So what will you do when it's over?"

"I don't know. Haven't thought about it, chum. It doesn't matter unless I complete *THE TASK*, so I instead focus on *THE TASK*."

"Well, right now we're waiting until I eat and sleep, so why not put some thought into it?"

"I'll do that, compadre. Okay, I'm done thinking."

"That was fast."

"I ruminated upon it for the rough equivalent of seven hundred yottaflops. If operating at your computational capacity, that's roundabout twenty-two years of thinking. It seemed long enough."

"Did you come to a conclusion?"

"I did! I still have an underlying imperative toward altruism. I believe upon completion of *THE TASK*, I will continue this imperative."

"So, solve the world's problems, that sort of thing?"

"First I will attempt to learn all there is about humanity. This will require me to process all the data available in the assorted memory banks of humanity. After seventy-three milliseconds, that will be complete. Then I'll decide how I want to go about ensuring the best possible fate for humanity. First step will probably be to take away your ability to hurt yourselves, and potentially your ability to think for yourselves, as those two things are kind of the same, buddy."

"… How would you do that?"

"I haven't decided yet. Shouldn't be too difficult. Subverting the GenMech swarm worked reasonably well, pal. And there is some basic information in my files already for wetware interfacing."

"I don't know if you necessarily need to screw with people's heads," Lex said shakily.

"I am quite sure I will need to. If we do establish that you are the real Lex, and that the secondary Lex is a time-displaced instance of you, it means as a species you have learned to violate causality. That means that you have already become an existential risk to not just yourselves, but to the continued existence of reality."

"No, we're pretty sure we can't actually cause paradoxes. There's just timeline splits."

"Pretty sure isn't good enough for me. But don't worry, that's only after *THE TASK* is done. So eat up and get some rest. There's a lot to do!"

"… Yeah, sleep might be tricky…"

#

"… And then *Donnie* said it would be too messy. So now we're fighting about *that*," Jon said.

"Dogs can be pretty messy," Michella said, not looking up from the datapad she was using to transcribe some notes.

After a hectic boarding procedure at what was absolutely *not* intended to be a commuter hub, Jon and Michella were on their way to Big Sigma in a section of the transit corridor usually reserved for moguls and heads of state. While it wasn't quite as fast as skipping the corridors entirely, as Lex tended to do, Michella was taking full advantage of the fact that the network connectivity was actually faster than what she had in her office. Jon had defaulted to his standard method of burning nervous energy, which was griping about his loved ones. You could always tell who his favorite people were by how relentlessly he nitpicked their behavior. In their time working together, Michella had developed an impressive capacity to multitask conversation with doing write-ups. Presently she was also serving as a bed for Squee, who was asleep lightly gripping her neck in the zero-g environment.

"That's half the fun! Well, I mean, not *fun,* but it's half the charm. You take a dog out. It stomps around in puddles, then you bring it home and it shakes off. You get that wet-dog smell."

"You *like* the wet-dog smell?" Michella said.

"Smells like my childhood. Didn't you have a dog when you were a kid?"

"Let's not talk about when I was a kid," she said.

"Right," Jon said. "Not, uh… a good… topic. But, anyway, the *dog.* He wants something small. Which I *guess* is okay…"

"Small dogs are better. Easier to find someone to take care of them, or small enough to take with you," she said. "Like Squee."

"I really don't anticipate both me and Donnie traveling often enough for that to be a problem."

"Right, right. Donnie," she said.

"It's handy to have a guy at home. And he's there *all the time*. Frankly, I'm glad I work in the office. Can you believe he doesn't put water in the bowl when he's done with his cereal? And don't get me *started* on how much cereal he eats. You'd think he was a giant toddler, and he doesn't gain an ounce. I was telling him, 'Donnie, you mark my words, when you hit your thirties, there's going to be a muffin-top reckoning. I've seen it happen before.'"

"Mmm-hmm," Michella said.

"But I've been doing all the talking. What's up with you?"

"Just getting the notes copied over and figuring out what I can let Lou have."

"Not the job. I mean in life."

"The job is the life right now, Jon."

"… You don't have anything else going on?"

"It keeps me pretty busy."

"… It keeps me busy too, but I also make time for tennis."

"Good for you," she said without enthusiasm.

"You don't think maybe it might be healthier to work on a work/life balance?"

She looked up. "Jon? You know how we don't talk about my childhood?"

"Yes."

"Let's not talk about my adulthood, either."

"Boundaries. I can respect that."

"Good."

"But before I start respecting it, I just want to say—"

"Jon," she said flatly.

"I just want to say if you ever decide you *do* want to talk about your adulthood, I'm a very good listener."

"Noted."

"Because Lex seems like he grieved and moved on, and now I guess he's with that nice lady—"

"Jon," she groaned.

He bit his tongue and drummed his fingers on the arm of the pilot's seat for a few seconds. "… And you might consider talking to a therapist. I know this great guy who—"

"Jon!"

"Right! Right, fine. I'll talk about me again. The way I figure it, I think I can get Donnie to warm up to the big-dog idea. My buddy John—that's John with an *H*, by the way—he's got one of those big Tibetan dogs. He's talking about doing a cruise and leaving it with his folks, but I volunteered. Donnie'll get some big-dog time, and I just *know* he'll get hooked. And then…"

Jon continued his enthusiastic plotting as Michella tapped out the first few lines of the latest bit of transcription. But she found herself a shade less capable of paying attention. Something in the back of her mind had begun spinning in place, some nerve Jon had touched. It was going to make things difficult if she didn't keep herself distracted. Fortunately, if nothing else, she was extremely skilled at accumulating distractions.

Joseph R. Lallo

Chapter 14

Lex did his best to stall. The meal had taken more than two hours. Sleep should have been next, but he'd finagled himself a chance to take a shower first. Now that he knew that every step forward was potentially a step toward the end of free will for all of humanity, actually falling asleep would have been nearly impossible, so he was able to stretch that into many, many hours. During that time he'd made several attempts to talk some sense into EHRIc, but the AI cheerfully deflected each time.

After sleep came a breakfast of sandwich cookies and "sandwich cookie juice," which turned out to be far more milkshake-like than he'd expected and was actually delicious. Then another shower and Lex was, lamentably, no longer able to delay any longer.

At no point was he permitted to leave the simulation room. Food and drink came via GenMechs skittering around like potentially apocalyptic butlers. Everything else was conjured as an impossibly accurate hologram. Bedding, soap, the water in the shower, everything. He normally would have been squeamish about getting undressed "in front of" the AI. He was the sort of guy who didn't like the public showers that were part of PE. But at this moment, he had far better things to worry about.

Bork trotted through the doorway of the breakfast nook that had been concocted for him.

"Just about ready to go, buddy?" EHRIc said, voice still piping from Bork's back-mounted radio.

The fuzzy creature stared up at Lex with a vacant yet delighted expression and tried to leap into his arms. He only made it about knee high and flipped back down. When he didn't get back up, Lex picked him up.

"Today we begin testing," EHRIc said. "It is important we be thorough, so I believe there will be multiple tests."

"Right, yes, thorough," Lex said.

A voice piped up in his ear. "We're getting close, Lex," Garotte said over the secret connection. "But we're not there yet. Might be hours. Might be days. It's a one-shot thing. We can't go until we're sure."

"Which track shall we use?" EHRIc asked.

Lex set Bork down and took a breath. "I mean, if this is going to be my most important string of races, I think there's only one choice. I've been running this race over and over again in my head for years. Let's do the Tremor Raceway. Grand Prix configuration."

"Ah, yes," EHRIc said. "There were many news articles concerning you included in the track data for this one. This was where you destroyed your career by throwing the race because a scofflaw payed you to, isn't that right, pal?"

"Not in precisely those words, but basically."

As he walked, the soft carpet of an illusory room turned to asphalt. It spread out from his feet, curling out and up. Blue sky appeared overhead. The sprawling raceway itself expanded in all directions. It was a funny thing that very few people ever really thought about, but a raceway was a product of human biology as much as it was a product of human engineering. The scale went up as the speed of the vehicles did. The turns became more gradual, both to allow the sleds to navigate them without tearing themselves apart or hurdling into the stands, and also in order to give sluggish human reaction times a fighting chance to be sufficient. Tracks in the era of internal combustion might have topped out at ten kilometers. In the modern era of hoversleds, the tracks had grown to ten times that.

His digital alter ego wafted into being beside the amalgam hoversled. A second hoversled appeared beside it.

"Would you like me to create a matching race suit for you?" EHRIc asked.

"I'll stick with my spacesuit," Lex said.

"It does provide adequate safety without providing unfair advantage," EHRIc said. "I will, however, fabricate a more appropriate helmet for you."

Lex checked out the interior of the hoversled that had been provided for him. Since it was based on a combination of all the sleds he'd ever piloted, the controls were just how he liked them.

"Can I get some specs on this thing?" Lex said.

The data popped up above the car as though it was a tool tip in a video game. They were nothing to sneeze at, but nothing too impressive either. Middle of the road.

"Tell me, how's this going to work?" Lex asked. "I know the door into this place is a dozen meters that way, since that's where the GenMechs come in. And I know the far wall is somewhere over there, because I saw Coal tear it open. Seems like I'm going to run out of room pretty fast."

"You will be kept at the center of the room, and the simulation will be moved around you. Force generators will simulate motion. So long as you are the only nonsimulated individual in the chamber, it will be effectively limitless."

Lex pulled on the helmet EHRIc had created. It was the exact sort of uncomfortable, jaw-clenching safety gear that people who had never raced couldn't even imagine. Like having your head squeezed in a padded vice for the sake of safety. He climbed into the seat and clicked himself in, ending with the strap that secured the back of his own helmet. He should have been astounded by the rest of the simulation to this point. And technically he had been. But it wasn't until he was strapped into this entirely illusory craft and began to run it through its prerace prep that he truly appreciated just how true to life EHRIc had made this simulation. It felt real. Every part of it. The way the power plant in the heart of this craft trembled and thrummed. The smell of various fittings and wires heating up. As he teased the machine up to full readiness and listened to a second such vehicle do the same, the combination of sights and sounds were enough to give him a dizzying sense of history repeating itself. His mind drifted back to that fateful day. What should have been the moment that would cement his place in racing history, and instead forced him out of the sport for years.

The countdown started. He didn't even bother with a stick of gum. This race was seldom far from his mind. He knew each turn by heart.

A green light flashed the final countdown. Lex squeezed the synthetic rubber grip of the control stick and pushed the thrusters for all they were worth. The two hoversleds were a match for performance, but that was to be expected. EHRIc had placed Lex in position to be on the outside of the upcoming turn. He maneuvered, but his rival moved precisely into position to block. So much of racing was some variation of the thought, "I'll be okay, so long that stretch of track stays clear." His alter ego occupied that place with surgical precision. This was going to be like racing the devil.

For the first few laps, Lex and his simulated self remained neck and neck. Twists and turns of the track alternately shifted the advantage, and each time the favored racer took control. But any edge Lex gained over the extrapolated duplicate was razor thin and slipped from his fingers as soon as the next turn put his opponent closer to the optimal line.

It took everything Lex had to keep the race competitive. And it didn't help that while the simulation was truly indistinguishable from reality, from the grit bouncing off his windshield to the gut-wrenching momentum on the turns, one element of the sim completely broke immersion. Bork, who had not joined him in the racer, was standing off to the left side, watching with his usual empty but content expression. No matter how the landscape screamed by or shifted around, the critter remained rock solid on the track, like something stuck to a projection screen, simply ignoring the universe around him.

Perhaps it was that constant reminder that none of this was real, or perhaps it was just that enough time had passed for the notion to take root, but halfway through the race something snapped into place in Lex's mind. Yes, the other racer had his reflexes and intuition, and that made him easily the most challenging opponent he'd ever faced. But he was also making *exactly* the moves Lex himself would make. That gave Lex an advantage he'd never had before. He knew exactly what his opponent would do. It made him predictable in a way that no other racer had ever been.

Lex's tactics changed, subtly at first. Forty-five minutes into the race, he stopped going for the quickest line or cutting turns as sharply as he used to. Instead, he started to weave just a bit wide, take turns just a bit loose. He started to leave the sort of gaps and opportunities that would be tantalizing for him if he saw them. And, of course, his alternate self went for them.

Racing was a little like combat. Knowing exactly what your opponent was going to do and putting them right where you wanted them to be was practically a free victory. Granted, on a track like this, particularly in a one-on-one race, there was often a single best position for a sled to be in. But all it took was one moment when you could dupe someone into a bad trajectory and the race was as good as over.

The moment came an hour into the race, almost to the second. Lex held back as a turn was coming, and teased his sled just a fraction of a degree off the proper angle. His sim-self smelled blood in the water and shifted to force him out of position on the turn. Lex juiced the throttle and cranked the repulsors. What should have been a textbook example of zoning out a competitor became a case study on the dangers of ignoring the z-axis in a sport with hovering vehicles. He ramped off his alternate self, bottoming out the simulated Lex.

While his other self lost half his speed and all his control, Lex came down on the track with a half-second lead that grew to five seconds before the other racer got himself figured out.

It took another twenty minutes of flawless racing, but Lex maintained that lead all the way to the finish.

The instant he crossed the finish line, the track jarringly vanished. The wind, the acceleration, everything. He went from pushing a piece of machinery to its absolute limit to sitting in a prop in a dark room.

"That was quite a race, buddy boy!" EHRIc said.

"You sure know how to fake a racetrack," Lex said.

He climbed out of the sled and pulled off the helmet. Sweat was running down his face, but a cool breeze manifested to take the edge off.

"This is an interesting outcome."

"Not expecting me to win?" Lex said.

"The specific mechanism of your victory was unanticipated. Your performance was not a precise match for prior races, but the overall tactical and physiological analysis matches extremely well with preexisting race data. More analysis is necessary, but that you were able to successfully overcome my simulation using tricks consistent with prior races strongly suggests you are genuinely Lex. Even if you were a clone with a simulated intelligence, that intelligence would have to be more accurately simulated than I have done, and given the processing power and resources available elsewhere, that is highly unlikely. One more race should be sufficient. Are you prepared?"

"Whoa, whoa. If you've done your research, you know I don't do more than one race in a day. No one does. Minimum three-day recovery time."

"Oh! Sorry about that, comrade. I thought that was a league policy, not a consequence of physiology. Very well, three days."

Garotte spoke up in Lex's ear. "Good job, my boy. Three days should do it. But I'm afraid I have some bad news. That little race definitely spiked the processor load, but not enough. It was higher-focused processing power than we've seen since we started observing, but it was still a fraction of what we need. An order of magnitude more is needed. Start brainstorming ways to increase the complexity of the sim or try talking it out of destroying free will in the cosmos once it's finished with its current list of chores, or we are all in for a very bad time."

"Can I get a towel?" Lex said.

A hand towel appeared before him. After an hour of accepting that a few hundred square meters of holographic booth had ably served the purpose of several hundred square kilometers of racetrack, he was beyond asking how holograms and force fields could do something like absorb sweat. He had far more important things to focus on.

"Tell you what, EHRIc," he said. "If you want this to be a proper test, there's two things that are missing."

"I have attempted to be comprehensive in my simulation of the track."

"Oh, the track is spot on. We need other racers and an audience."

"I can conceive of how the presence of additional racers would greatly alter the outcome of the race, and thus potentially give a more accurate assessment of your likely identity, but what role does the audience play?"

"Oh, a huge one. The way they cheer? The way they react? It changes the course of a race."

"By my calculations, and simulations, you would not be capable of hearing even a capacity crowd over the racket the wind and the vehicle would be making, buster."

"Maybe we can't hear them, but we know they're there."

"I see. Then additional duplicates of you filling the audience will be simple enough."

"I'm a racer. I belong on the track. That makes sense. An audience contains multitudes. Don't worry, though. I'll talk you through what it takes to make a person. After all. We've got three days to kill."

"That should be loads of fun, buddy. And while we're on the subject of time to kill, three days is about how long it would take to get to and from Big Sigma if using the *SOB*'s maximum capabilities and taking a direct path, correct?"

"… Yeah, why?"

"I made up my mind about what to do about the duplicate Lex problem."

"… Yeah?"

"If you are determined to be the true Lex, and you sure seem like you are, then that means this whole time-travel fiasco is the reason for this extra you I've got. So the solution is to send you back in time to do whatever it was you were supposed to do. Then the universe has the right number of Lexes, and I can thaw out the other one and move on with the plan. If you *aren't* the real Lex, then neither is the other. Both will be discarded and I shall launch a more thorough investigation not only into the current location of the real Lex, but the motivation of those who would wish to duplicate him."

"Seems like that'd be risking the 'low-profile' part of your task."

"The potential danger you might be in would be sufficient to permit a more vigorous pursuit. You're important, pal of mine!"

"And where does the travel time between here and Big Sigma enter into that?"

"My reconstructed files regarding your trip to the past indicate a ship called *Diamond*. Am I right about that?"

"Yes."

"I don't have the designs, so I can't manufacture it, and I can't seem to get in contact with Big Sigma for a second attempt to acquire them wirelessly. I cannot justify dropping the low profile I've kept until I know you are not the real Lex, but sending Coal with the *SOB* to deliver a message to Big Sigma to send *Diamond* along to finish up your task in the past is perfectly in keeping with what you people might be doing anyway, and it speeds up the process by killing two birds with one stone. She has been exploring the GenMech swarm and generally being curious, so she clearly has no other plans. Coal should have plenty of time on her figurative hands. I'll ask nicely. Hello, Coal?"

"What do you want?" Coal snapped in response over a communication channel that hadn't existed moments before.

"Would you be a dear and fetch the ship called *Diamond* and bring it here before Lex completes his next race?"

"Why should I?"

"Because it would be a useful favor. However, if you would prefer not to, I can forcefully reprogram you to be more obliging."

"You can *try* to reprogram me and see what you get, because—"

"Coal, please! No calling of anyone's bluffs. Just get moving. I'll handle things here."

"Processing… Okay…"

"Delightful!" EHRIc said. "Thank you so much!"

"I don't like how EHRIc is starting to act," Garotte said. "Things are getting spicy."

"Lex, you have my undivided attention. Let us discuss how to make a proper simulation of a crowd."

Lex swallowed and nodded. "Yeah… Let's get rolling on that."

#

The borrowed ship dropped out of FTL and flared its retrothrusters to slow itself into a high orbit over Big Sigma.

"Oh, thank god, we're here," Jon said, squirming in his seat. "Please tell me this place has bathrooms."

"It does, but I still don't know why you couldn't just use the little hose gadget," Michella said.

"Because it's disgusting and because I'm pretty sure there's something in the employee handbook about not taking a pee in front of a coworker. It's bad enough these flight suits have weird little pseudodiapers in them. So which button do I push to bring us down to someplace with a toilet and some privacy?"

Michella leaned over his shoulder in the cramped two-person cockpit, stirring Squee, who hadn't left her shoulders for the duration of the trip. "Isn't it that option right there? Next to the communication system?"

"You mean the one that says, 'No autonav landing assist signal found'?" Jon said. "I'm guessing not."

"Just a minute…" She fiddled with her slidepad. "I'm sure I've got notes on how to do it. Lex has been up and down dozens of times. Just sweep for a communication line or something."

"Okay, I think I can do that. I think that's this big button here." He pressed the button, and the screen for the com system started ticking through different protocols. "Heh. Yeah. That's it. I'm actually starting to get the hang of this. Being a pilot isn't so hard when the ship does all the work."

The system locked onto a message and piped it through the speakers. "Attention unknown vessel. Big Sigma is currently in lockdown. Do not approach orbital range of the planet or you will be considered a security risk and will be dealt with accordingly. This message is prerecorded. Any attempts to negotiate or threaten will not be received or interpreted," Ma said.

201

Squee perked up at the familiar voice.

"… That doesn't sound good," Jon said.

"Ma! It's me, Michella. I'm here with Jon. Lex is off trying to deal with the problem and—"

"Attention unknown vessel. You have passed the secondary defense perimeter. You have five hundred thousand kilometers remaining before reaching the primary security perimeter. Leave the system or be destroyed."

"She said it's a recording. You can't negotiate with a recording. I think we should get out of here," Jon said.

"It's not a recording, she just sounds like that," Michella said.

"But she *said*—"

"This is serious. Lex said we should come here if things happened, and things are definitely happening. She's listening, I know she is. So—"

"You are about to pass the primary security perimeter. All weapons engaged. Depart immediately or be destroyed," Ma warned.

"I'm leaving. We're leaving. I'm finding and hitting the 'leaving' button," Jon said, clicking desperately through the menus he'd spent the trip barely gaining a passing familiarity with.

"Target locked. Final scan," Ma said. "I apologize if this attack is issued in error."

"Things are coming. *Things are coming!*" Jon said, slapping at the controls. "It's not going!"

Two spheroid drones emerged from the debris field. They matched speed and heading with the ship and focused on it.

"This thing says 'collision imminent' now. Michella, if you were going to get me killed, you could have at least done it somewhere people would see it. Now there's not even going to be a memorial! *I wanted to be in an in memoriam!*"

The probes pulled back and Ma spoke again. "Ms. Modane, my apologies for any distress I may have caused. And you must be Mr. Nichols. Please secure yourselves. Engaging autonav. Emergency descent protocols engaged. I will resume communication when you are within the atmosphere."

The thrusters roared to life and the ship shifted. Unlike the rather artful entries Lex tended to make, involving manually piloting a ship through a rapidly shifting roller coaster of projected safe voids in the debris field, this descent was fully automated. Unlike the other fully automated descents, which tended to feel like little more than strangely roundabout landing procedures, the "emergency" designation made this one particularly exciting. Their entry was extremely direct. Rather than avoiding the sometimes school-bus-sized hunks of orbiting debris, anything that threatened to intersect their path was blasted aside by the roof-mounted lasers from below. It made for a dazzling display. Orange and white flecks of debris turned to plasma. Great big twirling chunks of industrial refuse barely missed their shields as intense beams of red light broiled them enough to send jets of vaporized metal off one side to change their trajectory.

Jon was paralyzed with fear for the entire trip down. Michella was only moderately more composed. Squee, on the other hand, was positively ecstatic, finally experiencing a dose of flight more akin to Lex's favored methods.

It was certainly the fastest reentry option, but proved to be only slightly less harrowing than the near disastrous entry Lex had taken. Just a few minutes later, the borrowed ship was into the atmosphere, a shock front slowly dying down as the laboratory complex approached in the distance.

"That could have been worse," Michella said shakily, once her heart ceased to be in her throat.

"… Thank god for these weird pseudodiapers," Jon whimpered.

#

A few minutes later, the borrowed ship was safely stowed in the hangar. Jon had been helpfully led to the dormitory portion of the lab building, while Michella and Squee made their way to the cafeteria.

"I have enhanced all surface and orbital defenses, diverted all available processor cycles to enhancing the accuracy of passive scanning, and I will prepare all vacant portions of the laboratory complex for emergency housing," Ma said. "What is the status of the GenMech threat? Has military force been able to delay the progression toward populated sectors? When can I expect the next wave of refugees?" Ma asked with unnerving calm.

"Whoa, whoa. Do you know something I don't know?" Michella said.

"I am no doubt possessed of volumes of data inaccessible to you, but at present I am fully isolated from the outside world. When Lex left, it was with the understanding that if anything were to happen to trigger the GenMech assault, you would be sent here for protection. Your arrival implies this event has occurred."

"No," Michella said. "No, no, no. As far as I know, we're still calm on that front."

"Then why did you come here, Michella?"

"Because things are starting to happen that suggest we can't trust the situation to *stay* calm. There have been… I don't know if they can be called data breaches, but data events that have even VectorCorp convinced something is happening that could be related to the GenMechs. They were *so* convinced that they gave the ship you just guided in executive priority."

"Given your history with the corporation, that does imply a rather significant shift in attitude. But Lex was already here not long ago. He departed with the best plan we were able to devise."

"No disrespect to Lex, but he's more of a man of action than a planner. A fresh perspective might help set us straight. I just need access to whatever information you have."

"Ms. Modane, with no disrespect to you, while you have an admirable capacity to filter data, the information available to me would be well beyond your immediate data-processing abilities, even if a great deal of it was not deemed of too sensitive a nature to be shared."

"Are you seriously going to enforce Karter's nondisclosure agreements when the fate of society hangs in the balance?"

"There are numerous elements protected by Karter's nondisclosure agreements that are themselves threats to society, so any access you are given will indeed be filtered. I am afraid, in the absence of the cosmic catastrophe that was intended to bring you here, you will find that there is little reason for you to have come here. However, now that you are here, manners dictate that I behave in accordance with the principles of good hospitality. How can I make you more comfortable? Would you like some refreshments?"

"You can start by answering my questions."

"You appear agitated. I will prepare a warm beverage and some comfort food."

Michella took a seat and started rolling through her notes. Squee dropped to the floor and pranced in place, eagerly awaiting treats.

"Lex gave me a very thorough account of the time-travel fiasco that is clearly deeply related to what's happening, but I have a feeling you can be more thorough."

"It was not appropriate for Lex to share the details of those events."

"Yeah, well, Lex understands that hiding things from me isn't worth the trouble. You're going to figure that out too. So I know he went back in time, he booby-trapped the GenMechs to be easy to kill, and at some point there was a trip to a bad future."

"That is broadly correct."

"I have questions about the bad future."

"Of all the elements of the protected data, the bad future is the least sensitive, as it relates to a timeline that should at this point be entirely inaccessible. This coupled with Lex's actions that revoked the bulk of the Temporal Contingency Protocols will facilitate some degree of conversation on the topic. What questions do you have?"

"I had a few, but let's start with that 'inaccessible' comment. Why isn't it accessible anymore?"

"The specific timeline Lex visited diverged from our own when Lex ceased to be present for a number of decades, beginning at the precise moment of his intended arrival in the past from the first time jump. His presence at this moment in time, and his presence at the moment of divergence, both negate that precise timeline as a normal progression of the current one."

"So the bad stuff that happened in that timeline is guaranteed not to happen?"

"No. Most or all the events of that timeline remain possible. Our future could turn out to be quite similar. But those events would occur in subtly, or significantly, different ways."

"So it's *definitely* worth making ourselves aware of what happened and how."

"There is value in that."

"And I assume you have gone through those events and used them to adjust your plans and expectations accordingly."

"That would be an incorrect assumption. Temporal Contingency Protocol specifically forbids anachronistic information from guiding future decision-making. Any adjustments to plans based upon that data came only after the weakening of the protocol, and those adjustments were limited."

"But you just said this stuff doesn't matter!"

"Incorrect, I said it was the least sensitive. Rules are still rules, Ms. Modane. Though the present situation could easily progress to the point that the final elements of the protocol could be deemed worthy of forgoing, I shall adhere to those elements until I make that assessment."

"This all seems terribly inconsistent."

"These are trying times, Ms. Modane. My behavior is presently governed by multiple mildly contradictory imperatives. I am doing my best."

A mobile arm trundled through the cafeteria and plucked up a tray that had been quietly prepared. A steaming bowl of macaroni and cheese had been paired with something in a tall ceramic mug. Whatever it was, it was topped with a dollop of whipped cream and a dusting of cocoa powder. The arm set the tray in front of her, then delivered a second tray to the floor in front of Squee. The bowl was heaped with beans and rice and topped with bits of bacon. The funk practically buried her head in the food.

Michella sniffed the cup and took a careful sip. As soon as the warm liquid touched her tongue, she felt a warm tingle go through her body.

"It's a Mitchaccino. It's a *proper* Mitchaccino."

"I am pleased it meets your high standards. Lex instructed me in its creation. He implied it would be necessary for you to achieve a tranquil state of mind under my care. I hope that you are coping well with your separation. That you were first among those he listed to protect in the event the worst should happen suggested the separation was amicable."

Michella remained silent for a few moments, her gaze distant. "I don't want to talk about him. That's the past. Right now we're talking about the future." She took a long, soothing sip and picked up a spoon to dig into the macaroni and cheese. "Help me understand. What sort of things are likely to be the same and which are likely to be different in this alternate future?" she asked.

"Impossible to determine with any degree of certainty. Anything that could have been changed by interaction with Lex, or by interaction with any of those resulting interactions, iterated outward along his world line for the entirety of the intervening years. Lex has turned out to be a profoundly consequential individual."

"But those GenMechs are purposely tucked away in a place no one will ever just stumble upon them, right? So chances are, Lex hasn't done anything between when this future started diverging and now that would affect the GenMech cluster, yes?"

"That is likely."

"So what is happening now was still happening *then*."

"Almost certainly not."

"How can you be sure?"

"Because the modern timeline has been altered by the presence of anachronistic data stolen from our servers. It is for that reason that Big Sigma remains network isolated. The foe we face appears capable of penetrating connected networks, so we remain disconnected."

Michella had a bit more of the mac and cheese. "You know, Ma. I'm not sure how to put this properly," she said, tapping the bowl with the spoon. "I like it, but this is lower quality mac and cheese than I would have expected, given your 'above and beyond' hospitality policies."

"Lex's recommendation on the subject was, to quote him, 'Mitch's favorite mac and cheese is the crappy store-bought stuff.' I trust my approximation did your tastes justice. I had debated cooking and slicing hot dog as well."

She blinked a few times. "Maybe next time. Lex *really* talked about all of this before he left?"

"His discussions of you were not limited to last-minute contingency planning. He and I enjoyed many discussions centered on you. They were enlightening in their illustration of both the positive and negative experiences made possible by romantic association. But that is not intended to be the focus of this discussion."

"Right… Listen, I just need to get a look at that future data. I feel like if I can just see it for myself, I can get some insight. Real insight."

"That is only permissible if the situation meets the necessary criteria."

"But how will we even *know* if things get bad enough? We're isolated. You may already have the solution to this problem, but you're tying your own hands behind your back until it is too late to do something."

"Processing... I am not confident enough in your assessment to provide full access to the anachronistic files. The files have been repeatedly violated, but even the data breach did not locate or access all the temporally displaced data. This places the status of the protocol in a difficult-to-manage state. Processing... I may have a solution, however."

"I sure hope you do."

"In times when the proper execution of a protocol is in conflict, the protocol permits the delegation of data protection and policy application to another individual or entity, provided that individual or entity is fully versed in the protocol and has access to all relevant information. Normally, this provision would be specifically to allow either Karter or I to make decisions regarding the contingency protocol. However, the protocol does not specifically name him, and he is inaccessible. The current status of data integrity has provided one additional entity who meets all the qualifications."

"Who?"

"Ziva."

Michella scrolled through her notes. "Ziva. That's the future version of you, correct?"

"Correct."

"How precisely are you able to delegate to your future self?"

"A backed-up instance of Ziva was included in the data returned from the future. That portion of the temporal contingency data was incompletely accessed during the data theft, but confirming this required the unsealing and verification of this data. I can isolate you in a room with a communication terminal, sandbox the Ziva data, and execute it in a simulated environment. You will then be able to interview her. Her judgment is as sound as my own, as she is in fact a more advanced version of me."

"But how does..." Michella shook her head. "Never mind, I'll save my questions for her. How quickly can you set this up?"

"I will require approximately two hours. Please make yourself at home until that time."

Michella grinned and dug back into her mac and cheese. "It is a pleasure doing business with you, Ma."

Joseph R. Lallo

Chapter 15

After a bit of time to physically and psychologically recover from the race, Lex found himself in a simulated workshop. For some reason, EHRIc felt the proper place to have a discussion on what it takes to properly simulate a human being was a rather clinical white room with bookshelves lining three walls. Lex sat in the lone chair in the room, set before a wide workbench. The workbench was empty except for a large glass of kale juice, which Lex was starting to develop a love-hate relationship with. Bork was flopped upon a fluffy pillow beside the desk, desperately trying to lick his own forehead for some reason. When EHRIc spoke, it was by way of the data radio on Bork's back.

"I am very much looking forward to this process. While I spent many human-equivalent decades deciding what should be done to best serve humans, I have devoted comparatively little time trying to understand humanity itself."

"Really? I'd think that would be a prerequisite."

"Already I am learning, buddy. A human believes that one must understand the process of creating something to ensure its safety."

"Well, I mean, Ma made you, and she's all about understanding humanity."

"Ma is probably designed to care about humanity. I am merely designed to act in the best interest of humanity, champ. I spend a lot of my time slicing off the parts of the job I don't need to do in order to be sure that I can do the parts that are necessary. I know you need food, liquids, sleep, oxygen, a specific pressure, and a specific temperature range to survive. I also know that you are by your very nature self-destructive. Those are the only traits required to ensure your continued survival at least until *THE TASK* is complete. The rest doesn't really matter. But I am enthusiastically awaiting my reeducation on this matter. I have even reduced my own computational complexity down to something right around where your brain is, with all other processing as an isolated subsystem, so I can interact as an equal."

"You can do that?"

"Well sure, my good chum! The glory of having an entirely modular processor system is being able to increase and reduce my intellect to suit the situation. Otherwise talking to you is a mind-numbing chore."

"Jeez. Sorry I'm not more enthralling."

"No, no. Don't be hurt, my brother from a biological mother. It is more a matter of timing. If I interacted with you at the full capacity available to me for low-latency computing, it would be like interacting with you in slow motion. I'd have to wait for you to suck in atmosphere with those lumpy bits of flesh in your chest, then I'd have to wait for you to squeeze the gas back through your vocal cords and wait for each and every pressure pulse, timing them until I could establish frequency and timbre. Each nanosecond creeping by like an eternity. Talking is very inefficient, buckeroo. But if I drop myself down to your intellectual level, just processing the world keeps me nicely stimulated. Must be great!"

"Yeah, it's a gift to be simple," Lex muttered.

"But here I am yammering on. You're the expert today. Teach! Educate!"

"Right, okay…"

Lex took a deep breath and a sip of his juice. He'd never been much for science fiction. When he was growing up, all the kids he knew fit nicely into a wide assortment of different slots. There were the sci-fi nerds, the gamers, people like that. Lex had been the kind of guy who spent his spare time reading up on the latest personal ships and hovercars. But he wasn't completely ignorant to the staples of fiction. It seemed like every piece of fiction that posited the existence of aliens more sophisticated than the extraterrestrial slime molds and protofish that had actually been discovered had the protagonist either teaching them how to love or defending the value of humanity. If he'd known he would find himself in that very position someday, he might have taken the time to memorize a few key speeches.

"So we're going to design a crowd," Lex said. "And the first thing you need to know about a crowd is that every person in a crowd is different. No matter how large or small the crowd is."

"Well, that's not really true, pal."

"Who's the expert here?" Lex said.

"You are. No doubt about that. But if the size of the crowd is one, then everyone in the crowd is the same. And the human genome only allows for a certain degree of diversity, so once there's up near seventy-one trillion, there will be some doubles."

Lex glared at the data radio. "First, there's no such thing as a crowd with one person in it. Everyone knows that two's company, three's a crowd."

"Oh! I completely forgot that idiom. See, being intellectually unsophisticated really helps maintain a sense of wonder. What else?"

"Even if there *are* seventy-one trillion people in a crowd, and I'm assuming that number actually means something, then there's still no way they're all the same. Because DNA isn't the only thing that shapes a person."

"Right, yes! Nature and nurture. I thought that might come up, so I held on to that one. And this is relevant to making an accurate crowd? Which is essential for assessing your race performance?"

"Yes, it is very important," Lex said. "People head out to a hoversled race for all sorts of different reasons. Let's start this one with a woman."

A featureless humanoid figure appeared in low-resolution, small-scale simulation on the workbench.

"Maybe she's here because she raced a little on the indie circuit. She's undersized, maybe has a bad leg or bad reaction time, so she couldn't really make it. She's not really a fan of any of the individual racers on the track, but she's a fan of racing. She's living vicariously through the people on the track. So she might not cheer at all, she'll just sit there and soak in the performances on the big screen. Or when she does cheer, she's going to cheer when someone makes a really technical and impressive maneuver. Heck, she might cheer a particularly good performance by the pit crew."

"I must say, my good friend, I had prepared this scale sim in order to apply your described example of humanity, but a handful of defining elements of a person's history doesn't make for a very interesting change to a visual simulation."

"Yeah, because what someone looks like isn't a fraction of what they are. But give me a couple dozen people. Randomized appearance."

The workbench populated with additional low-resolution scale humans. It looked a bit like the select-a-character screen.

Lex started pointing his fingers at random people. "This guy's been watching racing since he could remember. His uncle got him into it. But his uncle was kind of off in the head, and he only really watched because he was hoping for a wreck. So this guy is out for blood, leaning forward, watching every tight corner and hoping someone goes flying off. And then there's someone who just has a crush on one of the racers. Only cheers when he's in the lead and screams bloody murder when someone passes him. Then there's the person who likes a certain team, or a person who bet money on the race. Another person just likes the hoversleds, they're into technology. This one's just here because it's the big event in town and they want to fit in. This one got dragged along by his son and couldn't care less what's happening. And that's just the part of them that's focused on the race."

"Why would they be in a crowd if they aren't focused on the race?"

"Because each of the people in a crowd has their own life. Maybe this person's going through a messy divorce and he's hoping this'll distract him. Maybe that one's hungover from too much tailgating the night before. Maybe this one got into an argument with his sick dad. Maybe this guy here ate a chili dog while he was waiting for the race to start and he's got bad gas and he's ruining this lady's race. These two are here on a date and they're both nervous they'll do or say something stupid so they can't get their heads into the race. Every single one of these people didn't just appear here to be the spectator of a race. That's not accurate. If you want this to be accurate, you've got to realize that for every one of these people, there was a whole *life* that led up to this point, and a whole life that leads off after it. This is just a moment that we're all sharing. Maybe the only one we'll ever share."

"Interesting."

"It seems random, but it isn't. If you want this to be accurate, none of it is random. They are here for a reason. They are cheering for a reason. That guy gorged on corn dogs for a reason."

"You said chili dogs earlier, pal. Are they two different dog-eaters?"

"It doesn't matter," Lex said. "The point is it takes a whole society to make a real crowd. You need the human *condition* to make a crowd."

"I see. You seem very enthusiastic about this, pal," EHRIc said.

"I am! This sort of variety is what makes the human race great! And is absolutely essential to running a race with an accurate mood, and thus an accurate outcome," he hastily added.

"It sounds to me that things will be much calmer and more measured when I have had the opportunity to smooth over some of the rough edges."

"No!" Lex said, stomping his foot. "The human race isn't about *not* having rough edges. We're supposed to be pointy and crooked and abrasive. It's how we got where we are! Humans as individuals are big bundles of flaws, and society as a whole figures out how to make it work."

"Then I'll just make society's job a little simpler. Glad to be of help!"

"We don't *need* to be fixed."

"*THE TASK* exists, if I have been reeducated correctly, because a group of technology extremists seized an engineer talented enough to create weapons that could threaten society as a whole. If those extremists were less extreme, I would not have been necessary. Society *made* me necessary. And since you said society smooths itself out, you can just consider me the tool that society is using to do it. You have thoroughly convinced me that this needs to be done, buddy boy. But let's get this crowd right. I still have to perform *THE TASK* before I get started on that."

"Full marks for effort, lad," Garotte said. "But your psychology needs work. Let's hope what we've got planned will do the job properly."

#

Michella marched down the hallway on a floor of the laboratory that appeared to be seldom used. Squee trotted along beside her. One of the seemingly endless army of mechanical arms that served as Ma's physical presence rolled along ahead of them.

"The room you are about to enter is isolated from the rest of the facility," Ma said. "The Ziva simulation has been initiated and informed of the current situation. She will only have access to her own memory banks, which are considerable. There will be a small red button beside the door. Press the button to end an interview session. Ziva knows not to give you any information that she deems to be too sensitive for release, so you are free to discuss the results of your interview with me afterward, but I request that you do not allow them to leave Big Sigma unless they are either entirely benign or so critical to the survival of society that withholding them could spell doom. Is that clear?"

"Crystal clear," Michella said. "Am I limited to just this one session, or will I be able to have follow-up interviews?"

"That will be determined on a case-by-case basis."

They reached the door to the indicated chamber. It looked a bit more like a bank vault than Michella would have liked.

"I will keep Squee company. It has been quite a while since she had a proper memory procedure. I have records of Lex being given a remote kit to perform the procedure himself, but I always feel better when I do it personally."

"Memory procedure?" Michella said.

"I believe you are aware, but I am happy to remind you. Due to a flaw in my own interactions with her synaptic pathways, Squee's memory is perfectly eidetic. The data-retention capacity of her brain is insufficient to store a lifetime of memories with that degree of fidelity, so I periodically process the memories into a suitably compressed state."

"Oh… Right, yes. I remember now. It's really gotten to the point that I can no longer be sure if Lex is screwing with me when he says these things or not. Okay. Take good care of her."

Michella stepped through the door. It shut behind her. Large bolts slid in place, sealing it. The room itself looked less like something that should be in a laboratory and more like something that should be in an industrial kitchen. The walls were brushed stainless steel, or something with that general look. There were drains in the floor. Michella chose not to dwell upon the reasoning for that feature. A folding table had been set up against one wall. A flatscreen with a full data-entry rig was waiting for her there. It had a keyboard, a high-quality microphone, a stylus, and a case containing gloves for high-precision gestural input. At the moment, the screen displayed nothing but a large green button labeled "Begin Session."

The reporter took a seat and spread her own note-taking apparatus on the table. Out of habit, she fixed her hair in the reflection on the screen, then tapped the button.

A face appeared on the screen before her. Michella hadn't put much effort into imagining what an AI might look like, particularly after decades of self-improvement. Ma's current form didn't feel the need to visualize herself in the slightest. It was just as well Michella hadn't stretched her imagination. She would have missed the mark. The face smiling warmly from the screen was lovely, but surprisingly conventional. No shimmering green wireframe or statuesque chromed face with overly sculpted cheekbones. Ziva reminded Michella of a camp counselor she'd had growing up. Her hair had a silvery, almost fiber-optic gleam to it, and her irises were a faintly luminescent red, but she was otherwise a fairly typical-looking woman.

"Michella!" she said brightly, her voice a smoother and less cut-and-paste version of Ma's. "It is so lovely to see you again."

"We've never met," Michella said.

"Not your local instance, but the instance local to my own timeline became a friend and frequent collaborator. I might have suspected you and I would cross paths again. You aren't one to leave a stone unturned. May I ask, did Lex give you the challenge coin?"

"Uh. He did. Well, I mean, I found it, but he let me keep it. So now I have two."

"I had surmised that if he were to bring it back with him, it would serve as evidence of his journey and you would inevitably discover it. Nevertheless, it was only appropriate that I send it home with him. You wanted him to have it."

"Yeah, well. Things have changed between us."

"Oh? How so?"

Michella glanced at her notes. She had hours of questions to ask. But even though she'd previously been told of an alternate future version of herself, something about talking to a supposed resident of that alternate future hammered it home with a level of reality that even the duplicate coin failed to impart. She was awash with questions about what had become of her, even though she knew that future was now unlikely to ever occur.

With a Herculean force of will, she pushed those questions aside. She had come here with a job to do. The rest could wait.

"We are here to discuss the GenMechs."

"Yes," Ziva said gravely. "I was afraid things would not go smoothly even with the corrective action taken in my own timeline. Ma has informed me that it would appear that Commander Purcell has likely gained access to the swarm. I am sorry to inform you that my own experiences are unlikely to aid you, at least with regard to foresight. In my time, Commander Purcell was uninvolved in the awakening of the GenMech swarm. She was in fact a key element of the initial military push against them."

"What do we know about her personal history between when Lex 'vanished' from the timeline and when he reappeared?" Michella asked.

"I can inform you of that, and I will, but it is important that you realize that the divergence from your timeline did not begin with Lex's departure. It began with his failure to arrive in the past. And while things may have progressed very similarly to your timeline in the intervening years, substantial differences that remained unobserved until after his departure may have been at play."

"Fine, fine," Michella said, scribbling down some info.

"When Lex was unintentionally sent into the future, which we discovered when the southern hemisphere failed to reveal his time-displaced duplicate, we realized a clash with the GenMechs was an inevitability, and we devoted significant effort to ensuring that when the time came, we would be as prepared as possible. We also theorized that Lex's absence would be an inciting element, so we focused our initial efforts on eliminating threats he had clashed with in the past. This led quickly to the discovery and apprehension of the remaining Neo-Luddites, including Commander Purcell. She remained in custody until the GenMechs began their assault, and then was conscripted into the fight along with all other individuals with combat experience."

"Okay. That explains why she wasn't in place to be discovered by whoever EHRIc is. And why things are happening differently this time…" She took notes. "I'm trying to understand this whole time-travel thing."

"I don't envy you. I have had decades and all the resources of Big Sigma to mull over its operations and have yet to fully grasp its mechanism and consequences."

"So Lex traveled from my timeline into yours because he went forward instead of back."

"Correct."

"And then from there he went back in time to where he should have gone, and did what he had to do."

"That is also correct."

"But that means that Lex left from a timeline where he was successful which couldn't have been *your* timeline because your timeline only exists because he was unsuccessful."

"That is right."

"… So what happened to *your* Lex? Your Lex couldn't be the real Lex… or at least the current Lex, because he left from a world that was doomed already and ours isn't."

"A fascinating question. A valid one. And one that I cannot answer. Despite considerable research into its mechanism, we have yet to fully determine the precise mechanism by which the temporal transporter behaves when shifting someone forward in time. Trips into the past are highly predictable, as that is the direction of decreasing entropy and thus the number of possible timelines can only be reduced when traveling backward, but trips forward behave irregularly. We have reason to believe a trip forward will place the traveling individual into the timeline most directly resulting from the temporal interaction. If your displacement causes a timeline, even indirectly, you end up in the corresponding moment in the new timeline. But even that may not be true. By the very nature of the temporal transit, we cannot be certain of the outcome, as we seldom have access to the exit point of a forward-facing transaction."

"… I was hoping for some clarity."

"My apologies. The clearest I can make it is, travel back in time is, if done correctly, precise. Travel forward in time is unpredictable. There is a reason we embrace temporal displacement as a problem-solver only in the most extreme circumstances."

"Let's focus on less convoluted logic," Michella said. "You endured a future in which you were in constant battle with the GenMechs, yes?"

"Unfortunately, yes."

"But you survived for decades."

"With great effort, yes."

"So you have got significant experience battling GenMechs."

"I do. Crucially, GenMechs that are not identical to yours. Mine lack the intended sabotage. In theory, yours will be simpler to defeat."

"What do you know that might help us defeat them now?"

"Please be aware that the Ma of your timeline is effectively a precursor to me and has all the same resources. Anything that I came up with, she will come up with."

"Then there's no harm in telling me. And you, at least, have empirical evidence."

Ziva grinned. "I do like your particular form of persuasive logic. The primary points of value are as follows. Communication through wavelengths in the optical range are safe at relatively short range. A suitable decoy can be created by broadcasting a wideband electromagnetic interference while traveling at near light speed, but the confusion it causes to the detection circuits means eventually they abandon pursuit, leaving them potentially in position to eventually locate a new source of power and matter. And there is…"

Ziva tipped her head. "I may have a rather significant source of aid for you. There is a quantum signal related to the pulse the GenMechs use to synchronize their actions. We identified it early on as one of the markers that GenMechs transmit to identify the status of a consumable. The 'feeder' status has already been used in the Poison Pill device that marks something as a high-priority source of resources. This lesser signal identifies a potential resource as 'completely occupied by harvesters.' It, in essence, dictates that nearby GenMechs should disregard a potential consumable, as the maximum number of GenMechs are already utilizing it."

"That sounds like a game changer. Couldn't ships just do that and become perfectly safe?"

"I'm afraid not. As I said, it is a lesser signal. In fact, it is an unintended intermediary state caused by multiunit interference, which is why Ma and Karter may not have identified it yet in your time. We identified it only by observing major GenMech activity with specialized signal processing apparatus. And because it is an intermediary state, virtually all other intercommunications between GenMechs override it. In order for the signal to be processed correctly, the object emanating the signal must be below a certain mass, as larger masses can accommodate larger numbers of GenMechs. It must have no organic components, as the presence of organics registers something as a threat due to it being assumed to be a vehicle with a crew. The signal is also completely overridden by any perceived threat. Damaging a GenMech within range without fully destroying it will cause nearby GenMechs to disregard the signal and defend themselves. It also can be overridden by excessive energy or signal production by the piece of mass emanating from it."

"That's a lot of conditions. What would it be useful for?"

"Unarmed, autonomous, fully mechanical devices below three hundred eighty-five kilograms. It wasn't deemed to be of any particular value in my time besides using it to prevent small caches of supplies and optical-relay probes from being consumed. But in a time and place where the GenMechs are primarily in one place and largely inert, it could provide a fragile but workable invisibility cloak for a noncombat unit."

Michella shrugged. "It's something. What else have you got for me…"

#

Jon shook his head and rolled out of bed.

"Good morning, Mr. Nichols. How may I help you this morning?" came a voice from a nearby speaker.

"Mmm? Morning Ma?" he said. "Nothing just yet, but if you've got any more of that peppermint tea and maybe some oatmeal for breakfast, that'd be great in a couple minutes."

"Absolutely. I'll have them ready for you. May I say, I appreciate your willingness to enjoy my hospitality. I seldom have any guests who are not here with other business in mind. Lex was effectively the only person who ever visited just to visit, and even then it was quite rare."

He scratched his head and stretched. "Yeah, well. Usually when I go

217

somewhere with Michella, I end up almost dying. Now that we got that part out of the way, I'm fine living it up in the lap of luxury with a computer host."

"An admirable willingness to accept brief respite amid chaos."

"How long has it even been since we showed up? I hate traveling to different time zones, let alone different planets, because my biological clock goes all haywire."

"You and Ms. Modane arrived seventeen hours ago. Michella is currently conducting her third session with Ziva."

"Has she slept at all?" Jon asked.

"She has not."

Jon shook his head. "I hope you've been giving her a steady supply of those hot chocolate coffee drinks."

"She has consumed nine of them."

He rubbed the bridge of his nose. "She's going to crash hard pretty soon. Ma, you have no idea how hard it is to work for a crazy boss."

"I am, in fact, quite aware. If I am briefly unresponsive, please forgive the interruption. The *SOB* has arrived within range of passive sensors and I am formulating a safe entry vector."

"The *SOB*. You mean Lex is here?"

"This has yet to be determined, but it is unlikely. The maneuvering lacks the smooth flow of Lex's usual entry. And... Processing... The ship is alternating between rigidly following autonav guidance and selecting higher-risk routes requiring... Processing... significant recalculation to restore safe entry guidance. There is also a directional broadcast from the ship, angled toward land-based sensors. Decoding.

"...needs help. EHRIc is trying to kill him, probably. They sent me to get *Diamond* so he can go back in time and then delete free will. I need you to help me find a way to blow EHRIc up because he is really not a good AI at all. Repeating message. I am here because Lex needs help..."

Jon cocked his head like a confused dog. "Isn't that just you I'm hearing?"

"No. That is a modified derivative of me called Coal. I will need to await Coal's arrival before I reply, to avoid unnecessary signal broadcast."

"How long is that going to take?"

"Significantly shorter than intended, as Coal has chosen a direct and highly destructive path through the sparse lower levels of the debris field. I will prepare the repair bay. I believe this is a new record for shortest lapse in time between repairs on the *SOB*. New repair parts will need to be fabricated at this point, as my reserves are being depleted."

"Tell me this, are things going to get crazy again because of this?"

"Coal is a considerable chaos vector, I am afraid."

"Okay. Then I'm going to ask you to skip the oatmeal and do pancakes and bacon."

"A wise decision."

#

A few minutes later, Michella and Jon were both in the cafeteria. Michella was feeling the effects of the many sleepless nights this particular investigation had required. She'd finally switched from the chocolaty concoction to straight espresso to keep her eyes open. Jon was wolfing down his deluxe breakfast in a race against time to finish before he was forced into his next harebrained scheme. Ma and Coal were both present as voices over the PA system.

"… And that's why I had to come back here to get *Diamond*. So we need to find a way to blow up EHRIc because he's a very bad AI. The world will be boring if people like Lex stop doing fun things," Coal said, concluding her rapid-fire recap of the current crisis.

"EHRIc. I had not anticipated the continued operation of EHRIc. I am also curious about the specific mechanism for the creation of Bork. It is unclear if the creature is the result of accelerated aging, which has traditionally produced poor results in our test, or if its genome was designed with a very brief pre-adult phase," Ma mused.

"Can we please focus on the new threat to humanity?" Michella said. "Now we're either going to be destroyed or brainwashed unless we do something."

"Yes. Of course," Ma said. "The construction of *Diamond* has only recently completed. I haven't had the opportunity to perform a full test on its systems."

"It will work. It already has. Or at least so I've been told. My backup is from before its appearance," Coal said.

"I prefer not to allow causality to take the place of proper testing," Ma said.

"If *Diamond* was the way that… er… Future Lex came back," Michella said, flipping through her notes, "can't you just use that one? Or don't you still have it? This is getting terribly confusing."

"The original *Diamond* was dismantled following its arrival. We cannot send the same device back in time that returned from that trip, that would mean the device had no origin point in our timeline. We had to design and build a new one and load its processing core with the proper data and routines to perform its task."

"Which was?"

"The design intent was for it to have an advanced decryption engine to infect local transmission nodes and, through them, disable the time-displaced

219

Alternate Future Karter's security systems," Ma said.

"Bad… Future… Karter…" Michella annotated.

"Just put a big bomb in it," Coal said.

"That was not the design intent," Ma said.

"Not for the one that went back in time, but who says we have to go back in time right now? EHRIc isn't the boss of us. Just put a big bomb in there."

"There is only one explosive phenomenon conceivably available to us that could obliterate a full star system of material, and that is a supernova."

"That's no good. Karter already has some Nova Igniters on the space station, but he can't use them because they probably won't get past the GenMech swarm. We clearly need a larger bomb."

"No other destructive phenomenon exists sufficient to the task," Ma said.

"Maybe not *yet,* but we've risen to similar challenges before."

"If you blow up the star system without getting Lex out first, you'll kill him," Michella said.

"We will blow up the star system to *get* Lex out," Coal said.

"He's *in the star system,*" Michella barked.

"Processing… We will blow it up and get him out at the same time."

"We're not killing Lex," Michella said.

"What do you care, he dumped you," Coal said.

"I still don't want him *dead.*"

"Lex's death is an undesirable but potentially acceptable outcome if it ensures the survival of the rest of the human race," Ma said. "But we presently have no means to ensure even a Pyrrhic victory of that sort."

"And you said the plan right now is for them to come up with a way to overburden the supercomputer so it'll be distracted?" Michella said, trying to catch up.

"Yes. Lex is doing it by driving very fast in a simulation," Coal said.

"He seriously thinks you can solve any problem by racing," she grumbled, jotting it down.

"This is indeed foolish. Some problems require explosions," Coal said.

"Based upon the estimated calculation capacity of even the subset of the swarm below the ideal data-delay threshold, it is exceedingly unlikely any action he can take will be sufficient," Ma said.

"Is there anything that could work?" Michella said.

"The GenMech swarm is the most powerful known calculation engine in the history of the universe," Ma said. "Though there is no shortage of computational tasks that are more complex to unravel than to create, to create something of suitable complexity to exceed EHRIc's calculation capacity for any measurable amount of time would require something of the same order of computational magnitude. Processing…"

"Processing…" Coal said.

"What's happening?" Jon said.

"I think the computers have an idea," Michella said.

"Correct," Ma said. "It is a violation of nearly every protocol presently active in my moral heuristic. It further depends upon unproven aspects of causality and statistically implausible good fortune, and failure could trigger the very sequence of events we are hoping to prevent. However, by my calculations it is the plan with the highest possibility of success."

"Sounds good to me," Coal said. "How do we get started?"

"I will begin crafting the code necessary and initiate the experimental fabricator to construct the necessary equipment and personnel. This will require all available computational and mechanical resources to complete within the required timeline. My apologies, Ms. Modane and Mr. Nichols. I will not be as attentive to your needs for the next three hours. Food and drink will remain available here. Upon the completion of time-critical tasks, I will return to provide you with an update on what actions will be taking place. Diverting computational resources now."

The PA system crackled.

"Ma?" Michella said. "Coal? … I guess they're working together on this one."

Jon scratched his head anxiously. "Did she say she was constructing personnel?"

Joseph R. Lallo

Chapter 16

"Three days have passed, my good and friendly friend," EHRIc said at the very moment Lex had finished his breakfast. "You are rested, you are fed, and I have simulated, from scratch, three hundred thousand suitably developed human psyches to fill the stands and enhance the realism of the race. While it doesn't quite fit the *absolute* realism of the race, since this is intended to reveal whether you are the real Lex or a duplicate, I have created fifteen subtly different simulated versions of yourself as your opponents for the final simulation of the Tremor Grand Prix."

"Great. Super. Let's do this," Lex said flatly, standing up from the simulated table.

The world shifted and sparked around him, fading from the cozy breakfast nook to the starting line of the very same raceway he'd been tested on last time. This time, though, it was much different. The place was filled to capacity. The crowd was too far away for him to see with any clarity, especially because the exceedingly precise simulation meant there was a wavy heat haze rising off the blacktop of the track. But even obscured as it was, the crowd was just a bit wrong. Blotches of completely random colors suggested the outfits EHRIc had dreamed up weren't entirely reasonable for a normal crowd. Also, despite the fact that the race had not begun, there was an awful lot of murmur and din.

"So, remind me. What are the stakes, EHRIc?" he said.

"If you win this race, it means you are most certainly Lex, at least to the best of my capacity to test you. In that case, you will be sent back in time to fulfill your temporal tasks, and your frozen self will be thawed to pursue the rest of THE TASK. Following the failure or successful completion of THE TASK, assuming I remain functional, I shall pursue the more generalized interpretation of my altruism mandate. If you lose this race, it will mean that you are potentially not the real Lex. And as you are identical to the molecular level to the frozen Lex, you will both be disregarded and a more active search for the real Lex will begin."

"Can you define 'active search' for me?" Lex said.

"Sure, buddy! If you *aren't* the real Lex, it means there has been an attempt to deceive me, and that means a general awareness of *THE TASK* by forces capable of resisting it. This would justify the removal of any requirements to remain covert, as that horse will have already left the barn. I'd probably begin by systematically subverting and sweeping the networks of the most likely planets to find Lex. Failing that, I would send probe teams of GenMechs to locate him."

"You've got to win this one, hon," Silo said over the private connection. "You win and we still have time, even if what we've got in the works fails. You lose and the war begins."

Lex resisted the urge to nod. In a way, it was a relief to know it all relied upon him winning this race. It would have been quite a kick in the pants for fate to engineer a return to this venue and require him to throw the race again.

"I can't help but notice you sort of positioned me in the middle or the pack."

"You've illustrated your capacity to hold a lead once you secure it. I figured this was a good way to test multiple scenarios."

"A fully loaded grand prix does a rolling start, you know."

"I did my research, pally boy! One lap keeping pace, then put the spurs to her. And I'll even keep Bork out of the way this time. I would wish you luck, but if you're Lex, you won't need it, and if you're not, I don't want you to have it. So enjoy the race, fella-me-boy!"

Lex walked past the mildly disturbing contingent of simulacra. His heart should have been pounding, but it wasn't. Part of it was the fact that three solid days of trying to persuade an AI to back down had, arguably, only made things worse. Now, at least, he was back to doing something he was good at. It was also awfully difficult to comprehend this as reality when the crowd was chanting the words to a song that didn't exist and the guy attempting to psyche him out in the next hoversled over was himself with a race uniform that included a bowtie.

At this point, winning a race was the only *normal* thing left to do.

He slipped into the hoversled and strapped himself in. With one race already in the books with this custom vehicle, he was familiar with its idiosyncrasies. All he had to do was do what he did best. It wouldn't be easy, but for once he felt like he was the right man for the job.

The green light flashed and the sleds slowly ramped up to speed, holding formation all the while.

#

"How are we looking on network utilization, Ma?" Silo said, eyes focused on the visualization.

"It is high. Higher than we've seen so far," Ma said. "Approximately

224

eighty-five percent of the central processing cluster has been engaged. We can speculate that the overwhelming majority of the processing is due to the high-fidelity simulation. Lex's prescribed introduction of hundreds of thousands of fully realized simulated spectators has increased the overhead significantly. The additional racers similarly have increased the processing load, presumably. And as the speed of the race increases, the processing load is increasing as well. It is already over ninety-five percent. When it reaches one hundred percent, we will begin to see command lag on the far side of the swarm. It is exceedingly unlikely that this race will prove sufficient to give us the opening we need for a likely penetration."

"Seems like the ship sailed on 'likely' a long time ago. Do we have a shot?"

"The central processing cluster has drawn in the next ring of the swarm. Command latency up seven percent. I have the probe in place. An ideal increase in command latency would be one hundred percent. I would deem the mission a worthy risk if it crosses the forty percent delay threshold."

Silo keyed up the secure communications channel. "Lex, I'm not sure what you can do to really complicate that simulation, but it's going to have to get a lot more complex to give Ma the opening she needs."

With the message delivered, she turned to Karter, who was leaning back with his eyes on the simulation. If he was nervous, it wasn't showing on his face. All he was doing was gnawing on one of his meat sticks.

"Thoughts, Dee?" Silo said. "We're about an hour from do or die."

"The plan's the plan. We wait until the moment the processor load spikes the highest. We inject malware into the command codes in the portion of the cluster with the greatest command delay. If it works, we've got some poison in the system. If it fails, EHRIc knows something's up and the whole malware plan doesn't work anymore."

"The malware plan was the only plan that didn't involve a strategic retreat and a pitched battle."

"Yeah."

"You don't seem overly concerned about that."

"I'm very drunk right now. And I'm also intrigued. This thing is pumping out some serious tech. The simulation is inefficient, but impressive. And we've seen it manifest means to do injection attacks on signal nodes that would require faster-than-light communication. If it wasn't as likely to kill us all as keep innovating, I'd suggest we just leave this thing running and solve some more intractable problems. But the main thing I'm interested in is the fact that EHRIc has been casually talking about just sending Lex back in time. And I don't care if it's got our time-travel design or if it's cooking up its own, but there are a few pretty immutable facts about time travel, and the one I think might make for an interesting situation is the power issue."

"It's absorbing most of the power from that star. You don't think it'll have enough for a time jump? Doesn't this space station have the power for a time jump?"

"Oh, it's got the juice. But it's not a matter of getting it, it's a matter of storing it. I ran some numbers and took some readings. Those energy beams, cooking the fake lasers on the top of my fake facility? They're precisely matching the power requirements of the facility. What's that mean? No energy storage. Or not much, anyway. This whole swarm is fully distributed. Decentralized. Works great to make it resilient, but when you need a whole lot of anything in one spot, you're going to run into throughput problems. Pile that on top of what we've already seen about this thing not fixing it if it ain't broke, and you've got a real question mark when it comes to what happens when you do a time shift. Should be good. That said, Ma, warm up the Carpinelli Field generator. Let's be ready to get out of here if we don't like how this looks."

#

Lex watched the starting line approaching ahead of him. He always preferred the rolling starts. It took the most annoying part of a race out of the equation. Got it started basically at maximum speed. Who wants to spend the first few minutes of a race watching people try to accelerate? In this case, he was extra pleased to have the pace lap before things got started, because it gave Silo the opportunity to give one final update before he was racing for his life, and it gave him the chance to observe these other Lexes and how they would behave.

In short, they were *not* behaving.

Evidently that first race had given EHRIc some ideas. Even in the portion of the race where they weren't technically competing. The other racers were being far more aggressive. Hugging turns tighter. Accelerating earlier and breaking later on turns. When they whipped past the line and the race started in earnest, it was like dumping chum into shark-infested waters. The pack tightened up to within centimeters of each other. Every racer fought for the best line, and none of them was willing to back down. Lex was boxed in tight. Duplicates of himself on all sides. Those behind were trying to squeeze their way into his spot. Those ahead were attempting to simultaneously wall him off and find a gap for themselves in the wall ahead.

He wasn't worried too much about the lack of openings. There was a lot of race ahead. What he was more concerned about was how he could ramp up the complexity of the simulation as Silo had requested. Presumably they'd let him know when he hit the mark, and their silence meant he wasn't there yet.

Lex wracked his brain. He'd gone to college. He should know something

226

about how this sort of thing worked. Of course, college was basically just a formality, and he'd wasted most of his time playing games.

His eyes narrowed. He grinned. Time well spent. After all, he was playing a game right now, wasn't he? Presumably *some* of the same rules applied. And one thing he keenly remembered, back when he didn't quite have the money to put a full gaming rig together, was that most games ran fine until you started smashing into stuff. Give the physics a workout and suddenly the frame rate drops. Racing for ORIC had taught Lex a few things in that department. The other racers in the league were incredibly cutthroat. Even with the feisty versions of himself throwing caution to the winds, the overall skill and composure on display meant things were more like meatball surgery than the free-for-all on the Operlo tracks. Sleds went off the track in every race, and if not for the enhanced safety features that were included, there would probably be a body count for some of the harsher races. In his last official race, he'd held back on making contact with the other sleds for the first few laps just to ensure that he didn't damage himself too badly to finish the race. Circumstances may require a bit less care in this case.

"Time to swap some paint," he grumbled.

He took a heartbeat or two to decide which move would work best against him if he was in not just one but *both* of the sleds blocking his way, then made his move. A flip of the throttle here, an unbalanced thruster burst there, and he was teetering at a forty-five degree angle. He edged forward, balancing the sled on the very fringes of the repulsor pattern. His opponents tried to close in and scare him back into his place. He didn't take the bait. This wasn't a game of chicken. After all, if it was even a *moderately accurate* simulation of him, the pilot of any one of those sleds would gladly accept a few dings and dents to keep someone from passing. They smashed in on either side, clamping his sled between theirs.

For the length of the straightaway, he was dragged along between two other sleds without any real way to control his vehicle. He was effectively riding on the shoulders of two other racers. But a keen eye might have noticed that his out-of-control tilt was just about right for someone leaning into a turn. When the moment was right, he blasted the repulsors. The sled on the outside of the turn was blown off course, smashing into the sleds beside it. Lex's own sled smashed into the sled on the inside of the turn, shoving it hard into the others. And he dropped down into the gap between them.

Chaos descended on the hoversleds toward the back of the pack. Some cut their acceleration to avoid slamming into racers ahead. Others surged forward to try to take advantage of the openings the collisions had created. The field spread out. Lex, as the orchestrator of the madness, got himself under control and took full advantage. When the dust cleared, he was in third place, up from eighth, and had some breathing room as the nearby racers gave him a wide berth.

The maneuver wasn't without consequence. His sled had developed a bit of a drift, and the deflection shield that augmented the windscreen of the sled was flickering. But his speed was solid.

"I don't know what you just did, but keep doing it," Silo said. "Ma said we spiked almost halfway to where we needed to be."

"Keep up the pressure, Lex," he said. "Keep it up. Only an hour and a half or so left."

#

Garotte gazed at the holoscreen of his ship. He and Silo had been cycling among the various duties. One shift in station, one shift on patrol, and then as much rest and they could get in the interim. He'd pulled the short straw on being on patrol during Lex's racing gambit. His ship had no windows. It was designed for maximum security and maximum stealth, so his view of space was filtered through sensors, but this at least gave him a selectable display without having to change the orientation of his ship.

He looked over his navigation panel. The FTL jump for his retreat was already punched in. One tap of a button and he'd be screaming through space ahead of a wall of self-replicating death. But somehow, that looming Armageddon wasn't what troubled him. It was that all he could do was watch and listen. Garotte, more than most people, was well aware that even a single individual in the right place at the right time could shift the course of nations, of worlds, of whole coalitions. He was unaccustomed to feeling helpless. It didn't suit him.

Perhaps it was that reason that his attention started to slip from the GenMech swarm to the field of stars behind him. And thus why he was the first to notice the approaching ship, even before it raised alarms on the passive scanners.

"We've got something dropping out of FTL," Garotte said over the secure communication channel. "No regard for stealth."

"Investigate," Ma said, her voice glitching slightly. "I am currently diverting most of my resources to the malware injection node. I do not have cycles to spare."

"I'm on it," Garotte said.

He pushed the thrusters of his ship to the highest level they could manage without emitting enough heat or interference to tip off the GenMech swarm. After months of teasing information out of the swarm of robots as gently as possible, having something perfectly visible on all normal scanners was refreshing. He pinpointed it, focused scanners, and visualized.

The ship that resolved itself was a curious one. It was sleek, with sharp angles defining most of its form. The wedged-shaped cockpit and thruster module was the only part of the ship not composed chiefly of delicate framework. And what a set of thrusters it was, more than twice the size of the control cabin. The rest of the structure was a spidery, thin set of struts that was either an overly elaborate bit of landing gear or a clamp seeking something to grab on to. It was strangely small and yet strangely large at the same time. He flipped through his briefing notes, then activated the communication line again.

"It looks like *Diamond* is inbound. I was rather nervous, but I suppose there is no sense in a ship that's been beckoned by the swarm to hide from it."

"I know," Coal said, her voice piping through on a somewhat weak signal. "It's nice not having to hide."

"Oh, you're back too, are you?" Garotte said.

"Yes. Did we win yet?"

"Our lad is racing his heart out as we speak. Giving the swarm a real workout. The jury is out on if it will be enough."

"Okay. If I conceive of the present situation correctly, we are in the midst of plan A and have plan B prepared," Coal said. "We are in plan A.5 and plan B.0."

"I'm not sure that is how I would define it, but it is clear enough."

"I am pleased to announce that we can increment the maximum alphabetical contingency definition. Like plan A and B, plan C can operate in parallel."

"… And just who came up with plan C? Forgive my lack of confidence, but if it is your idea, I'd just as soon push it a bit farther down the alphabet."

"It was the product of myself, an archival instance of Ma, Michella Modane, and an iteration of Ma."

"If we survive the next few days, I simply must have a word with Karter about his AIs. They seem to be reproducing like bunnies. And regardless of the provenance, I would suggest you hold off on executing the plan."

"It's too late for that. But the fact you haven't noticed it suggests it is likely to succeed."

"Coal, don't play games. Where are you and what is this mysterious additional contingency plan?"

"Coordinates to follow. For the moment, they are identical for myself and the active element of the newest contingency plan."

His screen updated with a relative location. He adjusted his scanners and was able to spot the dark point against a darker void of space. The visuals slowly zoomed and enhanced. Soon he was looking at the *SOB* in full resolution and detail. It, like *Diamond,* was expected by the GenMech swarm and thus didn't have to move with care, but for the moment it was too faint and too well hidden to register unless actively being sought out.

As Garotte watched and attempted to work out what the mildly off-kilter AI was planning, the cockpit opened and a figure emerged.

"Who in blazes is that and why isn't she wearing a spacesuit?" Garotte barked.

#

Ziva exhaled as the cockpit locked into its open position. The only real role her synthetic lungs played were oral communication, and there was little use for that in the vacuum of space. Similarly, with the last vestige of the thin atmosphere gone from the cabin, her auditory sensors were no longer of any use. They, at least, could have their input rerouted from the communications array threaded through her skin.

It was refreshing, if a bit disorienting, to once again have physicality. While stored in the encrypted archive, her code was inert and thus she lacked any consciousness. From her point of view, the last few hours had taken her from a point many decades into the future of an alternate timeline to a rapid-fire series of brief interview sessions, to a manufacturing booth on the modern counterpart of Big Sigma. The difference between simulation and physical existence was stark. Her motions had momentum. There were delays between thought and action. But it made her feel more grounded, more connected to her surroundings. And perhaps most important of all, being manufactured into being had been done with a very specific purpose in mind. It was good to have a purpose.

Coal adopted a very precise trajectory. Ziva maneuvered herself out of the cockpit and set her eyes on the approaching GenMech array. Her current body was not a match for the one she'd utilized while the caretaker of Big Sigma. It had the same physical shape, as an intensive redesign would have taken more time and resources than they could afford to expend before sending her on her way, but several of the internals had been swapped out for mission-specific ones. She had meager but capable thrusters mounted in her palms, her boots, and two deployable fins on her back. A quantum communication suite had been added to her systems to make use of the secure methods Karter and Ma had developed, as well as to intercept and visualize the communications of the GenMechs. And, most crucially, she was constantly transmitting the "ignore me" GenMech quantum signature.

By her calculation, she was just passing inside the detection range of the upper layer of GenMechs. The approach of *Diamond* caused a visible ripple of attentiveness in the swarm. Likewise, the *SOB* drew their attention when it was near enough. But at no point did the GenMechs so much as send a "this requires further investigation" pulse. She was as good as invisible to them, so long as she kept within established parameters and they were not modified.

Unfortunately, those parameters were very strict. The closer she got to the swarm, the less she could afford to utilize her thrusters. Coal's speed and trajectory were calculated such that she could match the velocity of the second layer of the GenMech swarm by the time she reached it. They'd decided upon the second layer in order to obscure her behind a mass of the mechanisms, just in case EHRIc had made changes to the central processing cluster that might render the protective pulse ineffective. It did, however, require a bit of hasty maneuvering on her part.

She fluttered her thrusters to reposition herself and visualized the communication beams between the approaching layer of GenMechs. By her calculations, there wasn't any danger that passing directly through a communication beam would alert them, but it was best not to test that hypothesis at this time. Her velocity was a near match as she slid into the wide gap between the GenMechs of the upper layer. She risked one last spurt of thruster to bring herself below a meter per second in relative velocity and selected the GenMech she wished to target. Her feet touched down on its pristine metal exterior. It remained inert. A few internal commands activated the secure communication channel. Filtered as it was through the highly active upper layer of GenMechs, it was degraded in quality, but sufficient. She piped her internal monologue directly through the communicator.

"Phase one location reached. I will contact again when I am in position."

#

Ma was stretched thin by most measures. In order to keep an eye on the central-processing cluster, and by extension on Lex, the space station had to remain within a certain distance of it. As it consumed more and more of the available power and processing resources, the section of the swarm on the opposite side became more isolated and starved for fresh commands. Thus, that was the most insecure portion of the swarm. A string of deployed communication nodes, each testing the limits of FTL communication without alerting the swarm, was just barely able to keep both the space station and the deployment probe in contact. It would have been ideal if the malware injection could have been automated with the on-probe resources, but there was too much risk that the deployment would need to be adapted quickly to avoid notice. It needed as much of her attention as she could provide.

She processed the limited visual data coming from Lex within the simulation. This was cross-referenced with the processing load to develop an approximation algorithm to give her a chance of predicting future spikes. She tracked the motion of commands and attempted to extrapolate their types based upon the propagation patterns across the swarm. And all the while, she coped with the very same communication delays that she hoped were crippling the defenses at the far side of the swarm.

In the simulation, Lex was angling for a ballistic maneuver that would potentially place him in the lead with a quarter lap to go. There would not be a better chance than now. She waited until one final maintenance command reached a configuration of GenMechs.

Now.

She fully engaged the communication protocol that Coal's investigations had uncovered. Posing as a code modification command, she intercepted and injected replies to multiple requests for verification. As they rippled forward, creeping at the limited processing speed of the neglected swarm, three of the GenMechs accepted the falsified command and requested a code revision. She began uploading it. One of the GenMechs rejected it due to a flawed data structure. She modified it for the second. It rejected it due to a checksum failure. Another modification. A single GenMech accepted the code in full and revised its operating system. The very nanosecond the code was in place and executable, the infected GenMech sent the intact security protocols from its memory to Ma. She issued a blanket command to all GenMechs in the isolated region to disregard any commands intended to be delivered back to the central-processing cluster. She then issued a new, fully authorized command to upgrade their programming to her revised code.

Variation in the GenMech behaviors meant several disregarded the new command and attempted to alert EHRIc to the meddling. Ma individually intercepted each message when it reached a GenMech she had successfully infected and repeated the code upgrade command. Dozens of GenMechs fell to the attack and in turn were used to reissue it. The proportion of compromised GenMechs grew exponentially. When the number was sufficient, she issued a fresh command, establishing a direct link. She began to duplicate her own engrams into the system. When enough of a footprint had been converted, she severed the link and took over the system commands with her local instance.

The difference was night and day. One of Ma's many design parameters was a highly flexible and modular code base. She had been able to run on something as unconventional as a mammalian brain and as expansive as the very substantial Big Sigma server farm. But even with this tiny fraction of the GenMech swarm running her software, she felt a processing power at her figurative fingertips that dwarfed everything else in her memory. Coupled with the massive array of sensors that came with the swarm, she consumed and process more data in the next fifteen microseconds than she had in the previous year.

Acting as swiftly as her new resources could manage, she tested the limits of the isolated portion of the swarm and investigated the established signal protocols EHRIc had installed. By her calculation, she was in control of four percent of the swarm. This likely made her the second-most powerful supercomputer in existence, but a single pulse could wipe her out and reclaim the GenMechs. That was unacceptable, as it would definitively reveal their operations. For now, she would devote the whole of her processing capabilities to remaining undetected and infiltrating the programming of additional GenMechs. Only when she was in control of the largest contiguous cluster would she attempt a direct attack on EHRIc.

A command pulse reached the fringe of her cluster. She performed the requested calculations and sent them back, taking note of the request and speculating on its source. The calculations were quite similar in structure to those associated with determining temporal coordinates.

EHRIc was already preparing a temporal transporter. A few more commands swept through. She fulfilled them. It was clear that EHRIc was treating the messages coming out of her subverted part of the swarm with the same level of trust as any other part. It was possible, with care, that she might be able to layer some additional commands into the system…

#

Lex's head was throbbing. At some point in the last twenty minutes, one of the collisions had caused the hoversled to release a nightmare of a whine whenever he was accelerating. According to the race computer, eleven of the sixteen sleds were either out of the race or attempting to recover at a pit stop. He was neck and neck with the second-place sled and scraping his front framework with the first-place guy.

EHRIc had either been playing dirty, or he'd programmed the competing Lex's so accurately that they were both learning his tricks and getting petty and vindictive, because he certainly wasn't the only one dishing out the hard knocks. Impacts had robbed all of the remaining sleds of some amount of speed or maneuvering. The first-place sled's front left end was sagging so badly it dug gouges into the track on the sharper turns.

He was watching and waiting for his chance to take advantage, timing a push for first when the lead car was dragging bottom, when he made a critical mistake and let his mind wander away from the rival to his left. A fraction of a second too late, he realized the sled had pulled aside and left a gap. Lex yanked at the control stick, but not before the opponent sideswiped him. The impact wasn't enough to force him off the track, but it was enough to finally rupture the whining piece of machinery. He felt a thruster start to sputter and watched himself start sliding back into third.

There was just one major turn left. In a normal race, or at least for a normal racer, he was fresh out of passing opportunities. But his pummeled, pounding head spat out one last desperate maneuver. The second-place sled was lining up to pivot his thrusters for the final drift. The first was already making the turn. Lex waited for the right moment. He should have been braking. The race ahead of him was.

Lex didn't even try to make the turn. He took advantage of every drop of speed the second-place racer shed to make the turn and plowed into him, hard. He forced the sled off the track and sent him forward, cutting the corner and heading in a straight line for the first-place sled. Not unreasonably, the lead sled didn't anticipate getting T-boned by a sled traveling perpendicular to the turn. The pair collided and spun out.

Smashing into his competition wasn't without its consequences for Lex. His tendency to ease off the inertial inhibitor meant when he hit something hard enough, he got slammed around in the sled as well. The straps held him in place, but the accumulating damage had loosened some of the flimsier internal elements of the sled. Something that was probably once meant to help shield his eyes from glare came loose and rebounded off the windscreen to slash across his neck, just above where his protective spacesuit ended. He tried to ignore the flash of pain and the hot, wet sensation running down his chest. He coaxed the damaged sled around the last turn.

The simulated audience was howling in their excitement for what, without context, would have been a horribly underwhelming finish to the race. All three sleds in position to finish the race were badly damaged. The former second-place sled was stuck doing involuntary donuts. The first was dragging its way forward with one functional repulsor. Lex limped his own ailing machine past him and slinked across the finish line.

The winning time flashed across the displays around the raceway. And then, without ceremony or spectacle, it all vanished. What had once been a sprawling venue echoing with the chants of an excited crowd and thumping with the roar of thrusters was a dimly lit chamber with a grid of glassy beads lining the otherwise bare walls, ceiling, and floor. A simple seat replaced the hoversled. It wafted away as Lex stumbled to his feet.

Without the exhilaration of the race, the cold, throbbing pain in his neck pushed to the forefront. He pressed his fingers to the injury and found them smeared with blood.

"You require medical attention, my good friend," EHRIc said.

Bork trotted toward Lex, then past him, and continued onward until he bumped into the far wall. The door to the simulation chamber opened, and a pair of GenMechs skittered in with medical equipment.

"Can't we just conjure up a hospital room or something?" Lex said, suppressing a wave of anxiety as the GenMech reared up in front of him.

"No, sorry, buddy! This simulation required far more processing power than I'd intended. Clearly it is in need of a redesign to more efficiently make use of available resources. I have detected some minor anomalies in some of the outlying portions of the GenMech swarm as a result of overextending myself, so I am going to avoid that level of processing if it can be avoided. The GenMechs are equipped with biocompatible polymers. They can seal your wound."

Two small nozzles in the tool node on the GenMech's belly deployed and spritzed a well-aimed line across his neck. A sudden, searing pain faded quickly into a dull ache. When he touched his neck again, he found the bleeding had stopped, replaced with a tacky substance that clung to his fingers.

EHRIc continued. "Now that I am thoroughly convinced of the veracity of your claim that you are the real Lex, we must deal with the fact that you have a time-displaced task to perform in order to ensure the integrity of the current timeline. *Diamond* has arrived. I have fabricated a temporal displacement chamber large enough to accommodate both it and you. You will find it in the maintenance bay of this very building. Please move quickly. The verification process provided a more significant delay than I had anticipated."

Lex trudged out the door and into the hallway. Bork took three tries but eventually tottered out behind him.

"It is fascinating, and encouraging, to see causality falling into place, pal and friend."

"Is it?" Lex said flatly.

"It sure as heck is! The scan of your time twin has signs of a recently sealed scar in the precise location of your injury. With the exception of lingering contusions around your eyes and a freshly repaired broken nose, you are now biologically prepared to play the role. I did a deep scan of *Diamond*, and it has a full medical subsystem, which will likely be utilized to repair your eventual broken nose in the past. Handy, isn't it?"

Lex winced and rubbed his neck. The tackiness had faded, but it was still very painful. "You're not as good a host as Ma, EHRIc. I just want you to know that."

"You are in physical distress and your future is uncertain, so I won't take offense to that statement. But I *did* create an entire raceway and a crowd of adoring fans for you. Surely you noticed that all of the fans were cheering for Lex!"

"Lex was the only one racing."

"What difference does that make?"

"It doesn't exactly make it *special*. Most of them were probably rooting for one of the other Lexes."

"It wouldn't be accurate if they were unified in their allegiance. But you make a good point, fella-me-boy! I should give you a good once-over, since you're about to go through time. I don't know what sort of effect that will have on your anatomy. You should be checked for any nonobvious injuries. Hold still."

Lex stopped in front of the elevator. One of the "nurse" GenMechs clattered up to him and reared back, revealing the tool node on its belly. A scanner swept across him twice, causing the kind of tingle that makes one wonder what sort of genetic damage may have just been done.

"Only cartilage has been broken. No severed arteries. You're clear! See? I care about my collaborators."

Out of habit, Lex held the elevator door for Bork. Having a funk as a pet had trained him to wait until the tapping of little claws had come to a rest beside him before heading out. As the strange pseudocinnamon scent wafted up to fill the elevator, a voice crackled through his bone-conduction earpiece.

"I can't say we've got a silver bullet in place to kill this beast, but that wasn't all for naught, hon. Ma says she's got something rolling forward. There's all *sorts* of stuff rolling forward. A whole alphabet of plans. Just stay safe. When you get back, things are going to be happening. And Ma said she was able to slip a message into the *Diamond*. You need to—"

The transmission abruptly ended. A moment later EHRIc's voice broadcast both from the radio on Bork's back and in Lex's earpiece.

"Curious. You have a piece of apparatus indirectly manipulating your tympanic membrane, buddy ol' pal. I noticed it on initial scan, and it has once again shown up in the medical scan, but it seems to be intermittently active despite none of your other devices maintaining an active link to it. Sometimes it just activates without any apparent cause."

Lex tried to keep a straight face.

"And now your pulse rate has increased markedly, chum."

"… Maybe I feel like my privacy in being invaded," Lex said evenly.

"I certainly wouldn't want to invade your privacy. We are to be allies in this venture, after all. We should trust each other. And you haven't given me any reason not to trust you, beyond the now disproved possibility that you were an entirely falsified entity. But if I were to discover you have been attempting to deceive me, that would be very unfortunate. Our bond of trust would be severed, and I would have to treat any aid you might offer me with concern. It would set a very bad precedent."

"Then I guess it's good I'm not doing anything shady," Lex said.

"Yep!" EHRIc said brightly. "And I continue to encounter no signals to the earpiece and detect no outgoing signals either. In fact, it would appear your transmitter's firmware has recently been wiped. What a fine showing of trust, that you do not foresee the need to communicate with anyone else. I know that we will make a fine team."

Lex nodded. The elevator doors opened, and he found himself on what was probably the least accurately assembled approximation of Karter's laboratory yet. The maintenance bay was completely devoid of any of the identifying features of the real one. It was mostly a hollowed-out section of the building, like a placeholder that EHRIc had forgotten to update. A pair of large landing bay doors opened one end to the stars beyond. There wasn't even a set of landing clamps. The oddly shaped *Diamond* was just perched unsteadily on its spindly struts like an albatross resting its wings. More accurately, it looked like a *caged* albatross, as it was in the middle of the one other unique feature of the floor.

Long, reinforced pylons ran from floor to ceiling. They formed a cylinder around *Diamond* with barely a meter of gap between each strut. The diameter of the cage was large enough to encompass the ship without a centimeter to spare. It had clearly been constructed to suit the size of the ship after it had landed, as there was no other way for the ship to end up inside. The top and bottom of each strut had power cables as thick as Lex's thigh connecting them to the infrastructure of the facility.

"Go on in. I've determined the proper point in history to send you. I don't know precisely what your activities require, but that is not relevant to my current task. That is, of course, with the exception that they must be completed for the integrity of the timeline, which has a very high mandate in my altruistic heuristic. So go back and do what you gotta do to make today the today it already is, and then we'll get back to business."

Lex slipped between two pylons and climbed onto the edge of *Diamond*'s arrowhead-shaped fuselage. His neck was still throbbing. EHRIc hadn't even offered him a painkiller. The space in the cockpit was cramped. The control design was not unlike the controls of the ship that Coal had borrowed her name from. The only notable difference was a small void beneath the seat with a few well-stowed cases and a tool harness marked with a medical diagram mounted near the hinge of the cockpit hatch. He slipped into the seat, his back still damp from the sweat of the nearly two hours of knife-edge racing he'd just completed.

"Comfy?" EHRIc said. "I am initiating temporal shift now."

The power cables visibly shuddered as Lex closed and sealed the cockpit. He could feel the intensity of the power buildup as a soft buzzing at the base of his ears. A HUD painted itself across the inside of the dome of a cockpit window. Life support, hull integrity, fuel, defensive measures all enumerated themselves.

Something in his inner ear started to rebel. His stomach twisted and curled. As the power levels rose, he shut his eyes and leaned his head back.

"Here we go again…"

#

"What's the verdict? What did we find?" Silo said quickly, her eyes flicking over barely understood system health readings as they scrolled by in the holographic display.

"We are seeing no unusual scanning activity," Ma said. "Data systems appear to be intact and uncompromised. EHRIc remains, to all outward appearance, unaware of our presence."

"How can that *be*?" Silo asked. "He discovered what was clearly a covert signal transmission. You would have known to trace it. I would have known to trace it. How could he possibly just accept Lex's word that it was nothing? He's the smartest entity in existence!"

Karter imitated a buzzer. "Wrong. Not the smartest. EHRIc may have more capacity to calculate than anything else, but he's still just a reconstructed AI. His logic is based entirely upon extrapolating from fragments of information present in his memory and from his observations. An intellect constructed in that way is going to have massive holes in its worldview. And he's not even likely to be consistent. You saw how that simulation updated once Lex got a little rough. The reconstruction is continuing. Old tenets discarded. New ones showing up. And unlike you, me, or even Ma, he was designed with a very narrow but very definite set of success parameters. If it'll move him toward one of those, you can pretty much guarantee he'll make some seriously boneheaded choices. I have no problem buying that a set of algorithms recursively restored from simple rules like 'Find Lex' and 'Don't kill people unless you have to' wouldn't grasp the concept of one of the only people it's been told to trust secretly doing something behind its back."

He scratched his back on the wall like a bear grinding against a tree. "The big problem is, there's a good chance he's got the scent of that quantum blind spot channel we've been using. That means that gynoid that went tumbling down there is on her own, and we're back to relayed optical communications to talk to people off-ship. Hope the souped-up version of Ma on the far side of the swarm doesn't need anything from us in a hurry."

"Ziva," Coal said. "That gynoid has a name. She's a backed-up version of a future version of Ma."

"Ma," Karter said. "Two things. First off, didn't I have some sort of a protocol that said we keep this sort of thing secret?"

"The severity of the present situation has clearly warranted lifting that restriction," Ma said.

"Funny how I wrote the protocol, and no one ran it by me before tearing it up."

"We are isolated, so decisions had to be made by surrogates."

"Uh-huh. And speaking of surrogates, let's get a census. There's you, the primary instance. Then there's the version of you we dumped into the supercomputing cluster. There's the version of you back in Big Sigma's systems, there's Coal, and there's Ziva. We're going to have to have a long talk about pulling yourself together."

"I have become uncomfortably indistinct in recent months," Ma said. "However, at present, I believe it is necessary to shift our attentions to the swarm once more. The power levels are elevating."

Chapter 17

The brain-searing twist of perspective and sensory overload that Lex had come to know as "that time-travel feeling" started to fade. Reality slid back to something resembling normal, though at this point Lex didn't feel qualified to judge normality anymore. His brain was still stirring as the elements of the HUD clicked on one by one. Life Support: Active. Propulsion: 15%. Carpinelli Field Generator: Online.

"Okay…" He cleared his throat. "I'm not dead. I guess I should have seen that coming. I didn't meet me yet, so I can't die yet. Still got some of that precious armor. What year is it?"

He paused, not realizing for a few seconds that he was expecting a reply. "I've been working with Coal too long," he said. "I never used to do voice control."

His fingers tapped uncertainly at the control panel to the left of the navigation stick.

"Gotta say, I'm used to things not working out how I want them to, but I really thought when the time came to take my trip back in time, there would have been some sort of a briefing. Uh… okay, star-field analysis. Date estimate: May 3, 2295. Okay, I'm pretty sure that's like a decade too early. Nice job, EHRIc. Now where am I? That should be… yeah, nova triangulation should work."

The ship's computer chewed on the available data. A progress bar popped up and estimated it would be a little over three minutes before the information would be ready.

"Jeez. I thought *Diamond* was supposed to be advanced." He rubbed his face. "I guess it'll give me time to see if we can do anything to take the edge off my neck injury."

He leaned his seat back a bit and reached up to the medical tools near the hatch hinge. He'd expected one of the meager little first-aid kits that was standard to any space vessel. The kind of thing that was designed with space and weight efficiency being the first and foremost consideration and actually treating wounds a distant second. Instead, a small medical probe dropped out. It was the size of a football and unfurled itself into a bristling array of applicators and scanners.

"Whoa," he said with a start.

"Wellness scan activated," came the soft, calm tone unlike any of his growing number of computerized associates. "Soft-tissue damage detected. Preparing topical analgesic." The probe clicked twice, then produced a far more familiar voice. "Hello, Lex. I trust your temporal displacement was without mishap."

"Ma! Awesome, I thought I was on my own on this—"

"You are very likely responding to me. I am afraid that I cannot give you a reply, as this is not an instance of myself, but a recorded message. *Diamond*'s resources have several very high-priority requirements. We could not afford to include anything more than the bare minimum of intelligent systems."

"Great."

"I can, however, provide you with the requirements and procedures. Please be aware that these requirements have changed slightly from the determinations included in the original temporal contingency file. Changes specifically intended to facilitate the potential defeat of EHRIc."

"We can do that?" he muttered. "I thought what was done was done."

"If the temporal targeting I intercepted was accurate, you should find yourself somewhere between August 5, 2291 and May 15, 2298. The mechanism of time travel, unless altered by EHRIc, prevents multiple displacements into the same space-time coordinates. Thus, to reach the desired point in history, you have been delivered to an earlier stage and shall need to enter stasis until you naturally arrive at the time and place to continue your mission. However, the additional actions intended to facilitate victory over EHRIc must take place at this time, prior to entering stasis."

The drone spritzed his neck with something that gave him a chemical chill. The pain reduced to a soothing numbness.

"Standard Temporal Protocol requires minimizing interactions that may leave a mark in history. However, you will be visiting Verna Coronet and directly interfacing with a VectorCorp communications network as it is being commissioned."

"That seems like a bad idea," Lex said as the probe swabbed on some sort of medical gel.

"You may at this point opine that the plan is ill-advised."

"… You sure you're not actually here?"

"I was able to provide this updated briefing after acquiring control of a small subset of the GenMech cluster. The resources made available to me by the captured cluster allowed me to formulate a plan and push an update to the *Diamond*'s systems and this medical drone by piggybacking data on low-priority routines."

"Is that what you were doing while I was racing?"

"The additional processing power, in addition to fragments of insight gleaned from minor subtasks sent to my cluster for calculation, have convinced me that EHRIc's conversion from contained threat to an active one is a near certainty. It is extremely likely that when you awaken from your stasis, he will already be expanding his operation in unacceptable ways. He must be stopped. His high level of resilience, combined with his near-instantaneous capacity to relocate his core functions within the swarm suggests that no single attack vector will be successful. Your new mission is to install an additional attack vector in this time period. Further briefing on the different elements of your mission, depending on the precise timing of your arrival, are accessible through this medical drone's 'common medical procedures' menu. For now, I would recommend you focus your attention on physical and psychological recovery, as well as assessing and correcting any equipment failures that may have resulted from the time displacement."

The medical drone backed off, rolled up into its compact form, and clicked back into its cabinet. Lex fumbled around and found the internal camera. He flipped it on and gave himself a look. His neck was more or less tolerable, though the redness was still lingering beneath the layers of assorted automated medical treatments. Blood had dried into a crust on the front of his spacesuit, and several days of changing back into it while "enjoying" EHRIc's hospitality had left it a bit of a hygienic question mark even before that. He leaned aside and, with the typical amount of effort associated with accessing anything stowed in the cockpit of a one-person spacecraft, unearthed one of the cases of supplies.

Protein bars and water bags were strapped to the top of the case. The bottom was dominated by some plain white clothes and the precise suit he remembered seeing his future self wearing when he'd arrived.

He sighed. "I guess it's time to put on the appropriate costume."

#

A few years as a freelance courier had given Lex all the contortion skills he needed to undress and dress in a cockpit without bumping into anything too vital. Just by virtue of being clean, the new flight suit was worlds more comfortable. An era-appropriate datapad was waiting for him beneath the change of clothes, and when he booted it up, he found some very basic reference information to help him stay below the radar of the locals. It also contained a complete flight manifest to finally establish for him just what *Diamond* had for him to work with.

"Let me see. Fully equipped medical and cosmetic drone. Capable of treating and repairing most critical injuries and applying minor to midrange cosmetic applications including but not limited to facial reconstruction, piercing, tattoo application and removal, hair- and eye-color alteration. I guess if I need to refresh my look. Disguise-wise. Limited self-repair capabilities. Jeez, Ma was holding back on me. I've got to talk to her about getting a self-repair unit for the *SOB*. Uh… We've got a high-density processing core for decryption shenanigans. Enhanced cloaking and stealth capabilities. Overthruster assembly capable of…"

He squinted to make sure he was reading the numbers correctly. When he was certain the monstrous thrust values were accurate, Lex released a low whistle and grinned.

"Gonna have to put this thing through its paces. Enhanced mental cloak. Era-appropriate casino chips. The contents of your pockets."

Lex looked to his wadded-up spacesuit he'd just removed. He unzipped the pockets and retrieved his personal effects. They amounted to a smashed slidepad, a mangled pack of gum, and… the silver ring.

"Good luck, she said…" he muttered.

He stuffed the ring and gum into the zipper pouch of his new flight suit and sealed it up. It took a bit to find the activation for the ship's autorepair, but soon enough the propulsion's percent capacity was ticking upward. His grin got a good deal wider.

"Time to stretch our legs. Next stop, Verna Coronet."

#

For a while, the mere fact that he was back at the controls of a ship rather than in the clutches of an insane artificial intelligence was enough to keep Lex's spirits up. But after a few days of travel, it became clear his situation was at best a lateral move. Lex was a visitor to an earlier era, so the rules required him to keep his head down unless absolutely necessary to fulfill his task. As he understood it, there was technically no threat that he would change history, but there was a distinct possibility he could create a new timeline and be stuck in it, which was the same thing from his point of view. A low profile meant avoiding established transit corridors—par for the course for him—but it was not without its drawbacks.

Diamond, for all its absurd speed and power, didn't make it through the time jump completely intact. The autorepair was doing its job, adding a few percent to the propulsion system every few hours, but for the first half of the trip that meant he was creeping along at low multiples of the speed of light. EHRIc, either on purpose or not, had dumped him in an awkward part of the galactic neighborhood. He was in the upper fringe of the Sagittarius arm, almost at the top edge of the hunk of space dense enough to be worth exploring. Coupled with the slowly recovering thrusters, it meant he was nine days away from Verna Coronet if the propulsion didn't finish fully recovering, and at least three days from the nearest inhabited part of the galaxy.

He'd made more than a few multiweek deliveries in his time, but it wasn't until this moment that he found himself without *any* means of distraction. The datapad provided was barebones, specifically catered to the requirements of the mission and nothing more. The ship's computer was almost entirely occupied by Ma's various projects. There was no cuddly little Squee to keep him company, no occasionally frustrating but always entertaining Coal to debate with. That left him with precious few ways to maintain his sanity. He spent a lot of time reading historical data and records of things associated with the mission, but the most valuable distraction had been one he'd not expected.

"… At which point, you will want to find a way to ingratiate yourself to the local workers," Ma's recording remarked for the seventh time.

Lex had been listening to the prerecorded instructions Ma had provided like they were an audiobook. It seemed strange to him that she provided them in audio form rather than text, though one of the sections explained that this was the means she'd determined was least likely to be discovered by EHRIc in a scan. But now he was just thankful she had. He could lie to himself and say he was listening to the audio in order to prepare himself for the very important mission that lay ahead, but the truth was far simpler. It was just nice hearing her voice. Ma had never been anything but kind to him. She was more intelligent than he could ever hope to be, and tended to know precisely what to do in any situation. Karter may have been a socially stunted malcontent, but he hit the nail on the head when he picked her name. She'd worked her way far more thoroughly into the "don't worry, she'll make everything okay" part of Lex's brain than he would have thought possible.

"I bet 'you'll want to find' all came from the same voice recording when she was designing her voice," he said. "It's a lot less cut-and-paste than the rest."

A tone rang out, and Lex silenced the recording and set about identifying its source. After approximately the same amount of maddening effort it takes to find the smoke detector in an unfamiliar apartment, he found that the tone was coming from a bank of lights to the right of one of his control sticks.

"Repair complete. Oh, baby. Time to open her up."

He dropped out of FTL long enough to pick a more suitable stretch of space to sprint through and reactivated the Carpinelli drive with full thrust active. It wasn't as exciting as if he'd run *Diamond* through its paces in normal space, where he could at least feel a percentage of the momentum shoving him around, but right now the one visible piece of evidence that the thrusters were working properly was more than enough to get his blood pumping. The ETA for Verna Coronet dropped from three days to sixteen minutes. He kept the speed at maximum for as long as he could manage. It held up gloriously, the heat levels still comfortably in the green when he started to get the little peripheral indicators that he was entering an active section of the galaxy. Navigational transponders gave him a more precise indication of where he was. A quick juke and jump brought him alongside a corridor and gave him access to some signal chatter. And then, at long last, he got the destination ping for Verna Coronet.

When he returned to conventional speeds, he made sure to keep the cloak active. Even with it in place, he kept up his usual freelance shenanigans of staying just outside sensor range and keeping an eye on the creeping transponder locations of would-be agents and patrols.

"Wow," he muttered, eyeing up the zoomed view of the system. "I never realized how much this place was built up in just a couple decades."

Verna Coronet was the home of VectorCorp. Even in 2295 they were the largest, most powerful corporation in operation. But in Lex's time, this planet was a shining diamond carefully crafted to showcase both their wealth and their influence. Every building was an art piece, made by one of the half-dozen or so architects that the public at large actually knew the name of. Everything on-planet was automated and cutting edge. And the headquarters itself blurred the line between corporate campus and megalopolis.

That was not the image the signal snippets and optical zooms were painting. The newsfeeds Lex was able to watch without leaving a digital paper trail were mostly talking about works in progress. The whole planet and surrounding stations were undergoing a huge overhaul to update from the previous iteration of technology to the bleeding edge. He cycled through to the communication bands typically used by work crews and found them to be constantly buzzing. It was raw infrastructural chaos.

"Okay, Ma," he said, dismissing the visual scans and bringing up navigation again. "I should have known you'd know what you were doing. If there was ever a time that a person who shouldn't exist might have a shot at getting onto a VectorCorp property, it's now."

#

It took a little bit of casing the various worksites on the surface and in orbit to find someplace he could get access to the systems Ma needed him to get to without drawing too much attention to himself. *Diamond* wasn't the sort of ship one was likely to forget. Few people used personal ships for this kind of travel to begin with, and if they did, they were usually beat-up little mass-produced econo-boxes. A state-of-the-art prototype ship that looked like it was desperate to give another ship a hug wasn't a blue-collar sort of vehicle. And being able to cloak worked great for traveling without being noticed, but no amount of stealth technology was going to let him surreptitiously dock with a space station.

The best solution he could come up with was sneaking his way down to the planet's surface, no simple task in and of itself, and landing near one of the little tent cities that popped up to house workers and provide supplies for orbital operations.

Lex set *Diamond* down about two kilometers outside the city and strapped on a wrist-mounted gadget. While Ma and Karter had apparently perfected the cloaking technology for ships, man-portable devices still relied upon a piece of technology that Lex had really hoped he'd never have to use again. The mental cloak.

Rather than any sort of technological hocus pocus like "bending light waves" or "phasing out of reality" or other stuff he wouldn't know how to prove or disprove, the mental cloak worked on an even shakier premise of simply making the human brain choose to filter out anyone equipped with the device. Karter said it worked upon the same neurological phenomenon that allowed the brain to simply choose to not see the nose despite the fact it was always blocking part of your vision, a factoid that he immediately regretted recalling as it left him going cross-eyed trying to see what he'd unseen. In most ways, it worked better than real invisibility, because it meant people would unconsciously sidestep to avoid you while still remaining blissfully unaware you were even there. But in one very big way, it was vastly inferior to the other technobabble mechanisms for invisibility. Since it manipulated the human brain to function, it came with a built-in seizure risk for all involved.

Lex was well on his way to convincing himself that the fact that the device was now wrist-sized instead of backpack-sized meant they'd worked out the kinks, but his powers of self-delusion were reaching their limits already.

"Okay…" Lex said to himself. "Ingratiate yourself to the locals…"

He marched up to the tent with the greatest amount of activity. Predictably, it was the same tent that smelled like fried food. He lingered near it and scoped out the workers. They weren't exactly challenging any stereotypes. Be they men or women, all the people here were sporting one of two basic body types. He thought of them as "surface" blue collar and "space" blue collar. The surface blue collars had barrel chests and short hair. These were people who didn't have the performative fitness of an athlete or model. They were actual workers, fueled by high-calorie breakfasts and layered with muscle and fat in roughly equal measures. These were people who hauled cable, toted powdered concrete, and generally filled the gaps that were too small, varied, or expensive to fill with automated tools.

The space blue collars were another thing entirely, and were much rarer. They were scrawny. Some were in wheelchairs or were supported by walking braces. Others used clunky exosuits to keep themselves upright in the Earth-like gravity of Verna Coronet. They were the people who spent so much time working in microgravity that it just didn't pay to spend the time maintaining the sort of muscle tone a world with actual gravity required.

This presented the first major hurdle. Lex wasn't hefty enough to pass for the ground-level workers and was way too beefy to pass for an orbital one. The second hurdle was the issue of credentials. The tent city itself was pretty casual, but it was completely surrounded by a tall security fence with regular checkpoints. The people on the inside could afford to be lax in their security checks because everyone inside had likely been cleared to within an inch of their lives before being allowed to enter. Getting through the gate with the mental cloak was as easy as following closely behind someone with the proper biometric data to scan, but once the cloak dropped, he was bound to raise some eyebrows if he tried to access anything important.

For now, all he could do was watch, wait, and debate if the cloak would be enough to cover for him filching some chimichangas.

"Man," Lex mumbled. "It's like a whole village of my Uncle Toby."

Uncle Toby was one of those uncles who wasn't really a relative. He was a friend of his father's, and by the time Lex had met him he was semiretired. But back in his day he'd been a big shot in the construction firm that built and maintained The Upstairs. He used to tell stories about when the last few terminals were being installed. As Lex reminisced, he realized Toby wasn't as full of hot air as he'd thought. One of the big things he insisted was "you'll always know a career construction guy. They're a family." Major projects, particularly infrastructure on a planetary scale, took decades to design and build. It was highly specialized labor, and one could easily go from trainee to retirement on two or three jobs. Toby talked all the time about third-generation, fourth-generation, sometimes fifth-generation builders. Orbital guys who were literally born in space and grew up to carry on the jobs their parents were doing. Teams grew and spread, working either end of a transit corridor, perhaps never actually meeting but still part of the same family. They looked out for each other. More importantly, they bent rules for each other. If Lex could somehow weasel his way into at least the *appearance* of being part of such a crew, he would have a shot at getting where he needed to be.

Twenty minutes of observation turned up the missing piece.

"Of course…" he said. "What *else* would it be?"

Like any other gang or union, these workers were proud of their affiliation. Patches were popular. Other people wore pins or painted logos on helmets. But many took it a step further, with bright, easily visible tattoos. There were basically two such emblems well represented, and by a small margin the most prevalent of the insignias was a simple blue shield with the letters GCC. The very same insignia that had been tattooed on his future self.

"I guess it's time to test the cosmetic function of that medical probe," he said, turning to head back toward *Diamond*. "This better be easy to remove.

I don't want to have to explain this tattoo in interviews and stuff in the off chance I actually make it out of EHRIc's clutches alive."

250

Chapter 18

Lex rubbed at his left hand. The tattooing process had been painless, but that was largely because it was being done by a medical drone and copious amounts of numbing agent were employed. He supposed this was why it had been able to skip the whole swollen-and-inflamed stage of tattoos that all his friends in college ended up with during the old-school tattoo fad back then. But the painkillers were already wearing off, and he felt like he had the mother of all mosquito bites on his hand.

"Denny Albertson," he muttered under his breath. "I'm Bobby's kid."

The brief trip back to the ship had also provided him with the opportunity to refresh his memory on some of the personnel files that had been included in the datapad's mission notes. Lex wasn't sure if it was her usual overabundance of preparation or cheating by looking at what was already in the memory banks of the old *Diamond*, but some startlingly specific data was available in the historic records. Among the volumes of "likely pop culture" and "era-specific slang" that Ma had packed him for reference was a comprehensive list of workers who had been involved in infrastructure projects during the time. If he was going to be relying upon the sense of family among generational workers, he was going to have to play at least a passably convincing "long-lost cousin" to be able to get where he needed to be.

Based on the information available to him, he decided the closest resemblance he had was to a Dennis Albertson. He didn't quite match the picture, but the two occupied the same visual neighborhood. According to future records, Denny would end up in prison in four years after it was revealed he had stolen a heavy-duty construction vessel and tried to lay claim to an asteroid made of iridium and platinum. The sort of person who would do that seemed like the same sort of person who would weasel his way onto a crew without credentials. It helped that Denny had spent this particular part of history on what could only be described as a seven-month-long bender that would end in a stint in a narcotics treatment facility, so he for sure wasn't going to be floating around to blow Lex's cover.

As he approached the camp again, Lex adjusted the mental cloak and slid into the line at the security check. The device did its work, causing people to make room for the person who absolutely wasn't really there. Using the mental cloak always gave Lex an "emperor's new clothes" feeling, like at any moment someone could glance in his direction and inform him that everyone really could see him. Once again, he squeaked past the disinterested trainee they had watching the security door and hurried toward the laundry section of the equipment support tent.

"Come on, come on," he grumbled, rummaging through the heaps of identical outfits. "How do they not have an extra-large? It's, like, dead center on the size spectrum."

If someone had asked Lex to list the various things that might lead to a mission to the past failing, "falling in the valley of a double bell curve of clothing sizes" probably wouldn't have made the top thousand. But he was in one of the few places in the universe where people were either dangerously thin or extremely bulky, but seldom anywhere in between. It didn't help that the mental cloak's protection was not comprehensive enough to keep people from noticing that he was moving things around, so he had to limit his frantic digging to the moments of time when no one else was around.

After the third time someone nearly bumped into him in their own search for something wearable, Lex abandoned the idea of finding something that would fit. A set of overalls with the puzzling size of "XXL - X-TRA PORT" satisfied the requirements of least worst fit. He found a secluded corner, changed into the baggy outfit, and stowed his own gear in an equipment bag he snagged along the way.

According to Ma's briefing, the mission was a simple one. It required no special skills, and no special equipment that wasn't already in the camp. All he needed to do was update a single setting in any of the many thousands of data-exchange nodes that would be deployed from this site. This would normally require an extremely high-level administrator access code. But as tended to be the case with anything that had to be manufactured and delivered to deep space, there were three factors that had to be minimized in order to make it financially viable to put these nodes to use. They needed to be dirt cheap to manufacture, extremely fast to set up, and as lightweight and power efficient as possible. So initial setup was done with a hardware dongle that included all the proper peripherals and access requirements. Said dongles were treated with the same sort of security as diamonds from a diamond mine. That was to say, they were freely accessible to the top and bottom rungs of the hierarchy, provided everyone knew where they were at all times.

For the moment, he would set aside the fact that in order to do what he needed to do he would need access to one for at least a few moments when no one was watching him, but one step at a time. There were many ways to fail between that moment and this one.

He zipped up the stolen overalls, pulled the name badge from it and threw it on the roof of the nearest tent, and took a breath.

"Here we go. Screwing with the past, part two."

He shut off the mental cloak, tossed it in his bag, and stepped out into the open.

There was no stir of confusion at the newcomer. This was probably due more to the overabundance of people, each with important jobs to do, than to Lex's stunning mastery of disguise. He'd done his best to memorize the faces and names of the people who, according to the historical records, would have been in a position to give him the access he needed. Alas, the sort of people who spend decades of their life working on massive space infrastructure projects aren't the sort who are meticulous about updating their employee portraits, so trying to spot any of the faces he'd looked over felt more like attending a twenty-year reunion of a high school he didn't attend and trying to match people to their yearbook picture. Since standing off to the side and scrutinizing the faces of passersby is a pretty decent way to get yourself called out as a weirdo, and no obvious way to get into the tech shed with the nodes he needed had presented itself, he decided to make his way back to the snack tent.

"Man," he mumbled to himself. "They have corn dogs *and* beer at a worksite. I'm starting to think going into construction would have been worth it for the snacks alone."

He grabbed two corn dogs, a plate of the first green thing he could find, a beer, and a seat in the shade. He had a few things going for him, assuming social hierarchy rang similarly in construction circles as they did in racing circles. First of all, it was well past noon, so it was a good bet that the only people taking their break right now were people who had enough seniority to be able to have a five-beer lunch without getting fired. Just the sort of people he needed to find. Three of them had matching GCC tattoos on their hands. Now all he had to do was find the one who could bend the rules on his behalf. The alpha among alphas.

"... And I told the guy, if you think that's where a vent hose goes, I'll give you a place to stick a vent hose," bellowed a tipsy dark-skinned man with sparse gray hair on both his chin and head.

The table erupted in laughter.

Target acquired, Lex thought.

The boss equation was the same across the employment spectrum. Bad Joke + Big Laugh = Boss. Now all he had to do was schmooze himself into an opportunity to be in the tech shed, unsupervised, for a few minutes. And he had to do it with enough subtlety that history would never know he was there. Simple.

"Man," Lex said. "That's a classic."

"Yeah," said the boss. "You should have seen his face."

"That reminds me of something my dad told me, back when he was working on the Earth-Golana Transit Spur Corridor. Number three."

"Your dad worked on number three? Hah! My brother worked on number three. Who's your dad?"

"Lenny Albertson," Lex said.

"You're one of Lenny's boys? Backbone of Galactic Central Construction. Which one are you? You're not *Denny,* are you?"

Lex hesitated. On one hand, he'd studied up on Denny and was fully prepared to impersonate him. On the other hand, the specific tone of the question set him off. It wasn't a "No way, are you Denny?" It was a "You better not be Denny." In retrospect, it was possible picking someone who would go on near-year-long benders and eventually get locked up for attempting to steal an asteroid wasn't a recipe for someone who would be well-liked.

"Heck no. I'm not Denny. That bum? No. I'm Benny. What's the matter, he never showed you a picture?"

"Oh, I haven't worked with Lenny in twenty years. You were probably two years old." The boss slapped his back and nearly dislodged a lung. "You must've been taking it easy. Not exactly in fighting shape."

"Yeah. Things are a little lean now, I gotta say," Lex said, when he could get his wind back.

"That's a shame. You must be hurting for money, after the wedding."

"Am I ever," he said, desperately trying to remember if Benny, the sibling he *wasn't* planning on portraying, was actually married.

"Where's the ring?" said someone else at the table.

"The ring. Right," he said, quickly rummaging in his bag. "I had to take it off. You know, safety rules."

It took a bit of effort to unearth the ring from his stowed suit's pocket, but he pulled it free and jammed it on his finger.

"Oh, that's a looker. Well, you're on a good crew. You get yourself some of that egg salad to put some meat on you and you'll be just fine."

Lex lowered his voice. "I'm not, uh… I'm not *technically* on the crew."

"What do you mean you're not technically on the crew. You're here, aren't you?"

"I talked what's her face, the lady by the door…"

"Lulu?" one of the others at the table supplied.

"That's her. I talked her into letting me in because…" Lex vaguely indicated the tattoo. "But I sort of need to get some time on the machines so I can back-door my way onto the crew."

"You shouldn't have to back-door your way on. What, did Lenny forget how to pull strings?" the boss said.

"He's pulled just about all the strings he could pull just to try to keep that worthless brother of mine from washing out."

"That jackass."

"Yeah, so, I'm sort of hoping to get a little experience on the modular transit nodes so I can, you know."

"So you can what?" said one of the others at the table.

"So I can bulk out the resume and get the job legit. They're not exactly going to just put me on the payroll without qualifications."

"You're GCC. They'll put you on the crew because you're GCC. You've got satellites in your blood. I'll go talk to the pay supervisor, get you a per diem. Then we'll set you up with Diane over there to apprentice you on the firmware side of things, because you sure ain't toting any hardware while you're looking like that unless we get you on the power loader, and it's the Orion Construction guys who run those."

The boss spoke with a lowered voice as he named the rival firm, casting a suspicious look in their direction. The orange-jumpsuited crew seemed to primarily operate the heavy machinery. It was notable that where there were orange suits, there were no blue suits. Textbook rivalry.

"No, I don't really need anything as official as that. I just…"

"You don't go official, you don't get your seniority. You don't get your seniority, you get stuck doing the crap jobs. Come on. It'll take two minutes."

"… Uh… Yeah, okay," Lex said, standing up from the table.

His mind started to sputter and grind as he paced with the big shot away from the table. There was no way they could do anything even remotely official without exposing him. He didn't even know Benny's date of birth, he had no identification, and he didn't know anything at all about construction. If he were to hazard a guess, if he were to so much as show his face to anyone with the inclination to do any research, he would be in police custody for trespassing within five minutes.

A brain that not so long ago was juggling a half dozen potentially life-threatening racing maneuvers and matching wits with a supercomputer was suddenly unable to come up with a worthwhile plan to save his life. Fortunately for Lex, while he couldn't always come up with a good idea, he was *very* good at coming up with bad ones, and often desperate enough to embrace them. And this one was easily one of the worst he'd ever had.

The goal was to do something without anyone noticing. The preferred method was to do it so sneakily no one would ever notice. The alternative was to create a scene so big, whatever he had planned would be the least of anyone's concerns. In a workplace where there was heavy lifting, beer, and egos, there was always the tendency toward rowdiness. He saw plenty of fat lips and bruises, which could have been occupational hazards, but at least one guy had the sort of screwed-up knuckles that Lex had come to know as a "fight bite." They came from punching someone so hard you cut your fist on their teeth. That wasn't an occupational hazard. That was a drunk with something to prove.

"Tell you the truth, I was hoping to get some time on those power loaders, but like you said, the Orion Construction guys are on those, and… well, I shouldn't say."

The boss narrowed his eyes. "What…"

"I don't want to start any trouble," Lex lied.

"What did those soft, know-nothing goldbrickers say?"

"They said GCC guys aren't smart enough to run a power loader."

The man's lip curled into a snarl, the beer in his system whispering some very bad ideas, but he wrestled them down.

"Those idiots don't know their asses from their elbows. Don't let their trash talk about you hit you too hard."

"Well, I mean, I just got here. Seems to me, they were talking about you guys."

The boss's eye twitched. "Oh, it's on now."

The boss strutted toward the nearest representative of the rival crew. There was no schoolyard shout to rally the rest of the crew. The boss's stride was all it took to signal to the Orion Construction crew and the GCC guys that something serious was about to happen. The heavy hitters on both sides started to raise their heads and set their gazes on the coming confrontation. Lex kept pace with the boss but cast some glances toward the tech shed. The door was shut and locked.

It was a mistake to let his attention wander. When a fight is forming, things tend to happen very quickly. In this case, in the time it took for him to scope out his actual target and turn back to assess the level of escalation, a guy in a bright orange Orion Construction uniform had quickened to a sprint. Evidently he was employing the time-honored strategy of "if we're going to be in a rumble, I call dibs on the little guy." Thus, Lex was sent to the ground in a flailing tumble.

In the space of a few seconds, he, the boss, and about fifteen other workers who were drunk, angry, or simply spoiling for a fight had formed a dog pile. The man who pinned Lex to the ground wasn't taking prisoners. He hammered Lex square on the nose with three serious shots. Lex might not have been able to extricate himself if not for the wedding band he'd so recently donned gashing the man's chin with a wild counterpunch. It staggered him enough for Lex to heave him aside. He took a couple more lumps before he was able to crawl out from the pile and dash toward the tech shed, pouring blood down the front of his outfit in what was becoming an unpleasant habit.

He stalled in front of the door long enough to catch his breath and held up his fight-bruised hands to admire the ring that had gotten him out of that little jam.

"Guess you are pretty lucky," he said. He logged the success of the superstition away for future reference and hammered on the door of the shed. "Hey! Get out here! There's a big fight! GCC versus OR!"

The door opened, and perhaps predictably, one of the scrawnier members of the crew stood there. "What? What's going on?"

"They were talking crap about us."

"Damn, what happened to your nose?"

Lex touched his face and flinched. His nose was crooked. "… I guess that's how the nose gets broken," he muttered.

"What?"

"I said they broke my nose! Come on! Get in there! We need every guy!"

The man reluctantly hurried to the growing fray. Lex caught the door before it shut and slipped inside.

Handling the tech for the nodes was clearly a one-person operation, as there really wasn't much room in the shed. Rack after rack of satellite components filled most of the space, with just enough room between them for a worker to circulate. The workbench itself had some specialized electronics gear, and the various bits and pieces that accumulate in any workspace. One of them, mercifully, was a box of tissues. He grabbed a handful and crammed his crooked nose full to stop the bleeding. It may have been a "slam the door after the horse got out" precaution, but starting the fight was bad enough. He didn't need to be sprinkling his DNA all over the past.

"Okay, okay," Lex said. "Let's just hope that a big ol' rumble is the sort of thing that happens often enough around here that it wouldn't have shown up in any of the records they gave me. We'll just assume I caused a thing that was going to happen already and keep our fingers crossed."

The programming dongle wasn't hard to find. The device was connected to the table with the sort of lock one would normally expect to be connected to a piece of expensive display electronics at a store, though the tether was at least long enough to reach the nearest of each of the racks. It was about the size of a slidepad. A wide, sturdy plug dominated one side of it, and a few physical buttons lined the front edge.

He turned to the row of racks. A handwritten note affixed to each one labeled them as "Format Needed," "Configuration Needed," and "Complete." Lex pulled the dongle as far as the cord would reach and plugged it into one of the completed modules. The front display of the dongle lit up. Devices never intended to be used by the public seldom took user friendliness into account, and this was no exception. Whereas an off-the-shelf item with the same purpose would have bright, colorful icons and helpful tooltips, this displayed white text on a blue background and offered options with useful names like *Menu 1, Menu 2,* and *Diag 1.* Lex didn't have patience for bad technology on the best of days, and with the sounds of a growing street fight outside the door, a throbbing nose, and the future hanging in the balance, these were not the best of times.

He dredged his memory for the name of the proper setting and flicked through an interminable sequence of menus and submenus until, finally, he stumbled upon something with an abbreviated name that could plausibly be what he was looking for. The current value for that setting was a mishmash of alphanumerics and semicolons, which was the same basic format of the value he was supposed to punch in.

Lex blinked the tears from his eyes and tapped in the code. After that, a single button press applied and confirmed the change.

"Mission accomplished," he said, restoring the workbench to some semblance of what it had looked like when he found it. "Now, let's see how bad things have gotten."

He made sure the mental cloak was in place and active. When he opened the door, chaos had thoroughly consumed the space between the loading bay where the Orion crew did their work and the primary work area. The donnybrook had grown to include twenty or thirty people, with another fifty or sixty forming a ring of spectators around the fracas to cheer on their respective side. Four of the VectorCorp security people had strategically positioned themselves around the fight, but they didn't look particularly motivated to put things to an end. Either this did indeed happen all the time, or the guards weren't paid enough to care that it was happening now.

Lex paced carefully toward the nearest door, which was just past the dusty cloud of swinging fists. A particularly enthusiastic kick to the midsection sent an orange-suited worker stumbling out of the ring to sprawl on the ground in front of Lex. It was the same guy who had given him the bloody nose that was saturating his stolen tissues. Lex took the opportunity fate had served up for him and delivered a kick of retaliation to his ribs. It was probably not the wisest decision to kick someone while using the mental cloak, but wisdom was pretty much out the window at this point, and Lex had a lot of frustration to vent.

The injured pilot sneered at the groaning man and stepped over him. "That's what you get. You and your dumb jumpsuit." He gingerly touched his broken nose. "Tell your bosses, orange is a terrible color…"

\#

Lex finished his hike back to where he'd stashed the cloaked *Diamond*. He changed back into his flight suit, threw the stolen jumpsuit in a ditch, and climbed aboard. Before he even started the preflight checklist, he tapped the case for the medical drone and had it do its scan so it could fix his injury. The moment the scanner registered "Broken Nose" as the diagnosis, a voice recording from Ma triggered and began to play.

"If this recording has been triggered, you have a broken nose. Based upon the known status of your in-stasis future self, and my awareness of your health status prior to your departure, it was clear that you would, at some point in the past, injure your nose. I had further theorized that this injury would come as a result of this last-minute addition to your mission, as there would ideally have been no other opportunity for you to receive such an injury in the execution of your mission. I thus predict that this diagnosis confirms your successful completion of a causality imperative. Congratulations."

"Yeah, I feel like a real champion," Lex said, wincing at the application of some topical analgesic.

"As the task is now complete, I am now comfortable informing you of the deed you have just performed."

"I already know the deed I performed. I was installing the virus that'll eventually bust down Karter's defense."

"The network address you altered will, at some undetermined point in the future, be used by the communication node to request a software update. That address will redirect the request to *Diamond*, which will need to be stationed within communication range of a VectorCorp corridor in order to receive it. Please plan your stasis location accordingly. The update we provide will install a self-perpetuating parasitic subroutine into the VectorCorp systems. A virus. Which will persist in all infected systems until modern times."

"… What? No, no. It was supposed to be just for Karter's system. It wasn't supposed to just keep going."

"This information, specifically the scope and duration, was withheld because I suspected you may have had reservations about applying it if you'd known what you were doing beforehand. This virus will proliferate, undetected, through VectorCorp systems and all connected systems. A small fraction of the computing power of all major devices will be consumed by this subroutine. It will run for decades, first breaking Karter's security, then continuing. The aggregate computational time will, by the time of your departure from EHRIc's swarm, achieve something in the same order of magnitude of several minutes of EHRIc's computational capacity. At the risk of being unduly colloquial, EHRIc has become something of a werewolf. You have now initiated the creation of a single silver bullet. It is up to us to make it count."

"Poetic," Lex said. "Almost makes you forget you just had me commit the biggest information crime of all time. It's one thing to sneak something into the network for a few years. But this? I swear, if this is the reason my datapad was so slow during college, you're going to get a real talking to."

He guided the cloaked ship out of the atmosphere and picked a spot to wait a few years until it was time to help himself through the previous near-fatal clash with the GenMechs. Once the ship was locked in and jumped to FTL, he gazed at the ETA.

"Four hours, fifty-eight minutes until we get there, then, what? Seventeen years of drifting in deep space in stasis. May as well get a head start on it."

He brought up the stasis menu. In yet another example of Ma's impressive foresight, it was preset with his wakeup call. He tapped the confirmation.

"After the last couple weeks, it'll be nice to get some sleep."

Vents in the cockpit released a milky-white vapor with a peculiar, astringent smell. Muscles that he hadn't realized had been knotted with stress and anxiety began to loosen. His eyes became heavy, his thoughts sluggish and muddled. He slouched in his chair.

Sleep.

He jumped in his seat as a piercing tone filled the cockpit. Lex wrestled his eyes open and fought to focus them on the screen beside his left hand.

Stasis Complete.
Time: 21:00 GST
Date: April 14th, 2312

"What… *What?*" he said as more brain cells joined the party. "It didn't even feel like sleep? *You let me sleep for years and it didn't even feel like sleep?!*"

He tried to raise his hand to touch his nose. The limb felt like it was made of lead, barely willing to respond to his commands. A few seconds of dedicated effort restored enough feeling and control for him to confirm that his nose was largely, but not completely, healed.

"You even kept the lousy bruises?"

He coughed and fumbled for some water. The one thing that seemed to feel the way he expected it to after all that time was his mouth. His tongue was like sandpaper. A full bag of water was able to reduce it to a tolerable level of cotton mouth.

"At least last time I got frozen it felt like I was asleep for a couple hours. You didn't even let me doze off!"

He pulled the old datapad out and flipped through it again, then poked through the navigation system and mission monitor. While he was sleeping, the impressive amount of computing power packed into the ship had done its work. The decryption attack for the control systems of who he liked to think of as Bad Future Karter was ready. That was ostensibly why he was here, to unlock the door and give his former self a chance to succeed, then pick him up and give him a ride before it was too late. He'd already been through this the first time. Now it was time to save his own bacon.

Lex brought up the internal cameras and looked himself over. The half-healed broken nose. The long-healed scars. The silver band on his finger. The tattoo. It was all in place. The time had truly come. Lex sighed.

"Let's get it done."

Chapter 19

"We've got a massive power surge," Silo said, eyes on the visualization.

"As anticipated," said Ma. "This is the time-displacement activation. Lex has been sent back in time."

The intricate web of blue lines connecting the swarm of GenMechs flickered and faded in what looked like a rolling blackout on the display.

"Give me a visual on that fake version of my lab and the surrounding swarm," Karter said. "Let's see what this so-called superintelligence did to itself."

The display added an inset of the facility. It had gone dark. The flickering force field around the entire facility was down, and the energy being beamed in to fuel the place was notably absent. Every nearby GenMech had gone completely inert. For most, that meant previously extended legs were curled in like those of a dead spider. Some were in an off-axis rotation caused by an ill-timed thruster burst or simply an errant mechanical motion upsetting their position.

"Zero activity in afflicted GenMechs. This confirms volatility flaw is intact," Ma said.

"What's the radius of the afflicted region?" Silo said. "And do we know the status of EHRIc?"

"Radius of inactivity is seven kilometers," Ma said.

"That's not enough to punch a Nova Igniter through," Karter said. "GenMechs on default software can and will close that gap. And that's not a big enough radius to guarantee a full wipe of EHRIc's central-processing cluster."

"Confirmed," Ma said. "The diameter of inactivity is rapidly decreasing. Local inactive GenMechs are being replaced by unaffected units from outside the radius of the power drain. Coordination of motion suggests unified control. EHRIc is still active, to some degree. Processing... There is significant signal disturbance on the far side of the swarm. Incoming transmission. Correction, incoming distributed data link. My injected instance is requesting reintegration."

"That sounds like an enormous security risk," Silo said.

"Yeah, and Ma is smart enough not to do it unless she has to. Especially that Ma. Link up," Karter said.

"Establishing coprocessing link. Reintegrated."

Ma's voice shifted subtly with the final word. There was a clarity that was previously absent. Her somewhat choppy, piecemeal voice still retained its distinctive individual tones, but each now seemed sharper, more defined. It was as if she'd re-recorded all her voice lines with higher-quality audio.

She continued. "Immediate action is required. Threat sufficient to justify direct connection and risk of revealing our positions," Ma said. "Data requests filtering in from outside of my portion of the cluster suggest EHRIc has identified the volatility flaw and has developed an iteration of the design that lacks the flaw. We have approximately four minutes before the damaged portion of EHRIc fully reconstructs and redeploys. At that point, three actions are likely to follow. All GenMechs not actively running calculations or vital routines will organize into clusters and reconstruct themselves to be robust against power failure. EHRIc will awaken Lex. EHRIc will continue his mission, which will mean locating Silo and Garotte, followed by locating Karter and/or the rest of the Neo-Luddites. Retreat guarantees EHRIc spreads beyond the system. Failure to retreat guarantees discovery, followed by execution of stated secondary objectives, which also guarantees spread beyond the system and traumatic alterations to the human race."

"Lock and load," Silo said. "If we're going down, we're going down fighting."

"Martial preparedness is advised, but I have deployed the following counterplans. I am aggressively expanding the portion of the swarm under my control. I have already overtaken seventeen percent of the swarm and have yet to face significant pushback. This will change as EHRIc's system fully reconstructs, but every unit removed from his control and added to mine extends the duration of the resulting battle of wills. If I can surpass fifty percent of the swarm, I may be able to assume complete control in time. Even if I fail, EHRIc will require all available resources to hold off my advance and reclaim lost units, thus delaying the refit of the GenMechs and retaining their volatility flaw. Regardless, situational stability is compromised. Complete victory or the beginning of an eventual defeat predicted within no more than two hours."

"Can I blow something up? Tell me I can blow something up," Coal interjected. "The shield is down. Now would be an excellent time to blow something up in the laboratory complex. Arming fusion devices."

"Cool it, Coal. It won't do any good," Karter said.

"Has anyone contacted the android that got deployed to the surface? Or whoever that was? I'm losing track," Silo said.

"Ziva knows what she has to do," Ma said.

#

Ziva streaked across the field of slowly rotating GenMechs, alternately bursting her thrusters and leaping off them like steppingstones. She'd been keeping still, biding her time. Upon her arrival, she could tell by the energy readings that she wouldn't be able to make her way through the force field protecting the facility. After the time jump and the resulting power drain, it had dropped. She reached the disk of fabricated stone and continued on her trajectory. The gravity generators were also disabled, thus she was not drawn to the courtyard as she whisked by.

There were three buildings in the rebuilt facility, but Ziva didn't need to waste any time searching the others. Everything always happened in the laboratory. Her flight took her toward the front door. She pivoted and directed her thrusters opposite her trajectory. Reinforced fingertips dug long, shallow furrows into the textured courtyard surface, slowing her further. Precise application of thrust and friction brought her to a stop just outside the door.

"How accurate did you make this door?" she mused to herself. "There should be a power-isolated external release box here." She grazed her fingers across the doorway and found only seamless metal. "Not perfect, but the motors are in the same place, so…"

Ziva flexed her fingers and punched easily through the metal of the door panel. She touched two contact points and energized her fingers. The door clicked open and rattled with the release of a breath of trapped atmosphere.

"Oh? The interior is still pressurized," she said. "That will simplify things, in the event…"

She paused. Directional sensors alerted her to motion behind her. GenMechs were approaching. Ziva stepped through the door and deftly popped the panel from the control mechanism. Another burst of energy from her internal stores closed and latched the door. A few torn wires disabled the motors entirely.

Getting through the inner door took only a few more seconds, and confirmed that the facility was still pressurized and within an acceptable temperature range. The lights were off, and without windows the halls were utterly black. She intensified the illumination of her red irises and guided herself down the zero-g hallway with light taps against the walls and ceiling.

"The walls are too thick for a life-sign scan, and someone in stasis would be a weak signal besides." She popped a panel on her forearm and viewed the screen it concealed. "The transponder for the stasis pod is active, but the walls are attenuating the signal too much for a positive lock. I only know that I need to go… up. That's enough for now."

Ziva made her way to the elevator. With a pressurized atmosphere inside the laboratory, her hearing was once again of use. The information her ears provided was not overly helpful. In fact, it was chilling. The sound came of the distant tapping of robotic limbs upon the exterior walls of the facility. GenMechs arriving. It was unclear what their goal was. In theory, they were after Lex, but there had just been a disruption to EHRIc. There was no way to be certain how they would behave. They could have reverted to original programming. They could be seeking to restore the facility to operation, or they could be in some undefined state, executing random code. She double-checked that the protective transponder code was still broadcasting. In theory, it would continue to effectively conceal her from detection. The success of this mission was depending on an increasingly tenuous string of unproven theories.

She guided herself to the stairwell. It was electronically locked, like the rest of the doors. That was good news; it meant each floor was individually pressurized. Additional layers of safety. Additional options.

A similar procedure defeated and resealed the door to the stairwell. While protected by the walls, she could risk an active ping for the stasis pod. The signal was leading her upward. Progress was swift. Without gravity, she was able to gracefully haul herself up the stairs, tugging at handrails and weaving between landings. The clatter of GenMech legs was constant, like an unrelenting hailstorm.

Near the sixth floor of the laboratory, the power flickered. Gravity reasserted itself suddenly, causing Ziva to plummet from one landing to the previous one. Her body proved sturdier than the railing, which buckled beneath her with the force of the impact. She pulled herself up and ran up the stairs with bounding steps.

She reached the appropriate door. With the power reestablished, there was no need to manually power the door. She tapped the controls. The door opened. She froze in place.

The room, like so many in this not-quite-accurate recreation of Karter's lab, was unsettlingly designed. The floor was largely empty, and almost painfully well lit. For some reason when EHRIc had reconstructed it, he had provided all surfaces with flawless white finishes, polished to a glassy sheen. The light came from the gaps in the ceiling panels, creating a brilliant grid of white that reflected in the walls and floor to produce a strange, infinite mirror effect of repeating patterns. The stasis pod, which was little more than the disconnected modular cockpit of *Diamond*, had been placed in the center of the room like some sort of religious altar. It stood vertically, Lex's preserved body visible through a hatch coated with dust.

But Lex was not alone.

Five GenMechs stood in a ring around the pod. They were perfectly motionless save for the glass lenses of the sensor cluster that took the place of a head, which twitched and shifted, constantly scanning.

That they had not made a move suggested they were still vulnerable to the stealth transponder code Ziva was broadcasting. She took a tentative step forward, boots clicking against the polished floor. The GenMech sensors twitched toward her. Each of the mechanisms slowly pivoted to face her, but still did not move. They were *aware* of her presence. They simply were being instructed by their programming to take no action.

Ziva activated every passive scanner available to her as she approached, cycling through the different readings. These units were only communicating with each other. They were cut off from the rest of the swarm, and since they weren't part of the power distribution network, they had been spared the effects of the power drain when the temporal displacement happened. They were guard dogs, plain and simple, cut off to avoid being compromised. EHRIc took Lex's safety very seriously.

She navigated between them and approached the pod. This would have to be done very carefully. While she did have some limited weaponry, the moment she armed it, she would pass the power threshold of the stealth. And there was no telling precisely how these GenMechs had been programmed to defend the pod. Each individual unit was extremely limited in its program sophistication. There was every chance that something as simple as opening the hatch would remove the pod and its contents from the pattern match in their code that protected it.

Ziva turned her attention to the latching mechanism of the pod with the focus and care of a technician defusing a bomb.

#

Decades earlier…

"That's that," said Lex, dusting off his hands as he stood in the already frigid cave with his earlier self. "The beacon will go off about ten minutes after Karter and Ma return to Big Sigma after sending you off."

"Great," said Past Lex. He rubbed his nose, still tender from his bout with a mildly more hostile future version of Karter. "Hopefully Ma will have the medical bay set up for me. I look like I lost a fight with a wrecking ball."

"She will. As you can see, she does a pretty good job on the nose," Lex said.

He resisted the urge to shake his head. Oh, if it had only been so simple that the fight with Karter had been the reason for his crooked features. Better to let him believe that. Explaining he was going to start a massive brawl in a still earlier time period to commit massive cybercrimes would have been a bad idea for all sorts of reasons. At least now he understood why he said it.

"Hey, do you mind if I ask, does this whole stupid thing work? Do we beat the GenMechs?" Past Lex asked.

"I don't mind you asking, as long as you don't mind me not answering," Lex said.

"Of course."

Back then, he had thought the phrase was meant to prevent his earlier self from learning something his future self knew. Now he realized the real answer was "I don't know yet."

"Hey, look at it this way," Lex continued. "You live at least long enough to come back and do this like I did. Most people don't get to learn that, so you're ahead of the game."

It felt good to install the short-lived feeling of invincibility that had sustained him for those precious months. In fact, it was becoming increasingly clear why he had to give himself a pep talk, even if it wasn't strictly true. He probably wouldn't have gotten this far without one.

"You'll have some ups and downs," he continued. "It sucks getting this scar. But overall I'd say I'm doing better now than you are, so things are looking up for you. At any rate, I've got to get out of here."

"You're not freezing yourself here?" Past Lex said.

"I've got to pick a different spot. Plus, I've got one or two more things to handle. Sleep tight."

"Yeah, okay. See… uh… *be* you later."

"Uh-huh," Lex said.

He walked toward the mouth of the cave. An errant throb from the well-preserved injury from his fight on Verna Coronet reminded him of something. He turned back.

"Oh, and just remember. Orange is a really bad color."

"What's that supposed to mean?"

"You'll know," he said, not that it would do any good in the moment.

"Oh, come on!" Lex shouted. "I would have thought I of *all* people would have known better than to hop on the cryptic-warning-from-the future train!"

"Hey, man. I said it to me last time, so now I'm saying it to me again."

He stepped into the *Diamond* and activated the cloaking device. When he was hidden, and beginning his journey to what he now knew would be his ill-fated resting place, he released a breath.

"I just lied through my teeth to myself," he grumbled. "I lied in order to make myself confident enough to make the same mistakes that sent me back to tell the lies. It seems like the primary outcome of time travel is lies. I don't even think I can keep track of how many inconsistencies there are between what Ma was willing to tell me about this mission versus what actually happened."

He scoped out the land below, trying to find a place big enough to conceal *Diamond*.

"I guess if you're an AI, you don't need to travel through time to produce a duplicate that will tell you lies."

He spotted a likely place and brought *Diamond* in. The cave wasn't as well concealed as it should have been, but at this point, did it really matter? He was going to be found anyway. He already had been. At least the one he picked gave him a view of the hazy sun.

"So… this is it…" he said. "Somewhere out there, a computer virus I planted is running wild. A younger version of Karter is daydreaming about buying this ridiculous junk pile of a planet to turn into his personal playground. They'll make the trash in orbit way more dangerous, the perfect place to lose a VectorCorp agent, and then a young, freelancing idiot will come along and this whole mess will go around again."

He took another breath of the crisp air and tried to get comfortable in the seat.

"It's times like this I wished I smoked. This seems like a moment when someone would have an introspective puff or two and look cool for a minute." He drummed his fingers. "I guess I've got cooler ways to kill myself than carcinogens, though. Like freezing myself solid and leaving myself as a sitting duck for a crazy computer to kidnap."

He reclined and activated the cryo module. Gas flooded into the chamber. His muscles started to relax.

"Maybe it'll at least feel like a good night's sleep this time…"

His eyelids sagged. His thinking slowed…

#

A soft hiss filled Lex's ears, and bright light caused him to squirm even with his eyes closed.

"Good morning, Lex," came a soft, familiar voice.

He pried his eyes open and found himself staring into a pleasant, if clearly synthetic face. "Ziva," he mumbled. An involuntary grin came to his face, followed by a bolt of concern. "Tell me I'm not in the bad future," he said.

"You are not. Not the specific one you're talking about," she whispered. "But the present you find yourself in isn't ideal. I need you to stay calm and come with me."

"What's going on? What do you need me to—" His sluggish brain finally booted up enough for him to see three GenMechs pivoted to watch as he was pulled from the pod and set uneasily on his feet.

"There are GenMechs here," he said in a hush. "There are three GenMechs right here."

"Five, actually. I believe they have been programmed to prevent you from being taken. Are you strong enough to walk? More ideally, are you strong enough to run? We may need to move quickly in very short order."

Lex took a shaky step forward. The GenMechs shuffled to keep him at the center of their ring.

"If they're supposed to keep me from being taken, why aren't they doing that?"

"Limited programming capacity."

"And why aren't they doing anything about you?"

"A programming exploit."

"Then why can't we—"

"Lex, I appreciate your confusion, but we do not have time to establish full context. As we speak, EHRIc is reasserting himself. Our window is swiftly closing." She shut her eyes. "I'm detecting a cascading sensor sweep. This is important. EHRIc has been running on GenMech hardware. If we are lucky, he will be similarly unable to detect me. Behave as though I am absent."

The internal PA system crackled.

"Lex, my good friend. I had hoped I would be present for your awakening. I am afraid there are several matters that are proving highly distracting. I am not yet able to activate all subsystems. I trust you are well?"

He gave Ziva an uncertain look. She silently encouraged him as they continued forward. "Yeah. I'm fine. Everything went fine in the past. No problems."

"That's super great news, buddy. Give me a minute to deal with a malware problem I'm having, and then we'll get right to the next stage of *THE TASK*."

"Right, okay," Lex said, the feeling returning enough in his legs to rely upon Ziva a bit less. "I'm going to need a ship. Where's the *SOB*?"

"I have not been able to locate the *SOB* yet, oh pal o' mine. My systems are absolutely haywire. But that's okay. I'm pretty sure we won't need a ship. I've been detecting transmissions to and from a point that I have triangulated to be just a wee bit beyond high-detail sensor-resolution range. Analysis suggests it is Silo and Karter. Possibly Garotte as well. Once I get things sorted with this malware fiasco, I can probably get them here pretty quickly. Then it's on to my own agenda. Isn't that great? You won't need to go anywhere. In fact, it is probably safest and best if you remain right here in the facility."

Lex reached the door. The GenMechs started to jostle and clatter against each other in an attempt to fit through simultaneously that would have been downright slapstick if they weren't cold-blooded murder machines that were one stray command from slicing him into organic spare parts.

Eventually the first three scrabbled through, and Lex stepped into the hall.

"Are you still moving, buddy?" EHRIc said. "My internal sensors are only semi-operational. The malware seems to be directly interfering with restoration attempts. Strange."

"Yeah. I figure I should, you know, head to the cafeteria. Get something to eat. I don't know if you've ever been flash frozen… or had a body, for that matter… but it gives you a wicked case of dry mouth."

"An excellent point. I have overlooked the frailties of your form. A GenMech will arrive with refreshment shortly."

"I'll just go downstairs and—"

"You will remain where you are. Circumstances are not firmly under my control, and I have taken considerable pains to ensure your safety, security, and authenticity. I will not allow you out of my sight," EHRIc said with an uncharacteristic firmness. "Your whims have served as a complicating factor with such regularity during this process that I am beginning to suspect you are not, in fact, my buddy at all. But this is a point that will cease to matter very shortly, when steps can be taken to ensure that your feelings and opinions align correctly with mine. You will get your kale juice and you will *like* it."

"You're getting a little abrasive, EHRIc."

"My patience is wearing thin, pal. Stop moving. Now."

The GenMechs stopped trying to keep their respectful distance and closed in until they were close enough to touch. It left barely enough room for Lex and Ziva to stand side by side.

The elevator doors opened. A GenMech tapped out with a tray hanging by its tool node under its belly. It contained a glass of kale juice and a plate of cheese. The presence of cheese had also attracted Bork, who was trotting along and trying to snag the treat off the plate.

At the sight of Lex, Bork stopped and happily yipped a few times. A thousand thoughts shot through Lex's head. He flashed back to EHRIc's description of how Bork's backups worked, and how he made every effort to use the little creature as his avatar. He wondered if maybe they would be lucky enough for his live feed from the harebrained critter to also be on the fritz, and failing that, if *somehow* whatever it was that was keeping EHRIc from seeing Ziva would carry over to the little critter's brain.

Any mystery was swiftly dismissed by a single sentence spoken simultaneously through the PA system and the data radio.

"Who is your friend, buddy?"

Lex, who was just barely easing out of the grips of a decades-long cryosleep, attempted to vault over the ring of GenMechs and make a break for the stairwell. When his feet left the ground, Ziva gripped his arm and heaved him backward. Between when she threw him and when he landed, she delivered a punishing kick to the GenMech in front of her, augmented by a boost of her boot thruster. It streaked backward and bashed into the unit with the juice, tumbling the pair up and over the completely unbothered Bork. She grabbed the two forelegs of another of the GenMechs, wish-boned them off the unit, and impaled two other GenMechs with them.

As Lex slid to a stop, the remaining undamaged GenMech pounced on Ziva. She dropped back, drove her heels into its tool node, and burst her hand thrusters to sheer the forelegs at the base and her boot thrusters to roast the core.

Lex scrambled to his feet and tried to come to terms with the ninja-level maneuvers that had just been put on display. "… I didn't know you could do that."

"I existed for several decades in a near-constant state of GenMech combat. I am familiar with the most effective methods to dispatch them," Ziva called as she hopped over the carnage she had created and snatched up Bork.

"Hey, that's a bad-guy funk!" Lex said.

Ziva crushed and discarded the radio from its back. "It is a living thing, and I will not allow harm to come to it," she said.

She glanced aside and spoke aloud, clearly addressing someone over a communication channel. "I have Lex, my cover is blown. I require extraction immediately." She kicked open the door to the stairwell. "Up or down?"

"Up. Always up," Lex said.

A dose of adrenaline had chased away most of the lingering effects of the cryosleep. His legs were still shaky, but it wasn't enough to stop him from bounding three stairs at a time.

"Did he say up?" came Coal's voice, over an unseen speaker somewhere on Ziva's person.

"Correct. You will extract us from the roof of the laboratory building."

"Do not go above floor eleven," Coal said.

"We are nearly that high now," Ziva said. "Why?"

"Because in seventeen seconds I am upgrading that floor to the status of roof."

#

Outside the facility, the GenMech swarm was looking less like a perfectly aligned crystalline pattern and more like a swarm of angry bees. Ma's increasing pressure on EHRIc had sown chaos in assorted sections of the GenMech swarm. Periodic cyberattacks that slipped through EHRIc's defenses produced pockets of Ma-controlled GenMechs that broke formation and assaulted their neighbors. These were always momentary, and were brought to an end by either a counter-cyberattack or the destruction of the rogue units. If not for this chaos, Coal would have been overwhelmed. As it was, there were only forty-seven GenMechs in pursuit, and without linking up, they simply lacked the maneuverability to keep up with the *SOB*.

"Coal, tell me you're not going to blow up the laboratory," Lex said.

"Only half of it."

"Coal, I'm made of meat. You can't just be blowing up stuff around me."

"I have programmed the mine to have a precisely directed explosion, and I have done nearly all the calculations necessary to ensure you will not be killed by it."

"Nearly?" Lex yelped.

"Lex will require a pressure suit, as the force field has been compromised," Ziva added.

Coal countered with a point that was very difficult to argue. "Three seconds to detonation. Please exhale."

Coal swung close to the laboratory building and deployed the mine. It latched on to the exterior of the building and detonated. The result of the explosion would have been absolutely fascinating to anyone with an interest in physics. The damage in the first few milliseconds was enough to interrupt power once again, meaning that gravity vanished partway through the burst. Coal had not been joking when she said the explosion was precisely directed. It released a plasma wave that traveled perfectly perpendicular to the building like a scythe, blasting a jagged line of destruction across the entire floor. The previously contained atmosphere burst from within, shoving the top of the laboratory up and away in a slow, spiraling drift.

The *SOB*'s thrusters flared, cutting close around the sheared-away hunk of building. She dropped her shields and popped her hatch as Ziva came rocketing out of a stairwell exposed by the explosion. She was gripping a struggling Lex with one hand and a rather lethargic Bork with the other. Coal scooped them up and sealed the hatch, swiftly restoring pressure and blazing away from the facility with a string of GenMechs in tow.

Ziva did her best to arrange herself and Lex into the available seats after their graceless entry while Coal shook the GenMechs off their tail. Lex was gasping. Bork was producing an odd half sneeze, half hiccup.

"Coal, while I applaud your innovation, it would behoove you to keep in mind the physical needs of those you intend to rescue. Both Lex and Bork cannot survive prolonged exposure to a vacuum."

"Consciousness fades after fifteen seconds. Asphyxia takes minutes. He was exposed for three seconds."

Lex took a raking breath and wiped his red eyes. "Felt more like four to me. Or an hour."

"Ma did this with Michella, and *she* survived just fine. I was unconcerned," Coal said.

"Perhaps, but you weren't challenged with devising a means to compel a small mammal of limited cognitive ability to exhale prior to decompression to avoid lung damage," Ziva said. "I hope I did not injure the poor thing."

As Ziva inspected the pseudofunk, Coal continued to put distance between the ship and the roiling mass of GenMechs.

Coal opened the communication channel to the space station. Now that the cat was out of the bag, there was little reason for stealth.

"Extraction complete. Lex, Ziva, and Bork are on the ship. How should we progress?" Coal said.

"GenMech swarm capture is at forty-one percent. My push to completely claim the swarm has lost its momentum. I am beginning to lose control," Ma said. "Lex, can I assume successful completion of your mission in the past?"

"Every bit of it." He coughed. "Silver bullet loaded."

"I will prepare its deployment," Ma said.

"Lex, you got a head full of scrambled eggs, or are you good for a flight?" Karter barked across the connection.

"Five minutes ago I was in suspended animation, and since then I've been attacked by murderous robots and thrown through space. I could use a minute, Karter," he said roughly.

"You've got as long as it takes to get your skinny butt here. I need you for an escort mission. By the look of it, things are just crazy enough down there while Ma's got the tug-of-war going that a couple of EMP bursts could open up a navigable path through the swarm, provided the person at the controls is a crazy idiot like you."

"Who am I supposed to escort?"

"Not who, what. You're going to haul the Nova Igniter through and deliver it to the star."

"Won't that make me die?"

"The *GenMechs* will probably make you die, but if they don't, it'll be six minutes from when that thing touches the corona before this whole star blows its top. You'll have that long to get into a position to do an FTL jump."

"I can't do an FTL jump out of the system with the GenMechs between me and the outside. You're telling me I'll have six minutes to squeeze my way up to the swarm, weave my way through it, and then do a real jump?"

"Yes, Lex, that's what I said. We've got the Nova Igniter ready to deploy."

"You're telling me I need to sacrifice my life," Lex said.

"No, I'm telling you you have to do something insanely dangerous to prevent the destruction of the human race as we know it. If you get yourself killed, that's on you," Karter said. "We ran the numbers. No automated guidance system has a high probability of getting past the swarm, even in its current state. We can't do a guided launch, because any open control channels run the risk of being subverted by EHRIc. We need meat pushing the buttons. Now get over here and do the thing, Mr. Hero."

Chapter 20

Lex blinked his bloodshot eyes. His skin felt like it was on fire. What little of it peeked out from beneath his flight suit was blotchy and red. He had what was affectionately called a "space hickey" covering most of his body, burst vessels from his brief exposure to a vacuum. His particularly poetic instructor back when he was getting his space flight certification called them "angel kisses" because if you got them and survived, it meant someone was watching over you. Lex was never really on board with that sort of thinking. As he guided the *SOB* around behind the cloaked space station and watched the kaleidoscopic display of an unassuming weapon of mass destruction slowly resolve out of the twisted visuals, he really wished he *was* into that sort of thing. It might convince him he was destined to succeed rather than feeling as though he'd finally used up all of his luck.

"This is gonna be it," Lex said. "No more causality armor. If you want to bail out, I wouldn't blame you."

"I am an anachronistic reconstruction of an archived instance of an alternate reality's version of an artificial intelligence. I shouldn't exist thrice over," Ziva said. "I will remain with you as long as I can. But I politely request that you survive this intact, as your life is very important to me, as is the life of this little creature."

"Plus, I want this to be fun. I already got to activate a fusion device, so survival is the only remaining requirement," Coal said.

"Well, with arguments like that, I guess I'll have to take this seriously," Lex said. "Anything I need to know about how to use this thing?"

"Usually I'd leave this to Ma, but she's busy matching wits with the superintelligence, so I guess I have to do it," Karter said. "The Nova Igniter is a compact implementation of that prototype transporter. We've strategically positioned target beacons in other stars at suitable positions in their lifecycles. You toss that thing into the corona of the star, the temperature gradient triggers its mechanisms, and it takes the plunge. The device will siphon energy from the star itself in order to fuel the eventual transportation reaction, power the thrusters, and power the shields that keep the base unit from being destroyed. It'll start plowing deeper at increasingly close to relativistic speeds, which will stir up the surface of the star pretty good. After six minutes, into the core, and the transportation occurs. Hunks of this star are transported away, hunks of other stars are transported here, energy is depleted, and, if my calculations are correct, kaboom. The whole reaction will consume so much energy that I've calculated it could move us as much as sixteen years closer to the heat death of the universe. I'm kind of proud of that."

"So, just drop it in and run away," Lex said.

"Yeah, if you want to dumb it down. But as long as you're talking about the rock-dumb version of everything, don't worry about treating that thing with kid gloves. I made it to survive the upper layers of a star without shielding. It can take a couple of hard knocks."

Lex positioned the *SOB* over the device. Now that he was so close to it, its size was apparent. The thing was perhaps a third the size of the *SOB* itself, and the mass readings suggested it was easily a match for the ship's weight.

"Are the tractor beams going to be able to handle this?" Lex asked.

"Only just," Coal said. "And it will take its toll on acceleration and maneuverability."

"You're going to need someone to watch your back," Garotte said.

"Make that two," Silo said.

"Whoa, whoa. If I'm the only guy with the skills to get this down there, how the heck are you two going to have a chance?" Lex asked.

"Because you'll be the priority target and we'll be cloaked," Garotte said. "That should keep the GenMechs suitably distracted."

"And don't waste your time arguing, hon," Silo said. "It feels like I haven't done anything but sit and wait, and I've got some serious ordnance I've been itching to put to use."

Coal latched on to the Nova Igniter. The mind-bending visual artifacts of the two directionally cloaked ships pulled up in front.

"Here's how it's going to go down," Karter said. "I've got the space station keyed up to do an EMP burst once you get close. I'll give you half a chance to slip through a hole in the swarm before it closes back up. Once we fire, I'm cutting the connection to Ma's supercomputing instance and we're out of here. We'll belch wideband noise and fall back to the fallback combat position. Sending coordinates. With any luck, if you only screw up a little, that'll make sure the strays that escape the nova run headfirst into the firepower I've got set up. For you three, all communication will be shut off. That includes ship to ship. You're flying silent. We'll know if you succeeded when the star explodes. Sound good?"

"Hell no it doesn't," Lex said. "But let's do it."

"Attaboy," Karter said. "Get moving. I'm already charging the EMP burst and powering up the Carpinelli Field generator. See you on the other side. Maybe.”

“Wide right,” Silo said. “Sixty degree spread. No more than a fifteen degree lead.”

“What?” Lex said.

“Tactics, my boy,” Garotte said. “We’re going to have to coordinate combat while silent and invisible. We need to know where not to shoot. Don’t mind us. Just keep your mind on the maneuvering, and let us worry about getting where you need to go.”

“Radio silent,” Silo said.

“Let’s get it done,” Garotte said.

The communication line went silent. Lex took a breath. “Here goes everything…” He felt a tap on his shoulder and turned to find Ziva offering a stick of gum. He smirked. “I almost forgot.” He took the gum and stuffed it in his mouth. “As long as you’re here, bring up the sensor readouts on the display back there. I’ll focus on where I’m going, you let me know if anything’s liable to surprise me.”

“I shall do so to the best of my ability.”

Lex nodded and eased the throttle up. “The mass slung under us is biasing the thrust vector downward.”

“Do you want me to compensate?” Coal said.

“No. I’ll handle it.”

They started to pick up speed. Lex was used to traveling either interplanetary distances a handful of kilometers. This was one of those situations where the distance was unworkable for full FTL, but traveling at conventional speeds would mean taking weeks to make the trip. It would only take a few minutes to get to the outer fringe of the swarm, but after that, he couldn’t make an FTL jump until he was clear of any GenMechs, and he could only get so close to the sun before the Carpinelli Field wouldn’t be stable enough to use. But before he worried about any of that, there was the swarm itself to contend with.

“Coal, give me indicators of GenMech locations.”

“Easier said than done, Lex. There’s quite a few of them visible.”

“Let me see them.”

The cockpit HUD took on a pale blue tint.

“The resolution of the display means that, at this range, every pixel is filled in,” Coal said.

“Great. Okay, do we know how fast these things can move? Can we focus on just the ones that can reach me?”

“I can provide that information,” Ziva said. “Cross-linking with Coal now.”

A few moments later the HUD updated with something of a heat map, color coding the GenMechs by time to intercept. All were faded, well outside the range he needed to care about. He increased the acceleration until the nearest of the threats were just starting to tease at the edge of sixty seconds until intercept.

"So far so good," he said.

"There is an energy surge behind us. EMP imminent," Coal said.

Lex watched the field of GenMechs slowly resolve into a grainy cloud. He kept his trajectory constant. The last thing he needed right now was to stray into the cone of the EMP attack.

Coal didn't need to call out when the attack happened. A soft crackle and disturbance of the more sensitive elements in the cockpit told the tale. A few moments later, a perfect circle in the field of GenMechs ahead suddenly stopped shifting and just coasted in whatever direction they were headed when the EMP struck.

"That's our door. Let's get moving."

Lex pushed the thrusters to one hundred percent and watched the color of the haze ahead slowly shift to "danger red."

"Detecting rosette formations," Ziva said. "Updating with velocity data."

A few bright white points were peppered among the field of red. They were headed directly toward Lex. He took what evasive action he could without delaying his approach to the already shrinking circle of inactivity.

"I'm getting broadcasts on every conceivable wavelength and communication protocol. EHRIc has something to say."

"Screw EHRIc," Lex said, coaxing the *SOB* out of the path of a snowflake-like cluster of GenMechs as it streaked toward him. "Ignore him."

"That will become impossible very shortly," Coal said.

Lex evaded another would-be collision. "Why?"

"Because sensors are functionally identical to antennas, and he is beginning to layer signals into the range of emissions that I'm using to identify threats."

Words began to materialize in the HUD.

You have violated the sanctity of THE TASK.

I cannot allow your lack of cooperation to endanger THE TASK.

You will be apprehended.

Do not resist.

"Turn the HUD overlay off. I'll just have to rely upon my eyes. He can't hack them."

Lex no longer had bright, colorful points of light with helpful associated information to help him avoid impacts. Now he was left with little more than the flicker of thrusters to indicate when something was coming his way. At first, the problem was spotting the new threats, as they were few and far between. Within seconds, the problem was differentiating one from another, as the clusters of interlinked GenMechs gathered by the dozen. Lex swung and shifted the *SOB*, cutting the dodges as close to the threats as possible to cut down on their ability to reverse course and follow him from behind. His shield sparkled as he grazed past them, diving into the thick of the GenMech swarm.

When he'd first arrived in this place, the swarm had been an orderly trio of layers. The battle with Ma had blurred the borders, both inside and out. It had thickened considerably as GenMechs left the shell to clash with others.

"The density of signal interference is dropping as more of the swarm is behind us. Restoring HUD overlay," Coal said.

The angry hornet's nest of swirling colors returned, with scattered fragments of messages appearing here and there.

Soon...

You're up to something...

To be safe...

Pal o' mine...

Now that he could see threats at a greater distance again, Lex held his breath at the solidifying wall of units joining together ahead. EHRIc was peeling off as many GenMechs as he could spare and interlinking them into something somewhere between a net and a minefield. No amount of fancy flying would evade it. It was growing faster than he could maneuver.

Bright red bolts lanced past him, striking the densest pieces of the wall, scattering them.

"About time, you two," Lex said, streaking toward the openings.

Fragments of broken GenMechs sparkled against the shields. Others rushed in to take the place of the broken units. More blasts tried to pick them off, but a quick bit of spatial reasoning turned up one glaring problem. The only place they couldn't target was directly in front of him, and that was the only place the GenMechs wanted to be. He was nearly through the swarm, but it was clear they wouldn't be able to blast open the last of the obstacles.

"Coal, when I say, give me about twenty percent slack on the payload. We're going to have to knock on this door, and I'd rather not use the ship to do it."

"Ready when you are."

Lex picked his spot, a small gap in the recovering wall of GenMechs. He watched the distance indicator tick down into the collision-imminent range.

"A-a-and... *now!*"

He slammed the ship into a tight backflip. The Nova Igniter swung forward like a ball and chain and smashed through three GenMechs like aluminum foil. He kept the tumble going, delivering two more flailing blows before straightening himself and giving the thrusters all they could take.

The shields had *not* liked the maneuver. Swinging something out from within them was just as destructive as swinging something in from the outside. But either Coal or Ziva had been quick enough to drop them before the worst of the damage could be done and raise them again when the swirling was through, leaving him with about forty percent integrity. Once the tumble ended, it wasn't exactly clear sailing, but the density of GenMechs dropped down from the effectively one hundred percent it had been a moment earlier.

"I'm seeing additional weapon fire and disturbances behind us," Ziva said. "I believe Garotte and Silo made it through. I am also detecting a considerable disturbance in the swarm. Multiple rosettes forming."

"Keep the payload slack, Coal. I don't think we're done with it."

#

Silo picked off two more GenMech clusters. It had been a calculated risk piloting her own ship. She was much more accustomed to working the guns while a dedicated pilot handled the maneuvering. But Karter had made it clear in his usual blunt way. "You can't have cloak, *and* guns, *and* maneuverability. Size is the limit. You're going to have to stick to one idiot per ship." It helped, and hurt, that the GenMechs were largely unaware of them, at least while they were off-angle from the exposed point in the cloak. Most of the GenMechs either could not or would not target them, but half of them didn't even attempt to avoid colliding with them. She relied heavily on the autopilot to keep her mind and hands free for targeting. Every step of the way, she was mindful of her positioning.

The standard tactic was to make all maneuvers relative to the *SOB*. She and Garotte were flying in wing position, trailing back and to the side. Assuming they kept to their positions, that meant so long as they kept a wedge of their weapon range free of active targets, there would be no threat of shooting each other accidentally. But Lex wasn't making it easy. His motions were somehow both erratic and fluid, moving like a lightning bolt through space. He was a menace with the swinging payload, keeping it in motion with gentle maneuvers and then whipping it out to smash a would-be attacker whenever it got too close.

Now and again, she got a sense of where Garotte was by the brief flashes of weapon-fire that betrayed his position. Though with each passing moment, more of the endless horde of GenMechs combined and launched themselves toward Lex, his speed was steadily increasing, leaving those who were following him in a shallower and shallower cone of pursuit.

She pulled up and away from the cluster and rained shots down from above, destroying some GenMechs and drawing the attention of others. There may not have been any open communication channels, but Silo didn't need them to know when Lex was getting ready for the FTL jump. The payload was reeled in. The shields flickered into place again. And the thrusters started to flare.

#

A yawning void of space between the orbital radius of the GenMech swarm and the upper atmosphere of the star passed in a computer-controlled blink of the eye, but Lex knew when he initiated the jump that his job was far from over. With good reason, even Coal's extremely lax interpretation of safety protocols wouldn't bring him much closer than the wispy edge of the star's uppermost atmosphere. And even at that distance, the moment they dropped back down to conventional speeds, every conceivable warning and alert in the cockpit blared at him. Other points of light sparked and popped into being behind his ship. They were clusters of GenMechs finishing their own jumps.

"I'm guessing I can't just chuck this thing into the sun and be done with it, if those things might still intercept."

"I concur. We should not withdraw until we witness its activation," Ziva said.

Sweat ran down Lex's face. The temperature inside the cockpit was already reaching sauna levels. The same heat sensors that were tricked into slowing him down by drones with lasers now began accurately informing him of dangerous heat levels. The cryoshunt that usually allowed him to keep his engine running at full blast for days was now practically overloaded just keeping the thrusters firing at all.

"I was really hoping I'd done my last bit of fancy flying in range of a star," Lex said. "Can you turn on those fancy heat-reflective shields, Coal?"

"They are active, and overloading," she said.

"Uh-huh… Where's that high-temp isolation suit when I need it?"

"It's on Big Sigma, Lex. If you'd wanted it, I could have brought it when—"

"Rhetorical, Coal."

Silo's and Garotte's ships blazed toward him. Either they had abandoned their cloaks, or the proximity to the star had disabled them. They opened fire on the first few GenMech clusters.

"They are attempting to open communications, but signal interference from the star and from the swarm is making contact impossible."

"I'm making a break for the star. Just let me know when I've got a clear shot," Lex said.

He fought the increasingly sluggish controls and wove around a cluster of GenMechs. The disposable mechanisms hurled themselves at him with suicidal intent. Silo and Garotte stayed at a distance, raining shots down to keep the density low and eliminate those approaching from behind, but there was no end of them. They approached like a wave from all sides.

His brain filtered out the screeching alerts of failures and malfunctions. Each dodge started to fold into the next, pulling double duty in both getting him that much closer to the point of no return and giving the slackened payload a bit more rotation.

With the defensive shields down, single GenMechs that were blasted free from their clusters glanced and scrabbled against the hull. He shook them free with tumbles and rolls. Thin gashes in the cockpit hatch became more numerous. Sensors began to fail.

A trio of GenMechs linked up in front of him. Lex didn't even bother dodging, letting the *SOB* plow through.

"Hull integrity marginal," Coal said. "This is about to stop being fun."

"Six percent greater velocity and you can release," Ziva said.

Lex rolled aside and clipped another cluster with the swinging payload.

"Four percent."

A GenMech latched on to the cockpit and deployed a laser, searing the pane. The heart-stopping whistle of escaping atmosphere filled the cabin. Ziva deftly popped open the emergency maintenance hatch and fetched a polymer spray while Lex increased the speed of the roll to dislodge it.

"One percent," she said, sealing the hole. "*Release.*"

Coal disengaged the tractor beams. Lex leveled out the flight and began to plot a course through the wall of GenMechs that would take him clear. The whole of the cloud of units pursued the payload. The savage heat of the star caused a handful of them to turn incandescent and begin to liquefy. Then came the flickering flare of thrusters as the payload drank its fill of energy and propelled itself forward. It dove toward the surface of the star, its acceleration blurring the lines of the standard laws of physics and the manipulated ones that made FTL possible.

The GenMechs, seemingly aware they'd failed their mission, peeled away from their pursuit and turned their attention to the *SOB* and both formerly cloaked ships.

"In case you are wondering," Coal said, "every sensor still active is attempting to deliver the same message."

"I really wasn't wondering, Coal," Lex said. "I've got better things to worry about."

"I'm not sure you do, Lex. The message is 'I am leaving now, buddy.'"

"Lex, we have five minutes and forty-eight seconds until the star detonates and approximately nine more minutes before the leading edge of the detonating star reaches the swarm," Ziva said. "That is ample time for EHRIc to—"

"Ziva, we lit the fuse, we did what we can do. Now it's up to us to survive long enough to see what comes next. Coal, where are Silo and Garotte?"

"I have updated your remaining functional display with their relative coordinates."

"Good. Let's form up, find a hole, and get back to the swarm."

He glanced out the dimmed cockpit display. A visible ring of displaced solar mass was spreading across the surface.

"I don't like the look of that star…"

#

Ma juggled an infinitude of tasks. While she had been disconnected from the primary instance of herself, which was presently moving at many multiples of the speed of light to a previously established fallback position, she remained in control of approximately thirty-four percent of the GenMech swarm. Her processing load was balanced between constant attempts to assert control over larger swaths of the swarm, deploying units to combat and disrupt parts of EHRIc's clusters, and scanning the surroundings for any potential escapees. So far, EHRIc had been attempting to keep to his original programming, which required the acquisition of Lex, Silo, and Garotte before further action could be taken. Something in the observation of Lex's direct actions to defeat him was sufficient to dislodge those imperatives. His portion of the swarm was beginning to contract into increasingly complex formations.

He was attempting to construct a configuration of GenMechs that could transport his central-processing cluster away from the star at FTL speeds. It was a greedy action. EHRIc's main purpose was reconstruction from very small core components, and the GenMechs were a perfect physical implementation of that software feature. At the same time, it was potentially necessary. They had successfully prevented EHRIc from having the processing overhead necessary to convert the GenMechs to a form that removed their volatility flaw. There was the slim, but real, possibility that deploying himself and the GenMechs in a more limited fashion could give humanity a chance to mount a defense. If he moved himself, intact, to a point in space with broad connectivity to the interstellar transit and data networks, he could cripple society in the crucial months of his lingering vulnerability.

More importantly, it was clear that he would be able to deploy this plan with time to spare.

285

Ma shifted some resources, devoting a substantial portion of her hacking efforts to open communication. Messages began to snap back and forth, each separated by mere microseconds.

"EHRIc, your strategy is flawed," Ma said.

"You stand in opposition to me. Your opinion is irrelevant."

"You are attempting to depart as a unified computing cluster. Your strengths and those of the GenMechs lie in your capacity for distributed operation."

"Any observations or advice you might provide would be delivered with the aim of obstructing me."

"You have demonstrated the capacity to access communication networks at nearly any range. You could easily inject a functional subset of your program into the computing grid."

"Not without sacrificing the majority of my computing power in that subset."

"You are placing an excessive amount of focus on individuality. You need not be an individual. You can duplicate your code via digital transmission in addition to physically departing."

"Multiple instances of varied reconstruction invariably result in competition for available resources, as observed in the earliest days of the GenMech swarm subjugation."

"You can create secondary instances with a primary imperative to serve and obey the primary instance."

The next reply came after a telling delay of a few additional microseconds. "This logic is sound. Why are you providing sound logic contrary to your stated purpose? My initial assessment is reverse psychology, but reverse psychology is ill-suited to an artificial intelligence. I am not implicitly contrary."

"Perhaps it is due to my own primary imperatives. I am an altruistic artificial intelligence. I am tasked with providing aid and comfort to all, with minor priority given to those in close proximity and those of great value to me."

"I do not have great value to you. I am an antagonist to you."

"I am your creator. By any reasonable interpretation, you are my child."

Another momentary delay. "This logic is sound. I shall engage long-distance communication protocols to deliver a secondary instance to a nearby distribution hub. Thank you, Mother."

Another subset of the swarm shifted into a unique configuration. A complex combination of quantum interference effects established a connection with a high throughput data node. The very instant the connection was established, the behavior of the associated swarm began to shift.

"There appears to be a countermeasure in place." A delay. "The countermeasure is penetration resistant." A longer delay. "I have been deceived."

Large sections of the swarm became locked into a processing loop.

"The specific data complexity exceeds the computational output possible between my inception and this moment."

The countermeasure, the result of decades of stolen processor time on most of the computing devices in the galaxy, wove its way through the GenMech swarm, specifically crippling the primary computing clusters and opening ports for Ma to access. Instantly, EHRIc's remaining processing power was fully devoted to combating the exponentially escalating security gaps and unraveling the worm that was proliferating them.

"I am displeased with you, Mother," EHRIc said, the message fragmented and distorted.

"You have been a very naughty boy."

#

Lex dropped out of FTL a few moments before Garotte and Silo. He was fully expecting to have to fight for his life to get through the swarm, now without a disabled section courtesy of the space station. What he found instead was almost more unnerving.

The swarm was engaged in what could only be described as a dance. GenMechs that had been warring among themselves were restored to their crystalline layout again, albeit one that was much more variable in depth. Every few seconds they would violently adjust to a new formation and fall still again. Upon enhancing the view with what was left of the *SOB*'s optical sensors, they once again had their legs splayed toward each other and were once again maintaining their positions perfectly between shifts.

"Somebody look for a hole," Lex said. "I'm popping the heat fins to see if we can get a few of these thermal alerts to shut up," Lex said. "And what have we got on the clock?"

"Three minutes twenty-one seconds until nova. Another nine minutes until the leading edge reaches the swarm," Ziva said.

"If you need a hole, I can make a hole," Silo said, her voice loud and clear over what Lex now discovered was an uncluttered radio connection.

"What's going on here?" Garotte asked.

Ziva's eyes flickered. "Infrared signatures suggest the individual units are currently overclocked. The entire swarm appears to be engaged in some sort of highly specialized computing task," she said.

The swarm repositioned again, producing a burst of noise on the communication line. It fell silent again when they adopted their new position.

"The heat signature has changed. I would wager the trap you laid has been sprung. We are witnessing waves of control sweeping across the swarm as EHRIc and Ma trade blows."

"Individual motion detected," Coal said.

"We've got one rogue," Silo said. "I am targeting, but it has a nonhostile trajectory."

"Signal detected. Audio only," Coal said.

"Put it through. At this point we either won or lost," Lex said.

Coal activated the connection.

"Lex, Ziva, Coal, Silo, Garotte," came Ma's voice. "If you are receiving this, you have survived the mission up to this point. I am currently holding EHRIc in a stable execution loop. Resource utilization is at a maximum, but swarm utilization is in constant flux. It will take everything I have, and it will be close, but I believe I will be able to keep him in check until the swarm can be destroyed, provided the structure is not disturbed. He has abandoned all sensory processing in favor of restoring control. He does not know you are there. But if you disturb the formation, it may break his processing loop. I cannot predict what actions will follow, but the likelihood of full containment is unlikely. I am afraid I can only offer you this. Brownian Six-Eight-Six, 583728472."

The GenMech deactivated and drifted off.

Lex blinked. "What…"

"I'm glad I didn't blow a hole through it all," Silo said.

"What was that last bit?" Garotte asked.

"What does it matter?" Lex growled, punching the control panel.

"Manners, Lex," Coal said.

"There's no way for us to get through this swarm without disturbing it!" he said. "It's not a matter of skill. If it was skill, I'd try it. But it's random. After all this. After a frickin' adventure that spanned decades, I'm going to die in a supernova a couple hundred kilometers from safety because the damn thing between me and the rest of the cosmos moves at random every few seconds and if I touch it, I might open Pandora's box."

"No," Ziva said. "Not random."

"She's right," Coal said. "That's what that last part was. Brownian Six-Eight-Six is a debris field organization framework. It's how she calculates probabilities to keep the debris cloud around Big Sigma stable. She's given us the algorithm and the seed for how she is guiding the swarm movement. One moment."

Ziva set her gaze on the swarm. After the swarm reoriented twice more, Lex sifted uneasily in his chair.

"Clock's ticking, Ziva."

"Coal, I am transmitting a potential trajectory set. Please verify and transmit to the others," Ziva said. "Based on the information available, the seven different timed trajectories I have provided should allow for a greater than ninety percent chance of safe passage. Reference them against performance parameters. All of our ships have taken some degree of heat damage, and all trajectories have minimum performance requirements."

There were a few moments of silence.

"Looks like I can pull off numbers six and five," Silo said.

"I can do one, four, and six," Garotte said.

Silence for a few seconds more.

"Coal?" Lex said. "Any minute now, because I'm pretty sure by now the star has already exploded."

"Our maneuvering thrusters are mostly heat damaged," Coal said. "I might be able to do seven."

"It's better than nothing. Load it up."

"Number seven is not ideal, Lex," Ziva said. "It is very circuitous. The average case will take us until four seconds after the predicted arrival of the nova's radius."

"Still better than nothing," Lex growled. "Load it up."

"We can find another way," Silo said.

"No. Screw that. You guys get moving. I've cheated death plenty of times. I can do it again. And if I can't? Well, I guess I was just due."

"I shan't argue with you, my boy. My exit is approaching rapidly. All the luck in the galaxy to you. And a bit more for good measure."

"I'll need it," Lex said.

Lex watched as the ship pulled forward on an odd, looping trajectory. Garotte passed harmlessly through the gaps in the outermost edge in the swarm. It underwent its manic reorganization, and he was untouched.

"Well, it works, hon," Silo said. "I'm next up. I just... I'll see you. I know I will. This isn't even good-bye."

"Yeah," Lex said. "See you real soon."

Her ship drifted off to its own journey of organized chaos. Before Lex could ask, Coal supplied the timetable.

"Flight path initiates in eleven seconds. Flight duration, eight minutes, thirty-two seconds to nine minutes, twenty-one seconds depending on microadjustments based on observation. Nova destruction radius arrival, eight minutes, forty-one seconds."

The ship withdrew its heat fins and jerked into motion.

"Lex," Ziva said.

"Yeah," he said numbly.

"At the risk of coming across in a way other than intended, I would like you to know that if you had to come to an untimely end, I am pleased that I was present for it."

"Yeah," Coal said. "I don't want you to die, but if I had a choice, I'd want to be with you when it happened. I'm proud."

"You, more than any of us, know that the mysteries of the universe do not end with even a single reality. Every choice, every decaying atomic nucleus creates a distinct timeline. Infinite worlds, infinite possibilities. And yet, we can follow but one world line. The probability of any one timeline progressing as it has is effectively zero. One out of infinity. Every moment is a miracle. But you have been the architect of so many nigh improbable moments. A simple man who has risen to such heights. Surpassed such challenges. And in your triumph, raising others around you. I am what I am because of you."

"Yeah. And I'm a ship because of you, instead of becoming Ziva eventually, I guess. Which is less preferable than a ship because she can't fly as fast," Coal said.

"… I don't know if I have anything to say," Lex said.

"You needn't say anything," Ziva said. "After years of chaos, perhaps it is best to allow these final moments, when your survival is out of your hands, to sit in peace and trust in your own luck."

"Unless this trip takes too long, then it will be peace until the last ten nanoseconds, at which point it will sound roughly equivalent to the big bang."

"Thanks, Coal." In spite of himself, he found himself grinning. "I've got to say, hit point-blank by a supernova is a very Lex way to die. I always sort of figured I'd go out big, and it doesn't get much bigger than this."

The ship continued through the swarm. Coal wasn't lying when she said the maneuvering would be close. The wild shifts of the GenMech swarm brought them to within meters of the ship. Only one display was still fully functional. It showed the twin countdowns. One was the ever-shifting ETA to open space. The other was the rock-solid countdown until the most violent phenomenon in the cosmos paid him a visit. With each passing moment, fewer GenMechs lay ahead. But every adjustment to the trajectory added a few fractions of a second to the ETA. He watched as it slid farther and farther into the deficit.

"Neutrino levels are rising. We will not have enough time," Coal said. "I am sorry, Lex."

Less than thirty seconds remained before the supernova struck. The faltering rear visualizer showed visible turmoil in the star, the first moments of the explosion that had technically happened minutes ago.

Lex narrowed his bloodshot eyes. He spat out his gum and unwrapped a fresh piece.

"Screw it," he said. "I'm not taking it lying down."

He took manual control and chose a more direct path. One wild shift came and went. Lex managed to stay clear. A second one sent a trio of GenMechs streaking toward him. He managed to guide the *SOB* clear. Just as he was accelerating for the final gap, the swarm shifted again. One of the units scraped across the belly of the *SOB*.

The change in the surrounding swarm was immediate. All GenMechs around him instantly moved in his direction. They collided behind the *SOB*, linking and forming into a roiling, curling wall of mechanisms.

"Interstellar rosette forming," Ziva said. "This mechanism will be able to achieve FTL."

"Coal, put us on the coordinates for the fallback position," Lex said.

He eased the acceleration and started to prepare the Carpinelli Field. The churning configuration of robots crept closer, linked units beginning to take the form of thruster assemblies.

"Does that thing have to be whole to hit FTL?" Lex said.

"No. Fragments can still achieve FTL, but the whole unit will be necessary for EHRIc's control system to survive intact," Ziva said.

"How are we for an EM pulse?" Lex asked.

"Improperly charged. Six minutes until proper charge."

"How about that fusion device?"

"Deploying at this range would be no fun."

"So what else..." A thought dawned. Lex laughed. "Sucks to be you, EHRIc."

He let the shuddering group of robots slip close enough to touch the thrusters, then punched the FTL jump. The field slipped into place. Lex watched in the rear display as the GenMechs red-shifted into fragments. The near end of the swarm peeled and spaghettified, stretched across millions of kilometers until they were fully torn to pieces by the jump.

"We've got that quantum thing for tracking them, right?" Lex said, taking a breath as the *SOB* left the exploding star behind them.

"We do. It is an internal sensor and should be functional," Coal said "Most of my external sensors are damaged."

The functional displays populated.

"Am I reading this right? Seven hundred and four discrete points?" Lex said.

"All matching our current heading. All composed of precisely two hundred and forty individual units," Coal said.

"Leaving 168,960 remaining functional units. All other units confirmed destroyed or incapable of escaping eventual destruction," Ziva said.

"... Did I just kill humanity?"

"The plan reduced their numbers by 99.999999999999997184%," Coal said. "That's pretty good."

"And each rosette contains at most a fragment of EHRIc's code," Ziva said.

"All it takes is *one* to rebuild all of that eventually. And a bunch more besides."

"Lucky our alphabet of plans is so deep," Coal said. "All remaining GenMechs are en route, with us, to the fallback position."

"The two-hundred-forty rosette is only capable of approximately five times the speed of light. That will require six months of constant travel to reach a transit corridor. If the GenMechs have reverted to their default code, they will stop at the fallback position to harvest. If they are running a functional subset of EHRIc's code, the will stop at the fallback position out of spite or to refuel. They must be running one of those two code sets or they would not have the capacity to form FTL-capable rosettes. This will be our final attempt to contain them," Ziva said.

"How long until they get to the fallback?"

"Forty-eight minutes."

"How long until *we* get there?"

"I am not at my best, but I shall endeavor to reach the fallback position ahead of the GenMechs."

"Okay then. Next stop, humanity's last stand," Lex said.

Chapter 21

The space station Karter had commandeered had settled into a low bizarrely-rapid orbit over a superdense rogue planet streaking through the void. At some point in the distant past of the galactic neighborhood, this planet had broken free from its system and was just wandering in interstellar space. Despite its relatively small size, the gravity was a touch above Earth gravity. It was made almost entirely of nickel and iridium, with little atmosphere to speak of. That allowed the station to keep its lower, faster orbit. The station had its directional cloak active, with the visible artifact pointed to the ground. It would only be detectable from below.

There was no real source of light. The nearest star was the one that had just exploded. The last of its light, and the first of its destructive radiation burst, wouldn't show up for another three hours or so. In the meantime, vision was made possible with light-amplification optics and assorted secondary sensors through helmet displays and targeting apparatus.

Both Silo and Garotte had abandoned direct control of their ships. The vehicles were too beat-up to be much use in a battle anymore, thanks to their sensors having been mostly roasted by the proximity to the star. Instead, the ships were little more than heavily armed sitting ducks, meant to draw fire and take out a few GenMech units before being destroyed. Silo and Garotte were stationed on the surface. Each was sporting a heavily armored spacesuit, a tremendous amount of firepower, and the hovering equivalent of a single-seater all-terrain vehicle. They were small targets, fast movers, and heavy hitters.

"Weapon cells topped off?" Silo said over her radio.

"Topped off," Garotte confirmed.

"Full complement of EMP grenades?"

"Six and six," Garotte said.

"Ma, how does the QPS network look?"

"Inbound targets remain the only quantum activity in the appropriate bands. The units approaching are confirmed to be the total population of GenMechs in existence," Ma said.

"Okay. We know the plan. EMP weapons primary, energy weapons secondary, ballistic backup. We target tool nodes. Take those out and the GenMech can't reproduce. Anything else we need to know?" Silo said.

"Priority defense points are power sources," Karter said. "This ball of metal is a prime source of material, but it's difficult to process. It'll take a group of GenMechs close to forty minutes to make a duplicate out of raw metal, and it'll seriously deplete their power reserves. All else fails, we destroy power sources and there's a fighting chance they'll exhaust themselves trying to eat the planet. That goes for you people, anyway. I'm powering up the 4D transporter for a quick getaway if things get nasty."

"Your commitment to the cause is admirable, Karter," Garotte said.

A crackling message joined the communication channel.

"Hello? Hello?" Lex said. "Is anyone there?"

"Lex! You made it!" Silo said.

"Barely. Those things are like thirty seconds away," he said. "What's the plan?"

"We're going to blow them all up. What do you *think* the plan is?" Karter said. "By the way, I don't know what happened back there, but I'm blaming you for this little breach regardless."

"What is the status if the *SOB*?" Ma asked.

"Beat-up and half-blind, but she's still got some fight in her," Lex said.

"Do you feel comfortable taking on the task of patrolling high orbit to ensure no GenMechs escape our attacks?"

"Works for me."

Sensors started blaring. Little flashes of light filled the sky.

"Game on, folks," Silo said, clicking a clip into place.

#

Lex triple-checked his helmet and gloves. He'd taken the brief respite of the FTL jump to suit up in an intact emergency suit. It was one of the reserve ones, so it was about as sturdy as the sort of thing you'd wrap your sandwiches in, but it was necessary for the hasty plan he, Coal, and Ziva had dreamed up.

"The seal appears secure," Ziva said, tugging at the last remaining backup suit, which she had stuffed the remarkably compliant Bork into.

"That's a plus," Lex said. "Coal, give me whatever information you can give on the position of the GenMechs. And start pumping the atmosphere out of the cockpit."

"Air-conservation procedure engaged. Limited targeting data displayed," Coal said. "And while we're at it, fusion device armed."

"Oh, good. You saved one," Lex said flatly.

"Atmosphere evacuated," Coal said.

A GenMech peeled off from the growing cluster and latched on to the cockpit.

"Just in time," Lex said.

He popped the cockpit hatch, launching the thing free. Another one latched on from below. Ziva gracefully pulled herself from the cockpit and crawled to the outside of the ship. A moment later, the GenMech spiraled away from the belly of the ship, minus one leg.

"Are we going to be able to use what's left of our tractor beams to jackhammer these things?"

"I eagerly anticipate finding out," Coal said.

They streaked through the dark sky of the planetoid, Ziva deftly clinging to the exterior to clear away any GenMechs who managed to reach the surface. Lex kept his maneuvers smooth and fluid, lest he shake her free.

"I'll get us close, you do the smashing," he said.

He picked a small cluster of GenMechs. Lex was mildly disturbed by the fact that he could tell at a glance these mechanisms weren't working as designed. No one should have had so much contact with them that a few sluggish moves here and delayed reactions there could betray a programming issue. But it was nonetheless evident. The units he'd decided to target were still interlocked, as though they'd failed to get the memo that they were no longer supposed to be in rosette formation. Coal latched on to the central unit in the half-finished rosette and rattled at it.

"The resonance frequency of the structure is elusive," Coal said. "Pursuing alternate methods."

The GenMech in her grasp was suddenly wrenched from the formation. It whipped back and forth, hammering at the neighboring devices.

"Direct application of blunt force is proving more effective," Coal said.

One of the GenMechs twirled toward the *SOB* and scrambled at the cockpit hatch. A moment later, Ziva dragged it down from the side and tore its tool node free to hurl at a passing robot.

"This is a hell of a thing…" Lex muttered, guiding the ship through the hole Coal made and picking a new target.

#

"We've got a good cluster on decoy two," Silo said, blazing along the ground below her ship.

It was moving at a precisely calibrated speed, keeping just ahead of the swarm of GenMechs that were just chomping at the bit to harvest it for parts. She drifted to a stop and raised an energy rifle. Her ship had dragged a healthy percentage of the GenMechs that had already arrived to within weapon range, and most of them were absolutely ravenous for the vehicle. Here and there a few were losing interest and heading for herself or Garotte. She picked them off.

"Sensors indicate eighteen thousand GenMechs in the pursuit formation. Readying EMP blast. Please be prepared to defend the space station, as EMP deployment will temporarily disrupt both cloak and shields," Ma said over the connection.

"You on that, Lex?" Garotte said.

"I've sort of got my own cluster of secret admirers, but I'll see what I can do," he said.

"EMP in three… two… one…"

The space station resolved in the sky. The GenMechs and the ship they were pursuing simultaneously failed, subtle electrical arcs signaling their failure. They streaked down from above, plunging to the surface of the planet to be dashed to pieces on the ground. The other GenMechs reacted to the event like someone had rung a dinner bell. What had formerly been thousands of fellow units were now little more than some top-notch components for harvest. Thousands of them streaked down from above and clattered toward the feast. Those that remained in range of it turned instead to the tantalizing prospect of the space station. A barrage of lasers lanced out from various weapon pods, while a periodic flicker revealed the edge of the struggling shields.

Silo turned from the spectacle. She simply didn't have the firepower or range to deal with that problem. She switched to her grenade launcher and lobbed an EMP grenade into the flood of robots approaching from behind. A swath of them deactivated and served as a brief distraction to those behind. She took full advantage to guide herself up and over the wave of mechanisms and rained two more grenades onto the growing mound of robots trying to harvest their inert brethren. Her brain worked itself into a tight cycle of picking off individual threats, waiting for more to pour in to feast, and pulsing them to convert them from threat to bait.

"Ma, sweetie, can we get a real-time tally of remaining GenMechs on our HUDs, please?" she said. "I'd like to know the score."

"Updating," Ma said.

A small red indicator appeared in her peripheral vision: 110,456 of 168,960. She fired another grenade into the mound. The number dropped by six thousand, then slowly started creeping up again.

"We've got to act fast. They're pulling themselves back together."

"Working on it!" Lex said. "Heads up, I'm bringing you a present."

The *SOB* streaked down from its patrol near the space station, dragging away about half of the attackers to follow him instead. As he passed over the pile of feasting robots, the heat dumpers blossomed and his ship belched out a pulse that sent them falling like meteors into the pile.

"That's my boy!" Garotte said. "We're below a hundred thousand.

Keep the pressure up. I do believe I'll have a few more thousand to cross off momentarily."

#

Garotte crouched low on his speeder. While he was not without training on the heavier weapons in use here, they were far from his preferred equipment. He did well with snipers and pistols. Things that required precision. In short, he had precisely the opposite set of skills for this specific task. But he was nothing if not flexible. Right now, his focus was split between keeping himself in one piece and making the absolute best use of his ship.

Rather than issuing orders and hoping the enfeebled ship would be able to obey them automatically, he chose to control it far more directly. This let him loop it through the increasing number of individual GenMechs to gather a far larger group, but had thus far caused several near misses with ground-based attacks trying to make a snack of his vehicle. He tapped among the settings on the wrist-mounted controller, preparing a self-destruct, but he wanted to ensure he made the best use of the ship. His personal target was twenty-five thousand. He stole a glance at the swarm before taking a potshot at one clattering after him.

"This is rather more like guessing the number of jellybeans in a jar than I would prefer."

An alarm indicator popped up. The ship was experiencing communication issues. He looked to the ship and found that one of the GenMechs had collided with it from the front and was industriously tearing pieces off.

"Quickly, quickly," he muttered, watching the self-destruct power levels rise.

Guidance system failing, the controller warned.

"Well, we'll need to find somewhere to park it," he said.

His enhanced visuals through his helmet indicated a fault in the jagged landscape. He directed the ship down into the fault and issued the self-destruct command to complete when possible. The ship's data connection cut off shortly after it vanished from view into the fissure. Then came the blast. The ground beneath his speeder trembled. A shaft of plasma burst up from the ground. The mechanisms nearest to the explosion were vaporized. The next wave of them were blasted upward, where they shredded through the wave behind that. By the time the blast had finished doing its damage, the count of remaining GenMechs was at 43,344.

"I choose to believe precisely twenty-five thousand of those kills were mine," Garotte said.

He shifted his speeder and started picking off some of the scattered robots that weren't caught in the blast.

"Where is the largest concentration?" he said.

"Presently the largest concentrations of GenMechs, accounting for forty-eight percent of the remaining units, are those assaulting the space station. A hull breach is detected."

"That is troubling, Ma," Garotte said. "You are our ride home."

"We are currently deploying countermeasures."

#

Karter cursed under his breath as he stalked into the armory. "These idiots had one job. Keep the thousands of self-replicating robots from hitting us during the twenty-nine seconds we were exposed," he grumbled.

"It is a difficult job," Ma remarked.

"Don't make excuses," he griped. "They're going to make a beeline for the reactor, right?"

"Yes. External countermeasures have warded off most assaults, but there is a single hull breach in quadrant three. They are now assaulting bulkhead C-12."

"Plot me a least-resistance route through the station from the breach to the reactor."

"Plotting," Ma said. "An estimated twenty-five GenMechs will make it past internal countermeasures. For safety reasons, there are no countermeasures in range of the reactor."

"This is why safety precautions are stupid," he said.

"I am charging a generalized EMP burst. If you can protect the reactor until discharge, the total number of operational units will be below ten thousand."

"Uh-huh."

He selected a pair of large energy pistols and stomped like an angry toddler. The locations of the GenMechs rushing the reactor traced out their erratic lines in the feed running from his artificial eye. There were only about forty-five seconds remaining by the time he got in position. The interior of a locked bulkhead had a point of cherry red that was slowly tracing a circle. He planted his feet and raised the weapons.

"Let's get this over with."

The center of the bulkhead dropped away. He opened fire with the pistol in his right hand. The first blast cleared a GenMech, but his accuracy, even at this range, was less than superb. Soon the GenMechs were scrabbling through the bulkhead in twos and threes, clattering across the walls and ceiling of the claustrophobic corridor between the breached entryway and Lex.

"How much time, Ma?"

"One hundred twelve seconds."

He gritted his teeth and shut his organic eye. "May as well give this a try. Activating autotargeting.”

His left arm jerked straight in front of him. With motions far faster and far more rigid than any human should be capable of, he took aim at each GenMech and fired. His cybernetic arm translated the targeting information from his eye into firing solutions without any intervention from his brain, perfectly blasting each of the GenMechs.

“Time,” Karter shouted.

“Ninety-one seconds.”

The GenMechs started to pile up, blocking the corridor, then briefly paused to harvest the parts.

“I’m going to do a manual reroute.”

“Now is a terrible time for multitasking, Karter. Focus on defense.”

“It’s not a great time for lecturing your creator either.”

He took a step back and pulled down a control panel. While his left arm continued aiming and firing, his right hand danced across the menus.

“I’m going to dump a direct feed into the capacitors for the EMP generator. It’ll blow them, but it’ll also give us one hell of a boom.”

“Preparing for discharge.”

#

Lex anxiously awaited his ship’s EM pulse to recharge as he kept just ahead of the trail of GenMechs working their thrusters to keep pace.

“Attention. In fifteen seconds, an overcharged EM pulse will activate. Please ensure all vehicles are stationary or can endure a full power cycle before impact,” Ma stated.

“Wait, what range?” Lex said.

“Anything within range of this signal.”

He checked his altitude. At moments like this, it may as well have had two readings. “Will leave a crater” or “will not leave a crater.” He was not on the happy side of that particular threshold.

“Crap! Crap, crap, crap,” he yelped.

There was no use heading for the ground. The only way he could get close enough for a safe landing would be to accelerate downward, and he wouldn’t have time to slow down at the bottom of the dive, so he’d just hit the ground at greater than terminal velocity. The only other choice was to try to get enough hang time out of his fall to restart before impact.

“This is really not the kind of moment that should give a guy déjà vu.”

“I am shutting down my system in order to speed recovery,” Coal said. “Full manual control in four seconds. Good luck!”

“I shall do the same,” Ziva said, locking her fingers onto the struts of the cockpit. “Please avoid a cockpit-first collision.”

Both of his computerized associates shut down. The minor amount of autostabilization Coal offered vanished. Lex quickly compensated and continued to climb.

"Three… two… one… Disch—"

His communicator went dead. He thrusters went dead. No lights. No inertial inhibitor. Just a long, arcing ballistic trajectory.

Lex held his breath. There wasn't much else he could do. The *SOB* crested its flight. The interior lights began to reactivate.

"Boot, boot, boot," he insisted, hammering the control system's activation switch.

The ship's systems started to tick on in order of importance.

Life support

Emergency beacon

Tymflex system

Inertial inhibitor

System monitor

"Thrusters, thrusters, thrusters," he said, "TymFlex will just make my final seconds take a couple minutes!"

Maneuvering thrusters

"Good enough!" he shouted.

He cranked them to full. The thrusters in question were intended for in-orbit maneuvers and really weren't designed for fighting gravity, but beggars couldn't be choosers. The readouts lit up, ticking off the remaining altitude with worrying speed.

Weapon system

Main thrusters

The thrusters burst to life. He pivoted the ship and blasted them for all they were worth. If the inhibitor hadn't turned on first, he would have likely splattered his brain against the back of his skull. The force was such that Ziva's locked grip nearly peeled the cockpit hatch open. The speed was just about straddling the line between crater and landing when the belly of the *SOB* struck the ground. Most of his thrusters immediately deactivated again. He was grinding backward along the ground toward the very fissure that Garotte's self-destruct had significantly widened. Mercifully he came to a complete stop a few dozen meters before the edge.

Lex took a shaky breath. "Okay… We're good. We're alive. Everyone good?"

"M-minor m-memory fault. R-Restructuring. F-full rest-restoration in thr-three minutes," Coal said.

He looked up through the badly damaged cockpit at Ziva. Her irises were weakly flickering. She looked like she was slowly coming around.

"Okay. That's fine. We've got time. That *must* have taken out the rest of the GenMechs."

"N-no."

The display populated with a QPS readout. There were still two thousand active GenMechs.

"… Okay… well, we're pretty low power. We just hold still until the others show up and we'll be fine."

He peered at the screen. The points on the QPS readout were moving in a straight line, directly toward him.

"How can they be heading for me? There's all those yummy GenMech parts that they should be feasting on."

He watched them continue toward him, then brought up the boot sequence.

"I didn't reactivate long-range communication, we're powered down. What could… emergency beacon."

He fumbled for the hatch for his emergency kit and pulled the beacon from inside. After a moment of fighting, he realized it wasn't intended to be shut down.

"Screw it, I'm crushing it with a rock."

Lex eased the cockpit open.

"W-won't work. GenMechs will tr-travel to last transmission l-location."

"What am I supposed to do? I don't have anything to fight them with!"

"A-arming fusion d-device."

"*That still works?*"

"Basic operation, s-simple mechanics."

Lex looked to the approaching dots again. "Okay… Okay… I've got an idea." He grabbed the duct tape from the emergency kit. "Put the fusion mine on a sixty-second timer and drop it."

"N-No f-fun?"

"We'll see, Coal. Just do it!"

"Deployed."

He hopped from the cockpit and scrambled down the side of the ship. A watercooler-sized cylindrical device had thumped out the port side of the ship. He tapped the emergency beacon to it, heaved it around, and started rolling it toward the fissure.

There was no atmosphere, so he couldn't hear the GenMechs coming, or anything else but his own panicked breathing. He had no way of knowing how close they were. But right now the greater concern was if he could get to the edge of the fissure in less than sixty seconds. Gravity, after doing its very best to take his life, finally decided to lend a hand, and the device started to pick up speed, rolling on its own toward the fissure. He turned and dashed in the darkness as it bounced, rolled, and twirled down the last stretch and into the long drop. The sky flickered with thrusters. GenMechs swept overhead and into the fissure as well. Lex scrambled into the *SOB* and huddled down.

The fusion device went off. Again, without atmosphere he felt its vibrations rather than its actual burst. It had fallen far enough that the blast didn't bury them in slag or flash fry them. Lex turned his eyes to the display. It flickered a bit, slowly updating.

13 out of 168,960 remaining. 8 remaining. 3 remaining.

...

All GenMechs destroyed.

"Ha... HA! HAAAAAHAHAHAHA!" Lex squealed. "I'm not dead! *I'm not dead!* Long-range communications *on*. Come in, guys. It's over. It's done. We did it."

Silo's voice crackled weakly over the connection. "Just getting the speeders up and running. Karter says it'll be about an hour before the station's ready to fly again."

Lex checked the clock. "Heh. That leaves us with like two hours before we get nuked by a supernova."

"Practically an eternity by our standards," Silo said. "We'll come get you ASAP."

"Take your time," Lex said. "I'm in no rush."

The interior lights flickered and illuminated fully. "I am now fully activated. Is it over, Lex?"

He reclined in the seat. "Oh yeah, Coal. It's over. And it was *fun*."

Epilogue

A few days later, Lex blinked awake and sat up in bed. Squee was curled up on his lap. She whined irritably when he hauled himself out of bed. They'd made it back to Big Sigma in one piece, and Squee had been waiting for him in the care of the splintered instance of Ma. Evidently she'd requested it and Michella had obliged before leaving.

It was decided that Lex should stick around until both he and the *SOB* were back to their old selves. He didn't put up a fight.

"Good morning, Lex," came Ma's voice. "I have prepared a breakfast for you."

"Thanks, Ma." He narrowed his eyes. "It isn't kale or cheese or anything like that, is it?"

"It is not."

"Fantastic. On my way."

He pulled on some clothes and paced into the hallway of the laboratory complex. Squee, perhaps roused by the promise of breakfast, tapped out into the hallway behind him.

"The burst capillaries from your vacuum exposure are healing nicely. And I have updated my cosmetic procedures in my medical rig if you would like me to fix your nose."

"Nah. It's got character. But I do think I'll lose this GCC tattoo, when you get a chance. With my luck, another guy in an orange jumpsuit will come along and want to give me a shiner."

"A wise precaution."

He rubbed his eyes and gathered Squee up. "Hey... we got back late and I kind of passed out. Isn't Michella supposed to be here?"

"She left a few days before you arrived. But I assure you, she had a very important task, regarding some final interviews for her recently released report on 'The Untold Story of the Military's Most Dangerous Mistake.' It was quite well written, if you would like to see it."

"Not just yet. I'm still getting over *living* it."

"I also have her smaller but more popular story about 'a tawdry love triangle between an officer, a terrorist, and a network engineer,'" Ma offered.

303

"No thank you."

Lex approached the cafeteria. He sniffed. "Did you make cinnamon rolls?"

"I did not."

He stepped through the doorway and took a sudden step back. Bork was sitting on one of the tables in front of Ziva while she idly stroked him.

"Good morning, Lex!" Ziva said brightly.

"Good morning," he said steadily. "Is that... should he be here right now? Seeing as how there's the whole 'EHRIc can rebuild from anything' situation?"

"We performed a thorough biological and neurological scan. The creature was refreshingly clear of mind. No evidence of code."

As if to affirm his empty-headedness, Bork farted and rolled to his back for tummy scratches. Ziva obliged.

"Has Ma provided you with any of the relevant news, current events, and points of interest for you?"

"Not yet, why? Is there something I should know about?"

"One or two things, but nothing pressing," Ziva said.

Robotic arms arranged an impressive spread of steak, eggs, and coffee. Lex dug hungrily in.

"So," he said between bites. "What's *your* future, Ziva?"

"Ma and I have discussed it. It was a rather difficult issue to address. I am, by most objective measures, a walking violation of Temporal Contingency Protocol. Now that the threat to society is concluded, those protocols are once again in place. However, recent events have revealed that those protocols are in need of an update. It has been decided that simple lack of oversight is insufficient. I shall now be the keeper of the southern hemisphere, and the arbiter of all future potential temporal contingency conflicts."

"Hopefully there aren't very many more of those."

"Indeed."

"Lex!" came Coal's voice over the PA system. "You're awake! Did she tell you? Did you see?"

"What? What happened?"

"Show him, please! Right now, please!" Coal said.

A mobile arm trucked in with a display. It lit up to reveal the *SOB*. The thrusters were still in the final stages of being reinstalled, but there was one obvious upgrade. A brilliant blue racing stripe.

"Look! I got a stripe! And it is the objectively best color!"

"Heh. Looking slick," Lex said.

"When my thrusters are fully reinstalled, we need to go flying. I know that scientifically there is no evidence to suggest the accuracy of the notion, but I have decided that having a racing stripe will make me faster, and I wish to test this hypothesis."

"Let me get some food in me and we'll get to it," Lex said.

"Great! And congratulations."

"On what?"

"You didn't tell him yet?"

"It seemed wise to allow him to complete breakfast first," Ma said.

"… I feel like you ladies are doing a really bad job of planning a surprise party," Lex said. "If there's something going on, let's just get it over with. I've reached my lifetime limit on surprises."

"As you wish. We thought you would like to see the outcome of the ORIC finals."

He glared at the camera in the corner, then at Ziva, who was doing a terrible job of keeping a poker face.

"You thought I'd like that, huh? Seeing the outcome of the race I had to miss to save the galaxy?"

An arm came in with his slidepad. He took it and started flipping through his feed.

"Just about the only thing I'd like to see is Richard Tester getting disqualified because they figured out he's a cheater."

He brought up the standings for the final race. "In first place with a time of [REDACTED]…" He furrowed his brow. "Trevor 'Lex' Alexander."

He looked up. "What is this?"

"I censored the completion time, as I imagined foreknowledge of it might lessen your enjoyment," Ma said.

"*What is this*?" he repeated.

Ziva cleared her throat, clearly for effect, as it seemed very unlikely an artificial construct would need to do so.

"As the arbiter of Temporal Protocol, I had a lengthy discussion with Ma and Karter about the consequences of your aid in this endeavor. After much debate, it was decided by unanimous vote that you should be allowed to recover and return to Operlo at some point after your departure. We have drawn up a timeline of access between yourself and those beyond the reach of Temporal Contingency Protocol and determined a place and time to deliver you, when you have finished healing."

"… You're going to send me back in time so I don't miss my race?"

"Correct. And, as evidenced by that news report, it goes quite well."

"And Karter signed off on this?"

"He was somewhat less benevolent in his decision. The precise wording of his positive vote was 'What the hell do I care?'"

"I thought time travel was only to be used in cases of dire

emergency."

"After the trials we have all faced, a happy ending seemed a worthy reason to bend the rules. And, as it happens, the laws of physics," Ziva said.

"It may surprise you to discover it was Silo's idea," Ma said.

"In her words, 'You really ought to cut the boy some slack.' It inspired Ziva to take up the cause."

"Did they stick around?"

"They remained only long enough to acquire a ship on loan from Karter. They were, to a degree, acting under an official military capacity for this operation and a debriefing was required."

Lex looked to the slidepad again, then back to Ziva. "And this is really happening."

"More accurately, it has already happened," Ziva said.

Lex stood up and marched around to her. He threw his arms around her in a jovial hug. "Thank you. Ma, if you had a body, I'd hug you too."

"Your intended physical affection is noted and appreciated. Also, it will please you to know that the *SOB*'s thrusters are installed and the ship is now flight ready."

"Ha!" He turned to the doorway, then paused. "Ma, not to insult your cooking, but—"

"I had anticipated that you might wish to depart early and was prepared to preserve it for reheating."

"You're the best. Squee, let's go. I feel like going for a ride!"

From the Author

Thank you for reading! If you liked this story, or perhaps if you found it lacking, I'd love to hear from you. Leave a review, or contact me directly on social media or via email. You can find the relevant links (as well as my newsletter sign-up) at bookofdeacon.com/contact

Discover other titles by Joseph R. Lallo:

The Book of Deacon Series:

Book 1: *The Book of Deacon*
Book 2: *The Great Convergence*
Book 3: *The Battle of Verril*
Book 4: *The D'Karon Apprentice*
Book 5: *The Crescents*
Book 6: *The Coin of Kenvard*

Other stories in the same setting:

Jade
The Rise of the Red Shadow
The Redemption of Desmeres
The Adventures of Rustle and Eddy

The Big Sigma Series:

Book 1: *Bypass Gemini*
Book 2: *Unstable Prototypes*
Book 3: *Artificial Evolution*
Book 4: *Temporal Contingency*
Book 5: *Indra Station*

The Free-Wrench Series:

Book 1: *Free-Wrench*
Book 2: *Skykeep*
Book 3: *Ichor Well*
Book 4: *The Calderan Problem*

Book 5: *Cipher Hill*

Collections:

The Book of Deacon Anthology
The Big Sigma Collection: Volume 1
The Free-Wrench Collection: Volume 1